Acclaim for Jonathan Wilson's

A Palestine Affair

"A swift little mystery-romance. . . . Crisply written. . . . Wonderfully rich in period detail and atmosphere and wonderfully free of polemic, side taking, or blame."　　—*Seattle Weekly*

"Wilson is a talented writer with a gift for story, scene, and character."　　　　　　　　　　　　　—*The Boston Globe*

"Profoundly memorable. . . . Haunting. . . . *A Palestine Affair* is romantic, but darkly so, in the manner of *The English Patient*. . . . Wilson poetically evokes every aspect of Israel's scenery."
　　　　　　　　　　　　　　　　　—*The Jerusalem Report*

"Worth reading? An Englishman might say: 'Rather.' An American would put it differently: 'You bet it is!' "
　　　　　　　　　　　　　　　　　　　—Saul Bellow

"Well-plotted, this is a dark, romantic thriller whose author has an amazingly keen eye for the landscapes his characters get lost in."　　　　　　　　　　—*Detroit Free Press*

"Savvy. . . . Edgy. . . . Wilson excels at creating the atmosphere surrounding his story. He wears his research lightly but tellingly."　　　　　　　　　　　—*The Jerusalem Post*

"*A Palestine Affair* evokes, quite tangibly, the days of the Mandate. This is a true and touching act of the imagination. The book's very sexy, a nostalgic and provocative envisioning of that time. I recommend it highly." —David Mamet

"Gripping. . . . [A] moody, darkly romantic thriller with a haunting sense of place. . . . Wilson has always been a perceptive writer worth reading. . . . He has a grasp of period detail as deft and compelling as Alan Furst's." —*Forward*

"Enchanting. . . . Wilson has populated his captivating novel with memorable characters. . . . It is a compelling and powerful story of love and politics." —*Abilene Reporter-News*

"Cinematic. . . . Artfully written. . . . Intricate, closely stitched. . . . Wilson is a novelist with an eye for rich historical detail. . . . His writing is highly visual and tactile, with a painterly quality." —*The Jewish Week*

"How rare to read a novel that moves with the velocity of a thriller and that is, at the same time, so splendidly written. The characters glow with persuasive life, and Wilson exquisitely evokes the land itself as it seethed under British rule—a place stamped by history but unformed, too; an older world that seems younger because of all the possibility in it. Wilson's story of love and betrayal merges historical, political, and private passions to create a beautiful and timeless tale."

—Jonathan Rosen, author of *The Talmud and the Internet*

"Excellent and atmospheric. . . . It brings to life the fascinating complexities of the Land of Israel at one of the many significant junctures in its history." —*New Jersey Jewish News*

Jonathan Wilson

A Palestine Affair

Jonathan Wilson was born in London in 1950 and educated at the universities of Essex, Oxford, and the Hebrew University of Jerusalem. He has lived in the United States since 1976, with a four-year interlude in Jerusalem. He is the author of two previous works of fiction, *The Hiding Room* and *Schoom*. His stories, articles, essays, and reviews have appeared frequently in *The New Yorker*, *The New York Times Book Review*, *The Best American Short Stories*, and elsewhere. He held a John Simon Guggenheim Fellowship in Fiction in 1994. Wilson is chair of the English Department at Tufts University and lives in Newton, Massachusetts, with his wife and their two sons.

A Palestine
Affair

A Palestine
Affair

A Novel

Jonathan Wilson

Anchor Books
A Division of Random House, Inc.
New York

FIRST ANCHOR BOOKS EDITION, JULY 2004

Copyright © 2003 by Jonathan Wilson

All rights reserved under International and Pan-American Copyright
Conventions. Published in the United States by Anchor Books, a division
of Random House, Inc., New York, and simultaneously in Canada by
Random House of Canada Limited, Toronto. Originally published in
hardcover in the United States by Pantheon Books, a division
of Random House, Inc., New York, in 2003.

Anchor Books and colophon are registered trademarks
of Random House, Inc.

The Library of Congress has cataloged the Pantheon edition as follows:
Wilson, Jonathan, [date]
A Palestine affair / Jonathan Wilson.
p. cm.
1. Palestine—History—1917–1948—Fiction. 2. Jewish-Arab relations—
Fiction. 3. British—Palestine—Fiction. 4. Married people—Fiction.
5. Zionists—Fiction. 6. Artists—Fiction. I. Title.
PR6073.I4679 P35 2003
823'.914—dc21
2002035499

Anchor ISBN: 1-4000-3122-2

Book design by Johanna S. Roebas

www.anchorbooks.com

Printed in the United States of America
10 9 8 7 6 5 4 3 2 1

For Sharon

Acknowledgments

Two books in particular have been of inestimable value to me in constructing this fiction: Richard Cork's *David Bomberg* and A. J. Sherman's *Mandate Days: British Lives in Palestine 1918–48*. I am deeply grateful to both authors.

Jerusalem,
June 1924

1.

Bloomberg came out of the house in North Talpiot and bicycled toward the Arab village of Abu Tor. After ten minutes or so he dismounted and found a spot where the moonlight shone brightest on a stone wall. It was a clear night. He unstrapped his artist's box and retrieved his pallete. Back in London Joyce had carefully, kindly numbered the tubes in white so that he would be able to continue to paint even when the light grew dim. He couldn't love her anymore, although he wished that he could. His withdrawal from his wife was almost embarrassing—a man Bloomberg's age shouldn't be so damaged by the death of his mother. But he was. Late night at the London Hospital, the sky a sheet of midnight blue in the rain-streaked window beside her bed, and his mother, suddenly alert, recognizing him for the first time in weeks: "I will always remember you," she'd said. But of course it was the other way round. It was Bloomberg who would always remember her: the immigrant boy's mother ship and protector, the sails of her broad skirts and him cowering in the hold, gripping the cloth, his face pressed to the side of her leg.

Meanwhile, as he mourned, Joyce continued to make small supportive gestures that made him feel sick inside. Her concern and consideration only highlighted his impoverishment of feeling. He was numb to her, and haunted. His mother wasn't the only ghost. Her death had released the others. Six years on from the war's end and here were his dead friends, appearing, like Banquo's ghost, mutilated and bloody, whenever his head snapped into a dream or reverie: Jacob Rosen, his ripped face covered in tawny phlegm; Gideon Schiff, his sweet smile intact but not his body.

Bloomberg looked beyond the terraces across the dip and swell of the earth toward Siloam and the Mount of Olives, then set up his easel and canvas. As always before painting he executed detailed sketches of his surroundings. He sat on a rock and worked in his pad with charcoal and pencil. In the moon-flooded valley the olive trees were light gray, almost white.

After a while he heard footsteps on the goat path farther up the hillside and half turned toward the noise. Two Arab men walked side by side in animated conversation. Bloomberg watched them disappear round a curve of the serpentine path, then went back to work.

Twenty minutes must have passed before he heard more noise, this time from far down the terrace. Bloomberg got up from his work and peered between the trees. There was a flurry of activity a hundred and fifty yards below him, violent enough to stir up a small cloud of dust. He looked down and thought he made out two figures. Were they struggling? Making love? Bloomberg couldn't tell. The blanched narrow frame of a tall man emerged in a shaft of moonlight. Whoever it was dusted himself off and disappeared down the terrace into an olive grove. His partner must have followed shortly after, but by then Bloomberg was engrossed in his work again and had forgotten about them.

After sketching he painted for two hours without a break before stopping for the night. He cycled home past a line of half-built houses, one hand placed firmly in the middle of his handlebars, the other holding the small canvas he had produced. The bike wheels crunched on the graveled pathway.

The doorway to his house was lit by two garden lanterns in glass containers. When he entered Joyce was sitting on the mattress. The larger of the two trunks they had brought lay half unpacked at her feet. Her hair was pulled back and she was wearing one of the long, inappropriate winter nightshirts she had brought from England. Her friend and mentor, Leo Cohn, had told her that the nights in Jerusalem were cold, even in summer.

Bloomberg offered Joyce a sprig of jasmine that he had plucked from the bush beside the gate.

"A visitor," he said, "should always bring something, no matter how small."

"You're not exactly a visitor."

He kissed her on the forehead. Nothing he said came out right. He had to let her go.

"What did you do?" Joyce continued.

"The village, the trees."

Joyce lay back on one of two narrow beds that had been provided for them temporarily by Aubrey Harrison, the local representative from the Zionist organization in London that had brought them out here. It was warmer in the room than outside. A thin line of sweat trickled from beneath Joyce's chin down the open neck of her shirt.

Bloomberg turned his canvas to the wall, leaning it carefully so that only the top edge touched. He kicked off his sandals.

"What they want," he said, "the commission, I shan't be able to do it."

"Is it that difficult?"

Bloomberg produced his letter of instruction from his back pocket.

" 'A series of works depicting Life Under Reconstruction Conditions. Progress. Enterprise. Development.' In other words, inspiring representations of Jewish pioneers. In other words, propaganda."

"You'll have the nights to yourself."

"Hardly enough."

She didn't say anything but he sensed that she didn't think it would hurt him to do work on behalf of somebody else. And in this case, he knew, she happened to believe strongly in the cause. But she had decided that for the moment the kindest thing would be to keep silent. It was more kindness on her part not to mention the money, the sixty pounds advanced to him by the Palestine Foundation Fund. Hardly enough for the milk and honey that he had promised her.

"Tea?" Bloomberg asked.

"I thought maybe something else."

Joyce took a swig from the brandy bottle next to the bed, then sat up, pulled her nightshirt over her head and threw it behind her. She sat— bravely, Bloomberg thought—waiting for him to cross the room. It had been many weeks, maybe months, since they had made love. At first he didn't move, but when she reached back to gather her nightshirt again the movement of her breasts excited him. He took three quick steps and grabbed her wrist.

"If not now, when? Isn't that what the rabbis say?"

Bloomberg laughed, then bent his head and began to kiss her breasts.

After they were done (it was unsatisfying for her, he knew) Bloomberg got up and turned his painting around. It was still wet. He thought he'd got the moonlight on the rooftops rather well, but nothing else. He remembered the figures down the terrace and told Joyce that he had purposefully not sketched them in because he wasn't interested in figures anymore.

"You're a misanthropist," she replied. "What were they doing?"

"Love, or a local argument. I wasn't sure. They were a long way down."

There was a faint smell of turpentine coming, oddly, from the outside in. Bloomberg walked naked to the door and took a couple of steps into the garden. The borders of their thin lawn were dotted with shrubs and rockrose. There was a scent of lavender and the turpentine smell, which seemed to emanate from a grove of pistachio oaks. Joyce came up behind him.

"Not exactly the Garden of Eden," she said, encircling his waist with her arms and nuzzling her face into his back, "but it would be a shame if one of us were to get expelled. I love it here."

He unhooked her arms from around him and stepped away.

A soft moaning that might have been prayer started in their ears and grew louder as a bloodied shape tore through the hedge, rushed at

Bloomberg, held him in a hug and then crashed to the ground, trapping Bloomberg beneath. Joyce screamed, a long high note. Bloomberg shoved the weight off and rolled free. He was screaming himself and his entire body shook. The figure, a middle-aged man in Arab dress, twitched and grew still; his white djellaba was ripped and blood-soaked, so too the kaffiyeh pressed to his chest in a vain attempt to stanch the flow where blood poured from a knife wound above the heart. Joyce knelt down in the dampened grass. The dead, beaten face stared up at her open-eyed. She saw, to her surprise, pale skin, a full red beard, and the curled side-locks of an Orthodox Jew. Bloomberg rose and stood over her. In the moonlight she could see his face, chest, arms, legs and limp penis stained in blood.

2.

Saud, tall for his age, ran in long-legged strides down the hillside between the trees, breathless, tripping over rocks, caught from time to time in bursts of moonlight that felt to him like gunfire. Halfway down he stopped briefly in the shadows behind the Scottish church to strip off his bloodstained shirt, then he ran again, dropping the soaked ribbons of cloth behind him as in a paper chase. There was hardly anyone around— a young couple kissing under the globe of a locust tree, and far in the distance two mounted policemen trotting, mercifully, away from him. He reached the Old City and turned into its labyrinth of alleyways. Near the sesame-oil vats on Cush Street he thought he heard someone call his name. Saud increased his pace, although his lungs were bursting, and five minutes later he emerged through the Damascus Gate. His throat was dry and his heart beat so loudly he thought he might wake the neighborhood.

At the back of De Groot's house on St. Paul Street he climbed the stairway and pushed the door. It was locked, but the half-open window in the wall gave him access. Once inside he moved quickly to the small lamplit desk behind the sofa. He sighed with relief. His leather case containing his books—his name dutifully inscribed on the flyleaves—was there on the rug where he had dropped it when they began their lesson. He held it under his arm, moved into the kitchen and poured himself a glass of water from the pitcher on the table. He took the glass with him when he left and, as he ran, smashed it into the stone wall, adding to the rubble at the side of the street.

Not far from the Dung Gate, Saud turned a corner, grabbed a rope, pushed his feet against a set of stone tiers and lowered himself to the bottom of a cistern. He stood shivering in an inch-thick layer of silt, his back pressed against the wall. The hircine stink in the air that he had sucked in while running was replaced by a cool dampness. He would have to wait until the suq was busy, then climb out and lose himself in the crowd.

Clouds banked like a semicircle of black hills above his head and obscured the moon. He crouched down and put his hands to his head. His hair was matted with blood and sweat; he forced his fingers through the clots, then wiped his hands on the scraps of shirt he still held. The knife plunged and De Groot, spurting blood, released him from their embrace; he was running through the trees with De Groot staggering in the opposite direction. At first he didn't think that he was pursued, but then he heard a tumult of descent, heavy steps, shouts and, farther off, De Groot's cries. By the time he got to the church, nimble and fast among the rocks and tall cypresses, he had lost whoever had started after him.

Moments before dawn, a woman with a jug on her hip leaned her face across the rim of the cistern and dipped her hand in hopeless expectation that she might touch water. Saud lay stretched out in the silt, one arm curled under his head as a pillow, the other stiff by his side. Her cry woke him and, startled, he rose, picked up his leather case, and grabbed the rope. The woman recoiled from the muddied gray figure rising toward her, and then Saud was out and running again like a madman through streets and curved stone stairways, up to the rampart walkway that Governor Ross had built, where, behind him, the light broke in thin wafers of pink over the city's vaulted bazaars and cupolas.

3.

Robert Kirsch woke outside on the morning of his twenty-fourth birthday. In the middle of the night his room had grown unbearably humid and so, risking a body load of mosquito bites, he had thrown off his soaked linen sheet and dragged his mattress out onto the balcony. Now he sat up and stretched; he was surrounded by twisted thick-stemmed geraniums in window boxes. An olive tree pitched its branches over his head and tiny pink cyclamen grew in the crevices of the walls. He'd been lucky to get this place, smack in the center of town.

Kirsch's head ached. He'd had a hell of a night, alone with a bottle of arak. The letter from Naomi still lay on the kitchen table where he had sat and reread it between swigs: a bright chatty little letter, tennis with Toni, tea in the garden with Colin, little brother wrecking the peach tree by climbing on one of its branches, and only in the last paragraph the real news, engaged not to him anymore but to Jeremy Goldthorpe, out with the old in with the new. "Happy Birthday," she'd concluded.

What had he expected? You can't have love (especially long-distance love) and an independent fate: no one had asked him to go and be a policeman in Jerusalem and he didn't know what he was after when he had applied for the post—adventure maybe, someplace not England, some wildness to remember before he settled down.

He walked naked into the tiny kitchen that occupied a corner of his one-room flat and made himself breakfast: bread, olives, goat cheese and a cup of tea. He had one more go-round with the letter, then crumpled it in his hand and let it drop to the floor. Time to move on. There was the lovely Bukharian girl who worked at the corner grocery and leaned her bike on the wall outside his gate every morning; there was the young woman he had seen at the Polo Grounds in Talpiot fetchingly resting her head on her horse's shoulder; there was the American woman who had stopped him to ask directions while he was crossing the street outside the post office, older than he, thirty maybe, her hair prematurely gray, almost white, and a lovely, open face. "My first day in town," she'd said. He would have talked longer with her if the traffic policeman hadn't begun to whistle from his high pedestal and wave his white-gloved hands at them like a crazy mime.

Kirsch pulled on a pair of shorts and took his tea back onto the balcony. The sky, milk white when he had woken, was coloring up turquoise blue. In the distance he could see the zeppelin sail high over the King David Hotel; he watched its parachuted mailbags drift down like dandelion seeds. Twenty-five shillings if you found a lost and undamaged bag. He had written the reward notice himself, and had the handbill distributed all over the city and the province of Judea. The "undamaged" was important. Back in March some inappropriate people had come across some extremely inappropriate international post.

It was Sunday. Kirsch thought he might take a drive, maybe Jericho, or perhaps Hebron. He could invite someone along for a fruit ice. When she'd left him the American woman had headed in the direction of the municipal buildings. Suppose he went there and simply hung about in the doorway, perhaps she'd show up again. He had to do something to give this birthday the appearance of a purpose.

The phone rang as Kirsch was buckling the belt on his trousers. He listened for a moment.

"Goodness," he said. "Right away."

Kirsch sat at De Groot's broad walnut desk, which was covered with books, journals, newspapers, and a large number of scrawled-on manuscript sheets. It was hard to tell if the materials had been disturbed, or whether the mess was simply the reflection of a chaotic mind. The window in front of Kirsch faced south onto St. Paul Street. For the Jews in the neighborhood it was a regular workday, and the shouts of vendors mingled with the braying of donkeys and the occasional car horn. De Groot's body had been taken to the city morgue and identified almost immediately by one of the workers there, an Orthodox Jew from the Mea She'arim quarter. The victim was well known in those parts as a staunch defender of the faith.

Kirsch opened the pages of a leather-bound notebook; the looped handwriting presented itself in columns down the middle of the page under the heading *Kussen.* Kirsch tried to read a few lines, *"Het voorjaarbuiten is altijd zoel,"* then gave up. He'd studied German at school but this was double Dutch to him, or rather, he realized as soon as this thought came into his head, single Dutch. He began to move methodically through the papers, studying carefully those that were in English. In the small white-walled room behind him Kirsch's two sergeants, Harlap and Peled, were emptying the contents of a wardrobe.

When he had finished with what was on the top of the desk Kirsch began to go through the drawers. In one he found a brown velvet bag that contained the victim's prayer shawl, and in another, a smaller cloth bag embroidered with gilt Hebrew letters that held De Groot's phylacteries. The narrow drawer under the center of the desk was locked. Kirsch called Harlap over and in a few moments the sergeant had pried it open. Kirsch removed a folder and extracted a thin sheaf of typed letters, carbon copies of originals that had been posted to London. De Groot had been arranging a trip; the date of his departure, already put off twice, had finally been established as early next week. There was nothing shocking in that, except that De Groot's correspondence, with the exception of one letter, had all been sent to a rather familiar address: 10 Downing Street, home of the prime minister, Ramsay MacDonald. The other letter had gone to a marginally less distinguished recipient: Sir Miles Davenport at the Colonial Office in Pall Mall.

Kirsch closed the folder and stood up. "Are we ready to leave?"

Having gone through the pockets of De Groot's dark suits, Harlap and Peled were now bundling them back into his wardrobe.

"Did you find something?" Harlap asked, eyeing the folder in Kirsch's hand.

"Nothing incriminating. Poor sod was about to go on holiday. Booked to Rome on the *Sitmar* out of Haifa at the end of the month."

Kirsch locked the door behind him. The three men clattered down the narrow staircase and out into the street.

4.

Briggs opened Ross's door and poked his head round.

"He's here."

"Who is?"

"The painter chappee."

Ross beckoned Briggs into his office.

"Look all right, does he?"

"Overdoing the artist-type a bit. He's wearing a beret. And . . ."

"Yes?"

"Well, you know." Briggs made a quick gesture with his forefinger to indicate the size and curve of Bloomberg's nose.

"That's enough of that."

"Sorry, sir."

"Well, show Mr. Bloomberg in."

Ross selected one of the three seals that lay on the blotter in front of him. He stamped a document OFFICE OF THE GOVERNOR, then, as Bloomberg entered the room, he rose from his chair and came around the desk. "So glad you could make it."

The two men shook hands.

"I got Teddy Marsh's letter. You're out for, what is it? A year?"

"Longer, probably."

"Excellent, we'll have plenty of time to get to know one another."

On the wall behind Ross's desk was a photograph of Allenby entering Jerusalem, a map of the city, and a series of wood-framed, poorly executed pencil sketches. Bloomberg recognized the Dome of the Rock and the Church of All Nations at the foot of the Garden of Gethsemane.

Ross caught him looking. "Embarrassing, aren't they? I'm afraid I haven't your talent. But the passion is there. Hand simply won't do what the brain tells it."

"Sometimes that works better."

Ross laughed. "Happy accidents, you mean? No, mine are all unhappy. But do sit down." Ross paused for a moment to remove a cigarette from a silver case. He proffered the case to Bloomberg, who declined.

"Well, quite a welcome to the Holy Land! Embrace from a corpse."

Bloomberg tried to smile. He could still feel the weak arms wrapped round him and the bloody chest pressed onto his bare skin.

"Wife all right? Must have been a terrible shock. Terrible. Can't imagine."

"I think I was more frightened than she was."

"Were you indeed?"

"Do you have any idea who . . . ?"

"Victim, or murderer?"

"Well, both I suppose."

"The victim's rather well known, I'm afraid. Jacob De Groot. A Dutch Jew. He came out to Palestine as a journalist, sympathies all on the Zionist side, but as happens over here more than you would imagine, living in the place transformed him. For the last few years he's been singing the praises of the ultra-Orthodox. The black-hat chaps. They're not too hot on the Jewish state idea, as you must know: defilement of the holy ground, the holy tongue, et cetera. But De Groot was a benign enough fellow—a poet—you know, quite well known back in Holland. Not that I've read his verses." Ross shook his head. "Poor chap. Still, strange case, the Arab clothing and all that. Although we didn't find a wallet on him, so there's your motive, I suppose. As for who did it, we haven't a clue on the knifer. Hoping you might be able to help us. Our Captain Kirsch is heading up the investigation. You'll meet him. He's . . ."

Ross was going to add "one of your chaps," but stopped himself. Kirsch neither looked nor acted like a Jew. In fact, he had attended the same school as Ross's nephew—but his mother, everybody said, or was it his father? Must have been the father, otherwise where'd he get the name? And what did it matter anyway?

". . . terribly bright," Ross continued, lamely, he knew. In order to cover his embarrassment he began to speak faster. "Kirsch is young, but he's shot through the ranks. Chose to bypass Oxbridge and come out here. He's been with us almost since the beginning of the Civil Administration. Two years at least. Anything urgent he reports directly to me. There isn't a better man on the force. If anybody can track down the killer, he will."

Bloomberg, distracted by a hawker's cry from the street, looked toward the window behind Ross's back, where the heads of a clump of shy trees peered in.

Ross picked up two pieces of paper from his desk. He held up one of them, a flyer from the Whitechapel Gallery. "This show that you organized last year."

"Yes?"

"Teddy Marsh was terribly impressed. All Jewish artists, am I right?"

Ross began to read the list of names: "Lipchitz, Modigliani, Pascin . . . yourself."

Bloomberg could tell that the names were unfamiliar to Ross. And why shouldn't they be?

Ross shuffled his papers.

"And here Teddy tells me"—Ross moved his finger down the page, then found his place in the letter—"that the Tate bought one of your paintings."

"Only a drawing, I'm afraid."

"Well, even so. You're in elevated company there."

Bloomberg nodded his head. He could tell that Ross had no idea what kind of work he did, and he certainly seemed unaware of the way in which Bloomberg's reputation had taken a dip in the last year. His February show, something of an experiment, had been a disaster. He had been savaged and ridiculed in the press, made one sale that had barely covered the cost of his materials, and then he had foolishly agreed to give a series of gallery talks: the newspapers were waiting. He remembered the attack word for word: "ARTIST EXPLAINS WHAT HIS PICTURES MEAN: Mark Bloomberg, currently on the cubist bandwagon, is holding an exhibition at the Ransom Gallery, where, once a week, he explains his theories to visitors—an example which might be followed by cubists, futurists and distorticists generally, especially the foreign ones. We could understand their pictures then—perhaps."

"Well," Ross said, beginning to move a few items on his desk, "I'm so glad we could get acquainted. Anything I can help with you'll be sure to let me know. Meanwhile Kirsch will absolutely take care of . . . this inconvenient robbery, this murder . . ." Ross's voice trailed away. There seemed to be something that he wanted to ask but was afraid to. Bloomberg was surprised by Ross's nervousness, but in a moment the governor appeared to collect himself.

"Listen, old chap," he continued, "I don't know if you know, but I've been, well, and its hard to say this without sounding boastful, but, I've been, well, I and others, of course, restoring the city. We have a little society, well not so little actually, the Pro-Jerusalem Society, branches all over the place: London, New York, Chicago. We're trying to be very careful, no more stucco or corrugated iron within the city walls, and no more demolition. We've retiled the bare spaces on the Dome of the Rock, that type of thing. Brought potters in from Mutahia who still work in the old ways, built them a little pottery, found the kilns in the area of the Haram not long after we took the city. Terribly interesting process, wonderfully rewarding. What I was wondering, and of course you may not at all be interested, but perhaps, if time permits, a break from your other work, a rendition of certain spots, buildings, the Muristan for example. Naturally one could pay . . ." Ross, feeling that he had overstepped an invisible boundary, came to an abrupt halt.

Bloomberg smiled. "It's not really my cup of tea."

"No, no of course not, a man of your reputation, simply a thought. Well, jolly nice to meet you and if you should change your mind . . ." Ross blushed.

Bloomberg exited the office and at the foot of the stairs found himself being escorted to a waiting fawn-colored Bentley that showed government badges.

"Sir Gerald said to take you wherever you're headed, sir."

Bloomberg sat back in the broad leather seat. The strange thing was that since arriving in Palestine he had done nothing but paint realistically. Something was compelling him in what was for him an old-fashioned and unusual direction. Perhaps it was the beating he had taken in the London papers. Or something else. The obliterating white light.

He didn't know. Still, Ross was a strange one, seemed more interested in art than in the murder.

"Where's it going to be then, sir?"

Bloomberg gave the driver his address, then changed his mind and asked to be brought to the Old City.

5.

Joyce, wearing only a loose white shirt, long on her, that Bloomberg used to paint in, stood outside the cottage and breathed deep. Not even the memory, all too vivid, of the stabbed and bloody victim could entirely dampen her spirits. If she was honest with herself, and in this particular she wasn't quite ready to be, it was almost as if the murder, in its terrible drama, had already partially fulfilled the promise of excitement that her visions of Palestine had prompted. This place, Jerusalem, was the city that she had dreamed of for months and months, while she was chilled to the bone through London's damp winter and on into its dull spring, the watercolor evanescence of the metropolis's parks and gardens, its traffic honking like angry geese, all less real to her than the Palestine she had never visited, and on which she now pinned all her hopes.

She walked down the rough path broken through high grass to the point where De Groot had died. The police had scoured the spot and its surrounding area but found nothing. Joyce bent to the ground and rubbed her hand in the dirt, half expecting her fingers to come up bloody. She examined the dirt under her nails, then stood and wandered into the garden's wildest corner, where three flat rocks were overgrown with chicory and poppy. The air hummed and a black-and-white hoopoe darted flight paths across her line of vision, as if to sign, seal and de-marcate the area that belonged to Joyce and Bloomberg. She felt, as never before in the long history of her enthusiasms, that this time she would achieve a genuine accomplishment. On her last visit to a Zionist gathering—the rain, as always it seemed, drizzling onto their heads—a smiling Leo Cohn had told her that once she got to Jerusalem someone would get in touch with her, and the way in which she might make herself useful would be specified. Joyce couldn't wait to begin: she imagined how her talents might be employed; she could certainly teach, preferably art or dance, or if more physical work was required she could do that too. She wasn't averse to chopping or digging, or any kind of rigorous endeavor that might both test and strengthen her.

Mark had only the vaguest idea of her degree of involvement with Zionism, and he seemed to regard her fascination with Middle Eastern politics (such as he knew it) as a substitute for domestic entertainment: she had worked up an interest in helping to advance a homeland for the Jews, but she might equally have taken up bridge.

Joyce went back into the cottage. Its walls, pink in the dusk when she had first seen them, followed, so Aubrey Harrison had explained on handing them keys to the door, the governor's prescriptions for new city building: all-limestone under a tiled red roof. The cottage's general state of disrepair and temporary disarray appealed to Joyce, although its outhouse, a fly-ridden closet surrounding a hole in the ground, was, even after her experience of London's medieval plumbing, almost too much to tolerate. Nevertheless, in the thought that there was work to be done on the cottage and its surrounding garden she located a pleasure of identification with the Jewish pioneers whom she admired so much. Again, this feeling could not be relayed to Mark. "But you're not even Jewish!" he liked to remind her, a fact that her fellow Zionists at Toynbee Hall meetings had considered utterly irrelevant.

Light pierced the room's latticed screens and lay a pattern in dots and bars across the yellow matting on the floor. Joyce circled the cramped space, tidying up a little. The tips of the grass outside had rubbed against the back of her legs, and she stretched to scratch at itchy spots that had erupted in the sweaty pockets at the back of her knees. She stacked Mark's paintings by size against a wall. His stuffy kitchen/studio in Stepney Way, a room that smelled of boiled vegetables, had been perhaps only half the size of this place. When she had first visited him there, in the company of her friend Anne Marsden, its decrepit table had been strewn with drawings of a heavy woman with plain features—the only model he could afford, his mother—but the walls were covered with paintings, and on the longest space a canvas was stretched from floor to ceiling. The large work took Joyce's breath away; it showed figures emerging from the hold of a ship, but Bloomberg had presented them as jerky marionettes cast in reds, lavenders, blues, arcs and spirals. Nevertheless they were physical and alive. She lost herself in the painting.

Anne, in order to leave Joyce alone with the artist whose work she so much admired, had suddenly remembered an important errand that she had to run. Mark stood on a sturdy chair, his arm stretched high to a corner of the painting. He continued to work while Joyce watched. The poverty of her surroundings had made her nervous, but she was aroused by Mark's presence and waited impatiently for him to put down his brushes and talk to her, and perhaps, later, to embrace her. That was the beginning, to be followed by the weeks of high passion familiar to all new lovers. She wasn't sure now whether she had encouraged him to leave London for Palestine in order to save him, or save their marriage, or entirely for her own singular purposes. Whatever her motives, the new country, now that she had arrived, seemed alive with possibility.

There was a knock at the door.

"Come in," Joyce called, then, realizing that she was naked beneath Mark's shirt, scrambled to find a skirt to pull on.

A young man in a well-pressed but faintly grubby white uniform pushed the door open and stood on the threshold of the room.

"Oh God, I'm terribly sorry."

He turned away embarrassed while Joyce finished tugging up her skirt. He had glimpsed the top of her thighs and the triangle of her black pubic hair.

"My fault, I shouldn't have told you to come in."

Kirsch tried to collect himself.

"Mrs. Bloomberg?"

She nodded,

"Robert Kirsch. Is this terribly inconvenient? I could come back."

Joyce straightened her skirt and blinked against the flood of light that poured round Kirsch's long, narrow frame and through the door.

"You're from the police?"

"Well, yes, I am the police."

Kirsch, with a mixture of excitement and disappointment, had recognized Joyce. Her gray hair, tied back when he had run into her, hung loose on her shoulders now, and he couldn't mistake her blanched, appealing, heart-shaped face and striking gray-green eyes.

"Well come in, I suppose."

He had to dip his head to pass under the lintel. There were clothes and shoes all over the thin counterpane. One trunk, its contents no doubt packed away, had been placed at the foot of the bed, but another, with its lid open and almost empty, stood at the side. A few of Bloomberg's canvases were propped in a corner of the room. There seemed to be only one chair.

"Please," Kirsch said. "I'll stand."

Joyce pushed aside a pile of blouses, sat on a corner of the bed and gestured Kirsch toward the chair.

"This must have been a dreadful experience for you," he said.

"Pretty bad, but I'll survive."

Her American accent had an English inflection, which he suspected that she might be affecting.

"Would you mind very much?" Kirsch produced a small notebook from the pocket of his tunic.

"I've already answered a lot of questions."

"Yes, I know, but the first people out here—how should I say this without appearing disloyal? Well, those Special Constables are not the most competent note takers."

"I don't know what I can add. It happened so fast. He grabbed on to Mark and then there was blood everywhere."

"Did he say anything?"

"He was groaning. There was a terrible gurgling sound in his throat."

"But you couldn't make out anything that he might have said?"

Joyce thought for a moment. The dying man in the garden froze in her memory and all that she could recollect was her own scream.

"It was an awful confusion," she said. "For a moment, you know, I thought it was Mark who had been stabbed."

Kirsch looked directly at her. "Perhaps," he said, "we can go outside and you can show me exactly where you were standing?"

They stood in a patch of butter-blond weeds listening to the buzz and toil of invisible insects. Kirsch paced the garden, then knelt and crawled from the gap in the hedge toward the area that had been flattened by De Groot and Bloomberg's death hug. He took some notes, then snapped his book shut and smiled at Joyce.

"We've met before, you know."

Joyce gave him a quizzical look.

"In England?"

Kirsch laughed.

"In New York?"

"No, no. Here, a couple of days ago, in town. You asked me for directions. Actually, it was the same day that you had your unfortunate experience."

"There was someone far more unfortunate than me out here."

Kirsch, Joyce thought, looked momentarily like a scolded schoolboy and then he compounded the picture by fiddling with the folds on his white knee socks.

"Outside the post office."

Out of politeness Joyce smiled back at Kirsch; she had no recollection of their encounter.

"Well, you've been fantastically helpful."

"Have I?"

"And I was wondering when I might be able to find . . ."

"Mark?"

"Yes."

"He was supposed to be here an hour ago."

"Yes, I'd been given the impression . . . I mean I believe he left the governor's office . . ." Kirsch's voice trailed away.

"He rarely shows up when you expect him."

"Quite."

Was there a note of bitterness in her voice? Kirsch wasn't sure.

"Well," he said, "it's time for me to be leaving."

"I'm sorry that I can't offer you anything. We're really not settled in yet."

"Don't worry about it," Kirsch replied.

He hesitated a moment and she noticed him staring at her hair.

"I had influenza," she said, "during the epidemic. I was lucky to pull through. While I was sick all my hair fell out, when it grew back in it was white. But look"—she tossed her head as if shaking out the memory of her illness—"what do you want me to tell Mark?"

"Perhaps he could give me a ring."

Kirsch wrote down his number and handed it to her.

He had started to walk away when she called after him. Kirsch turned around.

"I'm sorry," he said, "I didn't hear what you said."

"I asked what you're doing here. Why did you come to Jerusalem, to Palestine?"

Kirsch smiled. "I'm not sure," he said. "Lots of reasons, none of them good ones, I'm sure."

She seemed satisfied with this response.

"And who do you think did this terrible thing?"

"I suppose it's my job to find out."

"And have you discovered anything?"

"We've only just begun the investigation."

He wanted to give her information that might impress her with a sense of his authority and competence, but all he had was his knowledge of the letters that De Groot had sent to England, and on that subject his lips were sealed.

"I see," she said. "And aren't you at all interested in why I'm here?"

Kirsch was about to say "your husband" but he knew that women didn't like to hear that anymore. The war had changed everything. Even his mother, formerly a paragon of compliance, had begun to balk at some of Kirsch's father's more egregious demands: she wouldn't roll his socks into a ball anymore before putting them away.

"I don't know why you're here," Kirsch said, "but I'm glad that you are."

He thought he saw her smile, but he turned quickly away, as if to erase what he had said.

———

After Kirsch had left, Joyce went back into the cottage, poured herself a finger of brandy, and curled up in the chair. She sat with her feet up on the bed. There was no doubt that Mark had abandoned her, in his head if not at home or in bed. The signs of coming disaster hadn't been hard to read: there was the failure of his last show, after which he had become depressed, the death of his mother and his subsequent rejection of sympathy or consolation. He had sat alone at the kitchen table in Vera's old flat sifting through a pile of her tattered clothes, then covering his head with one of her scarves as if it were a prayer shawl. Joyce had tried to encircle him with her arms but he had stuck out his elbows to keep her at bay. He preferred to cry alone.

And if he was gone, what did that mean for her? She refused to play the weepy, forsaken wife: her mother in the apartment on Riverside Drive after Joyce's father had left with "that woman," shutting down her life, inconsolable, playing at widowhood with the black streaming Hudson as backdrop to her melodrama, desperately hoping that Joyce, at eighteen, would take up the slack of her exorbitant loneliness. Well, she wouldn't do it for her mother, and she wouldn't have it for herself.

Joyce took a sip of brandy, shivered and roused herself. She stepped outside into a cloud of butterflies that twisted in the air above the plants like windblown confetti. The dead man's face floated through the trees and held her in his gaze. She stared right back until it moved on.

She hoped that Leo's representative wouldn't take too long to get in touch with her. Despite everything that had happened, more than enough for one week, she was eager to begin.

6.

Once inside the Old City walls Bloomberg quickly found a café, sat down, and ordered coffee and a small bottle of arak. The activity in the square before him—a predictable beggar, his long hair tangled, pursuing a group of tourists; two bearded men haggling over grocery prices in a whirl of argument and insult; a young boy carting a great basket of red peppers—was a corrective to loneliness. When they were in France his friend Jacob Rosen had spoken and written endlessly, wistfully, about Jerusalem. Stuck in the stinking trenches, waiting for the shells that might split any of their heads open, Jacob, stub of a pencil in his hand, had dreamed into his poems a Jerusalem he had never visited. Bloomberg wondered if perhaps he was here because of Jacob: bringing the dead home, taking the ghost on a tour of the market. If he was anything like the Jew he should have been Bloomberg would go down to the Wailing Wall and say a prayer for Jacob, then add another for his mother.

At the next table an old man in a red tarboosh was cleaning a pile of coins. He dipped cotton wool in olive oil, then rubbed the soaking wads over the coins. Bloomberg found him too picturesque to be true. Ignoring him as a subject he took out a small pad from a pocket on his tunic, broke a stick of charcoal and began to draw, in an accumulation of swiftly defined circles, a pile of watermelons on a nearby cart. He picked up a small chunk of moist bread that had fallen from someone's plate and began to use it as an eraser. He worked on a number of drawings, all of objects, until the square in front of him had emptied out. He looked up and saw the polar star glinting above the horizon. Two women passed, carrying brown earthenware jugs toward a pump farther down the street. They worked the handle strenuously, but to no effect. Eventually they managed to secure a thin liquid trickle for a minute or two. Bloomberg had heard that there was a diminished supply of water in the cisterns.

Bloomberg rose to leave, feeling irritated and frustrated. This was his last day of freedom and he had wasted half of it chatting to the upper classes. In the morning, equally boring, he would have to make the acquaintance of the pioneer socialists of the Jewish Women Workers Farm.

He should go home now. He had left Joyce alone too long, especially after what had happened. But what he had told Ross was true, he was the one who had been terrified for hours after the murder, trembling inside while Joyce calmly scrubbed the blood off his body.

A crowd of small boys, barefoot in shabby djellabas, glued themselves to him as he walked back toward the Damascus Gate. They tugged at his shirtsleeves and shoved their grimy palms in his face. He pressed a few piastres into one of the outstretched hands, shrugged off his charges, and increased his pace.

He passed through the gate, skirting the grain sheds and a line of parked tourist cars. He felt too tired to walk but was without money for a taxi. He started up the hill toward the nearest bus stop, then felt himself illuminated from behind by a pair of headlights that held him in their gaze while the car that owned them crawled behind him. Bloomberg turned. It was the same fawn-colored Bentley that had brought him here. The car drew alongside him and halted. The window rolled down and Ross's face appeared.

"Oh, good. I thought it was you. Can we give you a ride?"

Bloomberg wanted to decline but his legs ached and Joyce was waiting.

He settled next to Ross on the backseat.

"Have you been working?"

"Yes."

"Fascinating place, don't you think? Endlessly stimulating."

"I haven't had much time."

"No, of course not."

They left the poorly lit city streets behind, then turned toward Abu Tor, and without Bloomberg's having issued an instruction, headed in the direction of his home. Ross rolled down his window; a reek of burnt camel dung penetrated the car.

"Now, please don't take what I'm about to say amiss, but I was wondering. Your lack of studio space. Since you left today it occurred to me—the roof of my house, there's a covered, shaded area, altogether a large area. Ideal, really. View of the whole city. Stunning. No pressure, of course—paint what you like. I'm not trying . . ."

"It's kind of you, but I don't know when I'll have the time."

"Oh anytime, night or day, makes no difference. You won't disturb us, and I'd be terribly interested to see what you do."

"Well, I'll certainly think about it."

They sat in silence. Ross peered into the night. Oil lamps burned in the windows of scattered houses along the way. After a ten-minute ride they came to a stop.

"Now here we are, I believe."

Bloomberg got out and wished Ross good night.

"Perhaps you'll change your mind. Come anyway, see the view."

Bloomberg stood until the taillights of Ross's car had disappeared. Then he walked off the road and pissed in a grove of eucalyptus trees. A stray goat crossed in front of him, the rusty bell around its neck emitting a string of dull chimes. Bloomberg crossed in front of the window of his house. Joyce had thrown a lace cloth over the bedside lamp; she was reading in the chair. When he tapped gently on the window she looked up immediately, not startled at all, he thought, but as if she was expecting someone. When she saw that it was Bloomberg she quickly closed her book.

7.

Kirsch walked up toward Ross's house, where he imagined the party was already in full swing. He was late because he had sat at his desk for two hours after everyone else had left, sifting the meager evidence that his men had managed to accumulate in the vicinity of the probable site of the murder: a few bloody ribbons of cloth, sketches of indecipherable markings in the dust where the struggle had taken place, descriptions of stripped bushes and a broken path down the hillside that seemed to indicate the direction in which the attacker had fled, but no weapon and no eyewitness. It would take an informer to set things going.

For twenty-four hours his office had been remarkably quiet, and then, suddenly, all hell had broken loose: phone calls, a summons to the high commissioner's office, "very serious matter" . . . "city now a tinder-box" . . . "terribly sensitive situation" . . . "slaying of an important figure, could lead to God knows what." Kirsch had returned to his office to find Ross waiting for him, although Ross, as usual, hardly seemed to give a damn—spent half a hour describing his latest architectural project and the party he'd cooked up for tonight. Even De Groot's letters to Ramsay MacDonald didn't seem to interest him that much. "Prime minister has all kinds of supplicants. You don't imagine he was actually going to see the chap, do you? Marked absence of replies in your little folder." But despite Ross's own nonchalance he had managed to get out a "Pressure's on, old chap," just as he was leaving. Kirsch's bloody luck.

Kirsch rang the doorbell. He could smell the rich sweet odor of snail flowers emanating from a hidden spot among the heliotrope and flowering cactus. A butler opened the door and then Kirsch was inside, moving among the throng. All the Jerusalem grandees were there—the mufti, the kadi, judges and lawyers, both Jewish and Arab, and, of course, a number of British officers. Ross had persuaded some nervous Tommy to sing, and with the accompaniment of a single violinist, the stocky, freckled teenager was warbling the latest sentimental hit from London.

Kirsch moved quickly through the crowd, scanning for the face he hoped to see. After five minutes he was out on the spacious terrace. He looked down into the garden and in the light reflected from the rooms of the house saw Joyce wandering alone under the pepper trees. Her hair was twisted into a tight knot on top of her head. He called to her but as he did so her husband appeared from the shadows and placed his hand on her shoulder. Kirsch watched her turn toward Bloomberg and lean her head into his shoulder. It looked to Kirsch like a hopeless gesture, but maybe he wanted to see it that way. Bloomberg, only an inch or so taller than his wife, stood stiffly and spoke to her.

"Any progress, Robert?" It was Ross. He was at Kirsch's side and looking down in the same direction, toward the painter and his wife.

"Not much, I'm afraid, sir."

"Puzzling."

"Yes, sir."

"I mean, what the hell was De Groot doing all dressed up like an Arab?"

"They're comfortable clothes in this weather, sir."

Kirsch knew it was an idiotic thing to say as soon as he had opened his mouth.

"Witnesses?"

"What you see, sir."

Kirsch nodded in the direction of the Bloombergs.

"You've spoken with them, of course."

"Only the wife, sir. I'm seeing Bloomberg tomorrow, I hope. He was unavailable yesterday. Disappeared somewhere."

"Painting in the desert, I believe."

Kirsch felt a wave of irritation but refrained from asking why Ross hadn't forwarded this information earlier.

"Zionists are damned happy, of course," Ross continued. "De Groot was a thorn in their side. They detest all those Agudat people. Not hard to see why. De Groot and his people have the Zionists down as dangerous blasphemers, defiling the Holy Land."

Ross offered a tight smile.

"But listen, those letters, maybe I was a little hasty. Perhaps you should speak to someone in London?"

"I have, sir."

"Oh, really. Well done. Anything amiss? So what was our victim up to? He was certainly aiming high. Chat with the PM and another with Sir Miles. Ever since Weizmann got his foot in the door every Mediterranean with a beef wants to give our chaps an earful."

"It seems the original letters never arrived, sir. Nobody knew anything about them. You seemed to think he wouldn't have got an audience if they had."

"Yes, although it depends what he'd come to say, I suppose. I suspect it must have been something that he didn't want me to hear. I'm relying on you to find out what that might have been, Robert. No stone unturned, eh? Even if it means treading on some toes."

"Absolutely, sir."

"Bit of a hurry-up, let's get hold of this killer, nip things in the bud."

Ross waved to the Bloombergs, who had turned and were walking back toward the house. As they approached he shouted down: "Been up on the roof yet? Let me take you. There's enough moonlight. Should be able to show you something. You won't regret it."

Bloomberg stepped forward while Joyce hesitated. Kirsch heard him say, "I'll go alone."

Kirsch made his way to the terrace stairs and met Joyce halfway as she ascended. She almost walked past him without offering a hint of recognition but he touched her lightly on the arm.

"Beautiful evening."

She smiled at him. "Yes, isn't it just."

Joyce looked past Kirsch and toward the room. The serviceman had stopped singing and the violinist played on alone. Joyce climbed two stairs, then halted. Her shoulders relaxed and she turned to look Kirsch in the face.

"Tell me something, Robert. When the car came to collect us the driver said that there were nails all over the main road and he would have to take a back route. Who exactly is intended to be sabotaged?"

Kirsch smiled, happy to have a question that he could answer.

"There's a taxi strike. They're trying to prevent other cars from being taken out. If you know which roads to avoid there's not much of a problem."

"And do you have a car here?"

"I do, yes."

Kirsch tried to avert his eyes from the little vest under her white jacket that was buttoned just to the point of cleavage. How interesting and brave of her to dress so unconventionally at a party of conservative women, a slap in the face to the local spinsterarchy, all those old ladies sentimental about sheikhs. On the other hand, she was an artist's wife. Perhaps some daring or excess was expected.

Joyce smiled at him.

"How would you like to take me for a spin down some of those open roads?"

"But . . ." Kirsch stammered. "Well, very much, I'd like that very much."

"Then let's go."

"Now?"

"Perhaps you wanted to hear more of the violinist?"

Kirsch felt his face burn. Joyce began to move up the stairs.

"No need," he said. "We can leave through the garden."

"Good."

She followed him along a wall covered with flame-pink ivy geraniums. The wide sleeves of her jacket brushed against the leaves. Then they were out in the driveway.

From his place on the roof of the house, gazing out toward the Old City, Bloomberg watched Kirsch open the passenger door for Joyce. He saw her remove her jacket, fold it, and stretch forward to place it on the backseat. He watched as she sat, then swung her legs in. He saw Kirsch close the door, circle the bonnet, and take his place behind the wheel. It seemed a while before the engine turned. Joyce's bare arm was a white line in the window, then the line disappeared. The car pulled smoothly down the hill. Bloomberg watched until the Ford's taillights vanished around a bend in the road.

They sat in the car on a side road out near the British Police Training School. Kirsch didn't know why he had brought her here. It wasn't a beautiful place. A few dusty eucalyptus trees lined the road. There were tents visible in a nearby field, where construction of some new suburb was about to begin.

He killed the engine.

"Cigarettes, by any chance?" Joyce asked. "Please say you've got some."

Kirsch handed her a box of Player's. Joyce removed two cigarettes and offered one to him. He produced the matches from his pocket. Joyce inhaled deeply, then relaxed back in her seat; the simple warmth of the air was an unholy sensual pleasure. There was absolutely no reason in the world for her to feel that she belonged here, but she knew that she did. Some travelers discovered Paris or Rome or Mexico and felt that they had come home, but Joyce had known for a long time now that Jerusalem was her destiny, and the city hadn't, couldn't, disappoint her.

They sat in silence for a few minutes and then Kirsch, to fill the space (was it only to fill the space?) began talking about his older brother Marcus, killed April Fool's Day 1918—could she believe that? King's Own

Royal Lancaster. Damn army couldn't find the grave for two years. In the end they all went over to France, Kirsch, his parents, his cousin Sarah, stood around in the rain outside this little village, Fampoux. Father said Kaddish, never heard him speak Hebrew before. Army paid for the headstone but wanted more money for any inscription other than the name. Marcus had wanted to be a painter—not without talent as it happened. Mother wanted to put "Artist" on the stone—three and thruppence they charged them! Not the money of course.

Kirsch felt that he was prattling, yet prattling about things that meant a great deal to him and that he wished he could convey differently. In any case, she didn't seem to be listening. After all, he continued, it was probably Marcus who had led him to Jerusalem. Having the adventure his brother couldn't, getting away from his grief, his parents' grief, a heaviness in the home you can't imagine.

"Wait a minute," Joyce said. "Your father said Kaddish? You're a Jew?"

Kirsch nodded his head.

Joyce laughed.

"I'm sorry," she said, "I can't believe it."

"It's not something that I'm ashamed of."

Was he sometimes ashamed? Kirsch wasn't altogether sure.

"Well, no, why would you be? But you're a British policeman. I mean, aren't you, don't you feel that you're on the wrong side of the stockade?"

Kirsch looked at her and felt his face redden.

"I don't know what you mean," he said.

"Yes you do. You know exactly what I mean."

Immediately, Joyce regretted what she had said. She had gone too far. It was a fault of hers, a by-product of her zeal that she needed to contain, her rushes to judgment.

Kirsch looked straight ahead.

"Oh look, please forgive me," she said. "I've been here all of a week. I'm sorry about your brother."

The car windows were rolled down. Someone had left a pile of empty petrol tins by the side of the road.

"Thank you," Kirsch said.

Joyce tapped ash out of the window, then opened the car door to drop the cigarette and stub it out with her foot. In the moonlight she could see the walls of the training school barracks, asbestos slabs on a steel framework.

"Shall we get some air?"

She got out and walked a few steps, her mood lightening as she did so. No harm done. Kirsch came and stood close. He wanted to put his arms around her. A dusty fig cactus stretched its shoots like barbed wire in front of them. Although the night was still warm Joyce suddenly shivered. Kirsch returned to the car and grabbed his pullover from the backseat.

"Here," he murmured, placing it around her shoulders and knotting the sleeves at the front. "Your husband," Kirsch continued, "wouldn't he mind us being here?"

"I doubt it," Joyce replied. "He might even feel relieved."

"Why? Does he have someone else?"

"I don't think he wants anyone else. Not now, anyway."

"How could anyone not want you?"

Joyce laughed lightly. "You don't know anything about me," she said. "Or him."

Kirsch felt his hands trembling slightly. Joyce could have said anything to him, awful humiliations, and he would still have wanted to kiss her.

"Come on," Joyce said, "take me back."

They drove back in silence. He dropped her at the foot of the driveway that led to Ross's house. They had not been gone longer than an hour, and the party was still crowded. In all likelihood they hadn't even been missed. Kirsch was about to ask when he could see her again outside the investigation—when she turned to him.

"He spoke a name," she said, as if recalling a dream, "the dead man spoke a name."

8.

In the hour after dawn it was cool on the roof. Bloomberg wore the cord trousers and thick knitted sweater that had served him so well through several London winters. On his head he sported a wide-brimmed straw hat that Joyce said made him look like a gaucho. Ross had asked one of his servants to construct a shelter for Bloomberg, three sheets and a canopy that whipped and snapped like a ship's sails when the wind rose. The previous day Bloomberg had begun to set out the work in charcoal: the city spread out before him with the morning sun coming over the hills. He could do this kind of thing with his eyes closed—and perhaps that would be better. The money—that's all it was. But it wasn't. He had to admit that of the places he had found to paint—and been sent to paint—this rooftop was the most congenial. Bloomberg had hated the workers farm, the girls in their unattractive long black bloomers, the dullness and the monotony of the quarry work he was supposed to be sketching, the heat, his own boredom. As for his "real" painting—well, there wasn't any. By nightfall he was increasingly exhausted. He sank onto the bed, closed his eyes, and pretended to be asleep. Once Joyce pressed into him, reached her hand, cradled his balls, stirred the inevitable erection, and after a repeat of his quick, bad lovemaking, turned away. He was disappointing her, although somehow it seemed she was ceasing to care. That being so, he had no idea why she stuck with him. Perhaps she was waiting for him to release her. It wasn't that he didn't feel for *her,* more that he couldn't feel for anyone. Not anyone living, that is. Love had been stolen away by death: his mother's swollen knuckles, her hands red from wash day—and as for Mark, the forty-five-year-old mummy's boy, his eyes were wet with tears. Poor Joyce.

Certainly in his present state of mind it was better for Bloomberg to be up here above the gray domes and hewn stone than back at the cottage. Ross couldn't possibly have anticipated what an advantage it would be for Bloomberg to be set apart, tied to a place where people were so distant that they hardly marked the landscape. He would represent the

Holy City for his patron, and eventually, if he had enough time to himself, the "real" painting would return.

"Tea, sugar, lemon, bread, marmalade—and the latter locally made, would you believe?"

Ross stepped forward hesitantly, regretting that he had interrupted. He placed the tray down on the roof a couple of yards from Bloomberg's straw chair, then retreated as if it were Bloomberg who was the governor of the city.

Bloomberg carried on working. He wasn't averse to the interruption, or the breakfast, but it was best to let Ross think otherwise. He didn't want to interfere with Ross's exalted notion of the artist, not at this formative stage of their relationship, and certainly not until he had been paid. When Bloomberg estimated that Ross was halfway down the stairs but still within earshot he yelled, "Thank you."

But Ross was still on the roof, hovering in the background, watching as the shapes of the city were accomplished on Bloomberg's canvas.

"You know they were going to tear the old Suq al-Qattanin down when we arrived. It was originally the bazaar of the cotton merchants—hence the name, of course. Architecturally it's absolutely the most important of the old vaulted bazaars in all of Palestine and Syria. Utterly lovely. Preservation—so important, don't you think?"

"It depends what's being preserved," Bloomberg replied without looking up from his canvas.

"Oh, you've heard."

"Heard what?"

"Well, I do have my critics. It's been suggested that I exhibit a bias toward the Christian sites."

"Is it true?"

"Not at all. The Suq al-Qattanin is one example. Then we removed that hideous Turkish 'Jubilee' clock tower from the Jaffa Gate, not a damn thing to do with religious favoritism—simply an aesthetic improvement and a major element in restoring the walls. Some people seem to think the Pro-Jerusalem Society is proselytizing every time we strip some appalling Marseilles tile or rip up corrugated iron."

Bloomberg put down his brushes and wiped the back of his sleeve across his forehead. Ross correctly read the gesture as a cue for him to leave.

"I'm terribly sorry," he said. "Completely inappropriate of me. I'll let you get to it. Can't stop, you see. The place has taken me by the throat. I expect it will grab you too."

Bloomberg looked past the domes, towers and pinnacles to the austere mountains that framed his view. If you discounted the murder victim in the garden, then nothing much had grabbed him by the throat since he had come to Jerusalem, except the idea of putting a halt to the only activity that he was incapable of giving up: his work. "Death," a friend of his in London had once said, "is most welcome for the artist. It means he doesn't have to paint anymore."

"Stay as long as you like," Ross added, "and please don't worry about the tray, Nasr will take care of it."

Bloomberg painted for three hours, until the heat became oppressive. His thick cords stuck to his skinny legs, and his hands, clammy with sweat, could no longer hold the brushes without slipping. It was only nine o'clock and he was due at the workers farm again before they broke for a light meal at eleven. But really, if he had Ross to back him, why did he need the Zionist commission?

By ten he was back in the Citadel, which had quickly become his favorite Old City café, near the Jaffa Gate, with his sketch pad open on his knees. The water line was longer than ever. Ross had told him that in the last month street sprinkling had been banned and building construction virtually halted. At the American Colony Hotel, running water was available only on alternate days. Bloomberg watched the line shuffle forward, the women veiled, the men's faces lined and tight. All carried goatskins slung over their shoulders. The reservoir near the al-Aksa mosque was almost half a mile away and access was strictly regulated. These people in the queue were authorized water carriers who would distribute, like milkmen, all over the city.

By noon, the line had thinned and Bloomberg was alone in the café. He remembered, without caring very much, that, for the second day in a row, he had missed an early-morning appointment with Robert Kirsch.

Ross, who understood priorities, would take care of that. And in any case, what could he add to what Joyce had already given the policeman? The golden name.

After five nights of sleeping in the city's hidden places, its drained cisterns and empty vats, with only his case for a pillow, and days spent in the dark corners of churches, or on the move, venturing out at dusk to steal fruit from one stall, bread from another, Saud had returned home. He had arrived before dawn, taken fresh clothes from the line, then crept in and hidden his case under a mattress. His beloved books: he should have destroyed them days ago, but he couldn't. He had collected his goatskin from the room where his brothers slept, and then tried, using as little water as possible, to scrub his face and silt-stained arms. As he closed the front door he had heard his mother stir in her bed.

Now he shuffled forward with the others who were in line for water. It was best, he had decided, to go about his business because surely by now the police would be looking for someone hiding, or someone loose, scared and running. The important thing was that no one could have caught more than a glimpse of him scurrying down the hillside, he was sure of that. Once in the suq he greeted the merchants whom he knew and moved on, his lips parched and his eyes stinging from lack of sleep.

He had reached a sign advertising LIPTON'S TEA AND SHERBET when he saw the two policemen approaching. His instinct was to run, but sudden movement on his part would only draw their immediate attention. So he breathed in and turned to face the stall on his right, squeezing his feet into a space between the open sacks of spices as if he could be invisible among the cardamom and black pepper and, for a moment, when they called his name, that was how he felt, as if the word "Saud" had floated past him and attached to someone else, the stall owner in his red tarboosh, or the artist sitting in the café—or it had been absorbed by the stones, or swallowed into the narrow path of blue air that ran the length of the bazaar above him.

9.

Kirsch had not been inside a synagogue since his peremptory bar mitzvah at the Bayswater Synagogue eleven years ago. His father, going through with the ceremony in deference to his mother and the pressures from her family, had joked all the way through the service, and continued to do so when they had strolled in Regent's Park later in the afternoon. Now here was Kirsch in Jerusalem: endless visits to the Holy City without once crossing a holy Jewish portal. He had been in plenty of churches and mosques, mostly tagging along with Ross, where he had pretended to be interested during his superior's lectures on the Crusader lintels of the Holy Sepulchre or the startling arabesques of a mural on the Haram. He now suspected that by staying away from the temples, he had been trying too hard to demonstrate his impartiality. He wasn't much of a Jew, but for everybody here his religious affiliation, nominal as far as Kirsch was concerned, seemed to be the salient thing about him.

The room he now entered, which had the appearance and feel of a small damp wine cellar, could not have accommodated more than twenty or so worshipers. A thin curtain partitioned off the cramped, ill-ventilated area set aside for women. From this dank corner the wives and daughters of the pious could hear but not see the activities of their men. The sanctuary seemed to receive most of its light through a single window, although thin pencil lines penetrated from holes in the ceiling.

Rabbi Sonnenfeld occupied a seat before the crudely presented ark, which was no more than a wooden box draped in black velvet. Behind him against the wall stood a black marble table covered with phylacteries, prayer shawls and prayer books. Above that three rows of wooden pegs displayed at present a single black coat and hat.

As Kirsch approached, Sonnenfeld tapped his head, and Kirsch, who had removed his hat on stepping out of the sun, quickly replaced it. Kirsch looked around for an empty chair and pulled it up close to the rabbi.

"I'm sorry to trouble you."

The rabbi waved his hand.

"This is not a difficult case for you, Captain Kirsch. The descendants of Jacob employing the tactics of Esau. What will be hard is presenting the truth and getting your government to act on it."

"I'm sorry. I don't quite follow."

"What do you think? Yaakov De Groot, a wonderful man in case you didn't know. A great speaker on our behalf. Our enemies wanted him quiet as the grave, and now he is."

"Your enemies?"

"Who do you think? These murderers. Do you see the depths to which they have fallen? I've told my congregants again and again, 'Separate yourselves from this evil community of Zionists.' I advise you to do the same thing."

"Well I have some news for you. On information received from one of our witnesses we have rounded up a group of young men."

"Good."

"Young Arab men."

The rabbi opened and raised his hands in a gesture of exasperation. It was the kind of exaggerated motion that Kirsch's father would imitate when poking fun at London's ultra-Orthodox Jews.

"Then you have made a serious error."

"We think probably not."

The oil lamp suspended from the ceiling, symbol of God's eternal flame, emitted a subdued red glow. There was a rustle behind the curtain and then a kerchiefed woman emerged sweeping dust before her and out of the door. Kirsch remembered standing in Canterbury Cathedral with his father—a stopover point on one of the family summer drives to the south coast. "Look at this place," his father had said, throwing his head back to gaze at the vaulted ceiling. "It's an absolute wonder more of us didn't convert. Can't believe I didn't." He spoke like this in order to provoke and annoy Kirsch's mother. Still, in this claustral synagogue and its vista of enclosing rock, Kirsch saw how his father might have had a point.

"Give me a reason," the rabbi continued. "Explain why an Arab boy would want to do such a thing. Do you think the young Arab men simply kill a Jew whenever they take it into their heads?"

"The clothes. I hoped perhaps you might explain the clothes to me?"
Sonnenfeld shrugged.

"I've already told you the murderers, do I have to do all your work?"

"Would you care to be more specific about Mr. De Groot's enemies?"

The rabbi looked directly at Kirsch but without speaking. Outside, a bicycle bell rang, quickly followed by the skid of thin wheels, then came voices raised in anger.

"Mr. De Groot prayed here last Friday night?"

"This you know already, so why do you ask me?"

"And then he went home?"

"Ask the woman."

"The woman?"

The rabbi stood. He was taller than Kirsch had gauged him to be, only an inch or so shorter than Kirsch himself. Sonnenfeld took his hat from the coat peg. He moved toward the door of the synagogue, calling out in Yiddish to the woman sweeping in the back room. Kirsch laid his hand on the rabbi's arm.

"There are appetites that not everyone has the strength to control, Captain Kirsch, and that includes those amongst us, like Yaakov, who seek to do good."

"Where will I find her?"

"Not among us."

"Sit down, Rabbi," Kirsch said firmly. The rabbi glanced where Kirsch's hand lay on his forearm. Kirsch withdrew the offending touch, and reached into his tunic pocket for pencil and pad. He offered them to the rabbi.

"The name and address, please."

The rabbi sighed and moved back to his bench. He scribbled one word in the notebook.

"This is all I know."

Kirsch glanced at the paper.

"And the address?"

"Ask here." Sonnenfeld wrote again.

"Thank you." Kirsch tried to sound both policeman-like and conciliatory.

Rabbi Sonnenfeld looked up.

"British and Jewish Captain Kirsch, you're an interesting combination."

"I'm not sure that's how most people look at it."

"Then how do they?"

"More, I believe, as a *suspicious* combination." He was thinking of Joyce and how she had accused him of being on the "wrong side of the stockade."

Sonnenfeld smiled and immediately Kirsch regretted having let the rabbi draw him out.

"To the Jews, British; to the British, a Jew; and for the Arabs, the worst of both worlds. Is that what you mean?"

"Something like that."

Kirsch didn't like the way the conversation was turning and abruptly shifted direction.

"Did you know that Mr. De Groot was planning a trip to London?"

The rabbi returned a blank stare.

"Do you have any idea why he would be going? Was this trip the usual stuff, or something more?"

"The usual stuff being that all Jews, or maybe I should say *most* Jews, are not Zionists and that the British government needs to be reminded of this."

"And that's it?"

"Should there be something else?" Rabbi Sonnenfeld shrugged. "And you, Captain Kirsch. What's your position? Are you a Zionist sympathizer?"

"I don't have a position," Kirsch replied, again regretting instantly that he had spoken and then, despite himself, wanting to add, as if in explanation for his political naiveté, "My brother . . . my brother was killed." He stopped himself, however, and instead announced to the rabbi, "We'll talk again."

"Perhaps you'll come to pray with us," Sonnenfeld replied.

"I don't think so."

The one-room synagogue had grown oppressively hot. Or perhaps Kirsch was simply feeling claustrophobic. Kirsch's father had got that way in synagogues of any size, and nothing worked him up more than a congregation at prayer. Communal prayer offended him. He considered it the bleating of sheep, atonal blows from the thoughtless flung against the only edifice that Harold Kirsch valued: the shrine of individual personality. Kirsch tugged at his collar. He had to get out, away from this stick of a rabbi and his yellowing teeth.

"If you should hear anything that you think might be of use, please let me know."

The rabbi nodded and somehow managed to convey that he was unimpressed by Kirsch's air of self-importance.

Kirsch left the synagogue. His car was in the garage to be fitted with a new exhaust, a part that would apparently take a week to come in, and he had borrowed a motorbike from a friend in the constabulary. He kick-started the engine, looked again at the rabbi's note, then rode off in the direction of the Order of St. John Hospital. By the time he arrived it was dusk. Kirsch wandered down corridors whose walls were the color of tea, and on through the wards, past iron bedsteads where patients lay under tented mosquito nets as if in giant cribs. The nurses' black-and-white clipped-wing caps made them look like nuns—and perhaps some of them were. Although not De Groot's woman by the sound of it.

Kirsch didn't find her. The matron, a robust figure all in white who anachronistically still wore the old prewar Turkish crescent on her uniform, told him that Alice had gone to Nazareth to meet with friends of hers who were visiting from England. She was due back for the afternoon shift on Sunday, so perhaps she would be in Jerusalem tomorrow night, or on Sunday morning.

"Do you have an address for her in Nazareth?"

"Only in Jerusalem."

"May I have it?"

The matron stood up from behind her desk, took two steps to a wooden file cabinet and produced a sheet of paper. In large, hopeful, forward-leaning cursive letters she copied the address for Kirsch.

"Is Alice in trouble, Captain?"

"I don't believe so."

Kirsch asked her about De Groot. Had the matron ever met him?

"He came to the children's ward once," the matron replied. "He brought small presents and we greatly appreciated his doing so." Kirsch sensed that she had had no idea, until now, that De Groot was connected to a member of her staff.

"Didn't you think it strange," Kirsch asked, "an Orthodox Jewish gentleman carrying gifts to Arab children?"

"Not at all. In true charity we find no religious barriers, Captain."

On his way home Kirsch stopped to buy almonds from a woman squatting by the side of the road. It was late when he came into his flat. He sat on his veranda and shelled the nuts. The night was clear and the distant stars appeared to invite a compact with loneliness. The smells of the hospital, of camphor and iodine, were still with him. He remembered an air raid in London during the war. He and his mother had been caught in East London. Why were they there? Something to do with a jeweler. Kirsch was sixteen at the time. He had pulled his mother in the direction of the crowd moving in haste down the Mile End Road toward the London Hospital. They clattered downstairs into the basement and sat on the floor there. His mother folded her elegant red coat and used it for a seat. Patients in thick pajamas held each other's arms in order to remain ambulatory. Nurses lifted those who were in wheelchairs. Kirsch remembered an incessant coughing and the rank air. He was tall for his age and he sensed people looking at him with the special disdain reserved for those who did not serve. He wanted to blurt out, "I'm too young." After an hour or so the German zeppelins passed by and an all clear sounded.

Inspired by this memory, Kirsch began a letter home, but having collected pen and paper from the drawer in his kitchen table, he lost the energy of his good intention. The past was replaced by a fantasy of the future. Traveling somewhere with Joyce, her husband once more out of the picture. Kirsch conjured Joyce's face, her gray-green eyes and pencil-thin eyebrows, her white hair pulled back away from her face. Her slightly fleshy nose and full lips. He thought he was probably in love with her. It was absurd.

10.

"A hundred pounds?"

"Do you doubt the word of our governor?"

Bloomberg retrieved a crumpled envelope from the pocket of his trousers. He extracted a thin sheet of paper and read, as if he were barking orders:

Commissioned from Corporal M. Bloomberg, formerly of the 18th King's Royal Rifles, for view of the Mount of Olives. One hundred pounds. Half to be paid now, half on receipt of said masterwork.

Joyce laughed and grabbed the letter. It was as he had said, without the army references, of course, and without the last three words.

"And what will happen to 'Jewish Life in Palestine'?"

"It will continue without me."

They were sitting in the garden close to the fig tree and near the gap in the hedge that De Groot had burst through. Across the valley, the stone houses of an Arab village, half hidden in shadow, merged into the darkening landscape.

"You'll tell them I'm ill," Bloomberg added.

"Tell them yourself."

Bloomberg got out of his chair and kissed her on the lips. He sensed her disapproval but was unmoved by the content of her opposition. Instead he responded only to her manner, to what he liked to think of as her *American* feistiness, a characteristic that greatly appealed to him.

"When do you start?" Joyce asked.

"I've already begun. Ross has set me up on the roof of his house."

"Are you sure that this is what you want to do?"

Bloomberg didn't reply immediately. Instead he walked down the garden path to the front gate, swishing the high yellow grass with his hand, then he turned to face Joyce.

"I'm not going to paint picture postcards for government officials, if that's what you think."

Later, they lay side by side in bed, not touching. Bloomberg stared at the ceiling. There were brown patches left by the winter rains, a topography of stains that he found somehow reassuring. He should have remained silent but a desire to provoke her overtook him. When he spoke his voice was misleadingly gentle.

"How was your drive with Captain Kirsch?"

Joyce opened her eyes. "Oh, you saw."

"Was it exciting?"

"If it was, I didn't notice."

"He must be about your age, or perhaps appealingly younger."

Joyce raised herself onto one elbow. She was naked under the sheet. Bloomberg touched the back of his hand to the side of her breast.

"He lost his brother in the war."

"Careless of him."

Joyce turned away on her side. Bloomberg spooned his body into hers and reached his hand over her face, following the contours of her lips and nose as if he were a blind man.

"Now, when I was in the trenches . . ." Bloomberg adopted the story voice of an old soldier about to begin a long and resistible tale.

"Yes."

"There were demons dragging strangling wire."

" 'And you were stricken dumb.' Why do you have to make fun of yourself?"

Bloomberg had scribbled the poem on a sketch in blue crayon— the only work he had brought back from the war.

He let his hand drop between her thighs and rest there, then he touched his lips to the arch of her back and whispered:

"Put the gun to my foot and pulled the trigger." For emphasis he rubbed his left foot, with its missing toe, against the back of her leg.

"Oh, stop."

He touched his hand to her cheeks. If he was checking for tears he was going to be disappointed.

"What's going to become of us?" His voice was strained toward tenderness.

"I don't know," Joyce replied.

"You should leave me," he said.

"Perhaps I will," she whispered.

Joyce sat up in the bed and froze. There was someone outside in the garden, she was sure of it. There were footsteps, a flowerpot knocked over. She put her hand on Bloomberg's shoulder to wake him, then waited. The steps had moved and now seemed to be coming from the derelict piece of land at the rear of the house. Then there was silence. She laid her head back on the thin pillow. Perhaps she had been mistaken . . . A stray dog—she had seen so many—or a goat; the animals wandered loose, foraging everywhere, blocking traffic. She looked at Bloomberg lying on his back, the white sheet covering his striped pajamas and pulled almost over his face, like a shroud. She tugged it gently under his chin. Sleep softened his features. The look of injury was temporarily gone. Ten minutes passed, Joyce was on the verge of dozing off again, but this time the steps were very close. She turned in the bed.

"Mark!"

At the heavy knock on the door Bloomberg woke, startled, while Joyce plucked her nightgown from the floor and pulled it on.

"Who is it?" Bloomberg called.

"Police. I'm sorry to come so late."

Joyce lit one of the oil lamps by the bed.

When Bloomberg unlocked the door a man in uniform entered the room.

He introduced himself as Sergeant Harlap. He had been on a routine patrol, he said, but had been asked to pay special attention to the Bloombergs' house as he passed it. And indeed he had heard someone scrambling around nearby. Someone who had run off when he approached. Had Mr. or Mrs. Bloomberg heard anything?

"I did," said Joyce, "but I was half asleep."

As he spoke, Harlap had moved to the far end of the room. He tipped back a canvas that was leaning against the wall and looked at the work.

"Interested in buying?" Bloomberg asked, then added firmly, "If not, put it back."

Harlap turned.

"We have many wonderful Jewish artists in Palestine, Mr. Bloomberg. Perhaps you've met some—Zaritsky? Rubin?"

Bloomberg tried not to look surprised.

"I haven't yet had the pleasure."

Harlap laughed.

"You think a simple policeman shouldn't know about art? Not the kind of thing a London bobby generally understands?"

"I would think, given the chance, that your average London bobby would know a hell of a lot more than your average London art critic."

Harlap turned to Joyce.

"I know you've been asked before," he said, lengthening the syllable on the "ore" in the marginally singsong way of the Jewish Palestinians, "but would you mind if I asked again if you saw or even heard anyone else at all in the neighborhood on the night of the murder? You see, perhaps whoever was around here tonight was here before. They may be looking for something."

"I saw nothing except the victim. I heard nothing, except the name the victim spoke."

"And that name was Saud?"

"That's right."

"It couldn't have been anything else?"

"Perhaps." Joyce thought for a moment. "But I heard 'Saud.' "

Harlap smiled. He seemed pleased with the result of his little interrogation.

The oil lamp on the bedside table burned low. Joyce adjusted the wick, and the flame shot up momentarily, illuminating the entire room until she brought it under control.

Harlap moved to the bed. He sat down on Joyce's side and spread his fingers in the indentation that her head had made in the pillow. The gesture held a peculiar intimacy.

"And your husband," he continued, turning to Bloomberg, who had sat down on one of the empty trunks, "saw two Arab men earlier in the evening."

"I saw two men in Arab clothes."

"Ah, yes. One a Jew who liked to play dress-up, and one Saud."

"I have no way of knowing."

"Mr. De Groot had some money dealings with the Arabs. You know this, of course."

"I didn't."

"Perhaps he had other dealings too." Harlap had swung his feet up and was lying outstretched in a most unpolicemanlike manner.

There was silence for a moment.

"I may seem naive . . . ," Joyce began, but Bloomberg touched her arm and she paused in midsentence.

"Oh," she finally said, "*lovers*. Well, why didn't you just say so?"

"No, not lovers, a boy fucker and his boy. With lovers no one pays."

Bloomberg, on the verge of telling Harlap to shut up, bit his lip.

Harlap swung himself heavily from the bed.

"Don't worry. Sleep in peace. We will catch him."

After he had left, Joyce dimmed the lamp and returned to bed. Bloomberg lingered by the paintings that he had leaned against the wall. The brandy bottle was on a blue stool beneath the window. Bloomberg picked it up and swallowed a quick gulp. The cheap local liquor burned his throat.

"Jews make terrible policemen," he said.

"Why is that?" Joyce spoke from the bed, her face turned away from Bloomberg.

"Too cocky. Too much imagination."

"Isn't that what they say about you?"

"I have no imagination whatsoever. Hence the dour and laborious images that I frequently produce."

"That was one man in one newspaper."

She was tired of trying, fed up with stroking, boosting and encouraging him.

"In the right newspaper it only takes one man to kill a show."

Bloomberg continued to assess his paintings, turning them this way and that in the yellow light thrown by the oil lamp.

Joyce thought of De Groot and the man or boy who was perhaps his lover. "I kissed thee ere I killed thee." Was that it? Othello?

After a while Bloomberg set aside his canvases and got into bed beside her. He ran his hand once through her hair as if to soothe her, but it was he who quickly fell asleep.

11.

Saud crouched in a corner of the narrow, malodorous basement room. Next to him two fellow detainees played dice on the floor. The collection of bodies was absurd—fifty men and boys, all named Saud. One by one they left to be interrogated. By the time they got to Saud it would be the middle of the night. He had heard the muezzin's call to evening prayers hours ago. At street level outside the room's only window a screeching cat fight was in progress.

Saud's mother must be desperate to know where he was. His brothers had to have been out searching for him. Or did everybody know by now about the roundup? And if his mother came to get him what would she say? Would she say nothing at all? That would be the best. After all, why would she speak to a British policeman? But what about the woman who had seen him in the bottom of the cistern?

He had fallen asleep by the time they came for him, curled up with his head on a flagstone pillow. The strong arms of a man on either side lifted him to his feet. The policemen were short, squat individuals, their faces sunburned, especially at the tips of their noses.

"Forty down, ten to go. Don't look so scared. I'm Corporal Arthur, he's Corporal Sam. We're here to take you for walkies."

"This way if you don't mind, son."

The men hustled Saud down a broad corridor that led to a small office. They dumped him in a chair.

"Won't be a moment. The dentist is in the toilet adjusting his drill."

"I don't think he's got one, 'as he?"

"Well, if he has it's one of those funny ones, without the little spigot on the end."

"A drill doesn't have a fucking spigot."

Corporal Arthur lowered his head until his face was close up to Saud's.

"Ever been here before, son?" he half whispered, " 'cause I have a funny feeling I recognize you."

Saud responded with a blank look.

"No speak English, Abdul?"

"It wasn't you I saw last Tuesday with your hand in the charity box, then scooting out the back of the Holy Sepulchre, was it? 'cause it was certainly someone who resembled you. Skinny with black hair and looking like he wanted a kick up the arse."

Kirsch came into the office and the two men stood to a ragged attention. He saw that the boy was scared. And why not? Even without Dobbins and Cartwright, who enjoyed putting a little fear into "the natives." They weren't prejudiced, Kirsch thought, just stupid, or indifferent. Zionism and Arab pan-nationalism meant about as much to them as last year's snow.

"Saud number forty, sir."

"Thank you. You may leave. I'll call you when I'm ready for the next fellow."

When they were alone Kirsch poured Saud a glass of water from the jug on his desk. The boy couldn't have been more than sixteen.

Kirsch wrote down his full name, Saud al-Sayyid; his address, on the Street of the Chain; and then his age, which Kirsch had guessed correctly.

"Well, Saud, perhaps you'd like to tell me where you were last Saturday night?"

Kirsch tried not to sound patronizing, but he was fighting a long tradition.

"I was alone, and writing."

The answer startled Kirsch, not only for its content, but also for Saud's apparent fluency in English.

"Writing?"

"Poetry."

"So you're a poet?" Kirsch had rarely felt more stupid in the light of one of his own responses.

The boy shrugged.

"And where do you do your writing?"

Saud thought for a moment, then raised the index finger of his right hand and tapped twice on the side of his head. De Groot had gestured this way during their lessons, as an incentive to make Saud think.

Kirsch wasn't sure how to respond. Was the boy teasing him? Laughing at him? But it was Kirsch who laughed.

"Okay. Recite me some of your work. Anything."

"In Arabic or in English?"

"I think I'd better hear the English."

Saud, it seemed to Kirsch, shivered a little, and then, remarkably, he rose from his seat and declared, "Those are the golden islands for which we longed as one longs for a homeland, to which all the night stars beckoned us with the light of a trembling ray." The lines both astonished Kirsch and seemed vaguely familiar. But his knowledge of English poetry, if that's what the boy had stolen, or learned in school, was hardly deep enough for him to make an identification.

Saud sat down.

Kirsch looked at him across his desk, then glanced at his watch as if the time might offer an explanation for the peculiarities of the situation. It was after midnight.

"Thank you," Kirsch finally said. "That was extraordinary."

The interrogation proceeded. By the end of half an hour Saud had failed to supply much of an alibi for his whereabouts on the night of the murder—his mother had been sleeping when he came home and he had left the house to pick up water before she awoke—but the adolescent poet, charming and wistful, certainly didn't seem like a knifer. Nevertheless, there was something troubling that Kirsch couldn't put his finger on. He determined to let the boy go, but to keep him under observation.

12.

Bloomberg had been painting alone on the roof of Ross's house for about three hours when Ross contrived to interrupt him. The hills around the city were covered in a light white summer dust that seemed to parch and blind their viewers. Bloomberg was mixing white and ochre on his palette, trying to get the color that he wanted. Ross's hundred pounds, which had seemed like money in the bank, was proving difficult to earn. But only because Bloomberg remained so resolutely himself: ornery, dissatisfied, an East End arrangement of bravado and insecurity.

Eventually Bloomberg put down his knife and turned toward his visitor.

"A formidable prospect," Ross said.

Bloomberg didn't reply. It was unbearable to have to sing for your supper as well as paint for it.

"The stones quite cry out."

"Not to me."

"Really not?"

It was never Bloomberg's intention to embarrass Ross, but if that happened as a by-product of necessary honesty, then so be it.

Ross remembered something that Aubrey Harrison had said after an evening spent in Bloomberg's company: "His work makes a better impression than he does." One had to make accommodations for true artists—although there were limits.

The two men looked out across the landscape. Ross, hands behind his back, gestured to the east simply by raising his eyebrows and lifting his chin.

"First day I was on the job, about a month after we took Jerusalem, two representatives of local transport came in to see me. They were after a concession to run trams to Bethlehem and the Mount of Olives—right over there."

"I see that you didn't grant it."

"No, I told them that the first rail section would be laid over the dead body of the military governor."

"So they're waiting for you to die."

Ross laughed. "I expect so."

"Perhaps you'd like to be buried here?"—Bloomberg swept his hand in the direction of the Mount of Olives. "Not much shade, though."

Ross's features darkened. The British Military Cemetery was on nearby Mount Scopus. There were men buried there who had been under Ross's command during the war. But Bloomberg couldn't know that. After a moment Ross brightened again.

"Next to caliphs, Crusaders, and Maccabees? I'd be honored."

Beneath them, on the narrow ribbon of road that wound toward the Allenby Barracks, a woman walked, her thin arms extended by two heavy shopping bags.

"I suppose Mrs. Bloomberg is at home preparing for the Sabbath?"

"Mrs. Bloomberg is not Jewish."

Ross registered this information with a short intake of breath.

"Nevertheless," Bloomberg continued, "she does like to go shopping on Fridays, and when we visit observant friends she enjoys the false security of a white tablecloth, two challahs, and a pair of candlesticks."

"The Zionists themselves are rarely so beholden to tradition."

"Oh, that too—my wife considers herself a Zionist. In London she went through two winters of Thursday-night meetings at Toynbee Hall. I believe she once shook Weizmann's hand. She'd come home and report the content of the speeches. She's the one who convinced me to come out here. Joyce, bless her heart, thought I could do worse than use my meager talents to help the cause."

"Really? And have you been persuaded that such is the case?"

"My sentiments are of the less exotic, apolitical, and by now quite irritating, I'm sure, miserable-artist type."

Ross laughed but stopped short when Bloomberg added, "I'm essentially an East End Jewboy on the make. Someone made a mistake when they distributed the talent, and gave me a dollop."

Ross turned to examine Bloomberg's painting. It seemed to him to have precisely the mix of topographical style and conservative representation that he had been hoping to see.

"More than a dollop, I'd say." Ross looked from the painting to the view, and then back again to the work.

The words "Thank you" caught in Bloomberg's throat and came out as a cough.

There was a single puffy white cloud in the otherwise blue sky, some disruptive artist-angel exhaling his cigarette smoke over God's empty canvas. When the cloud moved over the sun it turned yellow and brown at the edges.

"Did you catch the knifer?"

"No." Ross paused. "We shall, although it would probably be advisable not to. Better, perhaps, simply to fish." Ross offered this tentatively, as if the idea had just come to him.

It had never occurred to Bloomberg, who imagined himself a cynic, that the negative outcome of a police investigation could be prearranged.

"What do you mean?"

Ross clearly wished that he hadn't extended beyond his simple "No," but now that he had, it would be cowardly to step back.

"Well, once we have the culprit all hell will break loose. The hostile camps are tense and waiting now, but as soon as we identify and arrest the murderer, we'll be for it. If it's an Arab, the Arabs will riot and protest his innocence. If it's a Jew, the Jews will be up in arms. Really, it is a shame, you know. The last three years have been rather, well, relatively quiet. An impressive number of wives and young children have been able to come out and set up house. Club's doing very well, Arab chappee won the tennis tournament this year, beat Warburton in the singles final. Perhaps you heard." Ross's voice trailed away. He had an alarming, and utterly false, apprehension that artists enjoyed only high talk. Real artists, that is, among whom Ross did not include the zealous painters of Palestine, most of whom, he found, had the temperament but not the qualifications of the truly gifted. Twice blessed, then, that a talent like Bloomberg's had chosen to eschew as subject the mechanized sower going forth sowing, or merry immigrants dancing around Old Testament maypoles: in their place, a hard cosmic stare at the actual.

They heard a motorcycle engine, and then the two-wheeler appeared from around a distant curve in the road. As it drew near, both Bloomberg and Ross, from the excellent vantage point of the roof, could clearly see both the driver and his passenger. Joyce's arms were wound tight around Kirsch's chest, and her long hair, covered only in part by a loose red kerchief, unfurled behind her like a banner. The road curled away and the speeding figures were lost. The two men watching were silent for several moments, then Ross spoke.

Ross extended his hand. "Better be going. Long trip planned for tomorrow, a hunt down at Ramleh."

Bloomberg didn't respond in kind; instead he turned his palms upward to reveal their yellow and white paint stains.

"Looks as if my wife got fed up preparing for the Sabbath."

Did Ross redden? It was hard to tell; his thin face appeared to carry a permanent sunburn.

After a moment's silence Ross began to speak again, his voice measured and constant. "We chase jackal, if you can believe it. Had almost fifty mounted last time out."

Ross would have continued but Bloomberg cut him short. "How old is Captain Kirsch?"

"Kirsch? Mid-twenties, I should think. He's a good chap." Ross almost swallowed the last words and they emerged in a whisper.

"I'm sure he is," Bloomberg replied, then added, as if in an afterthought for himself, "I'm not."

13.

Kirsch and Joyce left the motorbike at the foot of a valley whose edge was notched by a fingerlike spur; then they ascended on foot into the forest, or what was left of it. The Turks had destroyed great swathes, Kirsch explained. So much so that when Ross refurbished the governorate he'd had to import the necessary wood from India. Still, Kirsch knew a thickly wooded area of scented pines higher up—he'd been out there to pick mushrooms in the spring, a Sunday tour organized by Mrs. Bent-wich, the wife of the attorney general.

Kirsch felt he was talking too much, prattling again. But he couldn't stop. His body was still recovering from the conditioned intimacy of the bike ride.

When they stepped off a dusty clay path and into shade Joyce re-moved her red kerchief and shook her hair loose. There was a light, pleasant breeze, but hardly enough to disturb the tops of the trees. Her loose-fitting white cotton dress, gathered slightly at the hips, short-sleeved and calf-length, had been entirely inappropriate for the back of a motorbike. Still, when Kirsch had seen her—by chance, he said—as she was passing the sun clock on Jaffa Road, there had hardly been time to go home and change.

"Will he be wondering where you are?" Kirsch felt ashamed that he couldn't bring himself to mention Bloomberg by name.

"I doubt it. Although Mark's not entirely without concern in that area. If I'm not around, who can he . . ." Joyce paused; she was going to say "torture" but settled on the milder "tease."

Kirsch scaled a rocky elevation, then extended his hand to pull Joyce up. There was no view to speak of, only the encircling gray-green trunks of a pine copse.

They sat side by side on a flat boulder.

"Cigarette?"

"Later," she said.

Kirsch had already reached for the box in the top pocket of his tunic, but now he simply patted his shirt, as if he were frisking a suspect for hidden weapons.

He was going to ask her if she missed England, or missed New York. He was going to urge her to tell him everything about her relationship with Bloomberg, from how they had met to the current situation. He was going to tell her something about himself, something that, without seeming prideful, might cast him in an appealing light; but he didn't say anything because he was kissing her. Afterward he wasn't sure if she had reached up to pull his head toward hers, or if he had made the first move. If the latter, he thought, it wasn't him, but rather the heavy fragrant air pushing on the back of his neck like an invisible hand. For a few seconds her tongue worked furiously in his mouth, while he felt his own move slow and with adolescent clumsiness. Her body tensed, and then she withdrew from his clinch.

Joyce sat expressionless, staring ahead, as if nothing had passed between them except an exchange of small talk. The peculiar, and wretched, thought entered Kirsch's mind that if they were in England he might, at this point, have apologized.

"I met Mark," Joyce began, as if in answer to one of the questions that Kirsch had considered but not asked, "on Shaftesbury Avenue. I'd only been in London a month and I was staying with a friend of my father's, Felix Shubert, an art dealer. He was trying, without success, I'm afraid, to sell two of Mark's paintings. I suppose I had then a flair for the dramatic, by British standards anyway. I was wearing this cherry red dress and a black cape."

Joyce turned to Kirsch and smiled. He couldn't take his eyes off her.

"I'm one of those cursed people who have a little talent in a number of areas but not enough concentrated in any one. In New York I began as a dancer, then I studied piano. In Paris I tried to go back to dance but it was too late. By the time I got to London I had decided that art was my calling. I spent my month at the Shuberts' creating a portfolio of still lifes and line drawings. I planned to enroll at the Slade, if they would take me."

Kirsch reached for his cigarettes. The kiss, if it had happened at all, might have taken place a hundred years ago.

"Shubert tried to put me off. Too many impoverished artists had passed his way. When we bumped into Mark that day he tried to drag him on the bandwagon. 'Help me dissuade Miss Pierce here from painting as an objective—tell her there's no money in it.' I found this patronizing. I said, 'I'm not interested in money—I'm interested in painting.' Mark wouldn't give Shubert what he wanted. He said, 'If Miss Pierce is interested in painting and she's not interested in money, then I'm interested in Miss Pierce.' That was the beginning. He invited me to visit his studio, only it was hardly a studio. More of a kitchen. And I liked him ever so much, you know. He's handsome, you can see that; his eyes are very gentle. There had been a lot of women before me. And everyone admired his work. He didn't compromise. I'd never met anybody else as driven as I was—but for him it was all in one direction. In his studio there was a painting that covered the whole wall. I'd never seen anything quite like it. He'd taken a scene from the immigrant world, a ship disgorging its new arrivals at London Docks, but made it intensely modern. There was no sentimentality in the representation, everything was oblique, spare figures and wild color. I was utterly moved. The studio was so small that Mark's paintings took over the whole space. You couldn't escape, but you didn't want to."

Kirsch, whose job was to interrogate, found himself tongue-tied. It seemed to him that there was nothing comfortable about Joyce, no place to curl up and rest. Her body was taut, you could tell she'd been a dancer, and her mind was sharp and unsettling. He wondered if she ever relaxed.

She laid her right hand, palm upward, on his thigh.

"I'll have that cigarette now."

Kirsch, fumbling for the box, managed a lame question to which he already knew the answer: "So you lived together in London?"

"For three years, and another three after we married. I met him right at the end of the war. I did go to art school. But the superior teacher was at home. We wound up sharing a studio in West Hampstead. I think Mark liked it less when I ceased to be a student. He became quite critical, sometimes cruel—and petty."

"How so?"

"He'd steal my white paint." Joyce laughed. "I'd be in the middle of a painting, then perhaps I'd leave the house, go shopping, and when I got back my paint tubes would be squeezed dry. Still, he had a right, you know, he's the real thing. I'm a dilettante by comparison."

"I'm sure that's not true."

"Please don't . . . I hate falseness."

Abruptly, Joyce rose to her feet. She stubbed her cigarette out on a rock, and then brushed the pine needles from her dress.

Kirsch stood too. He wanted to hold her, but she turned away from him and began to descend the hill as rapidly as she could manage. Kirsch followed. When they reached the motorbike she turned to face him.

"Do you know what I think? The middle name of all men should be 'I'll disappoint you.' John 'I'll disappoint you' Smith, Mark 'I'll disappoint you' Bloomberg."

"Robert 'I'll disappoint you' Kirsch?"

"That's it."

"But I won't disappoint you." He had said the words before he could think twice; they were trite and absolutely predictable.

"Won't you?" she replied. "Well, perhaps I shouldn't give you the chance."

Kirsch felt a space of absolute hopelessness blossoming inside him. Without that "chance" he might as well pack up and go home, back to England and someone safe, like Naomi.

The sun folded its light under the green arm of pines that stretched along the hilltops. This time when the bike passed Ross's house the lights were up on the second and third floors.

Kirsch was going to take Joyce home but he brought her to his place instead. She didn't object. Far from it. She walked ahead of him through the small garden that fronted his house and clattered up the stone stairs that led from the side entrance to his flat. Once inside he thought to offer her a drink but she was already unbuttoning her dress. She slipped quickly under the thin sheet that covered his bed. Kirsch, still in his clothes, sat on the edge of the mattress. He felt, having got what he wanted, both ridiculous and awkward. He didn't know what to do first, kiss Joyce, or untie his bootlaces. She made the choice for him, and this time there was no mistaking which one of them was the instigator. She sat up and reached out, clasping her hands around his neck. Her breasts were exposed, bone white in the moonlight that shone thinly through the quartered windows interposed between bedroom and balcony. Kirsch bent his face to hers. He kissed her mouth, cradling the back of her head and cupping her left breast in his hand. Joyce lay back and closed her eyes. Kirsch moved his face down to her breasts, kissing and licking her nipples. He settled on one breast and sucked at it, taking it all into his mouth as if he might swallow it whole. Joyce's breath quickened. She tugged on Kirsch's hair and he brought his lips back to hers. He stroked her head with one hand and moved the other between her thighs, inserting first one, then two fingers inside her. Joyce arrested his movement by circling his wrist with her hand.

"I think," she said, "that it might be a good idea for you to get undressed now."

14.

Outside the Damascus Gate a semicircle of squatting women sold cut flowers and wild lilies. Bloomberg walked past them and into the suq. It was dusk and the shopkeepers were closing up for the night. Two men rolled a wide bolt of fabric, then stood it on end and walked it, like a drunk companion supported between them, into the back of their shop. Farther down the street, outside a butcher's shop where flies swarmed over hunks of exposed beef, a small group of vendors were gathered round a makeshift brazier, turning skewers of meat over hot coals.

"Here," he said to Jacob Rosen, his invisible companion, "is this what you wanted to see? I hope you're not disappointed." Jacob wiped the dried blood from his eyes and looked around.

Bloomberg walked on without direction. The intimate sounds, odors and visions of the market, diversions that at another time he too might have appreciated and admired, meant little to him now. But when was that other time? A month, a year ago? What came more vividly to his imagination was the scent of Joyce's body when she had woken in fear next to him early this morning. He guessed that she had been dreaming of the murder victim. Half asleep, Bloomberg had pressed his face into her neck, bumping and nuzzling like some half-demented pet. Now, he was out walking in order to give her time to collect herself, and become comfortable with the lies she was about to tell him. Lies he had encouraged her toward. He told himself it was for her own good. To let her go was the only altruism of which he was capable. It wasn't much, but it was better than doing nothing. In an hour or so he would return home.

At their moment of parting Ross had outlined to Bloomberg yet another commission that he had in mind. Perhaps he was feeling bad for him on account of Joyce's little motorbike escapade. At any rate, Ross wanted a painting, several works in fact, of ancient temples in some place called Petra that Bloomberg had never heard of. He was willing to send Bloomberg on an expenses-paid trip into Transjordan. Joyce could accompany him (a not so subtle diversion on Ross's part?) and the two of them would have support and protection from a couple of bedouin guards. The journey held some possible, if unlikely, dangers, hence the need for the guards. What did Bloomberg think? Bloomberg thought, wandering now through a short stretch of the suq that seemed devoted to cheap postcards and cigarettes, that he would rather a hole in the ground simply opened up and swallowed him. On the other hand, in for a hundred pounds, then why not in for five hundred? Only not with Joyce. If he went at all, he would travel alone.

He withdrew a sheet of lined paper from his trouser pocket. On it was a typed list of places that the Zionist organization had asked him to visit for the purposes of sketching Jewish men and women at work: the Lodzia sock factory (that would require a trip to Tel Aviv), the Delphiner Silk Looms, Raanan Chocolate Ovens, and Silicate Brick Kilns. There was also a kosher abattoir and the maternity ward of the Shaarei Zedek Hospital. Bloomberg crushed the paper into a ball and threw it toward a pile of stinking garbage, where it became part of the detritus of rotten vegetables settled at the entrance to a narrow passageway, a site that appeared to be home to a large coven of the city's stray cats.

By the time that he arrived home in Talpiot it was after nine. He expected to see lights on in the house and was mildly surprised to find the place in darkness. He went in, poured himself a quarter tumbler of brandy, sat on the edge of the bed, and downed the drink. After a while he dragged his favorite wicker chair outside, and sat slumped like a dozing sentry by the doorway. The gibbous moon offered enough light to draw by, but Bloomberg had neither the energy nor the inclination for work. He was half asleep when he heard light footsteps on the road. On hearing the gate swing open, he roused himself.

"Nice time?" he shouted toward a patch of darkness that began at the foot of the path and spread below a dense overgrowth of jasmine that hugged the perimeter wall and absorbed moonlight.

Joyce stopped moving.

"Is he better than me? Couldn't be worse, right? Well, come on. I'll make you a cup of hot cocoa. Tuck you in. Pretend we're in wintry London instead of this God-infested hole."

She remained motionless. Bloomberg rose clumsily from his seat, knocking it over in the process. He stumbled forward three steps. There was Joyce, pale and remorseful. Only it wasn't Joyce. It was an Arab boy. Bloomberg glanced quickly at the boy's hands. "Charge a gun, run from a knife." His father's words came back as if stored forty years for precisely this moment. But there was no weapon visible.

The boy knelt quickly, scrabbled around and appeared to scoop something from the ground; then he turned and ran.

"Hey!" Bloomberg shouted after him, and barged breathlessly toward the gate. He picked up a small rock, gestured as if to throw it after the intruder, but then thought better of the idea and let the stone fall to the ground. He looked around for a moment, as if utterly bewildered as to how he had come to this place. The stars slid in unfamiliar, unsteady formations across the sky.

Shortly after dawn, when Joyce finally arrived home, Bloomberg was asleep in their bed. She removed the empty brandy bottle from her pillow, undressed and, shivering slightly, slid under the covers beside her husband, if she could still call him that.

15.

Kirsch climbed the broad winding stairs that skirted the outer wall of the Church of the Holy Sepulchre. He felt pleasantly exhausted and his back itched under his cotton shirt. Joyce had dug her nails hard into him and left surface scratches as reminders of her passion.

He continued on up to the roof, following the bishop's procession as it curled past a set of anachronistic mud huts, their tiny windows cut in the shape of crucifixes. A tall thin monk, clad all in white, elevated a bright yellow umbrella above the bishop's head. Once inside the Abyssinian church, Kirsch stood at the back, separated by the width of a flagstone from the crush of worshipers who sang and swayed to a tom-tom's beat. He was there in search of De Groot's woman. He had gone to her home and been told by a neighbor that this was the service she attended some Sundays. Observing the congregation now, Kirsch could understand her impulse: the pink ceiling, the vibrant paintings on the walls, the ecstatic African music. It was a wonderfully sensual brand of Christianity. He felt like joining the wild hymn singing himself—but that, of course, was for another reason.

There were more than two white people at the service; the Abyssinian church was on the "must-see" list for new arrivals to the city. Kirsch noticed Helen Willis, who had come out to join her husband, Jerry, a fortnight earlier, and, seated in the front row, recognizable from behind by the monk's fringe that surrounded his bald pate, was Lawrence Milton, the new district officer for Jerusalem.

"Business or pleasure?"

For a horrible moment Kirsch thought it was Bloomberg's voice that he heard. But on turning he saw, to his relief, J. V. Rowlands, the mandate's antiquities expert. Rowlands was wearing an entirely inappropriate wool suit. Sweating profusely, he dabbed his forehead with an oversized handkerchief.

"Work, I'm afraid," Kirsch replied.

"The De Groot case?"

Kirsch half smiled. He wasn't about to say anything that could be reported back to Ross.

"I heard there were twenty thousand black hats at the funeral," Rowlands continued. "Can that be true? Didn't know the city had so many—although from the noise in the Jewish Quarter you'd think there were a half a million in there."

"It was a large crowd."

"Any suspects? They say your victim liked to play a little with the Arab boys. Of course he's not alone in that."

Out of the corner of his eye Kirsch saw a slightly overweight woman with unkempt hair make her way down one of the side aisles and into an already crowded pew at the front of the church.

"I also heard he owed money and didn't pay up. The Arabs don't like that, you know. They're very honorable people."

"Excuse me," Kirsch said. "There's someone I have to talk to."

"Absolutely."

The singing, loud and melodious, reached a climax, then trailed into silence. The drums stopped beating and the bishop gestured for the members of the congregation to take their seats.

"By the way"—Rowlands gripped Kirsch's arm—"what do you make of Bloomberg? Ross tells me his new work is superb."

"I'm sorry?" Kirsch whispered, pretending that he hadn't heard the question.

"Wife's a bit inscrutable," Rowlands continued, "which is odd for an American, usually they're transparent. Somehow, no one wants to have them to tea. Should we?"

"I wouldn't risk it," Kirsch replied. "They'll probably drink out of the saucers."

Kirsch brushed Rowlands aside and began to move forward. Alice was standing directly under a portrait of Jesus on the cross that took up almost half the wall. The blood from Christ's punctured hands dripped scarlet; the martyr's crown of thorns, bright green, circled his black forehead. It seemed right, Kirsch thought while working his way though the crowd, this naked black Jesus, better certainly than the draped and sentimentalized white figure of the British Jesus, who rarely sported even the hint of a tan. London at Christmas, rain usually, and Kirsch helping the other children glue cotton wool on hardboard to complete his class nativity scene: the windows steamed up, and the tubercular cough of Johnny Chisholm emanating from the seat next to him; the barely concealed disappointment of his mother when she found out what he had been doing all day—no less painful, Kirsch thought, than that of his present colleagues on their discovery that snow was as rare in Bethlehem as in the Home Counties.

Having gained his proximity to the woman with the braids, Kirsch took a seat. He was prepared to wait until the end of the service in order to speak to her, but shortly before the sermon began she rose from her place, and, wiping tears from her eyes, headed for the exit door. Kirsch followed. He caught up with her at the top of the steps that led back down to the suq.

"Miss Bone?"

"Yes."

"Robert Kirsch, Jerusalem Constabulary. I'm investigating the murder of Jacob De Groot. I wondered if we might have a few words."

The woman looked as if she might begin to cry again; then she looked away from Kirsch toward the foot of the stairs where a donkey was relieving itself against a stone wall, its steaming urine turning the pale brick brown.

"This is a terribly inappropriate time, I know," Kirsch continued. "I tried to reach you at the hospital. If we could only talk for a few moments."

He led her back through the suq and into a small café nestled close to the mouth of Jaffa Gate. Kirsch ordered tea but Alice refused his offer of a drink. Her replies, when he began to question her, were brief but to the point. She had, she informed him, nothing to hide.

"When did you meet Mr. De Groot?"

"Two years ago."

"And where?"

She blushed.

"At the Bristol Garden Restaurant. One of the *thés dansants*. All the nurses used to go—when we could, that is."

"At a dance?"

"Well, at that time Jacob wasn't . . . Surely you know? He wasn't a religious man when he arrived in Palestine. He was a socialist."

Kirsch looked at Alice's round open face. There was a thin line across her forehead, a scar etched above her eyebrows, as if left there by the tight fit of her nurse's cap. Her bushy brown hair was pushed behind her ears, her nose was broad, like a Tartar's. She was an unprepossessing woman in her features, but with a softness of manner and an intelligence in her eyes that was appealing. He guessed she was approaching forty.

Kirsch raised his glass of tea to his lips and immediately, evaporating the flavor of the mint, came the scent of Joyce's cunt, held on the tips of his fingers and under his fingernails. For a moment he was back in his bedroom, Joyce astride him, her eyes closed and Kirsch reaching to touch her nipples. He pushed her breasts together and lifted himself slightly as they fucked. Sweat accumulated in beads on her brow, then coursed down her face and neck. He wanted her breasts in his mouth but she pushed him back down, keeping her eyes shut tight.

Alice Bone continued to talk, telling him the story of De Groot's conversion from socialism to Jewish Orthodoxy and how he had relinquished everything in which he had once believed.

"But not you," Kirsch put in.

"Pardon?"

"He didn't relinquish you."

Alice's face grew taut.

"I don't mean to be obnoxious, but you must admit your relationship was unusual. A Christian woman and an Orthodox Jew."

"We were not lovers, we were friends. Is that so inconceivable?"

"Friends? But I understood . . ."

"What did you understand?"

She stared at him across the table. Her eyes brimmed with tears but she fought them back.

"Friends, I say," and then she added in a murmur, "How could it have been otherwise?"

"Because of his religion?"

"No." Alice turned her head to the side and, addressing the empty table adjacent to their own, whispered, "Because of the boy."

Kirsch was silent. Perhaps she was lying, perhaps not.

The waiter moved in smartly to remove his glass and replace it with a scrawled bill. The heat of the day had arrived and the bazaar was closing with a discord of screeching shutters, dragged chains, and heavy padlocks.

"I tried to warn him," Alice continued. "The families, you know, are very protective, and sometimes vengeful. And as to the boy himself, who knew if he could be trusted not to steal, not to . . . ?"

"Not to?"

"Not to stab."

Alice buried her face in her hands.

"Did you know the boy?"

"No."

"Did you ever meet him?"

"No."

"Did you ever see him?"

"Once, but from a distance. I came to the house. I wasn't supposed to. Jacob said he didn't want his lessons interrupted. He opened the door; there was a boy in the far room sitting at a desk. Jacob sent me away."

"Do you know the boy's name?"

Alice pulled her hands from her face and stared across at Kirsch.

"I didn't," she said, "until your roundup. Everybody in Jerusalem knows it now."

Kirsch thanked Alice, paid the bill and hurried from the café. His path was blocked by a procession of priests in long, girdled white gowns, all wearing identical sun hats and talking animatedly to one another in Italian. Kirsch pushed his way through. The boy must be picked up as soon as possible. Kirsch had ordered Harlap to keep an eye on him, but on Friday night, while Kirsch and Joyce were lowering themselves into the abyss of infidelity, Saud had apparently slipped away. In the meantime, until Harlap caught up with the suspect again, Kirsch needed to let Ross know of the breakthrough. Or perhaps he should wait until Saud was in custody.

The decision was made for him. Ross's fawn Bentley was parked outside Jaffa Gate. The governor stood beside the car, resplendent in his white uniform. He was deep in conversation with a tall, fair-haired, well-dressed young man whom Kirsch did not know. The two of them were poring over a map that was spread out on the car's bonnet. At the moment that Kirsch emerged from the Old City, Ross looked up. He gestured toward the crenellated walls, pointing out something to his companion, and then he caught sight of Kirsch. Ross began to address Kirsch when he was still only halfway across the road.

"Yes, I know. You expect me to be in church. And by rights I should be. Nobby Briant's reading the lesson over at St. George's this morning. Promised him I'd be there, but I'm afraid, like everyone else, I've been sucked in by the movies."

A look of utter bafflement crossed Kirsch's face.

"I'm sorry, Captain. I'm being obtuse. This is Mr. Peter Frumkin from the Metropolis Film Corporation."

Ross turned to his companion to complete his introductions.

"Mr. Frumkin, this is Captain Robert Kirsch. You may, I believe, find that you need his assistance on your enterprise even more than mine."

"Pleased to meet you."

The two men shook hands.

"Mr. Frumkin here would like to use these ancient walls to stage and then screen Titus's capture of the city. He'd also like to borrow a large number of our British Regiment legionaires, dress 'em up in palliums and helmets and have them stage the assault. What do you think? Shall we let Hollywood come to Jerusalem?"

"It sounds as if you've already decided to go ahead, sir."

"Governor Ross has been telling me all about the Pro-Jerusalem Society. The work sounds remarkable, precisely the kind of organization that we like to get behind. And I can assure you, Captain Kirsch, that by the time we've finished filming here not a stone will be out of place or a paint mark left where it shouldn't be."

"I believe you."

"We'd like to shoot in Jerusalem all next week. Right now we're down in the desert and we should be done with the camel charge by Thursday. I've got three hundred bedouin suited up and ready to go."

Kirsch nodded. The stupidity of it! When he turned to face Ross his heart was beating fast.

"A word, sir, if I may?"

"Ah."

There was an awkward pause and then Frumkin began to roll up his map.

"My apologies, Mr. Frumkin," Ross began, "but I'm afraid the captain's ominous tone suggests this is something that cannot wait."

Frumkin waved the rolled map above his head, and a car that had been parked waiting farther down the hill accelerated smoothly toward him. The driver halted, got out and came around to open the door for his boss. Frumkin hesitated, then turned to Kirsch.

"You're one of us? Right?" He winked broadly.

Kirsch, walking a couple of steps behind Ross, pretended that he hadn't heard.

16.

"I'm going away," Bloomberg said.

He tugged at his straw hat and pulled the frayed brim down over his eyes.

"Away from me? Away for good? Or just away?"

They were outside in the garden, seated at the rusted round table that had been bequeathed to them, along with four rickety wooden chairs, by the house's former inhabitants. Early in the morning, walking alone, horribly confused but unreasonably happy, as if she couldn't resist the honeyed new beginning that the warm, lissome day seemed to offer, Joyce had plucked a bunch of wildflowers at the path side. Now, set in a cracked white enamel jar at the table's center, the purple and yellow blooms drooped like a cluster of tiny bruises.

"To paint. It has nothing to do with Friday night. Keep seeing him if you want to."

She didn't need his permission—didn't want it, in fact. She preferred his drunken rage of the previous night to this return to indifference; at least his anger had passion. Perhaps her behavior had surprised him, although she knew that he liked to think of himself as unshockable. He had told her to leave him, but she expected he had never imagined that she would follow through.

A lizard, not more than two inches long, scuttled up one of the table legs. There was a bowl of ripe figs on the table next to the flowers. Aubrey Harrison had brought them over the previous day, arriving in the middle of Joyce and Bloomberg's worst argument. Bloomberg's shouting, if not Joyce's less histrionic responses, must have been audible halfway down the hillside; even so, Aubrey, out on a morning stroll in the neighborhood, had soldiered on, oblivious. However, by the time he reached the painter's door, the enormity of what he had somehow contrived to ignore had set in, and he had been too embarrassed to enter. He had set the figs on the doorstep. Joyce glimpsed him through the window, retreating down the path.

Bloomberg stretched his arm across the table, took Joyce's hand and stroked the freckled skin just above her wrist.

"Do you remember that boat we took up the Thames?"

"The posters-of-London idea? I rowed and you sketched."

"Yes, exactly. Well you've rowed enough. You shouldn't have to put up with me anymore."

Joyce remembered a cool breeze on the river, no one else in sight, on one bank a tangle of green and on the other cows grazing in a muddy field.

"I'll be gone by the end of the week. It's a money job. 'The Lost Temples of Petra' as executed by Sir Mark Bloomberg L.J.C."

"Latter-day Jesus Christ?"

"Lost Jewish Cause."

"How long will you be there?"

"Two, three months, maybe longer."

"And I am supposed to remain here?"

"If you want to go back to London, no one will try to prevent you, except perhaps your ardent Captain Kirsch."

Bloomberg tugged at the high collar of his pullover, then wiped his perspiring hands on his corduroy trousers. Why was he wearing such warm clothes on a day like this? It was simply a mark of his perversity, and of their ultimate incompatibility. Joyce could list a half dozen more off the top of her head. She liked to dance, he didn't. He was tidy, she liked to spread things everywhere. She loved to drive, he said he never wanted to. He hated opera. He hated museums, though she could wander through the long rooms for hours; and yet he would accompany her, if only to tell her continuously how little he was enjoying himself. He found her beloved English countryside too noisy. She was an American naïf, taken in by picturesque poverty: "All those damn ducks quacking." She had no understanding of class.

A year ago none of these differences would have mattered, but now, she thought, they all contributed to pushing them apart. For five years she'd never doubted once that she loved him, but a year of bitterness, resentment and, worst of all, inattention and unresponsiveness, had disturbed her certainty. Even so, it was possible that she still loved him, love being the resilient commodity that it was.

But if so, then why had she slept with Robert Kirsch? That, of course, was the one question that Mark hadn't asked her during yesterday's explosion. No doubt he thought he knew the answer, even if she didn't. He would have liked to consider himself one hundred percent responsible for her actions. His self-hatred worked better that way. But there was something else to be recognized, her own autonomous choice, her independent desire, and seeing it in action troubled her even more than Mark's confidence that it was absent.

"I'll stay on in this house," Joyce said. "I've taken to Jerusalem. I'm expecting to get a job." Surely it couldn't be long, she thought, before one of Leo Cohn's friends contacted her.

Bloomberg appeared relieved.

"That's good," he replied.

17.

When night fell, its hostile moon unreasonably bright, Saud hid behind a screen of asbestos sheets that leaned against his uncle's bakery wall. Peeking out, he glimpsed the face of the policeman who had followed him on Friday, and he shivered with fear. Saud had given him the slip and managed to reach the place where Yaakov had died, but here, only two days later, was the policeman again, a thick-armed squat figure, searching down the empty alleyways. He must have been to Saud's home, banged on the door, brought his mother, terrified, out of her sleep, then lined his brothers up to confirm once again that Saud was not among them.

In the end they would arrest him. He would be back in the interrogation room with the English officer, or perhaps he would not make it that far. He knew now how swift his death could be. One knife thrust in the heart, or his throat slit. Saud held his breath, the policeman passed, his boots ringing on the stone steps as he descended the Cardo. Saud waited for silence, and then he entered the bakery through its side door. In darkness, he felt his way past the open mouth of the oven, then crouched on rough stone in a narrow passage between two huge vats, one filled with sesame oil, the other awaiting a new consignment. Among the dark shapes in the corners of the room he thought he saw De Groot stumble and groan, the knife still plunged into his heart. Saud closed his eyes and De Groot was beside him, whispering in his ear as they embraced, murmuring his name, stroking his hair.

There was nothing to be done. Uncle Kamel would find him when he came to work. The policeman would return and sit in the café opposite, drinking cup after cup of sweet coffee, watching and waiting while his uncle's flour-whitened hands piled rounds of bread and spilled zaatar into paper twists.

18.

It was early on Sunday evening before Kirsh caught up with Ross. Now, they were being driven in Ross's car down Bethlehem Road, past the Protestant Cemetery and Bishop Gobat's School, on Mount Zion, and out, away from the Old City, toward North Talpiot. The stars were sprinkled like grains of light, handfuls flung into the face of the night.

"We have him," Kirsch said. He sounded blasé. Whenever he was with Ross he found himself involuntarily imitating the governor's studied nonchalance.

"Ah." Ross removed his glasses, produced a folded white handkerchief from the pocket of his tunic, and began to clean the lenses. "Things have speeded up, then?"

"Absolutely, sir. I believe we know the culprit and I've sent Sergeant Harlap to pick him up."

"Then you don't quite 'have him.' "

"Correct."

"And who is our murderer?"

"The suspect is an Arab boy, sir. Saud al-Sayyid. He was seen in De Groot's home. We're searching the area around the house again now. It's possible that al-Sayyid was De Groot's lover."

"How old is he?"

"Sixteen. I interrogated him on Friday and let him go, but under watch. Then some new evidence emerged. It's circumstantial in nature but I think we'll make fast headway."

"Do you now?"

Ross reached to the breast pocket of his tunic. The space in the back of the car, insulated by a glass screen that partitioned the driver from his passengers, had filled with dead, fetid air. Kirsch thought Ross was about to produce the handkerchief again, this time to wipe his brow, but instead he flourished an envelope.

"Would you mind very much if I read you something I received this morning from one of our police posts—not your district, I hasten to add?"

Kirsch smiled thinly.

"Not at all, sir."

"Fine, then." Ross took off his glasses, removed the letter, and began to read:

Dear Sir Gerald,

I beg to thank you in the name of the District Police Force for your very much appreciated gift of a football, which you presented on Friday last at a match, which was arranged for the purpose, on the Barracks Square. The teams were composed of Moslems, Christians, and Jews, captained by (a) Sgt. Schwili (Jew), and (b) P. C. Badawi (Moslem), and it is of interest to note that utmost harmony prevailed through 50 minutes of play. A knowledge of the rules of the game is not a strong point with the District Force at present, but the spirit of fair play and a keenness to be taught is abounding, and instruction in the art of football is being undertaken. Yours etc. etc.

" 'Utmost harmony,' you see, Robert, and it can sometimes be achieved with a modicum of effort, cheaply and efficiently. That's the good news. Now, when we light this tinderbox after the arrest of young Saud is announced, the ensuing conflagration could burn down the city. We had better be prepared. Sergeant Schwili and P. C. Badawi may not be shaking hands at the end of the match. A supposedly homosexual Arab boy murders a supposedly homosexual Orthodox Jew who just happens to be the Agudat's most powerful anti-Zionist spokesman—for money (De Groot's or somebody else's), for love, for who-knows-what—and everybody goes home quietly for dinner and a prayer? I don't think so, old chap."

"No, sir."

"And to be quite honest, if things really blow here I'm not sure that we've got the forces to contain them. Here we are on our 'sacred mission,' mandated to bring those less fortunate than ourselves up to scratch, but it can only work if we maintain the illusion that we are in control. An illusion that rests as much upon our well-deserved reputation for fairness as anything else. We are not the Turks. There will be no public hangings. The sad truth is, however, that Palestine is a rather unimportant and neglected outpost of our empire. Although not entirely unimportant. We are not, for example, going to pull out and let the French come in and start hanging around Suez; and in the meantime, while we are here, we can try to stop the Arabs and Jews from slaughtering one another. Nevertheless, as I say, there are, I assure you, positions of far greater authority and renown than my own both within and without the British Empire. What is our garrison here compared to that in India? What have I got in military and police? A handful of aircraft, six armored cars, a gendarmerie of seven thousand men to cover the entire country, and only two hundred of your chaps—that's not including the Schwilis and the Badawis, who can't be entirely trusted. And I shall soon run out of footballs. So, lecture over, what do you propose?"

"Propose?"

Ross looked down exasperated, as if he were dealing with the dullest boy in class. "About al-Sayyid."

Kirsch, in fact, had understood Ross's poisonous intentions perfectly well from halfway through the letter.

"Well?"

"I propose, sir, to have Saud al-Sayyid arrested."

"And if someone should tell you that was not a good idea?"

"Then I might find it necessary to speak to the high commissioner."

Kirsch had played his trump card. It was a dangerous move. Only Lord Samuel had power over Ross. And would he take Kirsch's side? There was no telling.

Ross smiled. "Jolly good, Robert. You're quite right. Stick to your guns. Justice above all."

Kirsch, feeling claustrophobic, rolled down his window. The car turned left toward Government House, where, in the moonlight, Kirsch could see the Union Jack on its high pole.

Ross changed the subject.

"I've asked Mark Bloomberg to go down to Petra for me. I want him to see the temples. I'm not sure that they have ever been represented in oils by an artist of his stature and talent. It's a major undertaking. He could be away several months."

Kirsch felt the blood rush to his cheeks, but there was nothing he could do about that.

"His wife will accompany him, of course," Ross continued, "unless . . ."

The car approached the gates of Government House. Ross tapped on the glass panel.

"Just one moment," he told the driver.

"Unless finances forbid. In addition, the hardships of the Transjordan desert are perhaps unadvisable for a young woman, especially at this time of year. I was thinking, however, that Bloomberg might, well certainly if his wife doesn't go, need an assistant. Someone to carry his paints and easel, a general dogsbody. Al-Sayyid would be an excellent candidate for the job. And there will be an Arab Legion N.C.O. and four men from the Camel Corps along, in case there's trouble along the way, or the boy gets a notion to stab someone else. All this, of course, if Bloomberg is agreeable to making the trip at all, and absolutely to travel without—what is Mrs. Bloomberg's Christian name? Jane. No, Joyce. Contrary chap isn't he, Bloomberg? Hard to figure. Although I believe I can persuade him. He's done rather well from our little circle of friends, and the work is truly, truly remarkable. To be honest I'm quite in awe of him, and I'm willing to foot the bill for this rather extravagant excursion. So we're in accord here?"

Kirsch grasped the door handle of the car.

Ross leaned over and grabbed Kirsch by the wrist. "Let the boy go, keep your mouth shut, and you'll find that you can spend as much uninterrupted time as you like with Mrs. Bloomberg. It's as simple as that."

Ross relaxed his grip.

Kirsch pushed open the car door.

"Well," Ross said, "no doubt I'll be hearing from you shortly."

Kirsch stumbled from the car and slammed the door behind him. Outside, the fields were covered with stubbled grass and dusty thorns.

He knelt by the roadside and retched. Ross's car passed through the gates and into the government compound.

19.

In his stifling windowless office at the station Kirsch sat and stared blankly at the wall. He had walked the three miles back from Government House; his cap, like a lost emblem of his former conative life, lay forgotten on the backseat of Ross's car. He sat now in the dark and felt the blood beat in his head. He knew what it was right to do, and he knew what he was going to do. If he let Saud travel to Petra with Bloomberg, then his job was a sham, and so was he. It crossed his mind that there was an ugly local precedent for such behavior. Hadn't King David sent Bathsheba's husband into the front lines in order to get him out of the way? The king got the woman he yearned for, but spent the rest of his life paying for his murderous deception. Kirsch, however, wasn't responsible for Bloomberg's journey into Transjordan and Joyce wasn't a slave to Kirsch's desires. Far from it. He had never felt more used in his life. Equally, he had never felt more attracted to another human being. And why? His soul had no answers. Even so, whichever way you looked at it, participating in Ross's scheme was wrong, and in some vague way Kirsch knew that his becoming a policeman had been, for him, a way to balance the scales of injustice that had tipped against his family when his brother had been killed. To bow to corruption now would provide a victory for those same malevolent forces that had taken Marcus.

There was a sharp knock on the door. Kirsch rose to switch on the light but Cartwright entered before Kirsch could call him in. Harlap hovered in the doorway behind him. Cartwright stood before Kirsch's desk, the door wide open; tea-green light from the dimly lit corridor surrounded Harlap's ample frame.

"We've got him. Lampard found him hiding in an empty sesame oil vat at his uncle's place on Cush Street."

Kirsch looked at his two sergeants, one English, one a Palestinian Jew, but they were both sloppily dressed in the local style. Cartwright's shirt was crumpled and his sleeves rolled up, while the top two buttons of Harlap's tunic were missing; the hair on his chest burst out like stuffing from a mattress.

"Is the boy here?" Kirsch asked.

"He's on his way."

"Good. As soon as he arrives you're to transport him over to Government House."

"This late? What for?"

"Never mind how late it is or what for, just do as I say."

As soon as Kirsch spoke Harlap left the room. Cartwright lingered a while, an expression of frustration and disdain etched on his sunburned face. Kirsch knew Cartwright was sick to death of taking orders from an officer ten years his junior, and a Jew to boot.

"Well, go on. What are you waiting for?"

"Just drop him at the door, then?"

"Members of the governor's staff will be waiting for him. The interrogation will take place at Government House."

"Right."

Kirsch had no reason to believe that Cartwright knew that he was lying about the interrogation; and yet he was sure that Cartwright did know.

"If you want, sir, I think we could probably get out of him all you want to know in the car on the way over there."

"We don't do that."

"No, sir, 'course not, sir."

The car, a green Morris Sports Tourer, one of only four vehicles owned by the force, sped down past the Convent of the Poor Clares, then slowed as Dobbins swung it onto back roads in order to avoid the scattered nails that the striking taxi drivers were still distributing on main thoroughfares. Saud sat in the backseat of the car flanked by Lampard and Cartwright. Dobbins drove in silence, breaking into speech only once to swear at a goat that was making its way slowly across the road. At the junction with a path that led to the educational farm they hooked up with the main road again and picked up speed, traveling in the direction of the Government Arab College.

Cartwright banged Dobbins on the back. "Speed up."

"Fuck off," Dobbins replied, "we'll get there soon enough."

"You're a stubborn bastard," Cartwright said and then the first shots came pumping through the glass, into Dobbins's arm, into Cartwright's head. The car skidded, veered off the road, then back on as Dobbins recovered enough to steer.

"Keep going! Keep going! Fuck! Fuck!"

The bullet that grazed Saud's head caught Lampard in his right shoulder. There was blood in the boy's lap where he involuntarily cradled Cartwright's slumped head.

"He's dead. He's dead. You fucking Arabs, you fucking bastard."

Lampard tried to lift his arm to swipe at Saud but the wound in his shoulder brought him to a scream instead. The hole above Cartwright's ear leaked thick dark blood down Saud's thighs and legs and onto the floor of the car. Dobbins was weeping; one arm on the wheel, he tore down the road toward the gates of Government House. Once there, he braked and leaned his head on the horn, keeping it there until the on-duty sentries came to prize the bodies, three living and one dead, out of the car.

The phone rang in Kirsch's office.

"Get Bloomberg now and bring him here. As soon as it can, the Petra party leaves."

Kirsch had never heard Ross so ruffled and agitated.

"What's going on? Why the rush?"

"Good God, man. Haven't you heard? Somebody shot up the car. I've got a dead squaddie and two others with bullets in the arm and shoulder."

"Who's been killed?"

"Your man Cartwright."

Kirsch closed his eyes and wiped his hand across his brow. Ross was silent on the other end.

"And the boy?"

"Right as rain. Lucky bugger."

"And who . . . ?"

"Were the shooters? How the hell should I know? That's your job, isn't it? My guess is Jews. Could be entirely unrelated to our nasty little cargo. Somebody took a shot at the same car when we were in Hebron last month, clipped the bonnet. I don't think I'm being modest when I say that it's probably me they're after. Or perhaps you? I imagine the local Zionists don't have a great appreciation for what you're doing."

Ross, realizing that he had probably gone too far, softened his tone a little. "Listen, get hold of Bloomberg and get him over here. Bring him in the back way. Tell no one what you're up to. And don't let on what happened. What Bloomberg doesn't know can't hurt him, and by the time someone spills the beans they'll be halfway into the desert."

"Lampard and Dobbins?"

"Lampard's arm's a mess. Dobbins has lost quite a bit of blood, but he'll pull through."

"Cartwright. I'll have to telegraph . . ."

"Do it in the morning."

There was a click at the other end. Kirsch hung up the receiver. Ross's explanation for the ambush didn't quite fit. This was the first Kirsch had heard about an incident in Hebron. As far as he knew, no one had taken a potshot at a British officer or an N.C.O. in over a year, and the last culprit had been a drunk playing silly buggers, not an assassin. The scenario was unlikely, unless things were changing and he, Kirsch, had failed to notice the shift in atmosphere. That was possible, especially as in the last few days he hadn't exactly had his ear to the ground. A subtle rearrangement of the political forces, and before you knew it you had an insurrection on your hands. Poor Cartwright. Poor sod. Once, in a moment of unpredictable sentimentality, Cartwright had shown Kirsch a family photo: Mum, Dad, and sister outside their narrow terraced house in Bermondsey. All of them, except the balding Dad, with Cartwright's sandy hair. The sister was pretty, a nice-looking girl with freckles and a wide smile.

Kirsch rose from his desk and walked out into the compound where his motorbike was parked. He was about to kick-start the machine when he remembered that he wouldn't be able to squeeze both Bloomberg and his luggage onto the backseat. All the other vehicles were out. Back in the office there was a somber air; news of Cartwright's murder had filtered through among the night staff. For some reason, perhaps the looks he felt that he was getting as he crossed the room, Kirsch sensed that at least one or two of the British policemen were holding him to blame. But he might have been imagining this.

He had to wait an hour for a car to come in, and it was almost nine by the time he set out for Talpiot. At first he drove with the windows closed, as if expecting bullets, but he quickly rolled down the glass on the driver's side and as he did so the heavy odors of Jerusalem at night, crouched by the roadside, sprang up at him: camel and donkey dung, honeysuckle and jasmine. But Kirsch, tuned at this moment to memory, caught only the smell of his brother as they sat by the coal fire in the bedroom that they'd shared as children: cross-legged in underpants, Robert and Marcus held their damp vests up to dry, blocking the heat with their clothes; shivering, the scent of Marcus's chest and the chill sweat in his armpits.

The car's tires ground noisily on the unpaved road that led to Bloomberg's cottage. In the beam of the headlights that followed the terrace curve Kirsch caught a thick wall of caperbush, its blaze of white night flowers in full bloom. At sunrise they would wither away. He parked the car and jumped out, slamming the driver's door in order to give warning of his arrival. He didn't want to catch Joyce in bed with Bloomberg.

"Hello! Anybody there?"

Kirsch heard the clink of bottle on glass and walked in the direction of the noise.

Bloomberg was sitting under a tree in a far corner of the cottage garden, a glass of wine in one hand, an almost empty bottle in the other.

"Ross sent me. I'm afraid you have to leave sooner than expected. In fact you have to leave now."

Bloomberg put down the glass and ran his fingers through his shock of curly gray-black hair. He was shirtless, and Kirsch was surprised by the powerful build of his upper body. He had thought of Bloomberg as skinny—perhaps he wanted him to be weak.

"Now? Well that's certainly sooner than expected. What's the hurry?"

"There's been . . . a change in circumstances. Some bureaucratic complication that Ross wants to avoid. I think it involves the Arab Legion N.C.O. who's supposed to accompany you."

Kirsch looked around the garden and toward the cottage. A lamp burned in one of the windows.

"She's not here. In case you were wondering. Strange thing is I thought she was probably with you. Maybe she's giving us both the runaround?"

Kirsch didn't know what to say. He could have understood if Bloomberg had tried to punch him in the face, but this was worse.

"You need to get your things together."

"Oh, really." Bloomberg took a long swig and drained the bottle to its dregs.

Kirsch stood over him and waited. Eventually Bloomberg rose and dusted off his trousers. Kirsch noticed that there was another empty bottle of wine on the ground behind him.

"Oh well," he said, "orders are orders." He stood at attention and effected a clumsy salute.

"Corporal Mark Bloomberg. Ready to paint, sir."

Bloomberg toppled forward and grabbed Kirsch's arm. He was half cut; Kirsch would never get him out of there in this condition.

"This way, Kirschele." Bloomberg laughed. "You know a bissel Yiddish? *Es nit di lokshen far Shabbes.* Don't eat the noodles before Shabbos. Lovely, isn't it. You get the meaning? Don't fuck the girl before the wedding. But you've already done that, haven't you? You've forked down a whole barrel load of *lokshen.* Come here."

Bloomberg dragged Kirsch by the arm.

"This is where he came through the bushes. Knife right in the fucking heart."

Bloomberg began to beat his breast.

"Right here. In the fucking heart."

Kirsch had been supporting Bloomberg, holding him up by the elbow. Bloomberg shrugged him off.

The moon hung above a copse of thin, sickly-looking acacia trees. Bloomberg's skin was horribly pale and his eyes red.

"Give me fifteen minutes," he slurred, and walked unsteadily to the cottage.

Kirsch saw something glinting in the dry grass. It looked like a coin that had probably fallen out of Bloomberg's pocket. Kirsch bent down to pick it up. It wasn't a coin, it was a button, a silver button from a policeman's tunic just like his own. Kirsch ran his hand to check his own jacket. No, he was all done up.

A thin beam of light bisected the darkness between the poles of the garden gate. Kirsch heard someone dismount a bicycle and ring its bell. He slid the button into his pocket.

"I'm ho-ome," Joyce called out, far too cheerily for Kirsch's peace of mind. Her voice was full of domestic confidence, even love.

Kirsch took two steps in from the corner of the garden and spoke softly: "He's inside packing. He has to leave."

Joyce, startled despite Kirsch's efforts, lost and then regained her grip of the bicycle. "Oh," she said. "It's you."

"Yes, I've come to accompany Mr. Bloomberg to Government House."

"Mr. Bloomberg?" Joyce laughed. "Are you arresting him?"

Bloomberg's voice carried through the open door of the cottage. He was singing: *In the morning, in the evening, ain't we got fun?* He sang off-key, and Kirsch heard the trace of Whitechapel cockney that Bloomberg suppressed when he spoke. Then he appeared framed by the doorway, a portfolio in one hand, a clutch of brushes in the other.

"Right, then. Off we go."

Joyce began to laugh again. Kirsch felt confused and angry. What game were they playing?

"You'd better take a change of clothes," she said.

"Gotcha." Bloomberg peremptorily dropped the portfolio and brushes, then turned back into the cottage. "Clothes, yes, but first a dance. Come inside, my love."

Joyce leaned the bicycle against a nearby wall and almost skipped up the garden path.

Bloomberg grabbed her around the waist and began singing again. *"I wonder can my baby do the Charleston, Charleston."* He twisted his knees and swung his heels sharply in and out on each step. Joyce did the same, and twirled an imaginary string of pearls. *"Fo do do deo do Black Bottom!"* They collapsed laughing on the bed. Kirsch stood a few feet outside the house, feeling utterly excluded, like a boy watching his parents drunk for the first time. He wanted to shout, "Get a move on, we haven't got all night!" But Joyce's presence discouraged him. Had he utterly compromised himself for nothing?

Eventually, the Bloombergs composed themselves and a somber mood descended. Bloomberg and Joyce, neither bothering to challenge further either the surprise of Kirsch's presence or the suddenness and finality of his orders, puttered about the small room gathering clothes, toiletries, paints, turpentine, brushes, rags, and canvases. Kirsch backed the car up to the gate and the two men loaded the boot while Joyce filled the floor and the backseat with Bloomberg's surplus materials. Husband and wife did not speak. Bloomberg walked from house to car and back again with knitted brow, while Joyce's face grew first gloomy, then blank and expressionless. By the time the car was ready Kirsch felt their silence as burdensome and oppressive, like a storm that will not break. He jumped into the driver's seat, turned the key in the ignition and the engine sputtered to life, overloud and thumping threateningly in an awkward rhythm that suggested the car was about to stall. Kirsch pumped the accelerator a couple of times, revving the engine to a smoother pitch.

Bloomberg bent to the window.

"We'll take a moment here," he said, then led Joyce by the arm back into the cottage. Once inside he kicked the door shut behind them.

Kirsch felt his heart racing. He wanted to get out of the car, break into the house and somehow interpose himself between Bloomberg and Joyce. But he did no such thing. Whatever was passing between them couldn't matter much. In five minutes husband and wife would be apart, and then time would place a wedge between them, pushing and pushing until the space was big enough for Kirsch to enter and occupy. If Joyce thought she still loved Bloomberg, Kirsch was convinced that she couldn't. What she had was a sickness, bohemian sickness, love of the suffering artist; it happened to women who read too much poetry, especially Americans, like Joyce. The torrid blue of an English winter, Bloomberg painting in an unheated room, a long scarf wrapped round his neck. Who wouldn't fall for it?

His reverie was interrupted by Bloomberg's opening of the passenger-side door.

"Let's go," he said.

The two men drove in silence. It was a short ride to Government House. Kirsch, mindful of Cartwright's fate, floored the accelerator. He took the curves in the road at high speed; the art supplies in the boot banged about. Kirsch thought that he should probably have something to say to Bloomberg, but everything that came to his mind concerned either Joyce or the ambush, so he kept his lips sealed.

At the rear of the house they halted. A Tommy with his rifle at the ready approached from the gate.

Bloomberg, who had been slumped in his seat, roused himself. He turned to face Kirsch. His short-sleeved blue shirt showed dark patches of sweat under the arms.

"She's a chameleon," he murmured.

Kirsch stared straight ahead.

"She gets involved for a while and then she lets go."

"I'll take the chance," Kirsch said.

"I wouldn't if I were you. I know her very well. You saw how she was tonight."

"If she's so fickle why did she stay with you?"

"Ask her," Bloomberg said.

The sentry was at the window of the car. Recognizing Kirsch, he waved them on. Kirsch wanted to press Bloomberg further, but Bloomberg was drunk, and in any case, as soon as Kirsch parked the opportunity was lost as the car was surrounded by a working party of men who stripped the boot and the backseat of their contents and transferred them to another, larger vehicle.

Ross appeared, coming down the concrete stairs at the back of the kitchen. If he had troubles on his mind he was doing a good job concealing them. Ignoring Kirsch, he turned his full attention to Bloomberg.

"Mark. So good of you to do this." He shook Bloomberg's hand energetically. "Apologies for the unforgivable rush. I'll have to explain it all to you when you get back. But do take my word, no way to avoid this. Listen, it's going to be two cars over to Amman and I've arranged a night's stay for you at Freddie Peake's place. The following morning you'll go on to Kerak and from there it's horseback and camel all the way to Petra. You'll have five Arab Legion chaps at your disposal. Muhammad Rachman's the N.C.O. He's absolutely reliable. Knows the desert like the back of his hand. You're going to be in the lap of luxury down there, no fetching firewood or water for you. Leave it to them. You get on with the painting, let them pitch the tent and make the beds. Take a look here . . ."

Ross produced a pocket torch and spread a copy of the order sheet on the bonnet of Kirsch's car for Bloomberg to inspect. By the light's thin beam Bloomberg read: *Always detail one man to be with the painter at the time he paints.*

"That's preposterous."

"Hardly. And let's not have an argument. Yours is going to have to be a guarded camp. Oh, and by the way, there's a boy going along to be your assistant, name of al-Sayyid."

"I don't need . . ."

"Come, come. All the Italian greats had their apprentices. Giotto's boys on their ladders. Why not you? Think School of Bloomberg." Ross laughed and patted Bloomberg on the back. "Well, let's not delay. Can't wait to see what you do with the place. Terribly excited. 'Match me such a marvel save in Eastern clime: A rose-red city—half as old as time.' "

Kirsch, who had heard these lines about Petra quoted to weariness since arriving in Jerusalem—rumor had it they were from someone in the military administration's (Harrison's?) Oxford prize poem—turned away and pretended to supervise the packing of Bloomberg's rolls of canvas into the boot of one of the cars. In the high pines and eucalyptus trees cicadas beat and whirred their invisible wings. Kirsch felt himself momentarily transparent, as if his own inner workings, the machinations of his mind, were visible to everyone in the courtyard. He shook himself free of this awkward sensation by yelling at a young subaltern to be more careful with Bloomberg's supplies.

Within half an hour the party was ready to leave. The group, absurd to most of its onlookers, and to at least five of its participants (a handful of armed men to protect a painter!) divided in two. The lead car, a large black Ford, was driven by Muhammad Rachman. Bloomberg sat up front next to him, sweat running down his face, while Salaman, one of the Arab Legion soldiers, a squat individual with a bushy black mustache, occupied the backseat; he was squashed in next to a cardboard box that stank of turpentine and contained Bloomberg's brushes and rags. At the last moment Saud was hurried out of the house and into the second car, where he sat in the rear flanked by the taller two of the three remaining Arab Legion men. Kirsch approached the car but Mustafa, the driver, waved him away and started the engine. Kirsch peered through the side window. Saud had been oddly disguised in some cast-off British schoolboy's outfit: a white shirt with an utterly incongruous red-and-black striped tie, and gray trousers; his hair had been combed back and a bandage was loosely taped on his forehead. If Saud caught Kirsch's eye he didn't show it, but stared blankly ahead of him. As the cars pulled around from the back of the house and away east down the Hill of Evil Counsel, Kirsch put his hand in his tunic pocket and came up with the silver button that he had collected outside Bloomberg's cottage. He had forgotten about it. He spread the palm of his hand, examined the button, then clenched his fist and, ignoring someone by the open kitchen door who was calling his name, got in his car and drove back in the direction of the police station. Half a mile down the road Kirsch changed his mind and veered off toward the Bloombergs' house.

Joyce wasn't there. He knocked hard, a policeman's wake-up call or a desperate lover's, unnecessarily loud for so small a house; then he peered in through the windows: an oil lamp had been left burning low, there were clothes strewn over the floor, the bed remained unmade. It looked as if Joyce had left in a hurry. Kirsch described a circumference of about twenty yards around the house calling her name as he walked. He returned to the spot where he had found the button and poked indiscriminately around in the long grass and adjacent flowerbed. What was it that Ross had said on the telephone about local Jews not liking what Kirsch was up to? As if, weirdly, Ross didn't like it either. And yet—contrary to Kirsch's expectations—in Palestine, thus far anyway, his Jewishness had been more or less irrelevant. He recalled his father's standing in the drawing room addressing Marcus on the day before he had set off for Aldershot. "You will be surprised by the irreticence of army life— particularly where Jews are concerned. I have sheltered you boys, too much no doubt, under the dark gray skullcap that covers this rather comfortable neighborhood." That was Kirsch's father, good-natured but endlessly ironic, although after Marcus died he wasn't ironic anymore.

The moon hid under a cover of black cloud. It was too dark to see much in the garden, not that Kirsch was really looking; rather he listened for Joyce's step or the tick of her bicycle wheels. The heat of the night was oppressive; earlier in the day a khamsin had moved in from the Judean desert, settling fine yellow dust on windscreens and windowsills. Now Kirsch felt his hair, regimentally short though it was, matted to his head. He ran the back of his hand across his forehead to rub the sweat away. Where could she be at this time of night? He hung around for almost half an hour, then drove away.

20.

The two cars headed down the old Roman road out of Jerusalem. The heat, stifling enough in the city, only grew worse with their precipitous drop toward the Dead Sea. Bloomberg shifted in his seat and tried to get comfortable. He was sweating off his drunkenness, his shirt and trousers were damp and clung to his body; his mouth was dry and he could almost taste the salt air on his blistered tongue. In the absolute madness of this moment, on his way, guarded by a bunch of armed men, to paint a place that meant less than nothing to him, and that he hadn't even heard of until a couple of days ago, Bloomberg couldn't for the life of him remember why he and Joyce had left London. Although that grand city was where he could have done with the armed men. Station a couple inside the Ransom Gallery. Wake the critics right up. Don't like what you see? Try this bayonet up your arse.

But had things really been so bad there? Well, yes, they had: no money, nowhere to show his work after the last disaster, no mother, no friends to speak of, half of them gone in the war—Jacob, Gideon, Norman Taylor the sculptor, his little group from the Slade blasted to pieces. The stupid war: he was working in the drawing office a few miles behind the front when a brigadier came into the room, looked him over, then started talking with the officer in charge. "What's *he* doing?" the brigadier had asked. "He's doing section mapping, sir. That's why he was brought in. He's an artist." "What's his name?" "Bloomberg, sir." And the brigadier had responded: "We can't have a man with a name like that doing map drawing." On the spot, Bloomberg was dispatched back to the front. Hard to believe, you could die for your country if you were a Jew, but you couldn't map for it. Even so, it *was* his country, and this place, with its lunatic Jews and Arabs, certainly wasn't.

The car hit a bumpy patch of road and stirred Bloomberg out of his reverie. "Where are we?" he asked.

Rachman, looking straight ahead at the road and navigating its dusty craters, replied in better English than Bloomberg had expected, "In a half an hour we will pass through Jericho, then cross the Allenby bridge into Transjordan."

Bloomberg slumped back in his seat. Rachman checked his rearview mirror; the headlights on the other car shone a hundred yards back, then disappeared and reappeared as the drivers negotiated the long serpentine curves that led, far too suggestively, Bloomberg thought, to the lowest point on earth.

In the rear of the second car Saud sat motionless between the two legionaries. The air in the vehicle reeked of stale tobacco and sweat. Suddenly, the driver pulled to a halt at the side of the road. The lead car sped on down the hill. Saud's blood froze. Mustafa got out of the car, he opened the rear door and the men climbed out, the last pushing Saud in front of him. Mustafa took Saud by the arm and led him to the edge of a small ravine. Saud heard two clicks behind him. The other men had loaded their rifles. The stars spun overhead. Saud turned wildly to see where he might run.

"Kneel down," Mustafa ordered him. "Now close your eyes."

Saud obeyed: the strangest anxiety entered his mind that he mustn't get the British schoolboy trousers dirty. Then there was his uncle, his apron stained with sesame oil, demanding to know where the policemen were taking the boy, and his mother, her face tearful in the angry crowd on the street, her arm reaching out to him. Much closer he heard loud laughter. Saud opened his eyes. In the glare of the car headlights Mustafa and the other two were pissing on the rocks a few feet down the hill. Saud rose and brushed off his trousers at the knees.

"Did anyone say you could stand up?"

They started laughing again.

Mustafa made a clicking sound with his tongue.

Saud cursed them out. They stopped laughing and told him to get back in the car.

"You think we'd shoot you? We'd rather shoot him." Mustafa grinned and nodded in the direction where Bloomberg's car had vanished at the base of the hill.

At dawn, as they passed the Ghor, Bloomberg woke with a pain in his left shoulder. He adjusted his position and looked out of the window to see a rushing stream bounding over rocks by a chasm of the Jordan. Then, as the highway turned through bare mountainous slopes on either side, he saw, a hundred yards ahead, what looked like a huge black upturned plow. As the car approached Rachman slowed and pointed.

"Jericho Jane," he said. "German present to the Turks."

"What?"

Then Bloomberg made out a giant howitzer rising behind fragments of barbed wire, rough patches of oleander at its feet.

"Is that what we called it?"

Bloomberg had almost forgotten that the war had been here too.

Rachman brought the car close to a halt.

"Allenby came here"—he gestured to the right, swinging his arm—"and the Turks ran away *there*." He pointed to his left.

Rachman looked slightly disgusted, as if, so Bloomberg imagined, the Turkish flight, desirable though it had been at the time, was a cowardly disgrace upon the whole region.

"And you," Rachman asked, "you were in the British army?"

"I was."

"Where were you?"

"Flanders. They brought me in to draw maps. I was thirty-eight, already a little old for the trenches, but in the end I was sent to the front."

"Did you fight?"

"For a while, and then I didn't."

"You were wounded?"

Bloomberg had no need to have this conversation, and yet he felt that he wanted to. If Joyce wasn't around, Rachman was a useful wall to bounce off. And why not go over it all again? One more run-through to see if he had been a brave man or a coward. Although, of course, he already knew the answer.

"I wounded myself. Shot my toe off. Deprived His Majesty of the services of a sworn member of his forces. Treason, in other words."

"Why didn't they shoot you?"

"They thought about it," Bloomberg said, and laughed. "Then they decided it would be crueler to let me live."

Rachman smiled. No one in this car, thank God, was going to feel sorry for him.

"Then what was your punishment?"

"Three weeks without pay, then light duties until the wound healed."

"And after that?"

"Back to the front with a vengeance, me old mate. Runner for the unit. Sketched the enemy positions."

Rachman nodded.

"You were lucky. Here they would have shot you for sure. If you were an Arab and you had put a bullet in your foot to get out of battle . . ." Rachman closed one eye and set his gunsights. "Firing squad."

"And if I were a Jew?"

"I believe that you already are a Jew."

Bloomberg laughed. All over the world there were fates more bitter than his, and they didn't make a damn bit of difference to his own stupid misery.

They drove south past small, sleepy Arab villages and on through a fair rolling plateau that seemed better wooded and better watered than any place Bloomberg had seen in Palestine. A castle appeared out of nowhere, rising on a rocky cliff above the river. Unlike the howitzer, however, Rachman didn't seem to think this construction worthy of comment. Bloomberg stared hard at the landscape, then looked down at his hands: they were trembling a little, he couldn't get them still. What would Joyce do without him? Be happy, perhaps. If happiness was an option for anyone—although Americans, whose culture assisted every illusion, seemed to believe in it. What he had done to her . . . The offer of love, the withdrawal of love; the encouragement of her work, the devaluation of her work; using her to vent his anger, spending her money: all this was despicable. In London, when he'd first met her, Joyce was spirited and adventurous, and to his enormous pleasure she had remained so despite the difficulties that he sometimes set in her path, but the last year in the West Hampstead studio had tested her sorely. He couldn't explain to her what had happened to him. He thought that she knew anyway, and she had done everything to accommodate him. All he hoped was that time would grant him an opportunity to make restitution to her before they parted for good. Or had they already done so?

One of the legionaries in the backseat woke and said something to Rachman, who drove on for a short distance and then stopped the car in the shade of some nearby trees. The men all got out to stretch their legs.

After a few moments the second car pulled up and its occupants spilled out. Saud stood stiffly by the boot of the car looking back in the direction from which they had come. He had undone the top button of his white shirt and loosened, but not discarded, the school tie that he had been given at Government House. The stained bandage on his head flapped loose and dried blood was visible on his forehead.

Bloomberg walked over to the car. "What happened to you?"

The boy took a breath and surveyed the group of legionaries who were crouched in a tight circle looking at a map. He was about to speak when Rachman rose from the circle and spoke sharply to him in Arabic.

"An accident. Nothing," Saud replied.

"Well, I'm Mark Bloomberg. I believe you're going to help me with a few things."

"Yes," Saud replied, "I'll help you."

"You won't have too much to do. I work alone and I mix my own colors!" Bloomberg meant this as a gentle joke and was surprised when the boy responded, "How could anyone else do that for you?"

"Right," Bloomberg said. "They couldn't."

The boy looked down and kicked his heel into the dirt. When he looked up again Bloomberg had the feeling that he'd seen him before: that lanky frame, thin face and shadow of a mustache on his upper lip were all familiar. He *had* seen him before, he was certain of it. But when and where? And the boy was looking at him strangely—but why not? He *was* strange.

Rachman folded the map and hustled the men back into the cars.

"I'll see you later," Bloomberg said to Saud.

The boy didn't reply.

From a hill on its outskirts Amman looked no larger than an expanded village; closer, Bloomberg saw that it sprawled somewhat, and was perhaps the size of a small London neighborhood. They drove past the royal palace, a building of incongruous Swiss architecture, and on through a railway junction that displayed signs pointing to the HQ of the Transjordan police force, and the camp of the R.A.F. Eventually they came to a halt in front of a faux castle that was the temporary home of Freddie Peake, who, to Bloomberg's amusement and marginal consternation—he hadn't voted Labour all those years for nothing—Rachman kept referring to as Peake Pasha. But in any case, Peake Pasha was out, away for a few days on government business.

Bloomberg's large room was lavish by the standards to which he had become accustomed in Jerusalem. The dark highly polished furniture appeared outsized, and a glorious red-and-ochre kilim ran the length of the floor. Bloomberg stripped to his underwear and lay on the broad bed under a huge slowly spinning fan. Morning light blazed through the windows' thin white curtains. Bloomberg closed his eyes. He was on the point of dozing off when he remembered where had seen the boy before—at the edge of his garden in Talpiot. Bloomberg had at first taken him for Joyce. But what had the boy been doing there? Come to rob the house perhaps? He would have been a disappointed thief. Bloomberg got up from the bed and walked to the window. Out on the street an old woman in a frayed black dress squatted with a wicker basket of grapes, or perhaps it was figs, at her feet. Not so long ago Bloomberg would have wanted to draw her, but that impulse was gone. He was after something deeper now and sought less and less of the world.

21.

For the second night in a row following two humid, insufferable days, Joyce sat with Peter Frumkin's party at a table in one of the tearooms in the Municipal Gardens. Frumkin had come by to invite her and Mark for drinks late on the previous evening, arriving with his lanky chauffeur, who looked more like a bodyguard, about forty-five minutes after Kirsch and Mark had set off for Government House. Frumkin had found Joyce sitting in the dark. When he called out, "Mr. and Mrs. Bloomberg," she had pretended to be asleep and kept silent. Her head was spinning. In a few days everything had turned upside down, mostly because of her. She wished that she had hated going to bed with Robert Kirsch, but that wasn't the case. She wished she had felt relieved when Mark had left— able to breathe, unburdened—but that wasn't the case either. Frumkin had called out again, and then, indifferent to the shocks that he might be sending through her system, he had entered the cottage and turned up a lamp. "I heard there was an interesting American couple in town," he'd said after introducing himself. "Only half right," Joyce had replied, try- ing hard to collect herself. "My husband's a Londoner." The floor was strewn with her own clothes and those that Bloomberg had left behind. She regarded them without embarrassment and did not rise to clear up. She knew that Frumkin's "interesting" was a reference to her and Mark's involvement in the murder hunt. *Tout Jerusalem* wanted to hear the story, and most already had. Still, she picked herself up and went with him.

She had to admit it was nice to be with Americans again, especially Californians. She needed their light banter and easy friendship. The other senior members of the *Titus* production crew were both, like Frum- kin, men in their late twenties. The three of them, Frumkin, Rex, and Harvey (Joyce could remember only Frumkin's last name), were full of jokes and, she guessed, loaded with money. On the first night she had largely observed their proceedings, and said little. They hadn't prodded her about De Groot, and she hadn't spoken of him. Tonight she felt loosened a degree, like the second day home after a long journey. Frum- kin, to whom the others clearly deferred, had ordered a third bottle of wine and then a fourth. Everybody toasted the Volstead Act. Joyce, more than slightly tipsy, thought she saw a sliver of her face flash distorted in the restaurant's polished silverware, her throat on a knife edge.

"So listen to this, Joyce . . ." Frumkin had placed his hand on her arm. "We're on this desert plain fifty miles south of Jerusalem and we're going to do the bedouin camel charge. I've got three hundred of these guys, they're all mounted, obviously we don't need costumes but we've given them each a gilt javelin. Harvey over here has measured the ground, the cameras are placed. 'Roll 'em,' he yells. The bedouin charge: it's great. They charge right across the plain, waving the fucking javelins and yelling: spectacular—the only problem is *they keep going*. The camera crew's going nuts, the director's having a heart attack and the bedouin just disappear into a wadi between the hills. The whole lot of them."

Joyce laughed along with the others.

"Then we're worried that all we've got on film is a dust storm. We've got to do it again. But there's no one to do it with! Not a fucking one of them. And they don't come back."

The days in the desert had tanned Frumkin's skin nut brown and blanched his thick fair hair. His teeth were movie-star white, even though he was only the producer. The previous evening Joyce had already sensed that he liked her, and she had to make sure not to encourage him. Robert Kirsch was quite enough for now. But what a pleasure Frumkin was: easy, fun, not at all like her intense Brits.

There was a short silence as the table was cleared of dinner plates. The three men looked at her—only Frumkin, she thought, with a trace of desire. They were from Hollywood and used to the company of stunningly beautiful women. Whatever interest she had for them would come from her personality, not her appearance. In a way, this was a relief. Robert Kirsch had stared at her as if he would never be able to tear himself away from her face; his doing so wasn't unpleasant, but adoration could quickly become oppressive. The waiter brought coffee and they all lit cigarettes. Joyce felt the moment coming when she would have to sing for her supper, relive once again De Groot's death rush into the garden. Of course she could demur if she wished, refuse to tell the story, retreat behind the shield of her ladylike sensibilities: "Too awful to speak of." But that was precisely the reason to speak: it was Mark who had shaken and cried after the event, not her. She adjusted the sprig of jasmine that she had pinned to the lapel of her jacket; the same scent had surrounded her in the garden as she sponged the blood off Mark's chest.

"So," Frumkin said, "we hear you've had a hell of an experience."

Joyce readied herself to respond, but before she could begin, the waiter—curt and aggressive like all the local Jewish service staff, or so it seemed—called Frumkin away. She watched him skirt two tables and walk a few yards toward the wide entrance doors where two uniformed policemen stood waiting for him. Joyce recognized one of them immediately; it was Harlap, the officer who had sat insouciantly on her bed a few nights ago and interrogated her about De Groot's last words. Frumkin touched the policeman's back and guided him through the doors. Joyce sipped her coffee.

"I guess I'll wait," she said.

"Might as well. I don't think Pete wants to miss this story," Harvey replied. "He's probably already wondering who he can get to play you."

Joyce smiled. "How about Zasu Pitts?"

"Not Lillian Gish?" Rex put in.

"And who for my husband?"

"Who would you like?"

"Ivor Novello."

"No hesitation there. I take it you've seen *The White Rose?*"

"We saw it in London. Two nights before we left for Palestine."

"Well, he's handsome, even for a Brit."

"So is my husband."

Frumkin returned to the table. Beads of sweat glistened on his forehead.

"All set up for tomorrow," he announced. "We're going to shoot the assault outside the walls at daybreak. Those guys will keep the inquisitive public at bay."

"I thought you'd already spoken to the cops," Harvey said.

Joyce looked across at him. Harvey was wearing a slightly baffled expression.

"Right," Frumkin replied. "They just wanted to check up on a few details."

"So no change of plans?"

"No change," Frumkin said firmly. "Let's just hope this lot stays put."

He turned to Joyce. "We're borrowing half the British legionaries in Jerusalem and turning them into Romans. Perfect, don't you think? One imperial army playing another. Paying them, of course, and for Sir Gerald"—Frumkin looked around the restaurant to make sure that he wasn't being overheard—"a substantial dollar contribution to his Pro-Jerusalem Society."

They headed back to the Allenby Hotel, where the Metropolis Film

Corporation had taken over two floors. Frumkin and Joyce walked slightly ahead of the others.

"What are your plans for the next few days?" Frumkin asked.

"I'm waiting," she said. "I'm supposed to be doing some work here. Possibly in one of the Jewish schools."

"Well, while you're waiting is there any chance that you'd like to help us out?"

"In what way?"

"Oh, there're a million things to be done on a film set."

"Well, that's kind of you," Joyce said. "I'll certainly think about it."

They approached the lobby of the hotel. Frumkin whistled and, like an obedient dog, his chauffeur responded immediately, pulling the hired company limousine to the front of the taxi line. Harvey and Rex shook Joyce's hand and said good night. Frumkin leaned over to speak to his driver, then opened the car door for Joyce.

"Aron here will take you home. I'm sorry I can't escort you back but I've got quite a bit of work to do before we start shooting."

"If it's all the same I'd really rather walk."

"Inadvisable to say the least. Too far, and too dangerous."

"Not at all," Joyce replied. She felt that she had fallen into her English self: overpolite to the point of self-mortification.

"Don't make me come with you," Frumkin threatened. "If you do, *you're* going to be responsible if we have a late start tomorrow. Do you have any idea what an hour of filming costs?"

He reached out and grabbed her hand, then leaned in and kissed her gently on the cheek.

"Good night, Mrs. Bloomberg."

Joyce got into the back of the limousine. The chauffeur closed the door and came around into the driver's seat. Joyce leaned back into the soft leather. Aside from the governor's, this was probably the most luxurious car in Jerusalem: rags to riches. Mark would be appalled. But there was something fresh and hopeful about these film boys. Joyce knew why: the war hadn't touched them. What was it Peter Frumkin had said during dinner last night? "We had the overseas caps but didn't make it overseas." The war had ended before they could set off for France. Three lucky American boys serving their time at Camp Taylor. Of course they didn't see it that way. They had, all three of them, wanted to be heroes. Mark could have told them all about that, or even Robert Kirsch, who had lost his brother.

The car pulled away smoothly from the hotel. The moon over the Mount of Olives appeared swollen and the hills seemed to falter beneath it. The place took her breath away, so much so that, along with her Zionist involvement, Joyce almost wished that she had religion to provide a home for her excess of feeling. And she so much wanted to *do* something here. It was frustrating. She missed the London meetings with their thrilling sense of urgency and companionship: raised voices, argument, and crowded rooms. And Mark, even though he didn't know it, had led her there. He had told her about Jacob Rosen, had shown her his poems and she had read them again and again until Jacob's hopeful, pioneer-proud, godless Jerusalem was hers. It was Jacob who had taken her out into the street and down to Toynbee Hall where a hundred black umbrellas were stacked up in the corner but the walls were covered with posters of sunny Palestine. But here she was, *in the place,* and her Zionism was quickly becoming a lonely thing.

The car moved forward. After fifteen minutes or so they arrived at the narrow, bumpy track that led to the Bloombergs' cottage. The driver halted twenty yards from the gate.

"Thank you, Aron," Joyce said.

The driver turned around in his seat. His chauffeur's uniform consisted of a white singlet, brown shorts, dark socks and scuffed leather shoes.

"Do you like Mr. Frumkin?"

Joyce was a little taken aback.

"Well enough, yeah, sure."

"He is a powerful man. And strong for the Jews."

"What do you mean?"

Aron raised his eyebrows and pursed his lips, as if to convey that he was privy to secret information.

"Not like the British Jews. They like their teatime too much. They can't change. One hundred and five percent English. All they think about is to be fair. No one is fair in the Middle East. Mr. Frumkin understands what has to be done here."

"And what is that?"

"Ask him. We've had a lot of talks."

Aron's response was locally typical: to lead you somewhere and then clam up. The British were similar. Joyce thought it might have something to do with the proximity of borders in small countries. Americans were expansive in conversation, they would tell you anything, the talk was continent-wide.

"All right, I will."

Joyce got out of the car and swung the door shut. She waited until Aron reversed and the purr of the engine had died away; then she walked up the path and stepped through a gap in the wall. The heat, if anything, seemed to have increased as the night wore on. There was a smell of ripe figs in the air. Nearby a branch cracked and she heard what sounded like a small cascade of stones. Joyce stopped short. Was someone watching her? She looked around. The fat moon had disappeared and the stars, usually so brilliant, were veiled with mist.

"Hello!" Joyce called out, but there was no reply.

It sounded as if a thousand locusts were singing in the trees. Joyce, refusing fear, walked slowly through the garden and unlocked the front door. She pushed it open, locked it behind her, and then, without turning up a lamp, flopped down on the bed without noticing either the folded note that Robert Kirsch had sheepishly pushed under her door an hour or so earlier, or the canvases and clothes that, at some other point in the evening, had been trodden on, split, and ripped, either by accident or intent, while someone, in haste, had searched the room.

22.

A huge pool of liquid sewage lay in Wadi al-Joz, the otherwise lovely valley that ran between the large house that belonged to Shaikh Isma'il,

Jerusalem's grand mufti, and Clive Barker's altogether less impressive abode. The priciest Moslem residential area in the city had been flooded with the drainage from Mea She'arim, one of the poorest Jewish neighborhoods. The local property owners, all Moslem, were up in arms. Kirsch couldn't fathom why Ross had sent him to deal with the problem; surely it was something to be worked out between the Zionist Commission, which had funded the Mea She'arim drain work, and the administration, which was supposed to have carried it through effectively. Settling down angry but nonviolent Arab petitioners wasn't police work, unless Kirsch's duties had been restructured without his knowing it. He should have been investigating Cartwright's murder. He had spent the previous morning composing a letter to follow up the telegram that he had already sent to Cartwright's parents, while phrases from the official missive that his parents had received about Marcus had danced through his brain. He was preparing to leave his office and drive out to take a close look around the site of the shootings, when Ross had called to tell him that as Cartwright's death and the wounding of Lampard and Dobbins was, so he believed, an exclusively military matter, he would be taking the investigation under his own wing. This was patently nonsense—even if Cartwright had been the victim of a terrorist act, or a political assassination, it was still police business—and Kirsch knew that Ross was covering something up, but as yet he couldn't figure out what that something might be. So instead, here was Detective Kirsch hard on the Case of the Overflowing Drain. Ross must have known that Kirsch felt like shit, and that must have been why he had given him shit to deal with.

It was nine in the morning and the sun was already too hot to bear. All Kirsch really wanted to do was find Joyce and pour his heart out to her; instead he was stepping through a foul-smelling, fly-ridden black pond of decomposing turds and other rotting sewage.

Barker was waiting at the front door of his own house, his commonly pale face beet-red under his broad-brimmed sun helmet. He was fuming.

"And pat he comes," he yelled, as Kirsch picked his way across the semiflooded garden, "like the Catastrophe of the Old Comedy."

"Now, now," Kirsch responded. He had never had much feeling for Barker, who carried his "civic advisor" title as if Jerusalem were his personal fiefdom.

"Now what? I spend from dawn until now sticking my knife up some worm-eaten timbers in the Al Aqsa trying to figure out some way to preserve the fabric of this city's most beautiful places, and I have to come home to this. It's a bloody disgrace. And I don't mind who hears it, you can tell Lord bloody Samuel for all I care, but I tell you if the situation were reversed and the drains of a Moslem slum voided into the best Jewish quarter there would be such a bloody outcry you'd be able to hear it on Wall Street and Park Lane."

A few months earlier a poem had circulated among the gentile upper-echelon mandate officers, and someone, ignorant of Kirsch's allegiance to the faith that the poem mocked, had passed it on to him:

Benjamin, and Levy, Cohen and Sassoon,
Lewis, Mond, and Meinertzhagen moaning all in tune,
Franklin, Montefiore, and Harrari in between,
Isaacs, Fels, and Israeli baying at the moon,
Ladenburg, and Schlezinger, and Trier, and Duveen,
All the tribes in harmony from counter, pale, and dune—
Was such sorrow ever known, or such a scandal seen!
Samuel, Schiff, and Rothschild twined in richer chords,
Mourning all together in a cry that is the Lord's.

Kirsch was sure that Barker had been the author; a second verse, apparently far more vulgar in its conception, and detailing the "scandal" alluded to in the first, had followed a week or so later to much local hilarity. Kirsch heard about it, but by that time his source had realized his mistake and wisely chose to leave Kirsch out of the readers' loop.

"Listen, Barker, Ross sent me down here because you told him things were about to blow. I don't see any street activity. What exactly is it that you think's going on here?"

The stench from the sewage was overwhelming. Kirsch stepped into the house and closed the door behind him. Barker had shut all the windows in an effort to keep out the smell, which simply meant that he was now suffocating.

"A story," Barker began, without making even the minimal overtures of hospitality—tea or coffee—that were common among the expats. "I get a request for a building permit and I refuse it as premature. It is followed by a petition. I go out to look at the site and I find the petitioner, a long, hungry-looking Germanized Jew who it turns out has been stealing his neighbor's boundary stones. The neighbors, all Moslem, are sitting around, some six of them, in the garden. In the usual Moslem way they had started to build without counting the cost, and then left their great stones lying around for heaven and the British administration to care for. So this Jew, a religious fanatic by the way, had conceived the idea not only of adding a wing to his house but also a foot or two to his land. The Moslem neighbors entered an injunction, but they were very kindly folk, and when I came into the garden tapped their foreheads significantly and said, *'Majnun'*—you don't know Arabic, do you, Kirsch? 'Quite mad!' *'Etfaddal!'* 'Pray be seated.' There was a great *Kalam* when the Jew who had it in mind that his was a prescriptive religious right sprang up at me and spread his great and very dirty paws, all the ten fingers extended, over my face. What did I do, Kirsch? I whipped out my little cane and rapped him soundly upon the knuckles. The Moslem claque on the garden wall shouted with fun at the play, but a fortnight later along came another petition, this time addressed to the chief administrator and passed on through the governor, asking for an investigation as to the reasons why a British official had maltreated an unfortunate Jew, and 'stricken him bloody' over the backs of his hands. Why am I telling you this? Because I have had it up to here. I can't stay in this house now—who could? And I'm about to be investigated by you people for defending myself against, against . . ."

Kirsch tried hard not to laugh. Poor Barker with his "Germanized Jew" and a toilet stink in every room of his house. He should never have left England. Perhaps none of them should ever have left England.

"These Arabs here"—Barker waved his hand in the general direction of down the hill—"just like my Moslem friends with their boundary stones, won't stand up for themselves, you see. So someone's got to do it for them and it might as well be me."

"What is it precisely that you want me to do?"

"You tell the administration that unless another house is found, and sharpish, I go. And they can forget the municipal office design."

"I thought your main concern was for your Arab neighbors."

"They don't know the ropes. Poor sods. But they will learn. And when they do, *Alhamdulillah!*"

As the hour was creeping toward ten, Barker decided that it was time for a G and T. Kirsch, declining Barker's offer to join him in a drink, decided that he'd better go and speak to the grand mufti, whose home was at the far end of the spill.

"Please yourself," Barker said, then added as if as an afterthought, "Guess who I saw at the gardens last night. The Bloomberg woman. God, she's a looker."

"Really, was she alone?" Kirsch tried hard to appear indifferent, but he sensed his cheeks reddening. He hoped Barker wouldn't notice.

"Good Lord no, she was with a crowd of men. Doesn't waste much time, does she? I hear Ross sent her old man off to paint Petra. Can't quite understand what Ross sees in Bloomberg: not a great talent there, if you want my opinion."

Kirsch was desperate to know whom Joyce had been with, but asking Barker would be giving away too much.

"Well, I'll be leaving."

Kirsch opened the door and let in a rush of sunlight that seemed to drag the stench on its back. At this time of year the valley was usually cracked and burned; any irrigation, except this kind, would have been welcome. Kirsch felt despondent. He had to speak to Joyce. He wanted to go to her right now, but, imposed or not, he'd already shown enough dereliction of duty. Two men sent by the municipality approached carrying shovels over their shoulders. Two men to clear up a river of shit: it would take them half the year. Still, to erase what Kirsch had allowed to be done with Saud would take longer. He stepped gingerly over a brown stream and began to make his way across the valley.

23.

The cars could take Bloomberg and his party only so far. They had set off shortly before dawn. By nightfall, it was hoped, they would be twenty miles or so from Petra. Rachman drove the lead vehicle as before. The road coursed through the Wadi-es-Sir, a deep valley that seemed to have been designed by a Romantic artist; there were even the picturesque ruins of a fortress positioned exactly where Bloomberg would have liked them had he been executing a painting of the place a hundred years ago. They drove past the black-haired tents of the local bedouin, on through the town of Madaba, where Bloomberg spotted a rash of church spires among the minarets, and from thence to Hesbon and on to Kerak, where the paved road abruptly came to an end.

They had driven in silence almost the entire way, as the transition from darkness to dawn, calling such profound and colorful attention to itself, seemed to require. Bloomberg, led back by the luxury of his previous night's accommodation to the poverty of his London childhood, had been thinking about his mother. There she was, vivid in his mind's eye, with her thick, strong washerwoman's arms, standing at the wringer putting through his wet clothes. She had covered the floor with newspaper to absorb an excess splash of water. Bloomberg's father had left their home on Christian Street hours ago and was hard at work pressing suits in one of the sweatshops off the Whitechapel Road. And he, Mark, the hungry prince of six children, the eldest son, sat with a tall glass of milk and a biscuit listening to his mother—sweat pouring off her face, her arms red—as she admonished him never, as members of some local families did, to take food or clothing from the Mission for the Conversion of the Jews. In the front of the car, the desert dawn advertising itself in staggered, rosy tints, Bloomberg smiled to himself: now he got his food and clothing from the private mission of Sir Gerald Ross in exchange for painting churches and Nabatean temples. His mother wouldn't have been too happy.

In Kerak Bloomberg and Rachman mounted horses, then waited while the other men and the boy loaded baggage onto the largest animals among the small caravan of camels that would follow. Almost immediately, Rachman's attitude to the trip took a drastic turn for the worse. He seemed to find something insulting in having to abandon his car for a horse. He barked orders, particularly at the boy, and refused to look at Bloomberg. By the time the loaded camels set off, however, Rachman's black mood seemed to have passed and he appeared to view with amusement (which Bloomberg shared) the strange sight of an artist's dismantled studio moving through the desert's morning light on the backs of a shuffle-footed ponderous camel line.

Bloomberg had ridden a horse only once before in his life, after his father had befriended the local milkman and the old geezer had let Mark sit on his dapple gray all the way from home to the Tenter buildings on St. Luke Street: clink of empty bottles in their crates, astonished cries from a group of girls that included his sister Lena, jeers from the barrow boys. Then, as now, the animal seemed to have a far better sense than Bloomberg both of direction and of the little that was required of the rider.

The horse plodded forward down one of a series of tracks that had been beaten hollow by the tread of a hundred thousand camels, and now stretched almost half a mile in width. Away on Bloomberg's right, and then falling behind the caravan, the rift of the Dead Sea seemed to present a mirage stretching into infinity.

Bloomberg had no chance to speak to the al-Sayyid boy during the day. He saw him during the men's occasional stops for prayer. The boy always knelt at a distance away from the others and seemed afraid of them. Frequently, when they stopped, he stood in the narrow shade thrown by his camel. The farther they traveled, the more Bloomberg felt an awkward tension in the group: almost imperceptible to begin with, it had risen with the heat of the day, but whether its source was himself or the boy or the simple inconveniences of the journey, Bloomberg couldn't tell. At the first prayer-stop Rachman had informed Bloomberg that they were traveling on the Darb-el-Haj, the ancient route of pilgrimage to Mecca and Medina. Although nowadays, he had added, most pilgrims took the boat to Jedda. After relinquishing this piece of information he clearly decided that he didn't want to play tour guide, and he left Bloomberg alone to examine the landscape.

To Bloomberg's surprise the stretch of desert that he had imagined as empty—a foolish sentimentalism, he now realized, to think that he was "going back in time"—was littered with dilapidated buildings and surrounding debris. It didn't take him long to gather that they were following the track of an abandoned railway line—or rather a rail line that must once have followed, with hardly a diversion it seemed, the direction of the Haj. All along the route were derelict station buildings; sometimes only their zinc water tanks remained with a few common huts beside. More often there were multiple signs of destruction, and once again Bloomberg was reminded, this time indelibly, that here too the Great War, his war, had swung a mighty arc and passed through: ruined buildings, broken tanks, roofless guardhouses, deserted gun carriages, shattered wagons; and around one station vast shell holes and half-filled trenches.

They saw no other travelers. Once, Bloomberg's horse, deciding that it needed a rest, halted of its own volition. The legionaries' camels overtook Bloomberg without a sideways glance, but the boy stopped, leaned from his camel, and with a few sharp clicks of his tongue and a whack on the horse's hindquarters got the animal moving again.

Bloomberg felt slightly ridiculous, a skinny Sancho Panza in a gaucho's hat. But a certain foolishness was appropriate, he decided, for the artist who had attached himself to an old-style patron. Before setting out from Amman he had reread the letter of instruction that Ross had given him, with its directives framed as requests: "You will not have forgotten the accurate architectural aspect of your paintings with especial reference, I hope, to the view of the Temple of Isis at the exit of the Sik when the light best suits it by day and possibly by moonlight." Even the time of day! Still, he wasn't ungrateful to Ross. At this time not too many in London would have shelled out to keep Bloomberg in brushes and paint.

As soon as the first stars appeared in the sky Rachman called the party to a halt and pitched camp. Two of the men set a small fire and began to make coffee. Mustafa untied one of the camel bags and distributed food. The men tore ravenously at the provisions, in the way Bloomberg had seen his fellow soldiers attack their rations in the army.

They sat in a ragged circle, the al-Sayyid boy tucked in between Bloomberg and Rachman. Such talk as there was took place in Arabic. Bloomberg was content to watch the stars multiply against their jet backdrop in a profusion he had never before witnessed. The moon hung above them, plump and yellow like an overly bold stage prop in a melodrama. Eventually the men began to disperse until only Bloomberg and the boy were left by the fire.

"You've seen me before all this, am I right?" Bloomberg asked.

The boy stretched out his long legs. He still wore the prep-school gray trousers and white shirt that Ross had given him. Goodness knew why.

The boy shivered. The temperature had dropped quickly since nightfall, but the air was still warm. Bloomberg noticed sweat on the boy's forehead and that his eyes were glazed. The bandage over his eye had long since fallen off. The blood beneath it had dried in a thin brown line.

"Perhaps in Jerusalem. My uncle has a shop in the Old City."

"Perhaps at my house, more like. You were there one night, weren't you?"

The boy paused and weighed his response before replying, almost in a whisper, "Yes, I was there."

"What were you up to?"

"I was lost."

Lost? Somehow that seemed unlikely to Bloomberg.

The boy drew his sleeve across his forehead. Bloomberg saw that the sweat was pouring off him.

"Are you all right?"

In reply, the boy simply dropped his head into his hands. He looked as if he might keel over. Bloomberg passed him his water bottle and urged him to drink.

"Listen, if you're not well I'm going to have you sent back. One of the men can accompany you."

"No. I'm hot from the journey. I will drink now and I'll be well. Don't send me back."

Bloomberg sensed an urgency in the boy's response but had no key to understanding it.

Rachman and Salaman returned to the fire. The boy stood and walked away. In a moment they heard him pissing on the sand.

"You like this boy?" Rachman smiled. Salaman, in contrast, spat in the ground.

"I've no idea. He seems fine. Is there something not to like?"

Rachman said something to Salaman, perhaps he had translated Bloomberg's reply. If so there must have been something funny in it that caused Salaman to laugh.

The boy returned but, as usual, sat a way off from the others.

"Why didn't your wife come on this journey?"

"She preferred to stay in Jerusalem. And besides, as you see, there is nothing for her to do here. But why do you ask?"

Again, Rachman turned to Salaman and this time engaged in a brief animated discussion.

"You didn't ask Sir Gerald for this boy?"

"Ask Sir Gerald? Quite the opposite; I preferred to travel unaccompanied, and believe me, if I'd had my way, I wouldn't have put you to all this bother. Although I do see that your presence makes this an easier trek."

Bloomberg's answer seemed to satisfy Rachman.

"But what is all this?" Bloomberg continued.

"This boy is well known in Jerusalem. He's been a wife to many men."

Bloomberg couldn't help smiling. The thought that Sir Gerald Ross had sent him off on a homosexual adventure was almost, but not quite, as absurd as the real mission.

"Really? Well, that's his business, I suppose. I don't think it will prevent him carrying my easel around, will it? And by the way, what is his name?"

"His name, to his father's eternal shame, is Saud al-Sayyid. Lucky his father is dead."

Bloomberg lay in his tent trying to compose a letter to Joyce. A letter that he knew would take weeks to reach her, if it ever did. Still, it was easier for him to show his affection when he was far away. He wrote in thick pencil offering a brief description of his journey thus far and he even included a quick sketch that he had made earlier in the day of one of the shattered gun emplacements.

His reading lamp threw shadows onto the canvas walls and the desert wind whipped them into dark predatory birds. He concluded the letter, in offhand fashion, "I may have found your Saud. But if so he doesn't seem like much of a murderer. I'll ask him tomorrow morning if he's ever stabbed anyone! My driver thought Sir Gerald had sent him along to keep me warm at night—remember that policeman who sat on our bed—'a boy fucker and his boy . . .' " And then with a flash of his old nastiness Bloomberg added, "Perhaps you'd better pass this on to the investigating officer that's keeping *you* warm. Or on second thoughts, maybe not. I wouldn't want him down here interrupting my work." He licked the tip of the pencil, then ran thick lines through the final paragraph. Why begin to torment her again? And in truth he *didn't* want Kirsch getting ideas. If Ross had sent this boy along to Petra he couldn't have suspected him of murdering De Groot. And then there was the boy's recent late-night visit to Bloomberg's house: why on earth, unless he'd spent a childhood reading English mystery novels, would a hunted murderer return to the scene of the crime? There had to be another explanation. Perhaps this Saud didn't even know De Groot. In the morning Bloomberg would ask him straight out. And what would Saud answer? "Yes, I stabbed the old Jew through the heart and now I'd like to turn myself in." Bloomberg smiled at his own foolishness.

He turned down his light. Two of the men snored loudly in the next tent. Over their noise came the demented yawn of one of the camels. What was it that Ross had mentioned about Giotto and his apprentices? This was far better. He would wear the hair shirt of isolation with pride. Under these wild stars Bloomberg felt, for the first time in years, that he was exactly where he wanted to be.

24.

Joyce turned up in Kirsch's office first thing on Wednesday morning. He was surprised to see her and also very happy. Her hair was pulled back and she was wearing a white shapeless kaftan that she must have bought in the Old City, but she had bunched the material and tied a red kerchief at her waist that accentuated her figure. Her skin, pale when he had first met her, was lightly tanned now, and in Kirsch's opinion set off her gray eyes perfectly. Seeing her let him forget, for a moment anyway, about Bloomberg.

"Where have *you* been?" Kirsch asked, trying to be jolly and not come across as jealous, although his heart was beating fast.

"Someone ransacked my cottage."

"Oh God. When was this?"

"Sometime Monday night while I was out."

"At the Municipal Gardens." Kirsch had meant to keep this information to himself, but the words had slipped out. When he was with her he lost control.

Joyce frowned. "Have you been following me?"

Kirsch laughed. "I've wanted to, but no. Clive Barker—do you know him, the civic planner?—well, he saw you there and happened to mention it to me."

"God, this place is a village."

Kirsch was about to offer a lighthearted rejoinder but then remembered that Joyce had come to report a crime.

"Your place, is there much damage?"

"Torn clothes, and three of Mark's paintings have been badly stomped."

"That's awful."

"Yes, but he won't care. He never does. He'll say it's what they deserved. I've seen him put ten paintings at a time out for rubbish collection. In West Hampstead I had to go outside early in the mornings and retrieve them."

"And the break-in was on Monday night?"

"Yes."

"Why didn't you contact me yesterday? I mean, this is a serious matter."

"I was busy all day. Peter Frumkin . . ." Joyce paused. "The filmmaker."

"Yes, I know who he is," Kirsch interrupted testily.

"Well, he brought me down to the Old City to watch the filming. Then he actually squeezed in a part for me."

Kirsch felt his face redden.

"Did he? I thought they were storming Suleiman's walls." Kirsch tried to make this sound like the worst Hollywood silliness.

"They were, but when the Romans break through to the Temple some of the local women get raped. I was the first victim."

Kirsch opened his eyes wide.

"That's appalling."

But Joyce had already begun to laugh. He couldn't tell if she was slightly hysterical or genuinely cheerful.

"Don't be such a prude," she said.

Kirsch remembered how before they made love she had told him when to take his clothes off. She must think him a fool.

"Very funny," Kirsch replied. "What did you really do?"

"I carried water to a thirsty man."

"I can see you doing that."

"Well, you will, I hope. There's a cinema *somewhere* in this town, isn't there?"

Kirsch stood and came around to the front of his desk. He noticed that Joyce was wearing a thin silver ankle bracelet. She looked altogether too well groomed and happy—quite a contrast to when he had seen her on Sunday night. She was a woman, it seemed, with an exceptional capacity for recovery. The ugly thought crossed his mind that she had spent the previous night in bed with Frumkin, and then the early part of this morning grooming herself in the luxurious bathroom at his hotel.

"I'd better come over to your place and take a look around."

"Oh, no need for that, I've cleaned everything up."

Kirsch sighed. "Did you find anything when you cleaned up? Something left behind?"

"Nothing at all."

"If you don't mind my saying so, you don't seem very disturbed by this."

"Should I be? I mean compared to the Big Day what's a little breaking and entering?"

Kirsch felt increasingly angry with her. "Did it occur to you that the two events may be connected, or that you may be in danger?"

Was he trying to scare her? Even as he spoke Kirsch felt ridiculous. How could the two events be connected when the murderer, as he well knew, was halfway through the Transjordan desert? Still, Joyce couldn't be aware of that.

"I mean, had you even locked your door when you went out?"

"I doubt it. We have absolutely nothing worth stealing. Apart from the paintings, of course."

He wished she would stop saying "we." "And you found nothing new there when you cleaned up?"

"I thought we'd already been through this?"

"Did you see my note?"

Joyce paused a moment and furrowed her brow. "Your note? I don't think so . . . no."

Kirsch's face fell.

"Of course I saw your note!"

She was laughing again. "But really, Robert, you miss me *that* much? I must be better in bed than I ever imagined."

Kirsch blushed, and looked toward the door of his office. It was definitely closed. He had never known a woman who spoke like this.

"You found nothing then," he muttered, "apart from my note."

Joyce stood. She moved close and kissed him on the lips.

"I want you to drive me out to Cremisan."

"To the monastery?"

"Exactly."

"When?"

"At the weekend."

"And until then? I won't see you?"

"Robert! I'm filming!" Her voice was teasing, but he didn't mind.

"You shouldn't stay in that cottage."

"And where should I stay? With you? Hardly proper, old chap."

The phony upper-class English accent in which she had delivered the phrase was off. Joyce sounded as if she were Welsh; Americans always got it wrong, he thought.

Joyce moved toward the door.

"Don't worry," she said. "I'll buy a guard dog, or you can send that obnoxious detective round again and have him stand sentry."

Kirsch looked at her quizzically.

"What detective?"

"The one you sent by to check up on Mark and me. He lay on the bed—don't look so shocked, I wasn't in it—and asked questions."

"I didn't send anyone."

Joyce shrugged. "I'm late," she said. "I have places to go and people to see. Saturday morning? Ten o'clock. Okay?"

"Wait a minute, this man, what did he look like? What did he say his name was?"

"Not bad-looking at all. Nice eyes, dark skin, and he was, I would say, a local Jew. He had a bit of a lisp."

"Black wavy hair and a bit stocky?"

"Yes. Robert, I'm leaving."

"Yes," Kirsch responded distractedly. "Go ahead."

Kirsch returned to his desk and removed a blank sheet of paper from the top drawer. He felt in his tunic pocket for the pencil that he always carried, but came up instead with the police tunic button that he had picked up in Joyce's garden. He heard himself asking her: "Did you find anything when you cleaned up?" and her reply, "Nothing at all." He stared at the button then put it back in his pocket. He stood up, put his hand to his mouth in order to remove the print of Joyce's lipstick, then opened the door to his office. The corridor was empty; its cracked yellow walls were covered in condensation, as if the building itself were sweating in the khamsin.

"Has anyone seen Harlap?" Kirsch yelled.

There was no reply. Kirsch walked down to the main office. The room was strangely quiet. Usually it was crowded with supplicants—relatives of the petty thieves who had been picked up that day, and complainers about one thing or another: reporting your neighbor for minor violations was a territorial pastime. On most mornings you couldn't hear yourself over the noise, but since Cartwright's death a stale, somber air had predominated. The local criminals seemed to have decided to lie low for a few days. No one wants to be around policemen when one of their own has recently been shot.

"Where's Harlap?" Kirsch asked again.

The desk sergeant, Mallory, looked up from a ledger in which he had been completing the morning reports. He blotted the page, then snapped the book shut as if he were the model of efficiency.

"He's down at the Jaffa Gate, sir. On detail for that Metropolis Film Corporation."

"Oh, is he?"

"Is he supposed to be somewhere else, sir?"

Kirsch shook his head.

"Did you know that the walls that they're storming weren't even bloody well there when Titus destroyed the Second Temple?"

"Excuse me?"

"Oh, never mind."

"If Harlap comes in, tell him I'm looking for him."

"Right, sir."

Kirsch made toward the door.

"And where shall I tell him you are?"

Kirsch paused a moment.

"Forget it, Mallory. Don't say anything. I'll find him before he finds me."

But Kirsch didn't find Harlap, neither that morning nor for the rest of the week. According to Mallory, the sergeant had phoned the station on Wednesday shortly after Kirsch had left to look for him. He'd told Mallory that Frumkin didn't need the police after all, filming was canceled for the day on account of an impending dust storm, and he, Harlap, was taking a few days off that he had coming. He was going to visit his mother in Haifa, she'd been admitted to the government hospital with some kind of breathing problem. The doctors thought . . . But Kirsch hadn't been interested in what the doctors had thought. There were far more pressing concerns. What on earth had Harlap been doing over at the Bloombergs poking around and asking questions? Was Ross up to something behind Kirsch's back? What the hell was going on?

For the rest of the week Kirsch tried, without much success, to conceal his confusion and apprehension. At the station he was snappish and petty; at home, isolate and inflamed with an ugly combination of guilt and envy. It was a physical sensation: alone at his kitchen table trying to read, he would think of Saud and his face would begin to burn, think of Joyce and the sensation would be repeated. He would get up, go to the sink, and splash cold water over his head. Of Bloomberg there was no word. Meanwhile, Frumkin's film crew, so he'd heard, had moved to a location site north of Tel Aviv. Joyce must have gone with them. Wherever she was, she wasn't at home. Ignoring her request to wait until the weekend, he had visited her cottage each evening. The window shutters were closed, and when he beat on the door no one answered. On Friday night, arriving shortly before sunset after a day spent doing virtually nothing, which, in Kirsch's present state of high nervousness seemed to exhaust him more than activity, he slumped into a wicker chair that Bloomberg had left in the garden. He watched the shadows deepen and lengthen. The declining sun shed its luster over the Bloombergs' overgrown garden, tinting the trodden green path with violet specks and turning the gray gate silver. Unbidden, the ghost of Kirsch's brother Marcus entered through the gate and sauntered down the path, hands in the pockets of his white trousers, straw boater angled jauntily on his head, as if he were setting off for a picnic on the river: only Marcus's shirt was buttoned to the neck and Kirsch knew the tightness was intended to hide the mortal wound in his chest. Marcus was singing "April

Showers," affecting Al Jolson's voice and pretending not to notice his younger brother staring at him from the garden chair. "So if it's raining, have no regrets—because it isn't raining, you know, it's raining vi-o-lets." Kirsch almost joined in with Marcus on the chorus, but it seemed inappropriate somehow to duet with the dead. The song ended and Kirsch woke with a shiver and a start. And suddenly he remembered that buttons had been missing from Harlap's tunic on the day that the sergeant had brought in Saud, and wasn't it possible that the button in Kirsch's pocket, the one that he'd picked up at the end of this very garden, had come from the same tunic? Harlap had certainly been up at Bloomberg's cottage; Joyce had described both him and his visit. But perhaps he had also shown up here before? Was it De Groot, fighting for his life, who had grabbed at Harlap's shirt? It seemed unlikely, but it wasn't impossible. That old rabbi, Sonnenfeld, had tried to tell Kirsch that the murderer was a Zionist and not the Arab boy, but Kirsch hadn't taken him seriously. And the letters. Somebody knew that De Groot was on his way to London and perhaps that same somebody wanted to prevent him from going. Kirsch had been a fool. Saud had presented himself so obviously as the culprit that Kirsch had stopped pursuing other avenues. He had known, because it had been instilled in him since the beginning of his stay in Palestine, that the politics of the place led plenty of Arabs to hate Jews and vice versa; but it hadn't really penetrated, although there was no rational reason why it shouldn't have, that, in ways that transcended the personal, Jews might hate each other enough to kill. His soul had been armed against such thinking, almost since birth. But if Harlap *was* involved in the murder of De Groot, for what precise reason, and to what end? And was it possible that Kirsch was imagining connections where there were none (the button!) in a pathetic attempt at self-justification: to blame Harlap and deflect his own responsibility for Saud's escape? And where did all this place the boy? Whatever the answers, the situation was dangerous. Whoever had shot Cartwright was still out there, Harlap was missing, and Joyce, Kirsch was sure, although he didn't know quite why, needed immediate protection.

Kirsch ran to the gate, kick-started his motorbike and raced toward the center of the city, heading for the Allenby Hotel on Jaffa Road. He had to find out exactly where Frumkin had taken his film crew. As he approached his destination Kirsch was obliged to follow a traffic diversion. The roads were blocked in the approaches to the Orthodox quarter of Mea She'arim. The Jewish Sabbath had commenced at sunset and the streets were thronged with kaftaned fur-hatted Hasidim making their way to prayers. In one particular spot, just beyond the Orthodox precincts, a dense crowd had formed and Kirsch revved the engine of his bike in order to attempt a passage. He remembered Ross telling him—it must have been during his first week in the city—that, whatever the reason for their formation, "crowds are not good in Jerusalem and should never be allowed to gather." Kirsch dismounted from his bike and pushed his way into the middle of a mass of shouting, gesticulating individuals. Once there, in a lacuna at the heart of the mob, Kirsch found a young Arab taxi driver earnestly claiming his fare.

"What's going on here?" Kirsch asked. "You realize you're blocking the whole road?"

"I bring him all the way from Jaffa! Forty miles! Now he tells me he can't pay."

The culprit was a tall, thin stick of a man, bearded, pasty-faced and, by dint of the expression on his face, without a trace of remorse for the petty crime that he had apparently perpetrated.

"He will pay him. He will pay him!" someone shouted very close to Kirsch's ear. "But not today. Let him come late tomorrow night, or better on Sunday morning."

"What's wrong with right now?" Kirsch asked the interloper. "Or are you suggesting that our friend here drive back to Jaffa then return to get his money on Sunday morning?"

Kirsch's words were quickly translated into Yiddish and received by way of reply several shocked looks and one or two shrugs, as if to ask, "And why not?"

The night sky had darkened considerably and where a moment ago only three stars were visible, now there were thousands. Little by little, in small waves of coherence that rolled in over the hubbub of noisy entreatment and dissent, Kirsch learned the essence of the problem. The Arab driver and his passenger had set out in good time from Jaffa that afternoon. But there had been endless delays and just as they reached Jerusalem the sun had set, the Sabbath had begun and no sort of financial transaction could take place. Thus, there was no real refusal to pay, only the genuine desire, as already articulated, to postpone payment. Why the Arab driver failed to see the propriety of his passenger's situation was a mystery, it seemed, to everyone save Kirsch and the driver.

The driver, who seemed a little dazed by now, had decided to take the weight off his feet and sit in the middle of the street. Clearly, like Kirsch, he understood little Hebrew or Yiddish, and no one in the vicinity, it seemed, knew Arabic. The swirl of translation into a butchered English that everyone might understand was beginning to exhaust all the parties. Kirsch too felt like sitting down, or better still, lying down. He had already spent half an hour on this absurd incident. It wasn't a hostile environment. In fact, to Kirsch's surprise—perhaps it was the aura of the sacred hour—everyone, noisy as they were, appeared even-tempered and well-meaning toward the driver, but a resolution, simple though it appeared it must be, had thus far eluded him. Joyce, he needed to remember, was his priority, but the implacable crowd had him stitched up and hemmed in.

"Oh, for God's sake, I'll pay," he yelled finally in a voice strong with gratitude for the inspiration. "And you"—he pointed at the passenger—"you'll come along on Sunday morning to the police station and you'll pay me back."

Kirsch reached for the leather purse in his pocket, but producing the money, while it brought a cluck of satisfaction from the driver, simultaneously elicited a gasp of horror from his passenger.

"No no no." Someone had hold of Kirsch's wrist. "A goy, a goy, it has to be a goy."

"Let go!" Kirsch stared down the speaker, and to his own astonishment found himself enunciating, "I am a goy. Understand? C. of E., if you must know. Now let me give this poor fellow his money and we can all be on our way."

Kirsch at this moment did not a care a jot if the Jews in the crowd believed him. And cared even less that he was violating the Hasid's yearning for a pure Gentile surrogate to do his business. All he wanted was a path to run his motorbike through the crowd. And then, as he was about to hand the three silver twenty-piastre coins into the outstretched hand of the driver from Jaffa, he spotted Harlap skirting the fringe of the crowd.

"Hey!" Kirsch yelled. "Stop right there."

Harlap turned, caught Kirsch's eye, and broke into a run.

Kirsch let the coins fall to the ground. He pushed his way violently through the circle of men that surrounded him and sprinted up Jaffa Road following in the direction that Harlap had taken. Outside the gates of the Municipal Hospital Kirsch halted, sweating and out of breath. He had lost his quarry. He walked slowly back to where he had left his motorbike. The haggling crowd had vanished. Someone had wheeled Kirsch's bike off the road and propped it against a corner wall. There were two dark mounds of garbage at the foot of the stone, and the smell of filth and the general air of shabbiness combined with Kirsch's physical exhaustion to send him slumping to the ground. He sat with his back against the front wheel of the bike, his breath coming in short bursts, certain of only one thing, that thus far he had got almost everything wrong.

25.

Bloomberg woke in the middle of the night to find the muzzle of a rifle sticking into his chest.

"Get up! get up!" Salaman screamed, and gave Bloomberg a hefty kick in the side. Bloomberg let out a yell and rolled over. Salaman snapped his fingers and spat in Bloomberg's face.

"Up!"

"What the hell's going on?"

Bloomberg stood clutching his side. Salaman prodded the gun in his back and forced him out of the tent.

A small fire burned inside a circle of stones. In its orange light Bloomberg saw Rachman, bound and gagged, sitting cross-legged. Twenty yards away two of the other men crouched stabbing at something on the ground, grunting and yelling as they did so. For a moment Bloomberg froze: he was sure it was the boy being sliced under those murderous rips, but then Salaman shoved him facedown and Bloomberg, spitting a mouthful of sand, scrambled forward to see that the victim was only an old khaki tunic, standard government issue.

With one heave Salaman tumbled Bloomberg's large canvas hold-all from the lead camel and unceremoniously dumped out the artist's supplies: brushes, paint tubes, cans of oil and turpentine. A second large bag soon followed. Salaman spilled most of its contents onto the sand: tins of meat, jam, milk and biscuits, and a small spirit stove, which was the only thing that he deemed worth taking. He called Mustafa over and together they bundled Rachman into the place on the camel's back vacated by the bags. Shortly after, Mustafa emerged proudly from Bloomberg's tent, where he had acquired a watch and an oil lamp, and then they were done. The big prizes, Bloomberg sensed, were the camels themselves.

In addition to his scattered supplies, they left him the fire, the skinniest horse, and a flagon of water. Bloomberg, still clutching his bruised side as the camels and their riders disappeared into the night, felt oddly grateful to his attackers. Wasn't being stripped bare what he was aiming for? Lear on the heath. You fuck people up, you get what you deserve. The stars hung above him in vast random clusters, as if God were a Hatton Garden diamond merchant rolling his stock onto black velvet bedding for Bloomberg's personal appraisal. But before he had time to collect his grand philosophic thoughts the boy appeared, from out of nowhere it seemed. The desert night was chill and Saud shivered.

"Poor Tom's a-cold," Bloomberg said, more to himself than to the boy, then added, "Poor sod," as if to console Saud for selecting such a shabby Lear as himself to be his mate in the wilderness.

Saud approached the fire. "I hid behind the dunes," he said. "I overheard them earlier in the evening. I wanted to warn you, but I couldn't. I had to hide."

"Not your fault," Bloomberg replied.

Saud held his hands out to the flames, then moved away and began to collect Bloomberg's art supplies and return them to the bag.

"I'll do that." Bloomberg tried to get up, but the sharp pain in his side sat him back down again.

"Here." Saud dragged over the flagon of water, unscrewed the top and held it out to Bloomberg.

"I've got something better," Bloomberg said.

This time he managed to get up and walk gingerly over to the food bag. He rummaged around for a moment, then came up triumphantly with his silver flask. A present from Joyce on their last day in London. He took a swig of the whisky, then offered it to Saud, who shook his head. The drink burned in Bloomberg's throat. He took another, longer swig and then a third. They sat in silence for perhaps twenty minutes until the fire started to burn low. The boy was still shivering but there were beads of sweat on his forehead. Bloomberg moved over and put his arm around Saud. He led him back to the tent, got him to lie down and covered him in two of the stringy army-issue blankets, among the items that Salaman, Mustafa and the others hadn't considered worth taking. Then Bloomberg lay down on his back beside Saud. A night from the trenches swooped, batlike, but mercifully passed in a beat. Instead he was in the Yiddish theater, the Majestic, on the Mile End Road. And what was the production in progress? "Hamelech Lear," *King Lear*, of course, and Bloomberg and his friends had tears running down their cheeks—tears of laughter. They were in hysterics at the appalling, pathetic substitute culture of their parents. In the West End there was genius and here in the East End there was the Yiddishe king—an entirely different bowl of kreplach. But which stage was Bloomberg on? Drama, or melodrama? The real thing, or ersatz? Everything that he had painted for Ross was a pile of shit.

Saud turned in his sleep and nudged Bloomberg fully awake. Bloomberg placed the back of his hand on the boy's forehead. His fever seemed to have abated. In the morning, when they found some help, he would send him on his way. Let him go wherever he wanted.

———

The dawn came bright and abrupt, a shutter lifted on the sky, not as in London, where the light staggered in tired and gray, like a drunk coming home after an all-nighter.

Bloomberg woke to pain. Where Salaman had kicked him there was now a wide purple bruise. He touched his fingertips to the spot and winced. His mouth was dry and his tongue felt as if he had dipped it in sand, which, of course, he had. He ran his hand over the two-day stubble on his face, then rose and pushed back the tent flap.

Outside, Saud had already repacked both bags and slung them onto the horse. Now he was sitting cross-legged on the sand waiting for the painter to appear. Bloomberg walked over to him and took the water bottle that Saud extended. He took a long swallow.

"Are you all right?" Bloomberg asked.

Saud nodded.

"No temperature?" Bloomberg heard the cadence of his mother's voice in his own.

"I'm well."

The air had warmed with the first touch of the sun's rays. Bloomberg looked around. He had only the vaguest idea of the direction in which they were headed, and he realized immediately the absurdity of his previous night's notion to let Saud go. In any case, Saud obviously had no intention other than to continue their journey.

There was no point hanging around. Together, they dismantled and folded the tent and within half an hour Bloomberg and Saud had begun their slow journey south, walking beside their horribly overburdened horse, who plodded forward with his head bent.

Once they set out on their way there was nothing much to say. Saud had told Bloomberg not to worry, that he knew how far it was to Petra, and that they should be there well before nightfall. They looked bizarre, which certainly didn't bother Bloomberg: Saud in his stained and wrinkled English schoolboy outfit, shirt out, the red-and-black tie given to him by Ross wrapped around his waist like a belt; Bloomberg with his own ripped shirt doubling as a kaffiyeh, and with his straw gaucho hat, mercifully left behind by his assailants, now perched on top. The presence of Bloomberg's hat was more than an act of mercy, it was a bona fide miracle, as beneath its broad black sash Bloomberg had pressed the banknotes that Ross had given him to cover the costs of the trip.

After three hours they arrived at an oasis that was more of a ghost village: a collection of empty shacks and a watering hole, host to a stray donkey that was quickly commandeered by Saud. Still, the view was stunning. They must have been high above sea level, for Bloomberg could see before him an immense crater out of which rose the sandstone mass that, according to Saud, enclosed Petra. Bloomberg ducked into the shade of one of the abandoned shacks. He brought over a packet of biscuits and used his penknife to open a tin. He spread the jam and offered the first biscuit to Saud. High overhead, on invisible currents of air, a lone hawk rose and fell in the cloudless blue sky.

Saud crouched close to Bloomberg and bit into the biscuit. His features were remarkably fine and, if it was true that he was a rent boy, Bloomberg saw that he must have been a popular one.

"What did you do?" Bloomberg asked, and when the boy didn't reply, he added, "Did you stab De Groot? Was it you?"

"No," Saud replied, "I didn't kill Yaakov." He paused for a moment, looked around him and then directly at Bloomberg as if he was weighing up not only the isolation of the place but also Bloomberg's sanity and trustworthiness, then he continued, "But I saw who did."

"And who was it?"

By way of reply Saud reached into the pocket of his creased and absurdly thick English worsted trousers. He retrieved a button, dusted off the lint, rubbed it a little on his shirt and extended it in the palm of his hand toward Bloomberg. Shiny and silver, the button, with thin strands of brown cotton still in its loop, showed the three-pronged crown that was the insignia of Jerusalem's police force.

"I went back to the place where he died," Saud said. "That's where I found it. Near the gate to your garden."

It was another four hours on horseback (they had transferred the load to the donkey) before they entered the canyon that gave access to the ancient city. The terrace on which Petra lay was pierced by a valley enclosed by two sandstone ridges. Bloomberg had come across colored sandstone before—it wasn't as if Britain didn't have any—but he had never seen colors of such depth and variety of pattern. The walls of rock reminded him of Eastern carpets, or some fanciful woven fabric. The deepest reds, purples, and shades of yellow were arranged in alternate bands, shading off into each other, and sometimes curved and twisted into astonishing fantasies. And he might have been overwhelmed, with awe or apprehension, except that his mind was elsewhere, anchored on the secret that Saud had revealed to him.

26.

Kirsch searched for Harlap all night in the sleeping neighborhoods of Jerusalem. Where he could, he rode his motorbike, and where streets were blocked off, closed to traffic for the Jewish Sabbath, he walked. There was no one, as yet, whom he could bring along to help. He didn't know who could be trusted. Harlap could have any number of accomplices. Kirsch knew too that his quest was futile; somewhere, Harlap was safe inside a shuttered and locked room. And yet Kirsch continued on, as if a solution to the crime, and not only to the crime but to his other, more personal dilemmas, could be solved by movement itself. It was the way he always acted when in despair—his running away to Palestine was a case in point, running from Naomi, who was lovely and deserved better, but whom he didn't love, and, more powerfully, trying to escape both his parents' unending grief, and his own, over Marcus's death. Marcus in waiting, hidden under the covers at the foot of Kirsch's bed. Kirsch, maybe four years old, his legs not stretching all the way down, and Marcus grabbing him by the ankles as he was settling down to sleep. Kirsch screaming, crying, then hitting out at his brother. Marcus's laughter turning to apology. "Come on," he'd said, "we'll play something": rolling the marbles over the carpet, the clink of glass on glass. Two nice Jewish boys. That's what Aunt Fanny had once called them. "Nice Jewish boy," they taunted each other with pokes to the ribs. Was that it? Was that all they had to say to each other about their Jewish lives? And Palestine? Marcus couldn't have cared less. Last words: "Dear Bobby, We are now in the trenches again and though I feel very sleepy, I just have a chance to answer your letter so I will while I may. I've been lucky enough to bag an inch of candle. Many thanks for book and chocolate. Both are being devoured with equal pleasure. I am sending you a good photo of myself in a day or two." And that was it.

Kirsch wandered—he wasn't really investigating anything except his own soul now—through the narrow alleyways and courtyards of Mea She'arim. The night was hot and the smell of sewage rode on the air and reminded him of the spill outside Barker's house in Wadi al-Joz. Here, the surrounding houses were crowded on top of one another in loose association: a Polish village, its tiny doorways, red roofs and clotheslines transplanted to the Middle East. Sabbath candles still burned in a few of the windows but most had given up their light hours ago. What on earth did Kirsch have to do with these Jews and their squalid compound? The answer, he knew, was nothing, and everything. Although he couldn't have explained why in either case.

Leaving the precincts of the poor and devout, he drove his bike down Jaffa Road. There were lights on in the offices of the *Palestine Weekly* but nowhere else until he reached the garage of the Nesher Automobile Service, from which taxis ran all night and where the local whores gathered, indifferent to Ross's attempts to ban them from the Holy City.

By the time he got home to his flat, the night sky was fraying at the edges and strips of pink poked through the blue-black on the horizon. Kirsch crashed fully clothed onto his narrow bed. He woke hours later in a heavy sweat, panicked (where was his bloody watch?!) that he had already missed his ten o'clock appointment with Joyce to go to Cremisan. The light in his room felt like the starched white sheet of midday, and the heat indicated the silent intense hour when most of Jerusalem took its siesta. He found his watch, its strap broken, under his bed—it was only nine-thirty. If he rushed he might make it. He stripped off his rumpled uniform and doused himself with water. There was no time to shave. He pulled on an old pair of khaki shorts and donned the less creased of his two white shirts.

Kirsch rode fast to North Talpiot, through dusty abandoned Sabbath streets. He made good time—there was only one traffic light in the city (Kirsch had been present for the ceremonial turning-on)—and on Saturdays there were far fewer of the carts and animals that frequently blocked the roads. Once at the Bloombergs' cottage, Kirsch leaned his bike against a tree and, although the heat of the day demanded a slow pace, he sprinted up the path. Ever since he woke he had been cradling a pleasant and insistent romantic idea of lifting Joyce up and swinging her around in his arms. But he was disappointed. Joyce had pinned a note to the door, printed in a hasty scrawl: "Robert," he read, "couldn't wait. Got a ride with Peter Frumkin. Be a sweetheart and meet me there."

The falcons at Cremisan—first pair in a hundred years, they said—were nesting in the pine trees behind the monastery. And for a city that had only one traffic light their presence was "an event." All manner of bird-watchers, the avid and the merely curious, had gathered behind a fence set up by the monks, and beyond which one could not step. The British contingent was large but not exclusive. Making his way through the crowd Kirsch saw that Aubrey Harrison was there, strutting around in his trademark white suit, passing bon mots to the Bentwiches and the McClellans, and then there were any number of faces that Kirsch recognized from Ross's parties. The atmosphere among the English was a little raucous, certainly indecorous; more football than bird-watching. Outside of England a kind of continental laissez-faire operated among the expatriates; the social system was fluid—not extravagantly so, but the restraints of the parish and the provinces were weakened. Maybe the war had done that, stiff upper lip for four years and then the emotions slowly loosening, like knotted bootlaces coming untied. Kirsch's father hadn't even wept until a year after Marcus had died, whereas now, if his mother's letters were accurate, he couldn't stop crying.

Nearest to the fence a group of servicemen passed around a pair of high-powered binoculars, and took turns training them on the falcons' nest. Farther back, among the fair-sized Jewish crowd, Kirsch recognized Professor Ben Dov, the historian who was tapped to head the

Hebrew University when it opened. He was standing under a striped umbrella chatting animatedly with two of his future colleagues, well-known scientists, and, if Kirsch wasn't mistaken, with Frumkin. But where the hell was Joyce? Kirsch couldn't see her. Close to him a few local Arab boys had mustered a cheap telescope from somewhere, and now they lay stretched out on the ground in a space between two pic-nicking family groups, each surrounded by a good number of empty and half-empty bottles. The monks, who made a perfectly adequate and some-what underpriced red wine, were doing a roaring trade. Meanwhile, the lovebirds, utterly indifferent to all this human attention, refused to oblige with an air show.

Kirsch pushed past the boys and approached Frumkin.

"Hey, Captain, nice to see you," Frumkin said cheerily, breaking off his conversation and extending his hand.

Ben Dov and the others greeted Kirsch less warmly. Kirsch, di-sheveled, unshaven, and with his eyes red and stinging from sleepless-ness, was aware that his appearance didn't offer a good first impression. Moreover, Zionists in powerful positions, whether academics or poli-ticians or both, were rarely sympathetic to people like him. To them, Kirsch knew, he was the enemy.

"You must be looking for Joycie. She's around here somewhere."

Joycie! It made Kirsch's stomach churn.

Frumkin swiveled around, using his six-foot frame to peer over the heads of the surrounding crowd.

"Joyce! Joyce!" he yelled.

"Forget it," Kirsch said. "I'll find her."

But Frumkin, with a quick apology to his interlocutors, took Kirsch by the elbow and tried to propel him away.

Kirsch shrugged him off.

"Oh, come on," Frumkin whispered. "Give me a break, these guys are boring me to fucking death."

"That's not my problem," Kirsch responded.

Frumkin sighed.

"What? Jealous Oberon?" he murmured.

Kirsch heard, but pretended that he hadn't.

Frumkin had succeeded in putting a few yards between himself and the Hebrew University enthusiasts.

"It's the money, you know. I made a little contribution to Sir Gerald's Jerusalem fund, and now they're all after me. Your boss must have spread the word. But, truth to tell, I'm here to shoot a picture and I'll do whatever's expedient. And unlike Sir Gerry, these guys"—Frumkin gestured behind him with his thumb—"haven't got a lot to offer my crew by way of location. In any case, the university's a dumb idea; there are already more than enough smart Jews in the world. Whaddya say, Captain K.?"

Kirsch had plenty to say, most pertinently about the way in which the company of Jews from other countries, particularly America, always made him feel terribly English. So much so that, listening to Frumkin, a kind of core voice, terribly upper class, and not at all his own, seemed to clamber up his throat and demand admission to the lambent air. "Good Lord," the voice wanted to say, "what utter balderdash!" But Kirsch, happily as far as he was concerned, managed to tamp it down and say nothing at all.

Joyce appeared. She was wearing a light, short-sleeved summer frock that accentuated the dark tan on her arms and face, which contrasted starkly with the white of her hair. By way of greeting she kissed Kirsch on both cheeks.

"You look as if you've had a rough night, Robert."

"Wild woman?" Frumkin asked, then added, "It can sure get hot out here."

"I need to speak to you," Kirsch blurted out, the poise and confidence that he had hoped to exhibit in her presence out of reach.

"Speak away."

"Uh-oh, time for me to shove off." Frumkin said, laughing. "In any case I think I've seen just about all there is to see of those cute birdies."

He turned to Joyce. "See you tomorrow?"

Joyce seemed unwilling to respond. Kirsch wasn't sure if this was a sign of her reluctance to commit to Frumkin, or simply an indication that she didn't wish to talk about her private arrangements in front of him.

"Well, think about it," Frumkin said, "think about it."

"Wait a minute," Kirsch said, touching Frumkin lightly on the arm. "Would you mind if I asked you something?"

"Fire away."

"My sergeant, Harlap, was supposed to be on detail last week at the Old City, but you told him he wasn't needed. Is that correct?"

"That is incorrect. I asked him to come with us to Haifa. He did a great job for me keeping the gawkers at bay in Jerusalem and I thought he might do the same up there. Don't tell me he didn't ask your permission?" Frumkin exposed a thin edge of teasing in his voice, then quickly concealed it. "Robert, listen, I'm sorry. My fault. I offered him more money than he probably sees in six months working for you. But I did ask him to clear it with you first."

"So he's been with you all week?"

"The whole goddamn seven days."

Kirsch turned to Joyce. "And you saw him?"

"Hey, what is this . . . ?" Frumkin interjected, but Joyce was nodding yes and he let his indignation fall away.

"Listen, don't be too hard on the guy. He's got a sick mother up there or something."

"Look here. Next time I'd damn well appreciate it if you came to me first before you started bribing my officers to take a vacation."

"Bribery? Whoa, hold up there, buddy."

"Don't 'buddy' me. You've got a bloody nerve."

For a moment it seemed as if either Kirsch or Frumkin might throw a punch. But then Frumkin suddenly held up his hands in mock surrender and started to laugh.

"You want to arrest me, Captain? Be my guest. But believe me, it's not a nice thing for one Yiddisher boy to do to another."

Kirsch, his face flushed red, nevertheless managed to calm himself.

"You'd be surprised," he told Frumkin. "I do it all the time."

Frumkin turned to Joyce, who had witnessed their exchange with growing impatience.

"You know how the Jews got to England?" he asked her. "The boat from Russia pulled up at the London Docks. Someone got up and shouted 'New York!' and all the dumb ones got off."

Joyce didn't laugh. Frumkin looked at Kirsch, who wasn't laughing either.

"Same boat, my friend. Your folks and mine. I wouldn't start getting snooty if I were you," Frumkin continued.

"My family are from Holland," Kirsch began. "We've been in England for two hundred years." As soon as he spoke Kirsch realized that he sounded ridiculous.

"Well, that's just great. Was great-great-grandpa pals with the Rothschilds? Perhaps *you* can lend Sir Gerald some money to help him rebuild Jerusalem."

A collective cry from the crowd closed off Frumkin and Kirsch's exchange. The falcons had taken flight and were swooping and plunging through the cerulean sky, the male in hot pursuit of the female, their long dun-colored wings fully extended.

"They fuck in the air, you know," Frumkin said. He looked directly at Joyce and added, "Imagine how great that must be."

Kirsch and Joyce lay together in bed in Joyce's cottage. Joyce was asleep, exhausted by their strenuous lovemaking. Kirsch, eyes wide open, the events of the last couple of weeks swirling dreamlike in his mind, stared at the ceiling. Joyce turned in her sleep and nestled into him, her head on his shoulder, her free arm flung across his narrow chest. He cradled her to him and inhaled the bitter smell of her hair. He wanted to make love to her again, but once they started, she was violent and wild, and while his pleasure was intense it was mitigated by the sense he had that, while Joyce liked him well enough, it didn't have to be *him* in the bed. And so he waited now, savoring this moment of quiet affection, even if she was dreaming herself in Bloomberg's or someone else's arms.

In the morning they sat together outside in two of the spindly garden chairs. Joyce had brought out a pot of tea and spread a plate with cheese and sliced bread. It was the first "meal" that Kirsch could remember anyone making him in months. The heat wave of the last few days, driven by hot winds from the desert, had passed through and now the air was fresh and warm. The garden, pristine in light, and settled under a clear sky, nevertheless had a nice English country clutter and disorder about it. The grass was high and there was hyssop growing in unruly abundance out of the stone walls. On either side of the door pink mallow sprouted from used tins of olive oil. For the first time Kirsch thought he understood why Jews from around the world might want to live here, although he was aware that his reasons for thinking so, which had nothing to do with politics, or persecution, or religion, or history, and everything to do with plants, sun, sex and love, were probably out of line with the majority opinion.

He let Joyce know some part of what was on his mind, but, as usual, she was severe with him.

"From what you're saying you might as well be in Italy, or any Mediterranean country with a nice climate, pretty flowers, and brightly colored birds flitting about. Don't you have any sympathy for the Zionists? I mean, they're not asking for very much, considering what the Jews have given to the world—and without, I might add, having received a lot of thank-yous."

"You don't have to lecture me. I *am* a Jew, remember."

"Well, you don't act like one."

"And how does a Jew act?"

"With pride and allegiance, I would hope."

"Zionist pride?"

"You could do a lot worse. What's so wonderful about being English? Well, I suppose you must love it, you get to police the empire."

"I don't remember your husband flaunting the Jewish company flag. For God's sake, he's painting churches for Ross."

"Shut up! Mark has nothing to do with this. And he happens to be a damn good painter. In fact he's a bloody genius."

"Artists are exempt, are they? What about your friend Frumkin? Is he going to help drain the swamps?"

Joyce, Kirsch noticed, seemed to falter a little, but she quickly recovered her equilibrium.

"I have no idea," she replied.

As if working to endorse Kirsch's view that nature was more compelling than politics, a hoopoe darted across the garden and fixed Joyce's attention. Then, abruptly, her strength seemed to ebb and she let out a deep sigh.

"I should probably have gone with Mark."

Throughout their dispute over Zionism Kirsch had been building toward a declaration far different from the type he had thus far expressed. He wanted to say, "I love you," and he had been on the point of doing so when Joyce had spoken. Now, he found himself momentarily struck dumb. The hoopoe, on its return journey, flashed black and white across the high grass. Kirsch tracked its flight. Out of frustration, or jealousy or the simple confusion that Joyce's presence induced in him, he replied: "You couldn't have."

"What do you mean? That he didn't want me to? Believe me, I could have forced the issue."

Kirsch had a choice now. He could own up to the deal with Ross, or he could take the cover that Joyce had unwittingly offered him. Yes, he could assert, he knew that Bloomberg had insisted on traveling alone. But what choice was there really? The blemish on his character was infinitely preferable to losing her.

"I'm sorry," he said.

"Don't be," Joyce replied, relenting a little. "I'm sure most people think that Mark left me behind against my will. In any case, the truth threatens them." She collected the breakfast things and brought them back into the cottage.

Somewhere not too far away a lone church bell tolled, inviting congregants to Sunday morning services, and soon it was joined by peals that thronged the air from all directions. Chapel at St. Paul's, Kirsch's school, in the year the war started: Kirsch, along with O'Keefe, a Catholic boy, was excused from services, but Kirsch went anyway. He loved the hymns: "Oh Jesus I have promised to love thee to the end," and his favorite of all, "To Be a Pilgrim." "He who would valiant be 'gainst all disaster," Kirsch had sung with gusto, "let him in constancy follow the Master." No one seemed to object to his presence, although occasionally his housemaster,

Jenkins, would give him a funny look, and once after Kirsch had lifted his voice in a particularly beautiful psalm turned song, Merlin-Smith, the choirmaster, a beet-faced Welshman with a booming voice, had stopped him on their way down the chapel stairs: "Enjoy the hymns do you, Mr. Kirsch? Well, your people wrote them. I suppose you can sing 'em!"

Joyce reappeared. She came up behind him and circled his shoulders with her slender arms.

"Robert, I have to go. Which doesn't mean that you have to. Sit here as long as you like. It's a lovely day."

"Got another date with Frumkin?"

"You really have no right to act like this, you know. You're the one with whom I'm betraying Mark, not Peter Frumkin."

Joyce lowered her head and kissed Kirsch on the neck. At that moment he couldn't have been happier.

"More film work?"

"He's given me a real job. I'm in charge of props. We're going back to the desert today."

"I thought he'd finished there weeks ago."

Joyce shrugged. "It's a short trip. Maybe they have to reshoot a couple of scenes. It can't be much, the stars took the steamship home from Haifa. Everything is winding up. Peter himself is going next week."

Kirsch, while delighted to hear this news about Frumkin, did not feel entirely at ease. Joyce was lying to him about something, he was almost certain. But, if she was, that made two of them with secrets to keep.

"I'll leave too," Kirsch said, and stood up. "Let me drop you off."

"No need, Peter sends a car."

"For the props girl? That's pretty fancy."

Joyce smiled. "You'd better go home and change, Robert, you're not looking very authoritative. In fact, you're starting to look like a painter."

Kirsch inspected his rumpled shirt and shorts.

"Yes, it wouldn't do to turn up at the station like this."

"Which reminds me, how *is* the investigation?"

It was Kirsch's turn to shrug. "We're making some progress," he said, "but it's slow. I thought I was onto something on Friday but . . . You did say Harlap was up there with you all week, right?"

The sound of a car horn interrupted him.

"Oh, that's me," Joyce said and began running toward the gate. She turned and blew him a kiss, then walked quickly toward the waiting car.

Kirsch went back inside the cottage, sat on the bed, and lit a cigarette. Bloomberg's paintings were stacked on the opposite wall, the top one facing Kirsch: Jerusalem by moonlight. Bloomberg had made the environs of the city look as desolate as the moon. Kirsch had to admit that the painting moved him. There was a loneliness in it even more intense than his own. He stood up and moved around the cottage, opening drawers and lifting piles of clothes. He felt slightly ashamed, quite uncertain if he was conducting this search as a policeman—after all, Joyce had experienced a break-in—or a jealous lover. Eventually, having discovered nothing of interest aside from Joyce's discarded underwear, his shame got the best of him and he left.

As soon as Kirsch got into his office the phone rang. It was Ross.

"Would you mind coming over?"

"I suppose not, sir."

Whenever he spoke to Ross, Kirsch had to suppress the rage that he felt; what came out instead was grudging obedience. Ross tended to respond magnanimously—a kind father giving his bolshy adolescent son time to come around.

"It's something rather urgent. I'd rather not go into it on the telephone."

"I'll come right away."

"Good."

Kirsch rode toward Abu Tor. He swerved left into the village, taking a corner faster than he had intended, and it was lucky that he did so, for the first bullet only grazed his arm and the others missed their target. Kirsch tried desperately to halt his skid. He felt the bike slide with him, an excruciating pain in his leg, and then he tumbled sideways, his body spinning into a sandy ditch at the side of the road.

When Kirsch came to, his head was cradled in the arms of an Arab woman. She had put down her basket of groceries and was wiping his face with a wet cloth. Looking around, Kirsch saw that she wasn't alone. A group of women were crouched around him, the embroidery on their black dresses an indecipherable tapestry of vivid pinks and yellows. The women were talking fast in what sounded to Kirsch like clicks and sighs. He raised his left hand to his head and felt no blood. Then the pain from his wounded right arm and his crushed left leg overwhelmed him, and he passed out.

27.

Joyce's driver took the Nablus Road north of the Damascus Gate. The windows were open and the city's wayward sounds reached in as punctuation marks on the obliterating white light of the summer morning: church bells, a donkey braying, the occasional klaxon from an automobile, and once what sounded like gunshots, rapid and distant. The car passed St. George's Cathedral and the American Colony and gained the first hill with its engine groaning; by the time they reached the summit of Mt. Scopus its chassis was shuddering and seemed ready to convulse. Joyce tipped sideways in the backseat and almost banged her head on the door frame. It was only after they had passed the village of Sha'afat that the road leveled and the noise diminished to a murmur, and they were already eight miles out of Jerusalem, heading toward Ramallah, when Joyce realized she was traveling not toward, but away from the desert.

She leaned forward. The driver was the same man, Aron, who had driven her home from the Allenby Hotel after her first dinner with Frumkin.

"Where are we going? What's this route?"

Aron slowed the vehicle a little.

"North: Nablus, Jenin, Nazareth, Haifa. Mr. Frumkin will meet us there."

"I understood our meeting was near Beersheba . . ."

"Haifa," Aron repeated laconically, as if Joyce's misunderstanding were of no consequence.

Joyce sat back in the leather seat.

"Do you have something to drink?" she asked.

"We can make a stop in the next village."

Aron parked in a small courtyard near the ruins of an old church. He got out and approached a small shop where boxes of cucumbers were on display under a tattered green canvas awning. Joyce watched him go in, then got out of the car herself and walked toward the dilapidated church walls. At the entrance to the site there was a thin wooden sign nailed to a pole, its message barely visible under a layer of dust. "Here the parents of Jesus missed him on their return from Jerusalem when he was a boy." The information struck Joyce as oddly tender and evoked a reflecting sadness in her. Her own mother had never seemed to care very much about anyone except herself, while her father, although he had done his best when Joyce was a young child, couldn't really wait to get her off his hands and into college. He had, of course, other interests outside the family. Had anyone ever "missed" her? Undoubtedly there was Robert Kirsch, poor puppy dog, but not Mark, almost certainly. He had loved her, that she was sure of, but the signal gaps in his life had always been paintings destroyed or not yet done. Joyce's absence, short-term or extended, weekend visits to friends, her one long trip to America to see her mother, had affected him about as much as a change in the weather outside his studio window; perhaps the light was a little darker and he was obliged to make a small adjustment to his palette, but nothing more. Joyce smiled at her own self-pity—feeling sorry for herself was an attitude she had long ago determined to renounce. The Jewish women on the workers farms certainly didn't feel sorry for themselves. At the dock in Haifa Joyce had seen a short-haired woman about her own age wearing a straight dress with a leather belt and sandals. She had a shovel in her hands and was filling bags of coal. It was her first glimpse of local labor—the descriptions of Palestine that she had heard in London come to life—and she had been filled with a kind of rapture. Mark had been less enthralled. She thought he was embarrassed to see women working this way.

Aron came out of the shop. He was holding a box of Player's and a box of matches. He offered Joyce a cigarette. She took it and inhaled deeply. Aron's fingers, she noticed, were stained yellow from nicotine.

"There's a spring at the foot of the hill," he said. "I'll fill a bottle there."

The water was cool and tasted good. Joyce poured a little onto her fingers and dabbed it, like perfume, behind her ears and on her wrists.

After about five minutes they crossed a narrow plain. Aron took one hand off the steering wheel and gestured to his right.

"In winter this is a pond."

Joyce surveyed the landscape. For a moment, perspiring in the Middle East heat, she remembered skating in New York, and the black corduroy dress that her father had bought her on her eighth birthday; it had a red velvet lining, sleeves that flared at the wrists, and a scalloped hem. She twirled on Ridgeley's Pond, the red lining flashing in the gray December light.

"Flash floods and then the water collects here," Aron continued.

They negotiated a barren ridge and suddenly she could see all the way to the Mediterranean: it appeared as a distant gray-blue band. Aron, glancing into the mirror, slowed down to let Joyce enjoy the view, but a lorry, its engine droning, accelerated behind them and tried to overtake. The Arab workers in the back of the truck cheered and waved at Joyce. Aron maintained his slow pace, stubbornly demonstrating that he controlled the road. The lorry driver leaned on his horn and gesticulated. Aron slowed further, almost to a stop. The driver pressed relentlessly on the horn while his passengers shouted and brandished their shovels and pickaxes.

Joyce bent forward and tapped Aron on the shoulder.

"Stop it," she said, "you're being ridiculous."

Aron shrugged. "Let them wait," he responded. "Believe me, they have nowhere to go that matters." Nevertheless he put his foot on the gas and pulled away.

A burst tire outside Nablus delayed them for more than three hours. While Aron negotiated with the mechanics at a nearby garage Joyce passed the time sipping mint tea in a small café. In both venues, prominently displayed, was a photogravure of Haj-Amin al-Husseini, the mufti of Jerusalem, and in both he appeared to be scowling. The cracked green walls of the café were additionally decorated with a mural of the

Old City, its great mosques disproportionately represented as occupying almost the entire area within the walls. There wasn't a sign of the Jewish presence. Each side, Joyce thought, mapped the other's invisibility. In terms of pure numbers the Arabs perhaps had more right to do so than the Jews, and yet, even though the Jews were a minority, it seemed to Joyce axiomatic that Palestine belonged, at least in its greater part, to them. How had she come by this idea? Sitting at her small wooden table, the scent of *nana* leaves rising from the steaming tea, Joyce felt suddenly and disarmingly aware that, back in London, it was possible that in addition to being enchanted by the practical content of Zionist dreams— pastoral, socialist, utopian—that were so movingly relayed to the packed, eager audiences at Toynbee Hall, she had also been seduced by the broad promise those dreams seemed to offer of an end to Jewish loneliness. And at the time this, as far as it directly concerned her relationship with Mark, was something to which she had been dedicated with all her heart. Was her commitment to Zionism then merely personal after all? An absurd desire to change Mark through changing the world? For the whole of this last year, it seemed, ever since he had turned away from her, Zionism had been both Joyce's hope and her sanctuary. Mark had no idea of quite how many meetings she had attended, and no knowledge of the murmured names, Arlosoroff or Buber, that were now as familiar to her as Cézanne or van Gogh. He must have thought, as she slipped out into Fordwych Road on weekday winter evenings and headed off in the rain for "the theater" or "to a concert" that she had a secret lover. And in a way she did, but only, surely, for his sake. But even so, her hopes were doomed. Mark had nothing but derision for Weizmann and his Jewish state, which is why she hid the bulk of her journeys from him. And yet he seemed to receive only pain from living as a Jew among the Gentiles of England. It was as if he drew the strength of his art from bitterness and detachment, and he was more frightened of losing those supporting structures than anything else.

By the time they reached Haifa it was dark. Near the port, the looming warehouses along the shoreline seemed to lean together like conspirators. The air was humid and brackish; Joyce felt as if her arms, legs, and face were covered in thin layers of oil and salt. The hair on the back of Aron's head glinted with sweat. In the beam thrown by the car's yellow headlights she saw a mangy dog rush into the road. Aron slowed to let it cross; then he pulled into an alleyway and turned off the engine. They were close enough to the sea that Joyce could hear water lapping against the concrete quay. Aron got out and opened her door. Her legs felt heavy but she stood and followed him down the alley. After a hundred yards or so he turned abruptly into a narrow passage not visible from where they had parked. He approached a metal door set two feet off the ground in an otherwise uniform high brick wall. Aron banged twice with his fist. Joyce heard a bolt slide back. Frumkin looked out; the moon, murky and veiled, threw a dim light across his face. When he saw Joyce he smiled and extended a hand to help her up.

"I knew you'd come," he said.

"Then you knew more than me," she replied.

When Frumkin lit two oil lamps the storage room revealed a stack of low flat crates all stamped PROPERTY OF METROPOLIS FILM CORPORA-TION. In addition, piled up against the far wall, there were many smaller boxes with Hebrew lettering stenciled on their sides.

Frumkin gestured toward the crates. "This is what you have to de-liver. The props. And here's a list of the actors to whom they have to be distributed."

Joyce took the sheet of paper. She looked down at the neatly typed names and addresses.

"What's in the crates?"

Frumkin gave her a long look.

"You said you wanted to help, didn't you? 'In any way that I can.' Isn't that what you said? I assumed that you understood."

"I *do* want to help."

"In any way that you can. Right?"

Joyce was shivering a little.

Frumkin walked over to one of the crates and lifted the lid. Joyce froze. Frumkin began to talk fast.

"You'll have to move them piecemeal. A few crates at a time. Not in the vehicle you came in, by the way. I don't want you seen again with Aron. If anybody asks, and I know you know someone who *will* ask if he should happen to get hold of you, I left you the old jalopy to run around in because you're doing all kinds of wrap-up business for the corporation. Kirsch, if he finds you, which he won't, will think that's bullshit. But if he does, he'll imagine I gave you the car simply to impress you with my wealth and beneficence, and obviously because I want to get you into bed. That's fine. Don't put him right, and don't try to come here to Haifa more than once every ten days or so. If it takes six weeks to get everything out, so be it. We can wait. The bullets will be easy. Take at least two boxes for every large crate."

Joyce stared at the guns.

"But Leo never said anything about guns."

"Leo? Who's Leo?"

Joyce looked at Frumkin; shadows from the flickering lamps danced behind his head. A terrible awareness shook Joyce and she began visibly to tremble. She was terrified but also disturbingly excited.

"Leo Cohn. From London."

Frumkin stared back at her, an expression of contempt on his face. "I don't know any Leo Cohn."

"A teacher. I was going to be a teacher." She was talking to herself more than to Frumkin.

"Look, you're in this thing now and you can't turn back."

Joyce's eyes searched wildly around the room. Her heart was pounding. There was nothing here of orchards to be planted or songs to be sung with needy children. The only desperate child was herself.

Frumkin continued to talk in a low, urgent voice.

"Before you drive up from Jerusalem, you'll call Shako Brothers, the tour service in Haifa. The number's 240. It's run by Aron's brother Motti. He will meet you and help you load up. You can start deliveries tonight."

"Tonight?" Joyce didn't know what she was saying.

"Why bring you here otherwise?"

"But I have no idea where I'm going," she stammered. "I've never driven here."

Frumkin put his hand on her arm. "Are you serious or not?"

"Serious. Yes, I want to be serious."

"Do you think we're not going to help you find your way? Everything will be made easy. All you have to do is follow a car for a while, then branch off on your own and make a few quick deliveries. The first one's in Ramleh, on the road from Jaffa to Jerusalem; then you'll follow someone else, and after it's all done you'll go back to Jaffa. Everything will be provided for you there: money, clothing, food. You're not to return to Jerusalem. Not until you hear from one of us that you can."

"And what if someone comes looking for me?"

"A room has been set up for you. No one will find you. And the movie wrap-up took longer than expected. You understand that?"

There was a faint smell of mildew in the room. The yellow light emanating from the oil lamps swirled suddenly green and black. Joyce felt she was drowning.

"I need some air," she said.

Frumkin pulled himself up to his full height and took a deep intake of breath, as if to accentuate Joyce's weakness: Producer of Movies, Director of Operations. He was enjoying himself.

"Let's get going," he said. "Here, put this on."

He handed her a wavy brown wig of the sort worn by Palestine's Orthodox Jewish women. Joyce pulled it on too low, the way she used to tug on her wool hat on cold days in London and New York. Frumkin took a quick step forward and made the necessary adjustment.

Then she was out in the salt-stained air, the stars whirling above her like crazed gulls. She managed to steady herself and slide into the driver's seat of Frumkin's car. The crates were speedily loaded in the back and before she knew it Aron had started the car in front of her and was signaling out of the window for her to get going. She turned the ignition and crashed the gears twice before the clutch caught and she began to move forward.

Hours later, in the first moments of a damp, blurry dawn, when night and day were confused in a gray-black cloudscape over the Mediterranean, Joyce pulled Frumkin's car into the protective shelter of a corrugated shack next to a small dilapidated house. Her mind was clotted with images and remembered odors: two men who had greeted her sullenly and with hardly a word, both wearing high-collared Russian-style shirts, but with Arab kaffiyehs on their heads to deceive any onlookers; back streets that she had followed to different destinations, each one shabbier than the next; the stench of a ditch she had crossed that led to a cesspool that a gloomy boy had helped her circumvent; figures that had emerged from nowhere to unload her crates and pack her boxes of bullets first into tins labeled THIN SOCIAL BISCUITS, and then into the bottom of straw baskets with sturdy handles, where they were quickly hidden beneath an array of fresh vegetables; vineyard supports that, stacked against a palm tree, threw the silhouette of a dark crucifix in the moonlight; and finally, at the last place she stopped, a corrugated lean-to at the back of a farmhouse barn, where suddenly the scent of wild honeysuckle overwhelmed her, as if to confirm her newly acquired hope that sweetness might emerge from violence.

Joyce entered the house and threw herself, utterly exhausted, on the closest piece of furniture, a long, narrow couch with a thin unadorned mattress. What would Mark have thought of her activities? Probably not much more than he had of her painting: the work of a desperate dilettante. And what did she think of them herself? She wasn't sure. Somewhere inside, a private heresy, she felt that she had betrayed herself. The gap had widened too far between her way of living and her feeling of what life should be: first bitter talk with Mark on a tumbled bed, and now her entry into a darkness where she discovered herself willing to do the dirty work for those who labored in the service of a great idea. And perhaps, after all, what she wanted was simple: love, peace, and quiet.

Joyce roused herself enough to pull off her clothes. She lay back naked on the couch and fell asleep as the birds began to sing.

August

28.

In the mornings Saud set up a bleached white linen tent in the spot where Bloomberg wanted to paint. They had bought it from a man returning to Amman from Mecca. Other travelers—pilgrims and tourists—passed through almost daily. Habobo Brothers ran a weekly motor and camel service from Jerusalem and Haifa, and Saud used Bloomberg's money to buy tobacco, needles, and soap from the company drivers. Bloomberg could have sent a message back to Ross at any time, but he chose not to. In fact, he had heard twice, in polite notes, from his patron, but he had chosen not to respond. He certainly didn't want replacement bedouin sent down to "rescue" him, and then there was the far more important matter of De Groot's murderers, but that was an issue that Bloomberg needed to think through; a solution that was safe for the boy—other than the current situation, that is—had yet to present itself.

At first, Bloomberg worked far away from the rock face; the distance was necessary in order to secure the "accurate views" that Ross desired.

But, sketched in this way, the massive temples and vast Necropolis looked tiny and unimpressive. By the end of two weeks Bloomberg had begun to move his position forward. Now, more than a month later, the effect of his work was reversed: The Temple of Isis, the amphitheater and the banquet hall lost their contours and became indistinguishable elements of the crimson rock from which they were hewn.

Bloomberg painted in purple, pink, red, and brown. He worked on a large canvas that Saud had helped him to stretch: his brushwork loose and expressive, he dragged the heavily loaded pigment across the canvas, his mind both free and utterly concentrated. For ten days he had worked at night and on into the early morning, sleeping through the heat of the day and asking Saud to wake him for dinner. But then, suddenly, he had altered his routine. Now he spent the mornings clambering over the rocks, treading paths that the Nabateans had cut and that, two thousand years ago, had brought them to the high spots that were their places of sacrifice. Bloomberg liked to touch the rough-hewn facades of the ancient buildings. He saw Saud watching him with amusement as he stretched his arms, like Samson, between two giant pillars, or placed his hands, as if attempting to make an impression, on the surface of a pink-and-white wall. Then, against Saud's better judgment, he began to paint at the hour of the day when the sun was most fierce. He wore his wide-brimmed hat, but even so the heat was intense and he frequently felt himself on the edge of fainting. But this was a precipice where he wanted to stand: unmoored in the blinding light, his head throbbing. He could paint at this time of day only for an hour or two. The problem was technical as well as physical: the oil dried too fast in the heat and he preferred it when the paint stayed wet and he could work it. But it was worth losing time for the magnificent abandonment that he was at last able to feel: a sensation of possibility leading to an honesty of expression that, he thought, he hadn't managed to accomplish since his student days at the Slade. Sometimes the wind whipped a hard rain of sand onto his canvas but, instead of despairing, he simply mixed it in; more than once he removed the canvas from its easel and placed it on the ground; then he scurried around it on all fours, painting with his back to the rocks that were ostensibly the subject of his work. Kneeling beside his wet canvas, his face, hands, and clothes stained with sweat and paint, Bloomberg felt transported: the overwhelming misery that had gripped him for more than a year had lifted, or at least it was in hiding. Here, as the weeks passed under the obliterating desert sun, he let the past go.

The painting was almost completed. He had poured his heart and soul into it, and it was, he thought, the first work of any significance that he had managed since his arrival in Palestine. He knew things were going well because he had lost track of the days, and because he was avoiding contact with others as much as he could. From time to time a tourist, usually British, took the long walk out to Bloomberg's perch in the rocks and hovered nearby, as Ross had done on the roof of his house in Jerusalem. Only one fellow had braved Bloomberg's hard stare and tried to engage him in conversation, but Bloomberg had firmly requested that he go away. The only person he spoke to was Saud. And what did they talk about? Nothing but daily things, and Bloomberg was completely happy with the quotidian: he wasn't ready yet, and neither was the boy, for any meditation on the future. They were like an old married couple, nothing much to say except, "What's for dinner tonight?"

This morning—he had been in Petra for perhaps two months; the moon, fat when he arrived, and full on one occasion since, had swollen again and was nearing the completion of her cycle—Bloomberg was planning to have Saud help him set up, and then he was going to put the finishing touches to his painting, but when he returned from his daily walk among the ruins Saud was nowhere to be seen. In his place Bloomberg found two visitors waiting in his tent.

The young man, who was dressed in a crumpled white suit that exhibited dark sweat stains under the arms, stood to introduce himself and the woman. He was prevented from reaching his full height by the confines of the tent. His hair, a wild mop of black untamed curls, brushed against the canvas roof.

"Michael Cork. I hope you don't mind, and this is my wife, Sarah. I'm so sorry but we couldn't help coming over and barging in. You see it's just an incredible coincidence. We've been on this tour, under rather peculiar circumstances, I'm afraid, but no need to go into that now. You probably don't know it, but you're, how shall I say this, you're a *sight*. All the guides mention you. And we are, well, admirers, and more, we're, well, thanks to Sarah here, we're *owners*. We possess a Bloomberg. Got it last year after we came back from Germany—that was our last trip, walking the Black Forest and then three nights in Heidelberg. Altogether happier times. Our honeymoon actually. God, I'm sorry! Anyway, your painting, I mean, the fact that you're working right here. You can't imagine how excited we are."

Bloomberg listened, but the words circled him like wheeling birds. The desert had thrummed its extraordinary silence deep into him, and the patter and speed of ordinary English conversation, sentences that rattled, squealed and swerved like a London bus, sounded alien, almost incomprehensible.

"*Barges on the Canal,* Sarah fell in love with it. She grew up near a lock. Iffley Lock in Oxfordshire? I don't suppose you've ever, by any chance, been there? There's a pub right over the bridge, the Green Man. At any rate, we had a choice between furniture for the new flat or your painting and I'm happy to say we made the right decision. God, I think she'd eat off the floor to own your work! Well, I should really"—Cork's voice trailed away—"shut up and let Sarah speak for herself."

He flushed red and turned to his wife, who rose from where she had been sitting cross-legged on the groundsheet. She offered a broad smile and extended her hand to Bloomberg.

"Sarah Cork. I'm so honored to meet you."

Bloomberg wiped his hands on his shirt. The young woman's face wasn't pretty, not in any conventional sense—her nose was too long, her lips too thin for that—but it was an open and attractive face. Her auburn hair was cut short in a bob, and her brown eyes had a somber quality that he immediately liked. Or, and the thought flashed bulletlike through his brain, did he already admire everything about her simply because she had purchased one of his paintings?

There was an awkward silence—that London bus halted at a red light—and then Bloomberg, remembering his tribal manners from some far-off place, asked: "Can I get you something? Tea? Coffee?"

Every morning Saud collected a few twigs and set a niggardly fire a few paces from the tent. He heated coffee in a small blackened pot, holding it over the flames by its long copper handle. As usual, Bloomberg had noted the fire on returning from his walk, so Saud couldn't be too far away, but Bloomberg had no intention of calling out for the boy. Any visitors were potential trouble. And moreover Saud was his assistant, not his servant.

"Tea would be lovely," Sarah said enthusiastically. She might have been at a tennis tournament.

Bloomberg stepped out of the tent.

He heated water over the fire, and when it boiled he poured it into two cracked floral-pattern china cups (Saud had scrounged them from a party of Dutch tourists—the handles had snapped off) and added sprigs of *nana* leaves.

He brought the steaming mint tea in to his visitors.

"Aren't you joining us?" Sarah asked.

"I'm not thirsty," Bloomberg replied. He didn't want to admit that there were only two cups, although that was hardly something to be ashamed of.

Bloomberg removed a box of cigarettes from his shirt pocket and proffered it to Michael, but it was Sarah who reached for it. Bloomberg pushed the box across to her.

"How long will you stay here?"

"I really don't know. Until the work is done, I suppose."

There was another silence that seemed as if it might, for all three of them, last beyond embarrassment and on into some speechless perfect destiny, but then the quiet was shattered by the backfire of a car exhaust echoing across the desert, and the noise ignited the conversation.

"And the two of you?" Bloomberg continued. "You mentioned 'peculiar circumstances.' "

Michael Cork looked across at his wife.

"We came out to Jerusalem six and a half weeks ago because my cousin was shot," Sarah said. "He's a policeman, Bobby Kirsch. My uncle and aunt would have made the trip, but they're not quite up to it, I'm afraid."

Bloomberg expressed nothing, but felt an inner jolt, as if an electric current had run through him. He collected himself by staring hard at the green groundsheet and smoothing a few crinkles with a pass of his hand.

"Shot dead?"

"No, thank God. In the arm. But it wasn't the bullet that did the damage. He was on his motorbike and he crashed."

Bloomberg looked at Sarah. She returned his stare. He thought he saw something in the way that she was regarding him, some recognition beyond the admiration that had already been expressed, but he wasn't sure.

"He's a mess," she concluded.

"Bobby sent us away," her husband put in—fearful, it seemed, that Bloomberg might imagine that they had been derelict in their duty to the sick. "I mean, gosh, Sarah was at the hospital every day. She's been wonderful. But he sent us away, he said Sarah deserved a holiday and he just couldn't stand our miserable faces around any longer. And he *is* on the mend, although it will be at least another fortnight until he's out of the wheelchair."

Bloomberg couldn't quite process the image of Kirsch in a wheelchair. The picture blurred in his head. This wasn't the fate that he had intended, or even imagined, for his wife's lover when he had left Jerusalem.

"Does your cousin have a lot of visitors?"

Bloomberg knew that the question must have seemed strange, and he wasn't surprised to see the Corks turn to one another with a shared look of puzzlement on their faces.

"Well," Sarah began slowly, "there's Sir Gerald Ross, he's been terribly concerned. He visits the hospital three or four times a week, and the nurses told me that at the beginning, when Bobby was first brought in, he was there every day."

"Ah yes, Sir Gerald. He can certainly be relied upon to do the right thing."

"Oh, do you know him?"

"Know him? He's the reason I'm here. All these vast worldly belongings that you see around you, including my goodly tent, the whole lot comes courtesy of Sir Gerald. He is, if you'll pardon the expression, my patron."

"So perhaps you've met Sarah's cousin," Michael offered enthusiastically, either choosing to ignore or simply missing Bloomberg's comic register. "Bobby's stick-thin and his hair's sandy, but otherwise his face is remarkably like my wife's."

"That's not true," Sara corrected. "Bobby's much better-looking than I am."

Michael Cork blushed again but responded immediately, "That's nonsense, Sarah."

Despite his better instincts Bloomberg admired him. Mr. Cork was clearly willing to battle two strong opponents—shyness and English reticence—on behalf of his true love.

"Yes," Bloomberg replied, directing his remarks to Sarah. "I have met your cousin. He was investigating a murder in which I played a strange part. I danced briefly with the corpse."

"Oh God, it was you. How extraordinary. But Bobby didn't mention your name. I think he simply said 'a local British couple.' He's quite changed. I don't know how well you became acquainted, but he's silent a great deal of the time now. Terribly depressed, of course. If you saw his leg you'd know why, it's half its previous size, as if someone had sliced it down the middle."

"I'm sorry."

The air in the tent seemed to have stopped circulating. Michael Cork removed his jacket: the sweat stains on his shirt matched those on the jacket. Sara, whose own clothes, a long loose cotton skirt and thin cream blouse, seemed far more appropriate to the place, wiped the back of her hand across her brow and rolled up her sleeves.

"And do they know who shot Captain Kirsch?" Bloomberg continued.

"No one knows anything," Michael Cork began, "but the city's a tinderbox. Everybody says so. There are rumors flying all over the place. We met a chap at the Allenby bar who once worked with Bobby, and he told us that all of a sudden Jerusalem is full of guns. No one knows where they're coming from, or who exactly has them, but they are there. And you must have heard about the riot."

"What riot?"

"Three weeks ago. Near the Wailing Wall? The news didn't reach you?"

"Happily, not."

"It started, if you can believe this, over an errant whack at a football in a village outside Jerusalem. A Jewish boy kicked it into an Arab family's tomato patch. A little girl grabbed the ball and hid it in a pile of laundry. When the boy came to retrieve his ball, the girl started screaming. Out comes her father, or maybe it was her brother, with an iron rod and smashes the boy's skull. Well, in these parts, as I'm sure you know, it's all an eye for an eye, so two hours later there's a young Arab boy out taking a stroll and suddenly he's getting smacked on the head with a blunt instrument. News spreads into the city and by nightfall everybody was going at it in the area by the Wailing Wall. Luckily for Bobby he was already in the hospital, because the district commissioner sent in ten chaps in steel helmets to take on four hundred Jews and Arabs going crazy, and only one of the policemen managed to escape a wound."

Sarah Cork gave her husband a harsh look.

"I'm sorry," he said, "I have an occasional tendency toward the foolish. Even had the misfortune to be born on April Fool's Day. I don't know how Sarah puts up with me. Of course, it's not lucky that Bobby wasn't there."

"Listen," Bloomberg said, "I have to get to work. But why don't you two join me tonight for something to eat? Or is the tour moving you on?"

"Not yet," Sarah replied. "Three days here, then a night in Al Aqaba, followed by Santa Katerina and journey's end in Cairo. But why don't *you* join *us* tonight? We do have a cook traveling with the group, he's been coming up with some marvelous meals, and we're not short on provisions."

"Thank you, but no," Bloomberg replied.

Sarah stubbed out her cigarette on the bottom of her shoe, then immediately reached for Bloomberg's Player's and lit another one.

"This is really too strange," she added, "sitting here with my absolute favorite artist."

Her husband smiled. "Gosh, Sarah," he said, "you're sounding just like an American."

"My wife's American," Bloomberg said.

The blood rushed to Michael Cork's cheeks again.

"Perhaps you saw her in Jerusalem. Her name is Joyce. She knows your cousin better than I do. They became quite good friends during the murder investigation."

The Corks looked at one another but said nothing.

"I'm afraid not," Sarah replied, but once again Bloomberg had the impression, perhaps utterly false, that she knew more than she was about to let on.

Was he finished with the painting? He thought he was done awhile ago, but in the mornings the painting seemed to be laughing at him for imagining the end. When would it be over? There was no plan, there were no stages. When the end came he would be able to smell it, touch it, and always, for some reason, the last brushstrokes came in the top right-hand corner, sometimes hours or days after the "original" last touches. He had represented the rocks, if they were still rocks and not the hard places of his own mind, in pink and blue, but now he saw that the top right-hand corner needed brown. Otherwise, the painting was boring. But brown in the place that he wanted to put it could lead to an entire reconfiguration, a new beginning. Of what Ross had requested nothing was left, no Tapering Columns, no Temple of Isis, no altar, pool and court, only the path to the place of sacrifice and the terrain that surrounded it.

Bloomberg worked in blazing heat as the red disk of the sun climbed through the brilliant atmosphere, tinged the peerless hues of the sandstone, crossed the impassable ravine, hid behind the towering cliffs, then emerged to occupy fragments of blue sky above. The effect of this experience on his mind, Bloomberg thought, would be enduring.

He painted for three hours until the sweat on his hands began to accumulate so fast that it was impossible for him to hold the brushes any longer; then he returned to his tent. At some point in the afternoon, while he was sleeping, Saud showed up. Bloomberg would not have known that he was there but for a stray camel that decided to stick its nose into the tent to sniff out food. Saud loudly shooed the animal away and Bloomberg awoke. He pulled his shirt over his head. His torso, while well muscled, was almost as skinny as the boy's, but Bloomberg's chest showed a crucifix of white hair. He wiped his perspiring face with the shirt then rolled it into a ball and threw it into a corner of the tent.

"I must go back to Jerusalem," he said. "The painting's finished. I have to deliver it."

Saud put his arms around his knees. His face took on a hopeless expression, as if he were an animal gazing through the bars of his cage.

"But you'll be perfectly safe. I've found some people who I think will take care of you, at least for a while. It will mean your traveling with them."

"And then?"

"Well, eventually, when all this is cleared up, I hope you'll return to Jerusalem and see your family. Perhaps I can make it happen. At any rate I'm going to try."

"The Zionists murdered Yaakov, they will do the same to me, and if you interfere, they will kill you too."

This was the first time since Saud's initial revelations and the discussions immediately following that either one of them had mentioned the murder. And yet it felt to Bloomberg, because he had thought about it so much, that they were retreading old ground.

"They won't find you and don't worry about me, unfortunately I'm indestructible. In the best of circumstances for the job not even the Germans or my own superiors managed to do me in. But listen, do you know anyone in Cairo? Any family there? Anybody at all?"

Saud shook his head. "Why Cairo?"

"That's where these people are headed. It's all right, they're trustworthy."

"And what will you tell the governor?"

"That I'm returning to Petra. That you're still there."

Saud closed his eyes and pressed his fingers to them.

"Then you go and see my mother," he said.

"I will. I promise I will," Bloomberg replied.

Was Saud a skilled rent boy, as described by Rachman, or De Groot's peculiarly precocious ephebe? Either way it didn't matter. Prostitute or poet, or both, Bloomberg was absolutely convinced that he was innocent of murder. And beyond the boy's word he had his hard evidence—the silver button with the royal crest that De Groot had ripped from his assailant's tunic. Not that *that* would convince anybody of anything.

"Well, look . . ." Bloomberg reached for his hat, retrieved from its headband what remained of the money that Ross had given him and started to count it. "If this works out, and it will, I'm going to give you the whole lot minus enough to get me back to Jerusalem and in for a couple of drinks. British pounds work as well in Egypt as they do here. You should be fine for at least three months. You'll send me your address, and if the time is right, I'll come down and get you myself. Oh, why don't you just take the money now?"

Saud stretched out his hand for the notes; then he rose, walked over to Bloomberg and kissed him on his forehead.

When night fell, the Corks turned up, "bobbed up," Bloomberg thought, as invited. They had spent the day wandering in Zibb Atuf, which contained the oldest tombs in Petra, and finished up farther north at the Tomb of the Governor: a place Bloomberg knew well because the mausoleum was constructed like a temple, adorned with four huge columns, as if death were the finest thing on earth.

The three of them sat outside the tent. Bloomberg opened a bottle of arak and, because of the cup shortage, simply passed it around so they could take swigs. The night was clear and stars gathered and clustered in an abundance that the Corks had never witnessed before.

"What a magnificent place this is," Michael said.

Bloomberg noted that both husband and wife had received mild sunburns during the day; the tip of Sarah's nose, in particular, glowed red and looked as if it must be causing her at least a minor discomfort. She *did* look like her cousin. It was their eyes, deep-set and remote, that created the resemblance.

There wasn't much to offer in the way of food. Bloomberg had opened two tins of beef and was heating the contents over the fire. There was fresh flat bread and onion to stuff in it along with the meat. On the pretext of needing something to make the meal more palatable Bloomberg had sent Saud off to one of the tourist camps in search of a bottle of wine. He planned to use the time the boy was gone to broach the subject of Saud's journeying to Cairo with the Corks. However, before Bloomberg could begin, Sarah Cork, her tongue loosened a little by the arak, or so it seemed, began to talk about her cousin.

"I think he'd recover much quicker," she said, "if he weren't so sad."

"Injuries like that can take a toll in lots of ways," Bloomberg replied.

The injured and the lost were all over Europe, he thought. Young men missing arms, legs, eyes—and worse, men who'd never make love to a girl again. Bloomberg had got away by giving up one toe—and he'd done it to himself. There they all were, a long sick serpentine line curling out from London into the countryside and on, all the way up to the gray cities of the north and beyond to Scotland; the half-blind and half-deaf limping along, and now Kirsch, only a few years late, had joined the ranks. You couldn't talk about physical suffering, of course, without thinking about the war. The Corks must have been thinking about it now. Half of Bloomberg's friends were dead, Kirsch's brother was dead. Who knew if this cheery young Michael Cork hadn't lost someone in *his* family?

But Sarah, as Bloomberg quickly became aware, didn't have the war on her mind. Her subject was closer to home, and at this point in time, even more compelling.

"No," she said, "it's not the injury. He's got a broken heart."

Bloomberg paused, he tried not to ask the inevitable question, but in the end he couldn't resist doing so:

"And who has broken it?"

"I don't know," Sarah replied. "He won't say. He's being very secretive. When we were young he used to tell me everything. Our families were very close. I was more like a sister than a cousin."

"So I take it there have been no visits?"

Once again the Corks exchanged glances. Bloomberg's obsession with Kirsch's hospital visitors was utterly mysterious.

"Not that we're aware of," Michael put in, "but who knows who came to the ward when we weren't around?"

Bloomberg both did and did not want to pursue the topic of Kirsch's broken heart, but either way, time was short. Saud would return soon with the wine. Hurriedly, he launched into a quick description of the plight of his assistant, who needed to get to Cairo in order to visit a sick relative. Could the Corks squeeze him in with their party? Naturally Bloomberg would cover the costs. The boy was an excellent companion, quiet, but if you got into conversation with him, preternaturally bright, he seemed to know a hundred English poems off by heart. He'd had a tutor in Jerusalem.

The Corks, as Bloomberg had expected, were generous and accommodating. They would absolutely arrange things. Bloomberg could count on them.

But in the meantime, where was Joyce? And where was her sympathy for poor Bobby Kirsch? How had her interest in him evaporated so fast? Was it Bloomberg's fault that she couldn't even show up at his hospital bed with a bunch of flowers? Had he drained all her passion away, left her empty and incapable of feeling?

Two more gulps of arak and the burning stars annihilated his questions. Michael Cork chatted on, and Bloomberg tried, as best he could, to pay attention to the young man's earnest and well-meaning assessment of the situation in Palestine. Then, in the space of an hour, Bloomberg fell in and out of love with Sarah Cork. By the time that Saud arrived clutching two bottles of cheap red wine, Bloomberg, more than half cut, was barely able to make introductions without slurring his words. Still, he wasn't about to let the boy down. He roused himself to the task at hand and outlined the plan. The Corks would play Saud's guardian angels all the way to Cairo. As for Bloomberg, he would return to Jerusalem with his painting.

"When you see Bobby," Sarah said, as if there was no doubt that Bloomberg, given his interest in "visiting," would indeed call in on her cousin, "would you give him our love, and tell him we'll be back soon?"

She rose and dusted the sand off her dress. "It's been wonderful to meet you. When we're all back in England I hope you'll come and visit. Or perhaps we'll see you in Jerusalem when we return."

Bloomberg stood and advanced shakily toward her. Sarah wasn't expecting him to hug her, but he did.

Barges on the Canal: the lugubrious vessels bumped into one another on the dark water; Bloomberg had stumbled down the bank side, sketch pad in hand, drawn by God knows what. He'd taken off his shoes and socks and sat on the quay, dipping his feet in the cool water.

"And your wife," Michael Cork added, "I hope we can meet her too."

"Yes," Bloomberg replied, "my wife."

29.

For almost two months Joyce traversed the country delivering wares from her supplier in Haifa. She knew, by moonlight only, the scented orange groves of Petach Tikva, and the clustered vineyards in Rishon Le Zion, and to each place, the homes of fruit and wine, she brought her own lethal diet of guns and bullets. She knew too the ragged shoreline from Tel Aviv to Jaffa, the silicate factory of the former, where camels crossed the dunes loaded with bricks, and the narrow bazaar of the latter with its meretricious offerings. On the outskirts of Jaffa, where she lived in a tiny, balconied house in the Jewish neighborhood, she knew precisely where to cross the tramlines and where to meet the messenger who came to give her the all clear. Mostly she stayed indoors during the day and slept, but one afternoon, stirred toward an antidote to the excitements of her nocturnal life, she wandered in the town by day and discovered to her surprise that the walls of some of the houses she had known only as looming shadows were plastered in ochre, sky blue, rose, and a kind of squashed strawberry. At dusk she walked to the shore and sat opposite an old, empty building that the sea filled with the tumult of its swell. She watched the local fishermen wade into the surf and cast, their djellabas bundled up above their knees: a day off for the conspirator, and she was perfectly content. It was madness, but she had to admit that, impossible as it seemed, she felt as if she had discovered her true vocation. For weeks her senses, intensified by fear, urgency and danger, had provided her with the kind of vivid experience that she had tried for so long to achieve, first through dance, then through painting, and ultimately, she supposed, through love and sex. Frumkin must have known what he was doing when he picked her. He had spotted that while her commitment to the Zionist cause, authentic though it might be, was sporadic at best, her allegiance to the temptations of excitement, and the excitements of temptation, while well masked for long periods of time, was absolute.

She thought about Robert Kirsch. Was he searching for her? She was his prey and target now. She missed him, missed both his unstinting admiration and the ardors of his infatuation. She missed him in bed. But her memory of him, and also, astonishingly, of Mark, was as of people from another life. She had tumbled into a clandestine world of murmur and rumor. She heard, and overheard, in the side conversations of her coconspirators, that there were riots in Jerusalem; that the British authorities were panicked, that there were no more garden parties or gymkhanas. Joyce imagined the widespread absenteeism among the serving staff of the colonial homes: no garden parties without the gardeners, no receptions without the servants. The Arab riots, so she understood, were a lucky distraction; the police were all tied up. And she imagined Robert and thought how he might handle himself in situations of violence and danger; but imagined him tenderly, as one might think of a child going into schoolground battles where the dangers were more imaginary than real.

Tonight, in the somnolent fading yellow light of a late-August evening, she had fallen asleep early. Around midnight she woke with a start; someone was in her room.

"Don't panic," Frumkin said, "it's only me."

He was sitting in a dark corner perched on the edge of a chair that was much too small for him. He was smoking a cigarette and when he drew on it the tip glowed orange. Joyce, who had been sleeping naked, pulled up the sheet to cover her breasts.

"Peter! Christ, don't you knock before you come in?"

She'd heard that he had left the country, and perhaps he had, for a while.

Frumkin stood up and came and sat on the end of her bed. "You've been doing a great job," he said.

"I suggest you go outside, wait five minutes, and then come in again. I'll get dressed." She said this in a teacherly way, and then disliked herself for having done so. She thought she had long ago escaped to far wilder places than the classroom.

Frumkin went to the paneled glass door and stepped onto the balcony, leaving the door open behind him. She swished the curtain across the glass, lit the small oil lamp next to her bed, turned it low, then pulled on a dress.

"Okay," she called out.

"It's lucky we've got you," Frumkin said, coming back into the room. "Every other British squaddie is selling arms to the Arabs; you'd be amazed how much matériel mysteriously disappears from army supplies, 'lost.' For the Brits it's a lucrative traffic."

"I thought you were in America."

"I was. The movie's almost ready for distribution. It's going to be a smash. I just got back here. Some problems with our cargo guy up at the port in Haifa. Extra funds were needed—salary increase. You can't blame him. But even so, things aren't going well. I have a feeling that the 'props' aren't going to get through for much longer—unless we can persuade Metropolis to shoot *another* film in Jerusalem, which is unlikely, don't you think?"

He stood close by her.

"Any problems at your end?" he asked.

"None. None at all," she replied. "And no sign of Robert Kirsch."

"Hardly a surprise."

"Do you think so? I worried that he would try to search me out. He's very persistent."

Frumkin looked quickly at her. He seemed taken off guard. She caught his glance but didn't make anything of it.

"Well, the riots. I imagine our captain must have it up to here."

"Don't mock him, he's a good man."

"Is he?"

"Maybe not for you."

"I can't understand a Jew who fights for the other side." Frumkin pushed his hair back from his forehead.

"I don't think he sees it that way."

"You don't?"

Joyce felt, for a moment, that they were all tangled together like badly cast fishing nets: herself, Peter, Mark, and Robert Kirsch.

Frumkin didn't wait for her answer.

"Listen, because of this developing problem in Haifa we're going to have to move to Plan B. And I need you to be a part of it. We've got to keep the supply going and, as I told you, the Arabs are doing a great job picking up everything the Brits have to sell and our people think it's time that we got in on the same business."

Joyce took one of Frumkin's cigarettes and lit it. Part of her couldn't believe what she was hearing. It was as if she were in a movie and she could see Frumkin's words appearing in frames beneath his heavy gestures. But her making it a movie was simply another act of translation, like the way she had shunted her own fear and proximity to violence into domestic banality: the extra care that she now took not to swim out of her depth, or the way that she sometimes hesitated before crossing the street.

"What do you want me to do?"

"There's a British Jew, a Major Lipman, he's more or less in charge of the military store in Jerusalem. The word is that, unlike your friend Kirsch, he's sympathetic—perhaps more than sympathetic. If you wouldn't mind, I'd like you to go back to Jerusalem and make friends with him. If and when the time is right, you'll simply pass him on to the necessary contacts and we'll take it from there. Compared to what you've been up to so far this one's a walk in the park. Oh, and leave the car here. We'll take care of it."

Joyce drew deeply on her cigarette. The whorish intimacy of the assignment depressed her. They were thrusting her back into the female realm, lipstick and laughter; it was the inversion of her solitary nighttime world. Frumkin was asking her to be charming—and she had never been much good at that. A week ago, somewhere near Ramleh, on her last assignment, coasting the last hundred yards down a narrow street toward an appointed rendezvous, her engine and headlights off, blasts of jasmine and honeysuckle filling the air, she had been stopped by a local policeman. Smiling, laughing, she had stepped out of the car, pretending to be a little tipsy, "on my way home from a party in Jaffa . . . pulled over for a cigarette, left the brake off. Silly me!" The young man, happy as all hell, it seemed, to have an attractive woman to talk to, had let her go with a few words of admonishment, and that was the closest she had had to come to charming a stranger.

"Will you do it?"

"I don't know," she replied.

"For Chrissake"—Frumkin tried hard to keep his voice down, but he was fuming—"it's not a fucking game. We're trying to make history here."

Frumkin said this, Joyce thought, exactly as she had heard him say "We're trying to make a movie here" to a recalcitrant actor high on the ramparts of Jerusalem—was it Titus himself?—who was refusing the direction to take his hands off the battlements and wave his arms.

"You know what's going on now," he continued, "and you know what happened right here in Jaffa three years ago. That was a bloody massacre, fifty greenhorns off the boat, five nights in a hostel and then a welcoming committee with knives from your neighbors and guns from your local constabulary. That's who was doing most of the shooting. The fucking Arab police. And people like Kirsch think they have to play it fair. Now imagine if it isn't only the Arab *police* who have the guns, and it already isn't. We have to be armed too. You know that. You obviously believe it. When the time comes the Jews here have to be able to defend themselves. Trust me, when push comes to shove, two hundred British cops aren't going to protect the Jews."

"And when will the time come? Because I don't think I want to be here when it does."

"Not for a while, but it will come. And you will have already done your part, for which everyone will be eternally grateful."

Frumkin stood up. He was well over six foot, heavily muscled in the shoulders but narrow-waisted. The cloth of his shirt was fine, and undoubtedly expensive, but the tight cut made him look something like an overgrown schoolboy.

He circled behind Joyce and put his hands on her shoulders. Softening his tone, he said: "No more gunrunning, all you have to do is meet the major once, and then, if you don't think you can pursue things, you don't have to. What could you possibly lose?"

He lowered his face into her mass of white hair and kissed the back of her head.

"You're a good one, Joycie," he murmured.

30.

Kirsch could walk now with the aid of a cane. If everything went well Dr. Bassan would release him from the hospital at the end of the week. Each day he took himself a little farther around the hospital grounds. This morning he ventured onto the patio. Four beds had been set up to provide sun treatment for tuberculosis patients, but only one was occupied. The beds, narrow four-posters, were draped in rectangular cotton screens with the canopy area left open so the patient could absorb the sun's healing rays in privacy.

He watched a nurse bring out and unfold a camp bed. Before setting it up she rolled up the sleeves of her white uniform. She must have been new, Kirsch thought, because he didn't recognize her. She was sleek and tidy-looking, her skin was pale, and Kirsch imagined that she hadn't been in the country all that long. Her hair was piled high, and twice she stopped what she was doing to pin her white cap more tightly into position. She disappeared through the patio doors, then returned holding a little girl in her arms. The child still had her shoes and black stockings on, her head was wrapped in a black-and-red kerchief. Her legs were stick thin. The nurse laid her patient very gently onto the camp bed. Immediately, the girl turned onto her side and pulled her white shift up to cover her head. The nurse tugged at the sheet.

Kirsch understood the impulse not to be seen. He didn't much want to be seen himself, not by most people, anyway. Nevertheless he couldn't resist the impulse to help. He took a few slow steps across the pebbled courtyard.

"Come on," he said to the girl, "come out of there, the sun's good for you."

"She won't listen," the nurse responded. "Rachel does this every day."

Rachel peeked out from beneath her self-constructed veil. Kirsch guessed she couldn't be more than nine or ten years old.

"I do listen," she said, in heavily accented English, and then she began to cough.

The young nurse pulled at the veil and this time Rachel offered no resistance. She let the nurse wipe the blood and spittle from her mouth. Kirsch looked at Rachel's face. Her long eyes slanted up toward the temples and were riveting in expression. She was going to die, and she knew it.

Kirsch walked to the patio wall and stared down into a neighboring building's roof garden. There was a petrol can covered by an embroidered cloth that served as a table, and on it wildflowers in a jam pot. Kirsch could see through a window into the spotlessly clean and tidy household: a little white bed and books piled on the floor. It was an image of domestic simplicity that, at this moment in his life, adventure having brought him down with a bump, touched him to the core.

"Would you like to live there?"

The nurse was standing at his shoulder.

"Right now I wouldn't mind at all. Although the place I let is rather nice. But this one seems more cheerful, must be because I'm not there."

Immediately, Kirsch regretted his wan expression of self-pity. He wasn't the one coughing up blood.

"I'm sorry," he murmured. "Inexcusable."

He looked at the nurse to see if she had already judged him an egoist. She was smiling. He liked her bright brown eyes and what he thought of as an eagerness in her expression.

"You're allowed to feel sorry for yourself," she said. "You've been here for a long time."

He couldn't make out her accent—Russian perhaps, but already re-tuned by Hebrew.

"I'll guess that you're newer to these premises than I am."

"As it happens I was here when they brought you in."

She had seen him at his worst then, crushed and bloodied.

"What's your name?"

"Mayan."

"I'm Robert Kirsch." Kirsch kept his right hand on the crook of his walking stick and extended his left, but he was a little unsteady and as a result the angle at which he made his offer seemed to invite informal hand-holding rather than a handshake.

Mayan laughed and took his hand in hers.

"Yes, I know who you are," she said.

To fall hopelessly in love with one's nurse was the greatest cliché of all—how many thousands of those back from the war had done it? Robert remembered Marcus's letters home, his paeans to the "tender lights" with their "sleepless passion" for the wounded and the dying. Now it was his turn to see how easily it could be done. And were it not for Joyce he would have fallen already, here and now, on this scorching white Jerusalem afternoon, while the two TB patients scratched a rough orchestral background of coughs and spits.

"Captain Kirsch," a voice called out from the hospital interior, "there's someone here to see you."

He let go of Mayan's hand and turned with the irrepressible expectancy that it was Joyce, even though he knew by now that his hopes would be dashed.

Not Joyce, then, of course, but Ross. The governor stood in his tropical whites holding a bunch of pale lilies and looking for all the world, Kirsch thought, like a colonial version of the angel of the Annunciation. But what had he come to announce? It was, perhaps, Ross's tenth visit to the hospital, and while the content of the first five had inevitably been limited to inquiries as to the state of Kirsch's health, expressions of concern and words of encouragement, the more recent conversations appeared to be circling a subject that Ross couldn't quite bring himself to pounce upon: namely, or so Kirsch imagined, who had shot Robert Kirsch and why? Ross, Kirsch couldn't help but notice, had become a master of the last-minute swerve: discussion of the recent riots would, miraculously, it seemed, lead into the latest cricket news from England; an update on how the police station was managing without Kirsch tumbled randomly, but not awkwardly, into "humorous" anecdotes concerning Ross's recent attempts to train a group of elderly Russian nuns from the Convent of the Ascension to sing Wagner. But Ross, Kirsch felt, need not have bothered to be so enterprising in his narratives. Kirsch should probably have told him that his tactful and politic deviations were a waste of time (he could hear Ross saying to his wife, "The chap must be given time to pull himself together"), as he had no particular interest in having the salient questions about his would-be assassins answered. The truth was that during this entire period of sickness and recovery his mind had been focused entirely elsewhere—on Joyce. But thus far he had said nothing to Ross, preferring to let him find his own way through the thickets of embarrassment that surrounded their meetings.

But here was Ross again, proffering his flowers to Mayan, as if he had brought them for her rather than for Kirsch, and once again Kirsch sensed a nervousness in the governor that implied the strain of avoidance.

"Well, you're certainly looking a lot better, color's back in your cheeks, walking with only a cane. Can't imagine they'll be able to keep you here much longer."

"Bassan said the end of the week."

"Home for the Sabbath."

Kirsch smiled. He couldn't remember another time when Ross had made direct reference to the fact that Kirsch was a Jew. "That would be nice," he said.

Mayan went in search of a vase.

Ross and Kirsch walked down a white-walled corridor and sat in two battered leather armchairs situated in a vestibule close to one of the children's wards: a mural before them showed the Pied Piper of Hamelin as a black silhouette with children of diminishing size following him out of town. Above them a ceiling fan revolved slowly and ineffectively. Ross's upper lip glowed with perspiration.

"There's something I've been meaning to talk to you about."

Ross coughed, then continued: "The day you were shot, you remember I'd phoned you. I needed to talk to you about something we were, still are, worried about. It's an ugly problem: guns coming in from all over the place, getting through at the ports, disappearing from army supplies. We caught three of our chaps—court-martialed them; one was a captain, Jeremy Billings over in Ashdod. The guns go to both sides, to whoever comes up with the money—and the sniper who took a potshot at you could have been Arab or Jew, although I have a hunch that it's the Jews who have it in for you. At any rate, at the time I rang you we didn't have a lot to go on. I was going to ask you to get involved, do a little sleuthing, make some inquiries, have you try to pin down who's running things in Jerusalem, find out who's taking bribes, look into who's doing the smuggling and who's bringing the damn weapons in. But here's the awkward thing."

Ross paused for a moment as Mayan wheeled past a trolley laden with medicines. Without thinking, Kirsch shifted in his seat, as if to turn his wasted leg away from her.

"A week ago, about two a.m., one of our your fellow officers, Francis Athill—he's out of Jaffa, but perhaps you've met?"

"No," Kirsch said.

"Well, he stopped a car in a Ramleh back street out near the cemetery, vehicle rolling along with no lights: the driver, to his and my surprise, was Mrs. Bloomberg."

Kirsch felt as if someone were choking him, but he managed to get out a derisory "And?"

"Well, 'and' not a lot, really," Ross continued somewhat sheepishly. "Said she'd been to a party or something. As it happens there are not a lot of parties going on right now. Still, perhaps she's lonely, both of you away, so to speak." Ross said this without the irony that Kirsch had anticipated.

"And were there guns in the car?" Kirsch said, laughing.

"Absolutely no idea. Athill decided not to take a look."

There was an awkward pause. Kirsch raised his eyebrows as if to ask, "End of story?"

Ross ran his hands through his thin gray hair, accentuating his widow's peak. "Well, I'm not being entirely forthcoming. In this kind of situation Athill was under instructions not to search. We know there are couriers, but what we really need to know are their points of departure and destination. Look. I know this sounds like rubbish and I'd be happier than anyone to learn that Mrs. Bloomberg has nothing to do with any underground activities."

"It's ridiculous."

"Maybe so, but not ridiculous that you were almost killed. The bullets fired at you came from an M17. They don't make those weapons here, and they're not ours either. It's a U.S. Enfield out of Ilion, New York. Our latecoming allies stored away about a million of these rifles in their government arsenal at the end of the war. Not surprising that some are going astray."

"Oh, and Joyce took a little detour and picked a few up on her way over from Southampton?"

"I understand that you're angry. And listen, as I said, there's no strong evidence to suggest that she's mixed up in any of this. Nevertheless I've had to keep a watch on her. She is a Zionist, you know, Mark made that quite clear to me. She's far more committed than he is."

"And what has your surveillance come up with?" Kirsch asked disdainfully. He had never talked to a superior this way before, but what did he have to lose?

"Nothing at all. And you may not think so, but I'm glad to be able to tell you that. Look, they're *friends* of mine. For God's sake, I'm probably her husband's biggest admirer in Jerusalem. And by the way, has she been here?"

"I'm not sure I'd tell you if she had. But I imagine the nursing staff can fill you in."

"They say you've had only one female visitor. Your cousin Sarah, I believe. But perhaps there was an occasion when they were mistaken."

Kirsch gave Ross a look of absolute disgust.

"I'm sorry, old chap. I had to ask. Cartwright's dead. You nearly swallowed a bullet. I'm trying to do the best for my men, for now and for the future, and what's more this thing is already out of hand, and we have to close it down. The PM's extremely unhappy with these bloody riots, the Americans are leaning on him about the Jews, the Foreign Office is over at No. 10 arguing for the Arabs. Joyce Bloomberg may be a small cog in a large machine, or no cog at all, but I have to follow through."

"So you had your riots after all," Kirsch muttered.

"What's that?"

"De Groot. Surely you haven't forgotten, sir. You shut down the investigation so we wouldn't have an eruption on our hands. And now you have one anyway."

Kirsch's leg throbbed. The pain came less frequently now, but when it did he felt sick to his stomach.

Ross measured his words carefully before responding. "I think," he began, "that once you are released from here you might consider taking a week or two off. Convalescence would do you good. You've been through a lot."

After Ross had left the hospital Kirsch, dizzied by the information that he had received, made his way outside, returned to the edge of the walled patio and sucked in a few deep breaths. He looked down: the idyllic room and roof garden below all of a sudden seemed horribly pinched, the flowers in the jam pot signaling a pathetic attempt to enliven incontrovertibly cramped quarters. Behind him Rachel woke and immediately began to cry. A nurse, less regarding than Mayan, ignored the child and walked swiftly across the gravel to attend to another patient. Kirsch touched his hand to his leg. Had Joyce provided the gun that had crippled him? Was it possible? It couldn't be so. Rachel's cries grew louder. As if in response a dog began to bark in the street. Kirsch stared down at the room. A woman entered, she put down a bag of groceries, took two steps, and sat on the edge of the bed. There must have been a mirror on one of the walls that Kirsch couldn't see, for the woman adopted the posture of someone who was looking at herself. She was middle-aged, wearing a long black dress, plump but not unattractive. He watched her raise her hands to the back of her neck and then, to his astonishment, she lifted off her hair. Under the wig she was completely bald. He felt a moment's revulsion. Nothing in this bloody place was as it appeared to be.

Thursday, and it was almost time for Dr. Bassan's late-afternoon round. A parched light filtered through the shutters. The other denizens of Kirsch's ward, three men—two Arabs, one Jew—who had been involved in the same traffic accident on the Jaffa road involving a donkey cart and a motorbike, lay dozing under their tented mosquito netting. Kirsch, who usually slept at this hour, was wide awake. He sat up in his bed and stared at the oil lamp that hung low from the center of the ceiling. When night fell it threw deviant shadows onto the tiled floor. In his first days at Shaarei Zedek, running a high fever from his infected leg, frequently delirious, and, as Bassan had later informed him, close to death, he had spent hours watching these shadows perform their danse macabre. They took him out of Jerusalem and ran him smartly back to his bedroom in London. He was six years old and in bed with the measles in the attic room that he shared with Marcus. Their father's battered old gardening hat hung on the back of the door and became by turns a grotesque face and an executioner's mask. Robert couldn't fall asleep until his mother removed it. His nice, softhearted mother who sang to him, stroked the hair back from his forehead, and brought him oranges that she peeled around the middle before slicing the fruit in two so that her younger son could suck the juice more easily. It was almost worth being ill to have your mother act this way.

And yet quickly, within days, both his dark shifting visions and the dream of maternal protectorship that they engendered had gone. In their place Kirsch had indulged a developing fantasy, fueled by Joyce's absence, of a life with her that was perfectly balanced between passion and domestic bliss. In this version, utterly predictable, he knew, the *contained* Joyce lost nothing of her wildness. (Where were they living? A flat in London—on that new road he had once ridden down on his bicycle near Wandsworth Common? Or perhaps a cottage in the countryside? That village beyond Ledbury out in Gloucestershire where, out on a ramble with friends, he had met some Americans—his first!—in the local pub?) Kirsch even found himself imagining introducing Joyce to his parents and being proud of the facts that she was divorced (which, of course, she wasn't), without direction, and older than he—all signs, certainly from his parents' point of view, of her complete unsuitability for their son. But now Ross's visit had all but put paid to these consolatory daydreams.

Dr. Bassan hurried into the ward accompanied by the head nurse. He wore a soft cotton shirt with a wide-open collar. The heat that exhausted everybody else never seemed to bother him. During the war he had worked at the old Anglican Hospital, sporting a Turkish crescent on his sleeve and a skullcap on his head. Kirsch had seen the photograph in Bassan's office. The bedspreads at the Anglican, Bassan had told Kirsch, were magnificent: "They decorated the ward like a concubine's palace— wall hangings, plants, glass decanters for your water."

The nurse roused the sleeping patients, who grunted and yawned into wakefulness. Bassan approached Kirsch's bed.

"You're not looking too happy."

Kirsch tried to smile. He liked Bassan, and it wasn't only the inevitable gratitude of the patient that drew him to appreciate the doctor, but also the straightforwardness of his personality. Bassan came from an old local family, brought from Vilna to Jerusalem by his great-grandfather more than a century ago, and his rootedness in this city of errant Jews and noisy new arrivals seemed to manifest itself as an engagingly quiet self-confidence. Bassan was of the place; even the Arab patients seemed to recognize this. And whenever Kirsch talked with him he felt calmed, *shaded*. Kirsch was well aware that, to a degree, he must have romanticized Bassan, and that in all probability the doctor's sterling character had nothing to do with his family past. Nevertheless, every time Kirsch saw Bassan approach the ward he succumbed to the notion, real or illusory, that in the doctor's powerful, squat figure the generations had molded a golem of kindness and integrity.

"Let's see if I can cheer you up," Bassan said. "First, I hear you've been walking all over the hospital, and second, that you have been holding hands with the nurses. These are both signs that you are ready to go home."

Kirsch laughed. "Only one nurse," he replied. "I don't have the courage for more."

"Ready?" Bassan asked.

A nurse came over and drew the screens around Kirsch's bed. She turned down the sheet. Kirsch pulled up his robe and exposed his left leg: thin as a celery stick and scarred from ankle to thigh. Bassan took a long, slow look and then proceeded to test Kirsch's range of motion, stretching and bending the leg. Kirsch grimaced, but the pain was bearable. For weeks Bassan had performed operation after operation to save Kirsch's leg. He had scraped away at the devitalized tissue, removing layer after layer. Without Bassan's meticulous surgery Kirsch would undoubtedly have succumbed to tetanus. There were other doctors, Kirsch knew, who had recommended immediate amputation.

"Let's see you take a walk," Bassan said. "Can you try without the cane?"

Kirsch swung his legs off the bed, rose and took a few halting steps across the ward.

"Don't worry," Bassan told him. "You'll wind up with a slight limp, that's all. Considering the alternatives when you came in here, that's not too bad, is it? Right now, it's your muscles that need strengthening. And to do that, let's get you out of this place. It's been a long road. Now it's up to you. The more walking you do the better. You can start this Friday night, walk over tomorrow from your house to mine for Shabbat dinner."

"That's so very kind of you. I owe you so much."

Bassan dismissed Kirsch's gratitude with a wave of his hand.

"That's settled, then. Come as close to six as you can. My wife lights the candles on time. If you see three stars in the sky, you're late."

The doctor moved across the room where his three other patients, victims of the clash between modernity and its enemies—was it the motorbike or the cart that had done the damage? Kirsch had been unable to ascertain the details of the accident—lay waiting for him.

Were it not for Joyce, Kirsch would have been in a state of high ela- tion. After all, he had been in the hospital for almost two months. Seven weeks of waiting for her. Could he even remember what she looked like? Her lovely face, which had seemed to Kirsch a pledge of Joyce's inner self, was blurred in his memory. But what was that inner self? As soon as he was dressed and packed he would go straight to her cottage, warn her that Ross was after her, hear her side of things. The story had to be nonsense.

In the dusty rose twilight Kirsch walked with care through the hospi- tal courtyard and out into the street. He navigated a pathway overgrown with burdock and nettles and skirted a dilapidated building with a rusty roof and half-collapsed chimney. After weeks indoors, the first blast of a nearby car horn came loud as Joshua's trumpet. Kirsch started, then steadied himself against the slats of a gray wooden fence. And then he remembered Frumkin's limousine driver parked down the road from Bloomberg's cottage gate, honking the horn. It was the last time that he had seen Joyce. She was going off to the desert to work as Frumkin's prop girl. Or was she? He had to find her now.

But Kirsch had no strength to get to Talpiot. As soon as he was back in his flat he collapsed onto the bed and slept. He awoke at mid-morning the next day covered in sweat (there was no fan above his bed to cool him, as there had been in the hospital), only to fall back asleep almost immediately. By the time he woke again it was late afternoon. The air rang with what sounded like gunshots, but the noise emanated from soldiers in Jerusalem's domestic army: Friday-afternoon housewives out on their balconies beating carpets, cleaning house before the Sabbath. Kirsch's throat was dry. He got out of bed carefully, walked into his kitchen, bent over the sink and turned on the tap. The water dripped out brown. Kirsch let it run until the color had improved to cloudy white and then he drank, stopping from time to time to let the water run over his head. There was no food in the flat, but no matter, he had an invitation for dinner, if only he could make it to Bassan's house.

Kirsch, washed, shaved and dressed, all without too much difficulty. The stairs down to the garden offered a challenge, but he made it safely. Once there, he paused in the shade of an olive tree whose uppermost branches reached the windows of his room. His downstairs neighbor, Dr. Klausner, a retired theologian from Germany, had planted hardy climbing roses in the narrow patch of earth that led up to the fence. The pink flowers were blooming, weakly, for the second time this summer, but Kirsch could still smell the heady scent that always seemed strongest at this time of day. Looking around, he felt as if he had been away from his place for years rather than weeks. Already out of breath from his awkward descent, he wondered if perhaps he had been wrong to send Sarah away. She could have helped him with shopping for a few days, got him back on his feet. But of course, he hadn't wanted Sarah and Michael to get in the way of his relationship with Joyce, and Michael, good-natured though he was, had been getting on his nerves. The Corks had been too polite, naturally, to ask about his love life. Or perhaps Sarah was being delicate; after all, the last time she had seen Robert at home in England he was engaged to be married.

He thought that he had given himself plenty of time for the walk to Bassan's home, which he estimated at only half a mile or so, but he found it necessary to take frequent rests, more than he had imagined, and by the time that he found the house on Habashim Street daylight was failing and the sky was dark with the first bruises of night.

The dinner table was set for four but Kirsch and the Bassans were the only people present. Bassan had given Kirsch a warm hug as he came in the door and then introduced his wife, a robust-looking woman whose long black hair was coiled into a smooth bun on the top of her round head. Kirsch watched as Bassan poured water from a pitcher over his hands and murmured a blessing. The walls were hung with dark framed photographs of family members, and a series of brightly colored whimsical primitivist paintings of the local milieu: swarthy goatherds in brimless pioneer hats, scattered red-roofed houses in Tel Aviv, each with a vivid blue door.

"We collect this artist," Bassan said.

There was an upright piano in one of the corners, and next to it a spider plant on a wooden stand. Kirsch had imagined a richer tapestry for the doctor's home life, but the only striking element in the room was its burnt-orange floor tiles.

There was a knock at the door.

"Ah," Bassan said, "she's here."

Mayan entered. She was wearing a very up-to-the-minute low-waisted white chemise, a cheaper version, Kirsch guessed, of the dress that Joyce had on when he had first taken her on his motorbike. The incongruities of fashion in Jerusalem never ceased to amaze him. With the addition of a long string of pearls Mayan might have been on her way out to a dance in London. And, God, Kirsch might have been accompanying her if he hadn't set his sights so firmly to the east.

"You look surprised," she said to Kirsch.

Bassan and his wife both laughed.

Kirsch looked at them, and then back at Mayan.

"No, no, Robert, she's not our daughter. But she is a newcomer to Palestine."

Mayan extended her hand and Kirsch, wanting to avoid a repeat of their rooftop confusion, gripped it far too hard, as if he were shaking on an important business deal.

Mayan laughed. "I'm happy to see that you have your strength back," she said.

Bassan handed Kirsch a skullcap. Kirsch put in on. He hadn't worn one since the day of his bar mitzvah; then as now the covering sat uneasily on his head. Bassan intoned the blessings over the bread and the wine. From time to time Kirsch's father, guided by a moment's nostalgia, or a desire to please Kirsch's mother, had engaged the family in Friday-night rituals, but they were always performed with a nod and a wink to the boys. Rain on the windowpanes and the taste of sweet wine. Jews in London, halfhearted, but still Jews. Would Kirsch have had it any differently? That great pillar faith, on which you could lean your misery and get support, had thus far eluded him, but so it seemed had a number of life's other familiar consolations: politics, art, business. To all outward appearances a young man who knew where he was going—uniformed, authoritative, composed—Kirsch most frequently apprehended himself only as a fool for love. How on earth had he got this way?

Kirsch looked across the table at Mayan. She was responding to a question from Bassan's wife about her family in Odessa. Her face grew serious. The news wasn't good: postrevolutionary Russia was turning out to be as bad for the Jews as life under the czars had been. Her Uncle Isaac, a small-time trinket merchant, had already been labeled a parasite by the Bolsheviks. Her father, a mild-mannered bookseller, now found himself in perhaps the most dangerous job of all.

Kirsch gazed at Mayan. Not a flapper, then, not even remotely close to one. She had missed the postwar party—hats in the air, everyone!— and so, of course, had he. The difference was that he had done so through choice. He couldn't dance and drink after Marcus had been killed, and even three years later his parents were still spreading their gloom over him, black clouds wherever he went. He'd had to get away.

"And now, Mayan, if I'm not mistaken, you have a week's holiday coming up."

Bassan was carving the roast chicken. As his profession dictated, he was deft with the knife.

"Yes, I have a friend from home who is living in Rosh Pinah. I'm going to visit her."

Bassan handed Kirsch a plate.

"Have you seen the northern part of the country, Robert?"

Good God! Bassan was matchmaking! And Mrs. Bassan was smiling at Kirsch across the table in a horribly expectant manner. Christ, he could see that she already had him married off to Mayan and bouncing a couple of kids on his knees. The good doctor and his wife were investing in the Jewish future of Palestine, and Kirsch was their bond. He wanted no part of it.

"I've heard Rosh Pinah's a bit of a dead village," he replied. "Set up with Rothschild money, wasn't it?"

He was sorry as soon as he had spoken. He sounded like an awful snob.

"Yes," Mayan said, "you're quite right, a haven for us poor persecuted Russian Jews. We have to take what we can."

Kirsch saw in her eyes that she understood everything—both the Bassans' eagerness and his adolescent response to it. She was telling him, "This has nothing to do with me," and suddenly, Joyce notwithstanding, he somewhat regretted that such was the case.

Dinner conversation ebbed and flowed, mainly around the subject of the hospital and its personalities: doctors, staff, and patients. It was a warm night and through the room's open windows came the sounds of the neighbors' families and their guests, gathered to eat and talk: the scrape of cutlery, voices raised and lowered, snatches of prayer, the silver shower of a young girl's song and the harsh gutturals of her elders. There were, too, the smells of cooking, odors that mixed strangely with the too-sweet scent of honeysuckle rising from bushes that overgrew the walls of Bassan's house. Kirsch felt suddenly unutterably tired, as if, after the deprivations of the hospital, he was suffering from an overdose to his senses. He got shakily to his feet.

"I'm sorry," he said, "but I really need to get some air."

Bassan was quickly at his side. "Of course, of course. Your first night out. We mustn't exhaust you."

Mayan stood, too. "I'll go with him," she said. "I'll walk him back. Don't worry."

"Yes," Kirsch murmured, "perhaps I will go home."

They walked side by side at Kirsch's slow pace down the slope toward Jaffa Road. He found it harder to use the cane on downhill stretches and was embarrassed by his awkwardness. Occasionally Mayan lightly touched his arm, as if to balance him. They stopped at the curbside. Above them the sky unfurled its nighttime banner: black ground with stars and crescent moon. Jerusalem's reply was the city's single traffic light. While Kirsch caught his breath the light changed to red. A car that had been speeding down the road skidded to a halt. The driver, head thrown back, laughing riotously, was a uniformed British officer and beside him sat a woman with long hair, her face half invisible to Kirsch and

Mayan; with her outstretched hand she was caressing the back of the man's head. It was Joyce! Or was it? The light went green and the car accelerated forward with a screech.

Kirsch felt his head spin. He broke into a sweat and his knees buckled. Mayan half caught his weight and helped him to sit by the roadside.

"Put your head down."

He obeyed. Gradually, his dizziness passed, but when he tried to stand Mayan put her hand firmly on his shoulder.

"Wait," she said.

He didn't have the strength to resist her.

Eventually she let him get to his feet. They walked on up the hill in the direction of Kirsch's flat. The air seemed to get heavier and warmer, as if someone had opened an oven door and released heat into a room that was already baking. By the time they reached his garden gate Kirsch had convinced himself that it was Joyce whom he had seen in the car.

He turned to Mayan. "Thank you so very much," he said. "You shouldn't have to be a nurse in your off-hours."

"Don't worry," she replied. "No special skills were involved."

"And listen," Kirsch cut in, a little quicker than he had wanted to, "that trip you're taking, I wondered, well, would you mind if I tagged along? Ross has given me a couple of weeks and Dr. Bassan's ordered me to get some walking in and . . ."

"I'll think about it," Mayan said firmly.

Kirsch's face fell.

"Oh, of *course* you can come"—she laughed—"as long as you promise not to bring the Rothschilds. Really, it would be too humiliating."

"You know," Kirsch said, "your English is truly remarkable."

Mayan laughed. "I was in Dublin for six months before I could get here. I lived in Rathgar." She pronounced it with a roll of the "r"s, in a way that made it sound to Kirsch like one of the most exciting places on earth. "Have you been there ever? Almost all the Jews are in the same neighborhood. My aunt owned Shrier's bakery on the Walworth Road. There is a pub next door, The Bull and Finch."

"And did you go into it?"

"A Jewish girl in the pub? The neighbors wouldn't have approved."

"No, I suppose not."

"So I only went in when I needed a drink."

Kirsch laughed. He had an impulse to kiss Mayan, but Joyce's face floated before him like a reproof, and even though at that moment he hated Joyce from the bottom of his heart, he held back.

"When do we leave?" he asked.

"The next bus is tomorrow evening, after the Sabbath."

"Well, I'll be there," he said.

Mayan began to walk away, then stopped and turned around. "Who was the woman in the car?"

"Someone else's wife."

"And you love her?"

"I thought I did."

Mayan nodded her head as if the answer, while not altogether satisfactory, would do for the moment.

"I'll see you tomorrow, then," she said.

Kirsch watched her until she turned the corner of his street and then he went up to his room. There was an envelope pinned to his door. Kirsch took it down and put it in his trouser pocket. He walked to his kitchen table, lit a candle and sat down. He slit open the envelope and removed an official-looking piece of paper covered in a very unofficial-looking hasty scrawl: "Heard you were out. Good show. Need to talk to you. Matter of some urgency. Please get in touch asap. Ross."

Kirsch rolled the letter into a ball and threw it away.

31.

In the rear half of his borrowed Ford with its top rolled back, Bloomberg had his painting wrapped in a heavy cloth sack. The car had come courtesy of Freddie Peake. That had not been a problem; the Pasha still had his Rolls, two Vauxhalls, and a Sunbeam, and he knew that once Bloomberg's painting had been delivered to Government House Ross could be relied upon to get the Ford back to him.

Bloomberg drove into Jerusalem around mid-morning. The larger military presence in the city was immediately visible: two armored cars stood parked outside the Damascus Gate in a space normally occupied by vendors offering figs and plums. Bloomberg skirted the walls of the Old City and turned onto Jaffa Road. After the silence of the desert he found the busyness of the shops and their customers to be dispiriting. Neither did he much care for the tiled roofs and small houses of the modern suburb that was expanding on either side of the thoroughfare; except for one or two buildings, the Jerusalem beyond the Old City walls was a place to disillusion the sentimentalist.

Before driving home to Talpiot he thought he'd stop in at the Allenby for a drink. He parked the car, leaving his painting on the backseat. The bar, at that time of day, was generally deserted, although the lunchtime crowd would soon find its way in: the American bankers and the Dutch engineers, agricultural experts from France, Germans selling machinery, anyone who was speculating on the new Palestine. Now he too was a man on a mission. Bloomberg patted his shirt pocket. The button was still there, wrapped in a torn square of canvas.

He approached the tall Sudanese doorman in his white robes and asked him to keep an eye on the car and its contents. In the lobby he recognized George Saphir, a reporter for the English-language *Palestine Bulletin*. He was deep in conversation with a bearded, black-veiled figure who Bloomberg guessed was the Armenian Archimandrite. Bloomberg had met Saphir at one of Ross's gatherings. The journalist, fresh out from England, had expressed an interest in doing a piece on Bloomberg and his Jerusalem paintings, but the project hadn't got off the ground. Saphir's bosses, the editors of the *Bulletin*, had little interest once it was revealed to them that Bloomberg had abandoned his Zionist commission to make paintings of local churches.

Bloomberg intended to pass Saphir by without speaking, but the young man abruptly looked up from his conversation as if he had known that Bloomberg was approaching.

"Mark!"

Saphir rose from his seat. The two men shook hands.

"When did you get back? How are the great temples? Ross has been bragging to everyone that he's about to own a masterpiece."

"This morning, got in this morning." Bloomberg felt that his voice had grown rusty through lack of use.

"Well, I'd love to buy you a drink and hear all about the trip. How long are you going to be propping up the bar?"

Saphir turned to the priest.

"Oh, I'm sorry, this is Father Pantelides. Father, Mark Bloomberg, the painter."

Not Armenian, then, but Greek.

"Father Pantelides has just passed on to me some information that might interest you. He tells me that our governor is on his way out. The rumor is a transfer to Cyprus. There's trouble brewing there, and they want to get Sir Gerald in early. Father Pantelides is just back from Nicosia."

"Sir Gerald will be the governor there, it is absolutely certain." The priest smiled. "Perhaps he will bring you to paint Cyprus."

Everyone, it seemed, knew that Bloomberg was a gun for hire.

"Perhaps I'll go myself," Bloomberg replied.

"How's your wife?" Saphir put in. "Haven't seen her about at all. Still, as you may have heard, nightlife in Jerusalem has got worse than ever. Probably more going on in Petra."

Saphir took a sideways look at the priest, who did not appear remotely offended.

"They even thought about canceling the teatime orchestra here at the hotel because nobody showed up during the riots. Wouldn't have been much of a loss, I admit, but dammit we have to have music."

"As far as I know my wife's fine," Bloomberg replied.

"Ah, then you haven't seen her yet; a little fortification first, that's the ticket. How long have you been away? Two months?" Saphir winked at Bloomberg.

Bloomberg went into the bar and ordered a double whisky. His funds were running low, but there were more than enough piastres left for a couple of drinks, and in any case Ross was about to replenish the war chest. The bartender poured the drink and Bloomberg swigged it back. The whisky burned his throat and felt good. A month ago the news that Ross was leaving Palestine would have come as both relief and a cause for panic—money had to come in from somewhere—but now he greeted it with indifference. He had lost his connection to Ross out in the desert, abandoned him at the moment that he had begun to paint his abstraction of the high place.

After a while Saphir came in to join him. He was, Bloomberg guessed, in his mid-twenties, a talker and a bubbly enthusiast for the Zionist cause. Bloomberg suspected that if he had any success as a journalist it would derive from the fact that his interviewees were unlikely to take him seriously—and that being so, they would relax and reveal their most precious secrets. Since coming to Palestine, Saphir, a Manchester University history graduate, had adopted the highly credentialed look of an agricultural worker: heavy boots, dark knee socks, khaki shorts, and a blue work shirt. He was betrayed, however, by his pale skin and soft hands.

The intervening moments had transformed Saphir, who, since the conclusion of his conversation with Father Pantelides, had grown gloomy.

"God, there are days when I miss England," he said.

Bloomberg had noticed before how Jews who were committed to Palestine frequently seemed nostalgic for their countries of origin, whereas Jews like him, who had no special passion for the place, were equally phlegmatic about their native lands. Perhaps enthusiasm for place, irrespective of politics, was itself an aspect of personality.

"What do you miss?" Bloomberg asked.

Saphir removed his spectacles and wiped them on his shirt. "It's hard to say. Things here are unrelenting, that's what makes them so exciting, but also so exhausting. You know, Saturday afternoons at home I'd like to relax and go and watch a football game."

"It was a football that started the riots here, wasn't it?"

"My point exactly."

A young man in a white turban peered into the bar and then moved quickly away.

"Listen," Bloomberg said, "have you heard anything new about the De Groot case?"

Saphir was looking toward the door, immediately distracted.

"De Groot? Oh yes, I forgot your involvement. No word there, the whole thing's more or less forgotten, especially now. Robert Kirsch was in charge of the investigation, and he's been shot. Poor bastard. Perhaps you heard?"

"His cousin came to see me."

"Really?" Saphir said, still staring past Bloomberg. "Look, I do believe that's the mufti. I wonder what he's doing here? I'm sorry, Mark. I was hoping we'd have time but . . . duty calls."

"So they've made no progress at all?"

"The Kirsch shooting? It's been weeks. God knows who pulled the trigger. Your friend Sir Gerald is the man to ask, and as of now he's on his way to Damascus. Off for a few days antiquities hunting with his wife, I believe. I expect he'll announce the Cyprus move when he returns."

Bloomberg didn't bother to repeat his question about De Groot.

"Well, nice to see you," Saphir said.

The relationship was always slightly awkward, Bloomberg thought, between the Jews who were staying and those who were only passing through: the reason, he suspected, was that no one was ever quite sure to which group they belonged.

Saphir walked quickly out of the bar in pursuit of his quarry.

Bloomberg ordered another double, gulped it down, then went outside. Should he drive to North Talpiot, or first pursue his business in the Old City? The sun was a white disk and the heat of the day, turning on the wheel of summer's end, floated like a wave over the city. Bloomberg's eyes were red and his mouth, despite the liquor, still tasted of sand. A lorry laden with building materials skirted a parked car and, out of habit rather than need, the driver leaned loudly on his horn. Bloomberg clapped his hands to his ears; sucking deep breaths, sweating profusely, and feeling that somehow a decision on where to go next had been made for him, he stumbled and swayed down the Jaffa Road in the direction of the Old City.

He entered blindly through the Jaffa Gate, shielding his eyes against the sun. The shutters of most of the stalls in the bazaar had been pulled down for the duration of the afternoon siesta, but some were only half or three-quarters of the way closed and offered, like seductively lifted skirts, a glimpse of their wares: a half sack of pistachios, thin crescents from a stack of copper plates, bottles of rosewater cut off at the neck. Saud had given Bloomberg directions to his mother's home, but finding the place was another story. The suq, once entered, demanded that you got lost, and for most of its visitors the obligatory derangement was a happy state: pilgrim, tourist or local shopper, the warren of alleyways would lead you eventually to the place that you sought, even if, at the outset of your journey, you were hardly aware that you had a destination in mind. In the first days after their arrival in Jerusalem Bloomberg had moved indifferently through the maze of the bazaar, but he had heard from Joyce how its objects—a rug, or gold-embroidered kerchief, or apricot papers—searched you out, rather than the other way round. He had dismissed such talk as romantic hokum, but now he saw how the feeling might be true. A donkey guided by a small boy clopped on the cobblestones in front of him, stopping once to unleash a powerful stream of yellow piss onto the wall of a long low-roofed windowless building that seemed to have its back to the alley. Eventually Bloomberg arrived near the Street of Chains without at all knowing how he had got there. Here the market was enclosed and its pink domed ceiling vaulted to a narrow opening that allowed light to fall in a bright shaft, as in an Old Master's rendition of celestial beams descending. Bloomberg, standing in the halo, laughed to himself: how his friends from the East End would have loved this moment, the arrival of St. Mark in Jerusalem.

He climbed two flights of broad, chipped and broken stone steps and knocked on the al-Sayyids' door. A skinny boy, no more than nine or ten, came to answer; his eyes were clouded by trachoma and there were little scars on the surface of his lids. Bloomberg peered past him into the home. He was about to ask for Saud's mother but the boy reached out and took him by the arm.

"Come," he said. "Yes, come."

He drew Bloomberg inside, tugging gently on his arm using the method of a dealer in the bazaar as he brought an anxious customer into the back of his shop to view a prize piece.

In the middle of the room was a round wooden table mounted on a wooden base but also supported by two stone blocks. A single low-backed chair was set against one of the walls. Five or six rectangular straw mats covered the cement floor.

The boy gestured for Bloomberg to sit in the chair, and then he disappeared into a back room. Sunlight sieved through motionless curtains. Across from Bloomberg someone had piled about a dozen thin checkered mattresses onto a narrow bed: they were kept in place by what looked like the frame of an old walnut bookshelf. On the floor stood various skins and jars, vessels for carrying wine, water, or milk. On the table there was a small copper bowl that held cactus fruit.

A few moments passed until the boy reappeared holding a copper coffeepot which he set down on the floor. Soon after, a woman came in, bringing with her a small plate of figs. She wore a long-sleeved black muslin dress, but her head was bare. Her long black hair was parted in the middle and tied into plaits. Was this Saud's mother? Bloomberg had expected an older woman.

"Mark," he said pointing at himself in a way that he knew was unutterably foolish, "Mark Bloomberg."

"She is Leila," the boy replied on behalf of his mother, "and I am Ahmad."

Bloomberg tried as best he could to explain who he was and what had happened to Saud. The woman and the boy both spoke a few words of English, and understood enough for Bloomberg to be able to communicate that Saud had been working for him, that he was alive and well and traveling to Cairo. More than once the mother got tears in her eyes. Bloomberg felt frustrated by his lack of Arabic. He had been a fool to come alone. He should have brought someone to translate for him. But whom could he have trusted to do that?

He drank the sweetened coffee, embarrassed that he had come empty-handed into the home. Was there nothing that he could give these people except difficult news?

Bloomberg smiled at Leila. "Thank you," he said.

There was a half-embroidered blouse on the floor, and nearby a small pile of linens waiting to be worked on. Bloomberg thought of his own mother sitting in weak light in the front room of their house on Christian Street, squinting, her fingers callused from sewing. And yet he could rarely imagine or remember his mother as young as this woman. For Bloomberg, his mother was almost always gray-haired, if still compact and resilient, like some tiny Atlas holding up her corner of the world. He had an overwhelming impulse to let Saud's mother know that he too came from a family who worked with buttons and zippers and spools of thread, but his yearning to communicate this connection would have to remain locked in his heart.

He stayed for perhaps an hour, desperately trying through repeated sentences and exaggerated gestures to reassure Leila of her son's well-being. He knew from Saud that the police must have visited their house, knew too that, for whatever reason, Ross had decided to let Saud go.

It was cool in the room. Bloomberg fell silent. Leila offered him the plate of figs and he took one. Instead of returning the copper bowl to the table she placed it on the floor, then she knelt by the table and gave a twist to the top. It shifted slightly to reveal that the wooden base was hollow. She said something to Ahmad; the boy reached in his hand and, one by one, retrieved four battered-looking books and one that was in better condition. Ahmad stacked the books in a pile and handed them to Bloomberg.

"Please," Leila said. "For Saud."

She spoke in Arabic to Ahmad.

"She wants you to bring them to Saud," he translated.

"But I'm not . . . ," Bloomberg began, but cut himself off in midsentence. "Yes," he replied, "I'll get them to him."

He looked at the spines: a geometry textbook, an English grammar primer, a poetry anthology, and two thin volumes entitled *Weespraak* and *Beemdgras*. Bloomberg opened to the flyleaf of one of the Dutch books. There he read an elaborate dedication from De Groot to Saud, not exactly a declaration of love, but close enough in feeling; certainly there was warmth, friendliness, and encouragement.

Bloomberg flicked through the anthology of English poetry. The dog-eared pages posted its reader's favorite places: "I met a traveller from an antique land," "Crabbed age and youth cannot live together." Bloomberg put down the poetry and picked up the other book of Dutch poems. It didn't look as if it had been read. As he opened it a folded piece of paper fell out. Bloomberg spread the sheet; it was the carbon copy of a letter addressed to the Colonial Office in London and signed by De Groot. Bloomberg glanced quickly at the contents, read through the letter more carefully, then refolded it and put it back in the book.

Leila and Ahmad watched him but out of either fear or trust, Bloomberg couldn't tell which; neither of them spoke.

"I have to go," Bloomberg said.

He patted the cover of the book. "Don't worry," he said, "it's nothing."

Saud's mother stood. Bloomberg held out his hand but she modestly lowered her eyes. Impulsively, he took two steps forward and hugged the little boy.

Bloomberg descended the stone stairway and turned into the suq. The alleyways were still more or less deserted. He hurried toward the Jaffa Gate, holding the books to his chest. De Groot had information so dangerous that it had got him killed. And now Bloomberg knew it too.

32.

"Come on, hop in," Lipman shouted cheerfully. "We don't want to miss the first race. It's the most important."

His voice had the timbre and inflection of Mark's. They probably hailed from the same part of London. Over the years Joyce had become fairly adept, if not expert, at identifying English accents, so finely discriminated by class, region, district and even, so Mark always claimed, religion.

She walked down the path, and there was Johnny Lipman, her stooge, standing by his car, grinning. He rushed around to hold the passenger door open for Joyce, performing an exaggerated bow as he did so.

"Milady," he said.

Joyce got in.

Lipman was almost six feet tall but didn't look it because while his torso was elongated, his legs were surprisingly short. He had a large head topped with thinning brown hair, a fact that he seemed to find amusing (the previous night he had encouraged Joyce to touch his bald spot—as if the experience might excite her!), but his gray eyes were rather hard and Joyce didn't altogether trust him. Of course, it should have been Lipman worrying about her dependability, and not the other way round. He had also brought to her attention a scar on the bridge of his nose, as if his face and head were fascinating old maps: "Walked into a greenhouse door when I was five. At least it wasn't a shithouse."

Joyce had hoped that the morning following her "date" with Lipman would be fresh and springlike. She had wanted to wake up to air that had been scrubbed clean of every scent except the wash of dawn showers, but instead there arrived the inevitable hot, oppressive August day, sun beating down, her body already soaked in sweat, and the cottage that she was newly returned to pervaded by an extraordinary mixture of smells, the most powerful of which seemed to join goat shit and excrescence from a drain sunk in the road a hundred yards away. Clearly, the weather was not going to provide a symbolic negation of her night's work, and as a result she felt obliged to put on a clean white dress.

At the end of the evening Lipman had tried, in a halfhearted, first-date "I know you're not that kind of woman" way, to get her into bed, and no doubt Frumkin would have been pleased if she had let him do so, but Joyce had murmured a half sentence about the "time of the month" and he had quickly retreated, happy to set up a second rendezvous for this morning.

It hadn't been hard to pick him up. Frumkin had told her that Lipman liked to take an early lunch at the International on Fridays and that's where Joyce had "bumped into" him. They had spent the afternoon walking in the Old City (Joyce's eyes had darted everywhere, half expecting, half hoping that she would see Robert Kirsch) and it was there, toward dusk, as they watched the Jews in fine cloaks and sable hats make their way to the Wall for evening prayers, that Lipman had come up with the bright idea of a trip to a race meet in Lydda scheduled for the following afternoon. If he was surprised by the alacrity with which she had accepted his offer so soon after meeting him, he hadn't shown it at the time. Perhaps he thought of himself as an irresistibly charming man. If so, that was all to the good.

As they began their descent out of Jerusalem a black Ford, identical to their own, pulled in behind them. It was there as Lipman slowed to negotiate the hairpin turns cut into the Judean hills, and still there when they crossed the valley of Ayalon. Near Ramleh, as the town's square Lydian tower came into view, the Ford disappeared in the direction of the English camp, only to reappear moments later from behind some sheds at a place where the road ran parallel with the railway track that linked Jerusalem and Jaffa.

"Look who's back," Lipman said, glancing into the driving mirror. "They are going our way after all. I knew this race would pull a few from Jerusalem. Andrew Nathan hasn't lost yet, and I'm sure there are chaps who can't wait to see him get his comeuppance."

Joyce stared out of the window. There, hidden in a grove of olive trees, was the white cemetery where she had made one of her gun deliveries. It made her shiver to think of it, even if by day the place was empty of atmosphere. Increasingly, Joyce experienced the vacant feeling that she knew well from the times when her previous enthusiasms, whether art, dance, or even love, had begun to decline. She didn't will these moments, but they came nevertheless, a horrible falling-away that she tried to resist but couldn't; there might be years of dedicated commitment, and then, dramatic as a leap from a high precipice, came the dreadful realization that nothing she did held any meaning other than its value as an antidote to her own chronic boredom. It was awful to have to admit to herself that she was a chameleon, her beliefs thin as tissue paper, and this time around she had truly convinced herself that in Zionism, even though she wasn't a Jew, she had found something that might turn into her life's work. But the warm stones in Ramleh's cemetery seemed to be telling her otherwise. Was it time then to stop her involvement with the Zionist cause? Frumkin had indicated that she had almost done enough. She would soften up Lipman, try to tease out the extent of his Zionist sympathies, then turn him over to Frumkin. That would be that.

They drove for another fifteen minutes down a bumpy stone road. By the time they reached the club the trailing motor vehicle was once again nowhere to be seen.

The meet had not yet begun. A military band, midway through a selection of patriotic tunes, broke into "What is the meaning of Empire Day?" Lipman, in high spirits, jumped out of the car and began to sing along: "Why does the trumpet sound?"

He turned to Joyce.

"They're the Ninth Queen's Royal Lancers," he said admiringly, "best band in the Middle East."

Nighttime parties in Jerusalem may have been suspended, but from the cheerful attitude of the circulating members of the Ludd Hunt, and the intense demeanor of the officers who were about to race for a cup to be presented by no less a personage than Air Commodore E. L. Gerard, you wouldn't have guessed that anything was amiss in this hot corner of the British Empire.

"Lipman," a voice called out from the paddock. "Want to make a wager?"

"Frankie! Was that you driving behind us? I thought I recognized your ugly mug."

"How about a tenner?"

"Do you think I'm made of money?"

"Alright, a fiver that Goggin brings in Ladybird ahead of your pal Nathan."

"Who's Andrew on?"

"Scots Grey."

"A fiver it is."

Lipman couldn't hear the note of condescension in Frankie's voice, Joyce thought, or if he did he chose to ignore it. Or worse, now that she thought of it, Joyce was certain that Lipman had given Frankie exactly what he wanted. For, unless she was mistaken, Lipman had allowed a little Stepney to slip into that "Do you think I'm made of money?" and his Jewish intonation was like a cat offering its throat in mock submission. "That's right," Lipman had said. "I'm a Jew, let's leave it at that." And suddenly, despite the inner landslide of misery and indifference that had afflicted her only twenty minutes previously, Joyce felt unambiguously glad that she had engaged in her subversive activities. The smugness of the British, bad enough in England, was unbearable here. What on earth did they think they were doing at this club, sitting on lawn chairs with their G and T's, and their week-old daily papers from London, slapping each other on the back and oh so happy to be set apart from the locals, whether Jews or Arabs? She couldn't understand why their attitude of exclusion didn't bother Mark more, or why it didn't appear to trouble Robert Kirsch much, or affect this new chap, Johnny Lipman, at all. The English Jews, unless they were here to settle Palestine, all wore blinkers, she thought. It was easier for them that way. The English hated them. Frumkin, for all his pumped-up self-importance, had got that right.

"The first race will be the Members Heavy Weight Race. Distance two-and-one-half miles over the point to point course. Catchweights thirteen stone seven pounds. In lane one, Colonel A. J. MacNeill on Sweep. In lane two, Lieutenant Colonel G. R. E. Foley on Jimmy James. In lane three, Squadron Leader J. S. Goggin on Ladybird . . ."

The voice boomed on through the megaphone until all seven riders had been announced. Joyce watched the officers jostle their horses into line. Twice, when they were settled, one of the horses made a false start and they had to begin again. The crowd, which must have numbered over two hundred, began to get impatient, but at the third attempt the starter fired his pistol and they were off in a thud and swirl of hoofbeats and particolors.

Lipman had disappeared somewhere farther down the course to get a better view of its only water jump, an artificial shallow brown pool under a low bank, its singularity a concession from the course designers to the water shortage that was afflicting the entire country. Joyce stood alone. She followed the race as the field spread out, but her mind was elsewhere. In this little colonial enclave she felt uniquely uncomfortable and homeless.

"If friend Andrew holds that lead I'll be out a fiver."

Joyce turned.

"Francis Athill. Old mate of Johnny's. From the station in Jaffa." He held out his hand.

"Joyce Bloomberg."

They looked at each other.

Athill laughed. "You don't remember me, then? Not surprising, I suppose. You were in rather high spirits."

Joyce stared at Athill's ruddy, smiling face. She was quaking inside. "Oh yes," she said, "Ramleh. It was kind of you to let me go."

"If I'd known you were tied up with Johnny Lipman I'd have arrested you on the spot."

Athill laughed. But not before Joyce had stuttered, "I'm not, I'm not tied up with him."

She felt herself audience to her own bad acting.

Half a mile away the horses, lengths apart from one another, rose heavy and silent, chestnut and gray against the blue sky, and splashed down into the water.

In the distance Joyce saw Lipman turn at the head of a small group and begin to run back toward a loose ring of spectators that had formed near the finish line.

"Shall we go over?" Athill asked.

Joyce walked beside him over the dry yellow grass. Athill chatted on about his yearning to see America, his cousin in Chicago, and where was Mrs. Bloomberg from? Ah yes, New York. Something was wrong, Joyce felt it with every bone in her body. Something in the way this sunny young man kept the conversation so unobjectionably upbeat and superfluous.

Joyce touched his arm.

"If you'll excuse me a moment."

She walked in the direction of a small tent that had been set up as the ladies' toilet. Inside, she splashed her face with water from one of four large canteens that had been placed on the ground. A small shaving mirror attached to an air vent with a piece of string showed Joyce her face; the bags under her eyes were darker than she had hoped. She heard two men enter the adjacent tent.

"They say he lost the leg."

"Did he, now? Poor old Kirsch. Poor bastard. I liked him. He wasn't . . . you know."

"Like the rest of them? Well, given half a chance."

"Yes, you never know, I suppose. Still, I wouldn't wish that on anybody."

Joyce felt her heart beat fast and the blood rush to her head. She ran out of the tent and sprinted back toward the finish line. The horses were coming down the straight at a gallop. The crowd cheered wildly. Joyce grabbed Lipman's arm and almost spun him around.

"Robert Kirsch. What happened to him?"

"What's that?"

Lipman tried to turn away. The lead horses were neck and neck. You could hear the thwack of whip on flank.

Joyce dug her nails into his arm. "Robert Kirsch, you know him, don't you? You must. Where is he?"

"For God's sake!" Lipman stared at her as if she were a madwoman.

"Come on, Andrew!" he shouted in Joyce's face, then he wrested himself free, turning in time to see Ladybird win by a head.

"He's in hospital in Jerusalem. He's been there for weeks." The voice belonged to Athill, who had been standing nearby. "He was shot last month in Abu Tor."

Joyce tried her best to remain composed, but she felt a scream rising within her.

"Which hospital? Where?"

"Damn and blast," Lipman said to no one in particular, "and here's your bloody money." He reached into his pocket, but Athill grabbed his wrist.

"Forget it," he said.

"Absolutely not."

Joyce felt her head spin. She looked hard at Athill.

"Take me there," she said. She wanted to say, "Whatever your business is with me, I'll cooperate, just take me to Robert," but somehow she
managed to keep the words from bursting out.

"What the hell?" Athill had let go of Lipman who had begun again
to try to pull a five-pound note from his pocket.

"Very well," Athill replied, as if he knew exactly what Joyce had been
about to say, "I'll take you."

They drove in Athill's Ford. Lipman hadn't put up any resistance to
Joyce's departure; in fact he had been glad to get rid of her. Now she sat
with her head leaning back on the leather passenger seat. Her eyes were
closed.

From time to time Athill looked across at her. Was she feigning sleep
so she wouldn't have to talk to him? Perhaps. Either way, he decided to
let her be. There had been nothing false in her response to the news
about Robert Kirsch.

They had begun the climb to Jerusalem when Joyce awoke.

"Do you have a cigarette?" she asked.

Athill reached into his tunic pocket, removed a Turkish pack that fea-
tured a picture of a harem girl on the cover, lit a cigarette himself, then
passed Joyce matches and the pack.

"You know, before the war I never saw any women smoking—and
now you all do."

Joyce lit a cigarette and inhaled deeply. She couldn't conduct any
small talk. All she wanted to do was get to Robert.

The automobile climbed, its engine gasping with exhaustion, as
Athill zigzagged through the arid landscape: boulders and scrubby vege-
tation, relieved on occasion by a coppice of cypress trees or a block of
houses that appeared to be clinging to the rock. The sky, blue over Ramleh, was parchment white on the outskirts of Jerusalem. The elevation
should have relieved the burning heat of the afternoon, but a khamsin
was blowing in from the desert, a wind that was no wind, blowing a suffocating stillness and dropping a rain of yellow dust.

Athill wiped the back of his hand across his brow. "How long have you known Robert Kirsch?" He tried to maintain a neutral tone, but they both knew, he was sure, that he wasn't asking out of mere curiosity, and that this was the first of many questions to come.

"I met him at the beginning of summer, not long after we got here," Joyce replied.

She drew on the cigarette. The "beginning of summer" felt to her aeons ago. Mark on his bicycle coming up the path gingerly holding his still-wet canvas, her heart in hiding, and then, before the cottage had become much more to her than a borderless agglomeration of treats for the eye, visual pleasures that were in any case inadequate compensation for her inner state, the rough mad arrival of the stabbed and dying man. *Then* Robert Kirsch. She couldn't begin to explain to Athill, and why should she?

"And Major Lipman is a more recent acquaintance?"

"That's right."

"You seem to have a lot of friends in the police and military."

"As do you, I imagine," Joyce replied.

Athill smiled.

Joyce looked straight ahead at the desolate hills; they looked like skeletons of places that had once been green. How could anyone call this a land of milk and honey? Frumkin! Peter Frumkin knew about Robert and he hadn't told her. "Hardly a surprise," he'd said when she'd commented on Robert's absence. If there had been more moonlight in the room, or the oil lamps had been turned up, she would have seen his face clearly and she would have known. Frumkin knew Robert had been shot; everyone in Jerusalem must have known, but she was ignorant because she had been either stuck in Jaffa or out delivering Frumkin's guns. She was the fool of fools, and Robert Kirsch had lost his leg, that poor lonely man who wouldn't hurt a fly. And who had shot him? An ocean crashed the flimsy seawall inside her.

"Stop, please stop," Joyce begged.

"There's nowhere to stop here, it's too dangerous. We're on a hairpin."

Joyce's face turned white as her dress.

"Then slow down!"

Athill brought the car to a crawl. Joyce leaned out of her window; the petrified world turned circles beneath her as she retched and vomited.

A quarter of a mile farther on Athill hit a stretch of smooth straight road and brought the car to a halt. He reached onto the backseat, knocked a kit bag to the floor, and came up with a canteen of water.

"Here," he said.

Joyce's white dress was spattered with vomit. She put the canteen to her lips.

"Not too much," Athill urged her, "a little at a time. You probably went too long without drinking. Have to drink all the time here."

"Yes," Joyce replied. "Thank you."

"And this road, twists and turns enough to make anyone sick."

"I'm all right now."

Athill searched again in the back of the car and came up with a dry rag. Joyce took it, folded it over to avoid an oil stain, poured on a little water and began to dab at her dress, wiping off flecks of vomit but leaving small brown stains.

"I'm all right," she repeated.

"I had the feeling," Athill said, "that you were about to tell me something."

Joyce continued to touch at the blemishes on her dress.

"Perhaps," she replied, "but it's gone now."

The hospital, when they arrived, exhibited a late-afternoon torpor. A few members of the Sabbath staff were visible in the corridors, but Joyce felt as if the airless whiteness outside had penetrated the building and brought with it a sleeping sickness. It seemed, running up to the front desk, as if she were wading through water. A middle-aged woman with bright red hair and freckles all over her face was writing in a ledger.

"I'm looking for Robert Kirsch. Captain Robert Kirsch."

"Wait a minute. I have to finish with these people."

Joyce looked around. On a nearby bench sat an Orthodox Jewish couple. The woman had her face buried in the side of her husband's coat. She was sobbing, and he was trying to comfort her.

"Please go and sit down."

Joyce sat for less than a minute, and then she was up, walking fast through the hospital, stopping whoever she saw and asking for Robert. Athill trailed behind, apologizing to bewildered nurses as Joyce hardly waited for their replies before moving on.

She turned down a dimly lit corridor; several figures, doctors and nurses she assumed, were gathered at its end. As she approached them, a narrow bed was wheeled from a side room into the corridor. One of the nurses had tears in her eyes. The body on the bed was covered and took up only a little more than half the length of the mattress.

"I'm sorry to bother you," Joyce said, "but I'm looking for Robert Kirsch."

One of the doctors turned to her, his face showing both anger and surprise. He took two steps away from Joyce and continued his conversation with a nurse, which Joyce had interrupted.

"Yes," he said, "of course I'll talk to them. Where are they? In the front?"

He turned back to Joyce, taking in Athill with a quick glance.

"Now what do you want?"

Joyce repeated her question.

"He's not here. He was discharged by Dr. Bassan yesterday. He's been sent home."

"Home? To where? To England?"

The doctor shrugged. "Wherever his home is."

A porter had arrived to wheel the body away.

Joyce looked wildly up and down the corridor as if Robert might appear walking toward her.

Athill watched the porter push the bed away. "How old?" he asked.

"Nine," the doctor replied. "A little girl." He raised the palms of his hands in a gesture of futility.

33.

The bus carrying Kirsch and Mayan pulled over to let an armored car overtake. In the open back sat half a dozen Hindu soldiers on their way to the camp at Rosh Pinah. They had been brought to Palestine as reinforcements in case of further unrest. Kirsch leaned slightly over Mayan to look out of the window. The soldiers stared straight ahead. In Nablus the charabanc had burst a tire and they had not restarted their journey until dawn. Between his cramped leg and his attempts to remain upright and not fall asleep on Mayan's shoulder Kirsch had spent the long night in a state of great discomfort. He remembered a lot of shouting and small fires burning by the roadside. All the disturbance had been related to the bus, but in his dreams, when they finally came, a full-fledged riot had been in progress, one that he was powerless to prevent. Now, it appeared, he had slept again. He did not know how much time had passed. Mayan in her thin blue dress looked as fresh as when they had set out from Jerusalem. She held on her lap a broad-brimmed straw hat with a red ribbon. Kirsch's walking stick, provided by the hospital, lay on the floor beneath their seats.

The bus trailed the armored car until it veered off toward a barracks on the right. Kirsch saw one of the soldiers clasp his hand to his head in order to prevent his hat from blowing off.

"We're here," Mayan said.

"Thank God for that," Kirsch replied.

The driver brought the bus to a halt. Ahead of him Kirsch could see the pioneer colony spread out on the slope of a hill, its small stone-block houses surrounded by eucalyptus saplings that threw off scent but, as yet, not enough shade. He took in the narrow path that snaked up the incline. He wasn't sure that he'd be able to make the climb in the blistering midday heat that, since the bus had stopped, seemed to advance in ten-degree jolts.

Kirsch and Mayan waited while the other passengers—two nuns and a large Arab family—got off; then Kirsch rose slowly to his feet. He winced as he straightened his leg. Mayan preceded him off the bus.

She offered her hand to help him down but he ignored it. Nearby, they could see a white-walled hostelry shaded by pine trees. Mayan pointed toward it.

"You can stay there tonight," she said, anticipating Kirsch's problem in ascending the pathway. "In the morning, when it's cool, I'll come and help you up the hill."

"And you? Where does your friend Rosa live?"

"She works at the Manor"—Mayan gestured toward a large house at the top of the hill—"in the administrative offices of the colony, and for now they let her live in one of the rooms. But if you're a rich tourist you can still sit on the terrace and have tea."

"Good," Kirsch replied. "If I can get up there, that's what I'll do. In fact I'll make it my business to make that climb before we leave. And because I'm so wealthy you can come along as my guest."

"I'd like that," she replied.

Now that the enforced intimacy of their bus ride together was over, Kirsch felt a little uncomfortable. It had been a rash decision to accompany Mayan, and the oddity of what he had done was made stranger by his arrival in this pioneer outpost. Although everything in Rosh Pinah was clearly committed to the future, he felt as if he had taken a step back in time, or out of time. Even so, he was terribly glad of Mayan's company, her nice open face, her keen intelligence. She seemed like someone who might erase the complications from his life—although, of course, she couldn't.

"Come on," she said, "I'll walk with you to the hotel."

Mayan lifted both her bag and Kirsch's. He protested mildly, but she acted with the authority of a hospital staff member, and he had been conditioned for weeks to obey.

She put on her straw hat and they walked a hundred yards down a broken path toward the entrance of the hostelry.

"Do you cheer everybody up," Kirsch asked, "or is it just me?"

Mayan put the bags down between two large pots of pink and white mimosa.

"Are you flirting with me?" she said.

"I'm not sure," Kirsch replied.

The walls of Kirsch's room were chalk white, too much like a hospital room for his taste, but he didn't have a choice. In any case, the place was clean and the bed was not uncomfortable. He had been shown in by a young girl with long plaits who might have stepped out of a Grimms' fairy tale. She was the daughter of the proprietress, a diffident Polish-Jewish woman with an unusually long, thin face and pale green eyes. While Kirsch had signed his name in the register, the girl's father had sat on a stool in a corner of the room noisily munching a pickled cucumber. Opposite him a middle-aged Arab man in black turban and kaftan sat at a table half covered with porcelain plates and sipped at a tiny cup of coffee. It seemed that Kirsch might be the only guest.

He lay on the bed and waited. Mayan had gone to find Rosa; if Rosa was available the two young women would return to have dinner with him, otherwise Mayan might come alone. Kirsch had taken off his shirt and trousers and hung them over a chair. He almost fell asleep but a mosquito buzzing in his ear kept him awake. Kirsch slapped at the side of his face and the noise stopped, only to begin again a moment later. He sat up and looked at his withered leg, twig-thin and bone white. The wrenching thought crossed his mind that perhaps injury and hurt were what he had been searching for when he came out to Palestine, not escaping his brother's fate but trying to replicate it. Well, if so, he had got what he wanted; and now he knew, as everyone who went into the war had quickly learned, that the experience wasn't worth it. He lay in the room fighting a losing battle with self-pity: Philoctetes and his suppurating wound. He pulled the white sheet over his body and up to his chin, as if it might obliterate everything that had happened in the last months.

Before undressing he had deposited the contents of his pockets in a glass ashtray on his bedside table: the key to his Jerusalem flat, a few coins, and the policeman's tunic button that he had found in the Bloombergs' garden and which he kept now almost more as a talisman than as evidence. A nurse at Shaarei Zedek had taken it from a pocket of his trousers after she had cut away the cloth from his leg. Now he stretched out his arm, picked up the button, examined its crest, then set it down again. It was possible that Joyce had lied to him from the very beginning. The image of her in the front of the car stroking the back of the soldier's head returned to him, and once again he felt his face burning.

After a while he got up from the bed and walked over to a window. At the outset of their bus journey Mayan had told him that in spring the hills here were covered in red flax and blue sage and that on her first visit, only days after her arrival in Palestine, she had seen fields of grasses criss-crossed with ivory and yellow flowers; looking at the dried-out landscape before him, stone and dusty oil-stained ground shimmering under ripples of heat, Kirsch found it hard to imagine such an abundance of color. But perhaps his ability to conjure beauty or the joy that it could bring had evanesced. Since the accident he was always looking for patches of darkness, not only in his own soul but also in the lives of the people he knew. He suspected anyone who, like Mayan, displayed a sunny exterior, of masking layers of trouble.

From his window he could see out to the main road. Where the bus had deposited its passengers a solitary stork had taken a dignified stand, as if waiting for the next ride into town. While Kirsch was watching, the armored car that he had seen earlier pulled in next to the hostelry. Kirsch assumed that the Hindu soldiers had been dropped off at the camp and only their driver was left. To his surprise, he suddenly felt desperate for conversation with someone from England. He pulled on his trousers—no easy task given the difficulty he had in bending his leg—threw on his shirt, and stepped barefoot from his room. He crossed toward the hostelry lobby, using his stick and moving as quickly as he could, but by the time he arrived, the British driver, a short, wiry man with a shock of curly red hair, was already making his way back toward his vehicle. In each hand he carried an open bottle of beer from which he took alternate swigs. From the high color of his cheeks it looked as if they weren't his first drinks of the day.

"Hey," Kirsch yelled, "are you from the camp?"

The driver turned in his tracks, held the beer bottles behind his back, and gave Kirsch a hard stare. Kirsch noted the sergeant's stripes on his shirt.

"What's it to you if I am?"

"Oh, nothing at all. Just looking for someone to have a drink with."

The sergeant looked suspiciously at Kirsch. "Oh, yeah."

"Look," Kirsch said, "I couldn't give a damn about . . ." He indicated the hidden bottles with a nod of his head.

"And why should you 'give a damn' "—the sergeant did his best to imitate Kirsch's accent—"to begin with?"

Kirsch shrugged. There was no way to explain his yearning for companionship and then to introduce himself as a member of the Jerusalem constabulary.

"Listen, gimpy," the sergeant said, "whoever you are, why don't you just fuck off?"

He took two steps toward the armored vehicle and climbed into the driver's seat.

"Wait a minute," Kirsch called out, "I think we've met before. Didn't you come into the station in Jerusalem? Weren't you a friend of Sam Cartwright?"

The sergeant had been about to turn the key in the ignition, but he stopped and looked across at Kirsch. A thin smile of recognition crossed his swollen face.

"And you're the sod who got him shot," he said. "What the fuck are you doing up here? Not that I give a shit."

"Got him shot? I certainly . . ." Kirsch wanted to say, "I was shot myself," but the case was already closed.

The sergeant turned on the engine.

"Bastard," he yelled at Kirsch. "I'd rather have a drink with my nig-nogs."

Kirsch went back to his room, propped himself up on a pillow against the tubular metal headboard, and waited for Mayan to return. He hadn't even thought to bring a book with him. Somewhere nearby a hostelry worker emptied a rubbish bin. The scent of mimosa that had faintly wafted through the open window was quickly overwhelmed by a bitter odor: someone smashing beer bottles outside a London pub.

In his dream there was an old Jewish woman with a satin perúke and cashmere shawl. Her face was something like his mother's and, from her seat in the snug of the pub, she was explaining her plans to set up a fly-catcher factory in Palestine. It couldn't fail, she said, because the country was full of flies. Kirsch, who at first seemed excited by the idea, soon found himself urging her not to go. Who would be left to look after him and his brother? They were only children. How were they supposed to fend for themselves?

A persistent knocking at the door of his room brought him out of sleep. Mayan was calling his name.

"Hold on," Kirsch said.

He got to his feet and opened the door. Mayan stood there alone. Kirsch looked at her through bleary eyes. She had washed her hair and pulled it into a shiny black braid that hung down her back. While Kirsch was sleeping the sky had gathered toward darkness and only a thin dying ember glowed over the distant mountains.

"Well, shall I come in?"

She was wearing the same white dress that he had seen her in at the Bassans' house. Kirsch suspected that there were not a whole lot of clothes in her wardrobe.

Mayan smiled at him. Even after months in Palestine her face was still pale (Kirsch had noted that she wore a hat whenever she was in the sun) and in contrast her lips appeared very red.

He held the door open for her. She entered the room and sat on the edge of his bed. He moved to the sink in the corner of the room, splashed water on his face and looked around for a towel.

"What happened to Rosa?" he asked.

"She's still at work. Perhaps you'll meet her later."

Mayan touched her fingers to the glass ashtray on Kirsch's bedside table. She picked up his keys, then put them down again.

Kirsch stood before her.

"Is there somewhere nearby where we can eat?" he asked, but before she could answer he had bent over to kiss her. His stance was awkward and the kiss clumsy. To make things easier for him, it seemed, Mayan stood up from the bed. He kissed her again.

"Wait," she said.

She stepped away from him, undid the hooks and buttons of her dress, and pulled it over her head. Underneath the dress she was naked.

Kirsch watched her fold the dress over the back of his chair.

"I don't want to get it creased," she said.

She walked over to Kirsch and let him embrace her. Her small breasts pressed into his chest.

"Here," she said, "let me help you. Sit down."

She undid his belt buckle and the buttons of his fly, then pushed down his trousers and pulled them off.

Kirsch lay back on the bed. The room's only light came from outside, a handful of stars that barely lifted the darkness. Kirsch touched his hand to the back of Mayan's head. Her hair was still wet. She moved her face down over his stomach but before taking him in her mouth she moved her head to the side and kissed him very gently all down his withered leg. Later, when she lay facedown, sleeping beside him, he saw, by the yellow moonlight that the room boxed and filtered, a track of white scars that ran like a ladder across her back.

34.

"Where do you think you're going with that?"

The young sentry, newly assigned to his post at the gate of Government House, gestured with his rifle toward the wrapped painting in the back of Bloomberg's car.

"I'm making a delivery."

Bloomberg knew that he didn't look like a credible delivery boy: he hadn't shaved in days and his hair was matted with sand from his journey.

"What is it?"

"A painting for the governor. He's not going to be pleased if you don't let me through."

"Isn't he?"

"Listen, I know he's not here. He's traveling to Damascus . . ."

"Now how would you know that?"

"For God's sake."

"Let's take a look, then."

The sentry walked around to the back of the car. Bloomberg untied the ropes around the heavy cloth sacking. He had only to reveal the brown-and-red top right-hand corner of the painting for the sentry to interrupt his activity: "All right, that's enough. Take it out of the car and you can leave it here at the gate."

"I'm not leaving it here."

"Then you'll have to go on home with it and come back with a proper pass."

Bloomberg was about to tell him to get hold of someone in authority, and that this business about a pass was nonsense, but he held back. He didn't want to speak to anyone except Ross. He couldn't be sure what others knew or didn't know about Saud, and he didn't want to be peppered with awkward questions.

"You wouldn't like to tell me when Sir Gerald is returning, would you?"

The sentry acted as if he hadn't heard.

"Didn't think so."

"Move it. You're blocking the way."

The road behind Bloomberg's vehicle was empty of traffic. All that he blocked was the sun's path to the shadowed dirt in front of him. Bloomberg backed his car up and turned it around. Freddie Peake would have to wait a few more days to get his Ford back.

Bloomberg drove back to the cottage in Talpiot and parked the Ford close to the garden gate, then he carried the painting down the path and leaned it against an old olive tree with a convoluted trunk. He went back to the car and retrieved the books that Saud's mother had given him. He didn't know what he was going to say to Joyce when he saw her, and when he opened the door he was almost relieved to find her not at home.

The room was more or less as he had left it, in a state of untidy calamity: the bed rumpled and Joyce's clothes strewn on the floor. There was a food-stained plate in the sink and two empty bottles of wine under a chair. Next to the bed Bloomberg found a third bottle, half consumed, and took a healthy swig. He sat on the edge of the mattress and retrieved De Groot's letter from his pocket for what was now his fourth or fifth read. Bloomberg skimmed the typewritten sentences that he had almost committed to heart: "in view of the present situation I urge you . . . weapons that the Zionists are bringing into Palestine with the intention . . . desirability of my leaving Jerusalem without delay . . . may only be possible for a short time . . . great personal danger . . . must make it clear that His Majesty's Representatives here do not hold me in high esteem . . . reasons for my contacting you directly . . . whatever action you may decide upon as the result of this warning . . . must tell you that the longer you delay the more dangerous the subsequent . . . guns arriving through the port of Haifa but I do not know . . . urge you toward the utmost vigilance . . . I am, sir, Your obedient Servant—" The signature space was blank; presumably De Groot only had reason to put his pen to the original letter, which had undoubtedly been intercepted by his killers. De Groot knew that guns were on their way. He knew that a group of radical Zionists was planning to use them for a series of assassinations to be followed by an insurrection. He knew that he himself was a target for murder.

Bloomberg put the letter back in his pocket, then stood and walked around the room absentmindedly collecting Joyce's discarded clothes and piling them on a chair. He had to clear his head and think what to do. But this was easier said than done. He had been in Petra for only a few weeks but it was long enough to impart a spacious unfamiliarity to this place to which he had returned and this punctuated his general disorientation. He turned in the room as if it were a flimsy stage set whose walls might collapse if he pushed on them. The Jerusalem light pouring through the windows that in the first weeks after their arrival from England he had found harsh in the extreme now seemed mellow and springlike in comparison to the desert's blanched and effacing glare. In the shadowed spaces between their trunks and the bed he stumbled and groped like a blind man. Bloomberg's face burned and his head itched.

He tripped and fell to his knees; in a delirium of strangeness the solidity of the floor seemed momentarily unreliable, as if it might turn to sand and suck in his hands and feet. He pulled himself up with an effort and approached the corner of the room where he had leaned his canvases. He tipped one back. The work, a small painting completed only three months ago, was adequate, but not much more. He had been a careful observer of the landscape, not yet in its grip.

He was about to go outside and bring in the new painting when he heard someone walking up the path. The door flew open. Bloomberg looked up expecting to see Joyce. Instead a tall, stocky man with a shock of blond hair entered the room.

"Who the hell are you?"

It was Frumkin who posed the question.

"I might ask you the same thing."

Frumkin took in Bloomberg's disheveled appearance and sunburned face. "Oh, Christ. You must be the husband. Just back?"

"And if I'm the husband then you must be . . . ?"

"No, no, don't start getting the wrong idea. I'm Peter Frumkin from the Metropolis Film Corporation. Joyce has been doing some prop work for me. She's been terrific. Wish I'd met her at the beginning of the shoot. Half my crew was incompetent. Your wife was a godsend."

"Is that why you nearly kicked the door in?"

"Sorry about that. You know how it is here, politeness out of the window, it's infectious."

Frumkin looked around the room as if Joyce might be hiding somewhere. His eyes fell on the sheet of paper that lay on the bed. Bloomberg froze for a moment, then took two quick steps, picked up De Groot's letter and stuffed it into his pocket. If Frumkin noticed that Bloomberg was less than nonchalant in his gesture, he did a good job of concealing the fact.

"Joyce coming back soon?"

Bloomberg shrugged. "Couldn't tell you, I'm afraid."

Bloomberg kept his hand in his pocket, and crumpled the letter into a tight ball.

Without having been invited to sit, Frumkin slung his long frame onto the bed, propped himself up on the pillows and stretched his arms above his head, clasping his hands together.

"So," he asked, "whaddya make of the Holy Land?"

Bloomberg relaxed a little.

"The land interests me, but not the holiness."

"I feel the same way. Speak any Hebrew?"

"Not a word."

"You should try, you know." Frumkin managed to sound both non-chalant and critical. "It's the language of the future for this place."

"Then you think the Jews will triumph?"

"Oh," Frumkin said firmly, "we'll triumph all right."

Bloomberg smiled.

"Ah, come on. That's right, I said 'we.' You Brits are unbelievable. You can't spot us, can you? But I'll bet your cold island buddies would pin you for a Jew in two seconds."

"You're right about that."

Outside, a small plane crossing the sky broke the silence of the afternoon.

"Hey," Frumkin said, "that was a nasty business you and your wife went through with Mr. De Groot. You were the talk of the town for a while there."

Bloomberg tried to remain calm. Was this man as easygoing as he seemed, or was something else going on?

"Were we? I'm happy to say I missed most of our celebrity."

"They ever catch the killer?"

"You'd know that better than I."

Frumkin nodded. He got up from the bed and gestured toward the stack of Bloomberg's paintings.

"Mind if I take a look?"

"Please yourself."

Frumkin crouched down to review the work, flicking the canvases toward him as if he were moving hangers in his wardrobe. He stopped at one of Ross's early commissions.

"Wouldn't have figured you for a church man. But you've got that dreary place, all right. Scottish hospice, right? How come you don't paint your wife? She's a beautiful woman."

Bloomberg chose not to respond.

Frumkin stood. "Well, I'd better be going. Listen, gotta piece of paper? I'd like to leave a message for Joyce."

Instinctively, Bloomberg tightened his grip on the crumpled letter in his pocket. "You can give me the information," he said. "I expect she'll be back soon."

The sound of a sputtering engine filled the air. At first Bloomberg thought it must be another plane, but the noise grew closer.

"Maybe that's her now," Frumkin said.

The engine cut and both men heard the garden gate swing open; then came the sound of two voices.

Frumkin moved quickly to the door and pushed it open. Joyce was walking down the path in the company of a uniformed British army officer, but it wasn't Lipman who accompanied her.

Bloomberg pushed past Frumkin into the sun-filled overgrown garden.

"Mark!"

Joyce ran toward Bloomberg and held him in a long embrace. For the first time in more than a year he felt that he could hug her back and mean it.

Athill and Frumkin watched the couple's reunion, Athill with mild embarrassment, Frumkin in a state of mounting apprehension.

Joyce, spying Frumkin over Bloomberg's shoulder, was the first to break away. Frumkin spoke before she could say anything.

"Nothing important," he said, "nothing that can't wait."

Joyce gave him a look of withering hatred. She wanted to spit at him, but she knew that she mustn't, and in any case her tongue was like a heavy stone inside her mouth.

"But I thought you wanted . . . ," Bloomberg began.

"Doesn't matter," Frumkin interrupted firmly. "I'm late for a meeting at the American Colony. They want my advice on selling cinema films to tourists."

He turned toward Athill. "You know Gerry Ross? Good friend of mine. I'm a contributor to Pro-Jerusalem. Tell him Peter Frumkin from Metropolis says hello."

Athill nodded, a slightly baffled expression on his face.

Frumkin set off toward the gate. It was a short while before they heard him kick-start a motorcycle that he must have left in the grove of eucalyptus trees a hundred yards or so down the path.

Bloomberg noticed that Joyce's dress was badly stained and that her eyes were red, but whether from tears or exhaustion he couldn't tell. She slumped down into one of the garden chairs.

"Well," Athill said, "I should leave you two alone. Mr. Bloomberg, very glad to meet you, sir. I hope your trip south was productive. I'm an admirer of your work." He looked at Joyce. "I expect we'll talk again very soon."

They were back where they had started in the wild garden with the sounds of the muezzins drifting up from the mosques in the nearby Arab villages. A late summer evening chill was in the air. Bloomberg fetched a blanket from the bed and draped it around Joyce's shoulders. The sun had set without its usual fanfare, or perhaps they simply hadn't noticed. Bloomberg's wrapped painting still stood where he had placed it against the olive tree. He had brought out what remained of the wine and they took turns swigging from the bottle. He had a pack of Lubliner cigarettes and Joyce chain-smoked until there was only one left. He wanted to tell her about Saud and De Groot's letter but she looked so beaten that he decided to wait. Finally, it was Joyce who broke the silence.

"Robert Kirsch was shot," she said.

"Yes, I know. He's in Shaarei Zedek. He's all right, though."

"How do you know that?"

"His cousin was passing through the desert, you know, as people do . . ."

Joyce laughed, surprising herself because she thought that she had lost the capacity to do so.

"Anyway, she looked me up, gave me the news from Jerusalem."

"I want to find him," Joyce said, her voice trembling a little, "if he's still here, that is. He's been released from the hospital. He might be on his way back to London. But I have to find him."

"Ah, then nothing's changed."

"Meaning?"

"Meaning, I suppose, that you're in love with him."

"But that would be a change, because I wasn't, you know, to begin with or even when you went away."

"But you love him now."

"I don't know," Joyce said. "Would you care if I did?"

"You probably won't believe me," Bloomberg replied, "and you'd have every right not to, but I think that I would."

Joyce shivered a little, even though she was the one who had benefit of the blanket. She had the sensation that she was being closely watched, although there was no one in the vicinity.

Bloomberg got up from his chair and walked over to his painting. "In the morning I'll show you this," he said. "You need to see it in the daylight."

He carried the wrapped canvas into the cottage and set it against the wall. When he came out Joyce had risen and was squatting in a corner of the garden. He could hear her lift her dress and then the sound of her pissing on the ground.

Joyce headed back toward the cottage; she could feel the damp hem of her dress touching the back of her legs.

"What did you do while I was away?" Bloomberg asked. "Apart from falling in love, that is."

"Nothing," Joyce replied. "Nothing at all."

She came and sat in his lap, laying her head on his shoulder. He put his arms around her and rocked back in the chair. He breathed in the almond scent of her skin, then ran his hand through the tangles in her hair.

"I'm sorry," he whispered. "I'm so sorry."

There were tears on her face.

"Don't," he said, but then he realized that the tears belonged to him. "I've left it all too late, haven't I?"

Joyce kissed him gently on the forehead. "I don't know," she said.

She stood up from his embrace and went into the cottage. Bloomberg followed and watched her light the oil lamp.

"I know who killed De Groot," he said. "It wasn't anybody called Saud. It was Jews."

Joyce stared at him; she didn't seem the least bit surprised.

"Which Jews?"

"Jews who wanted him dead."

He pulled the paper ball from his pocket and began to smooth it out on the bed.

"Read this," he said.

Reluctantly, it seemed, Joyce took the letter and held it near the lamplight.

"Jews assassinating a Jew." Bloomberg spoke while she was reading. "That's not supposed to happen, is it?"

Joyce held a corner of the letter near the top of the oil lamp.

"What are you doing?" Bloomberg said.

Her hand dipped the paper toward the flame, but at the last second she changed her mind and withdrew it.

"What are you going to do?" she asked.

"Give it to Ross when he gets back. Along with this."

He pulled the silver button from his pocket and showed it to Joyce.

"De Groot ripped it from the tunic of his assassin. Saud found it in our garden."

Joyce took the button, held it for a moment in the palm of her hand and then handed it back to him along with the letter. Bloomberg wasn't sure if she had been about to burn the letter or not.

Joyce sat on the bed; the flames from the lamp threw tall leaping shadows on the wall behind her.

"Will you help me find Robert Kirsch? Please, Mark, I don't know who else to ask. And it's important."

Bloomberg thought for a moment; then he reached to the floor and scooped up a loose page from an old *Palestine Bulletin* that he had used to wipe his brushes. He held the paint-scored newspaper up so that the light ran through it.

"HUSBAND SEARCHES FOR WIFE'S MISSING LOVER," he read.

They fell asleep in their clothes, only to wake and tear them off in the middle of the night in a frenzy of lovemaking that by morning was remembered by them both more as a vivid dream than an actual event. Bloomberg didn't know if the first time he had made love to his wife in months would also be the last time in their marriage. They fucked as strangers, desperate and excited, tugging at each other's hair, a confusion of mouths and juices as if they might lick and suck each other into oblivion. They lay bonded by sweat and come, first Joyce's head on Bloomberg's chest and then his face at her breast. Toward dawn Bloomberg pulled a thin blanket over them and when, in her sleep, Joyce turned her back to him he spooned into her and gently kissed the back of her neck.

They were woken by someone banging at the door. Bloomberg pulled on his shorts and walked across the room through shafts of light that darted like yellow birds across his path.

Athill had returned with two other policemen.

"I'm sorry," he said to Mark, "but we're going to have to bring Mrs. Bloomberg in to answer some questions. Please don't make a fuss. I'm hoping this won't take long."

"Questions pertaining to what, may I ask?"

Joyce had sat up in bed, the sheet pulled around her. "I'll go," she said, sounding almost relieved.

Athill took his men outside in order to allow Joyce to get dressed.

"Tell me," Bloomberg said, "tell me quickly what is going on."

"I can't," she replied, in her confusion pulling on the stained white dress that she had worn the day before. "But find Robert Kirsch. Please, Mark, I know he can help me and there's something that I have to tell him."

"Why do you need help? What have you done?"

Athill banged on the door and pushed it open an inch or so. "Ready, Mrs. Bloomberg?"

Joyce kissed Bloomberg on the lips.

"Find him," she said, then she almost rushed out the door and into the custody of her escorts.

Bloomberg followed down the path while Joyce hurried toward the car ahead of the dallying policemen; a reversal of intention that was almost comic. Bloomberg shouted after her but she ignored him. Then he turned on Athill, and tried to push his way past the two broad-shouldered policemen who blocked his way.

"How dare you! What the fuck do you think you're doing? Joyce! Joyce! You fucking bastards."

Athill whispered to one of the men who stopped in his tracks to restrain the flailing Bloomberg. The others got into the car. Finally the policeman shoved Bloomberg to the ground, then jumped into the front passenger seat.

Athill reversed the Ford down the road. Bloomberg rose and gave chase as best he could, stumbling with his slight limp into the high grass along the beaten path, but in the end all the opposition that he could muster was a large stone that he grabbed and threw into the cloud of dust that the car kicked up. He went immediately to his car and turned the key in the ignition. The engine stuttered and died. For a moment, in a state of baffled exasperation, he sat taking deep breaths. What could Joyce have possibly been up to? Had he missed something so egregious that it had been staring him in the face? Had her affair with Kirsch led her into some dark place? It was impossible for him to imagine that such was the case. He took out the starting handle from the toolbox, went around to the front of the car and gave three quick cranks; the engine emitted a long snore, then fell asleep. Ten minutes passed before Bloomberg realized that there was no petrol in the car.

Bloomberg arrived at the police station almost two hours later, having walked almost all the way into the center of town; he was sweating profusely and his throat was dry. The waiting room contained a noisy crowd debating in three languages; heated, accusatory, gesticulating individuals, Jews and Arabs alike, threw themselves against the desk with angry demands and tearful pleading. They waved papers and shouted requests. Bloomberg could barely make himself heard above the din. When he finally managed to shove his way to the front the desk sergeant, surly and indifferent, claimed to have no knowledge of either Joyce's arrival or her whereabouts. He suggested that Bloomberg take a look outside for Athill's car, but when he did so the vehicle was nowhere to be seen. Bloomberg returned to the melee and once again maneuvered his way forward.

"Where's Captain Kirsch? At least tell me that."

"Kirsch? I have no idea. In the Jewish hospital, isn't he?"

An English voice from far back in the room called out, "Hey, Matthews, how's the Monday crush?"

The desk sergeant replied by waving two fingers in the direction of the speaker.

"Is there anyone here who knows where he is? Or where my wife might be?"

Matthews, faking exasperation, shouted across the room to the policeman who had just come in. "Charlie, any idea of the whereabouts of our beloved Captain Kirsch?"

"Heard he'd gone to Cyprus with a nice looking nurse."

"Reliable source?"

"In this fucking place?"

Matthews turned his attention back to Bloomberg.

"There you are then, there's your answer." He winked at Bloomberg. "Worth taking a bullet sometimes, I suppose."

The man pressing into his back had managed to slip his arm under Bloomberg's and was proffering a sheaf of papers to the sergeant. There was more jockeying for position and Bloomberg looked momentarily like an octopus, his tentacles the waving, beseeching arms of the strangers who surrounded him.

He extricated himself from the crowd and forced his way outside. Where had they taken Joyce? Perhaps she had been quickly released, all a misunderstanding; while he was walking and hobbling in from North Talpiot, she was on her way back home. But wouldn't she have passed him on the way? He couldn't remember seeing a single car on the road. He walked in a daze down and across Jaffa Road. Without noticing where he was going, he wandered into the midst of an open-air art class. Two dozen students had set up their easels, the men in long khaki shorts and white open-necked shirts, the women in cotton dresses. Without at all expecting to be, he found himself distracted by their work: even as he negotiated a path through the cluster of aspiring artists he wanted to stop and correct a line or suggest an adjustment. It was madness. On Jaffa Road he bought a fruit ice at a kiosk and sat for a moment to collect his thoughts. A tattered poster on the opposite wall showed two smiling pioneers, a man and a woman, one holding a rake, the other a pickax. The man was dressed rather smartly, a Sunday stroller in the English countryside; the woman, in knee-length skirt and blouse, wore a kerchief on her head. The rolling fields behind them were green, neatly furrowed or dotted with sheaves of corn. In the far distance a village of sparkling whitewashed homes nestled in a valley. The caption was unequivocal: REBUILDING THE LAND OF ISRAEL. It was the theme that Bloomberg had been paid to come and paint in Palestine; what would the serious students on the other side of the road have thought of him?

He was contemplating his next move when Athill sat down beside him. "I'm glad I found you," he said. "I didn't want it to be like that this morning."

"Where is she?"

"At the governorate. She's fine there. We didn't want to treat her like a common criminal, you know. I'm Francis Athill, by the way."

The members of the art class were washing brushes and packing their materials into wooden crates. Their model, a tall, skinny woman with bobbed black hair, relaxed her pose and stretched her arms to the sky. Bloomberg would have given anything to be among them: to begin again.

"Why have you got her?"

"We believe that she's involved in helping the Zionists run guns."

Bloomberg suppressed a laugh. "Joyce? You're mad."

"If she cooperates I'm sure we can work something out. We're after bigger fish than your wife."

"And what is your evidence of my wife's involvement?"

"She hasn't been charged with anything as yet. But I would suggest that in the near future you think about finding her some legal advice."

"I'll do better than that. I'll get Sir Gerald Ross to have her released this minute."

"It was Sir Gerald who ordered me to keep an eye on Mrs. Bloomberg."

Bloomberg took this information in with a sigh as if he were inhaling smoke, and indeed he began to cough uncontrollably. Athill poured him a glass of water.

"And what did your eye see?" Bloomberg asked.

Again Athill declined to answer.

"Let her go," Bloomberg said. "It's preposterous."

"I can't do that unless Sir Gerald orders her release."

"And he's in Damascus."

"Not any longer."

"Then he's back?"

"No, Sir Gerald has traveled on to Cyprus. He has some matters to take care of there."

"Yes," Bloomberg said, "I heard. He's going to be the governor."

Athill furrowed his brow but decided not to ask about Bloomberg's sources.

"And when is he due back?" Bloomberg continued.

"In a week. Don't worry, nothing will happen to your wife while she is being detained. Only questions."

Nothing fitted. Was it possible not to know someone at all as you thought you did? Joyce in London: snags of memory, insubstantial as the blue smoke wafting from autumn braziers on the allotments behind the railway lines near their flat; half-heard names that she had mentioned in passing, her acquaintance with Jewish activists, thinkers and writers, journeys that she had taken, her Monday-evening outings, her long enthusiasm for Zionism (muted for him!), which he had deemed foolish but insignificant. And if it was true that she had been running arms, was he proud or ashamed of her? In any event, she had evaded him; her character, which he thought he understood to its core, had proved elusive—but how could it not do so when for years he had been so severely concentrated upon himself?

Bloomberg looked wildly around at the traffic challenging the narrow confines of Jaffa Road: horse, cart, car, and bus; one of the carts piled high with parsley, the bunched and piled greenery like the waving head of a tree, the cart's driver flashing his whip at the skinny blinkered animal plodding to market before him. Too much charged information clogged Bloomberg's brain: Joyce and De Groot, guns and murder. He heard the blast from his own revolver and winced at the memory of wrenching pain, his toe blasted to the bone, blood seeping through his sock, the stench of shit and death in the trench. Two men lying next to him, dead as doornails.

"Who did she mean this morning," Athill was asking, "when she urged you to 'find him'?"

"Robert Kirsch," Bloomberg murmured, drawn back into the present.

"Yes. We went to the hospital to look for him. He wasn't there. And your wife thought he might be of help?"

"Yes."

"Then perhaps you had better seek him out."

"I'll do that," Bloomberg said.

35.

Kirsch sat on the manor's wide terrace looking over a tree-filled sloping garden. He had begun his climb well before the heat of the day, confident that he could manage the ascent. He had been in Rosh Pinah for four days. Mayan had divided her time between nights with Kirsch and days working to help her friend Rosa. This seemed to be her idea of a holiday. Kirsch could understand the nighttime part; her choice of daytime drudgery he found somewhat excessive, although not out of keeping with the pioneer spirit of the place (regnant in Jewish Palestine), in which labor was revered as an end in itself as well as a means to an end. He also had a sneaking feeling that despite the latitudinarian zeal that was often the cream on a Zionist worker's coffee, Mayan had not told Rosa where she was sleeping.

Kirsch had intended his walk up the hill to surprise Mayan, but on his arrival at the manor neither she nor anyone who might resemble Rosa was visible among the small staff of middle-aged men and women who, thanks to the beneficence of Baron Edmond de Rothschild, hustled through rooms looking busy and purposeful.

At this moment, out of breath and with the muscles in his good leg sore and aching, Kirsch didn't have the strength to do more than take in the view; he stared past the narrow trunks of the garden's small black cypresses with their dusty, curled foliage, and down the narrow trench occupied by a brown and unappealing trickle of stream. In the far distance, no more than a white point on the horizon, was the city of Safed. Kirsch wasn't unhappy: how could anyone be who had spent the last four nights as he had? He thought of his lovemaking with Mayan as both a triumph over his physical awkwardness and a tribute to her patience. The accommodations that they had made for his condition, and the tentative movements inspired by those accommodations, had supplied a virginal aura to their fucking, an atmosphere which had its own pleasures. Thus far Kirsch hadn't plucked up the courage to ask Mayan about the scars on her back, perhaps because he wasn't yet ready to relinquish his status as "the wounded one." This was a thought that he wished would go away.

Since his arrival in Rosh Pinah he had passed the days in desultory fashion, mainly in the dull company of the family who ran the hostelry. But the general air of boredom suited his mood, and he was glad that the family tended to leave him to himself. If the proprietors, who were both, so they told him, from the Polish town of Lodz, were disturbed by Mayan's nighttime visits they certainly didn't make Kirsch aware of their discomfort. In the mornings they greeted him with friendly smiles and busied themselves behind the desk, while he drank tea and read the *Palestine Bulletin*. He found that he was not much interested in the news. One afternoon the small group of Hindu soldiers from the local camp made their way into the bar, unaccompanied by Kirsch's nemesis with the red hair. Their drinking and socializing led to an impromptu cricket game held on the patchy grass that passed for a lawn, close to the hostelry's laundry room: an upturned wastepaper basket for a wicket, a tennis ball, and a battered half-strung racquet for the bat. The soldiers had roped Kirsch in as umpire and he had enjoyed himself until they had urged him to take a turn at bat ("Let's see what England can do"). He had declined on the unassailable grounds that he "couldn't run."

"If you're injured, then you're eligible for a runner," one of the soldiers said. "Make the shots and have someone run for you. That's a perfectly legitimate part of the game."

Kirsch had shaken his head no. He knew that he was being absurd: the game they were playing was fun and improvisational, but it had exposed the gap between the person he had been before the shooting and who he was now, and once he looked into that black pit he was susceptible to a paralyzing self-pity.

In the early evening while he waited for Mayan to arrive he sat on his bed and composed a letter to his parents. When he put pen to paper he was surprised to discover that he no longer felt the need to reassure them of his well-being. And why shouldn't they hear the truth? After Marcus's death he had tried to protect them from his own troubles; there wasn't room in the house, and rightly so, he supposed, for anything less than great tragedy. But now he poured his heart out and did not spare them his misery of the past few weeks. Was he angry that they had sent Sarah and Michael out to visit him in the hospital rather than make the long sea journey themselves? He didn't think so, but there was a wide space in him now that they couldn't cross. The space was enough; he tore up the letter.

And where was Joyce? She still haunted his imagination, but the force of her betrayal, like the force of their affair, was rendered increasingly spectral by the presence of Mayan. It was Mayan who stamped Kirsch's days with the indelible memory of her voice, arms, legs, face, hair, lips, breasts and cunt, so that whatever domestic banality he practiced—tea and the newspaper, a game of chess with the local sheikh in his black turban—the scent of sex from the previous night embraced and surrounded him.

He watched from his high-backed chair on the terrace and saw

Mayan moving with her characteristically determined walk through a far corner of the garden. She was wearing her straw hat with its brim pulled down over her eyes. He waved even though he knew that unless she looked up she wouldn't see him. He was going to call out to her but then decided to wait. He followed her progress as she disappeared around the back of the manor.

Ten minutes later, hatless and wearing a rose-patterned apron, she was standing at Kirsch's shoulder.

"Would you like tea, sir?"

Kirsch twisted around.

Mayan laughed. She pressed her hands on his shoulders and kissed him on the neck.

"You climbed the mountain," she said.

Kirsch looked down the path, which was no more than half a mile long. A week before his departure for Palestine he had taken a train to Wales and traveled alone on a two-day walking excursion in the Brecon Beacons. It had poured on both days, the rain coming down in sheets as Kirsch made his way through flocks of grazing sheep up to the sandstone peak at Pen-y-Fan, but despite the weather, or perhaps because of it, Kirsch had enjoyed his outing, and what is more, he now thought, it was the strength of his own body taking on the elements that he had appreciated the most.

Mayan sat down in the chair facing him.

"Where's your friend Rosa?" he asked. "I'm beginning to think that she doesn't exist."

"She'll be here. We're on double duty today. A party of great Jewish philanthropists from your own country is due to arrive and we shall be the picturesque pioneers who serve them."

"What are their names?"

"Look." Mayan pointed to the bottom of the hill. "Here they come."

A charabanc had pulled in next to the hostelry. Kirsch saw three people get out; one was a woman in a large floppy hat. The driver came around to lend her the added protection of a blue-and-white parasol. The men were in white summer suits; the taller of the two wore a pith helmet.

"And who did you say they were?"

"I didn't," Mayan replied, "but whoever they are you must be very nice to them or the poor Russians here won't have anything to eat tonight."

"You won't let it go, will you?"

The visitors had begun their climb, the driver relinquishing his parasol to one of the men who chivalrously continued to hold it over the woman's head as she stepped gingerly up the rock-strewn path. Kirsch felt an apprehension at their approach, and a small wave of anger, as if the newcomers were trespassing on his property.

"I'll be back with your drink," Mayan said.

"Let me get it myself. I don't want you . . ." Kirsch interrupted, but she turned swiftly away.

The English party was within twenty yards of the terrace when the man in the pith helmet spotted Kirsch.

"Bobby? Good Lord, Bobby Kirsch. Well, I'll be damned." He turned around excitedly to the woman.

"Look, Miriam, I'll be damned if it isn't Harold Kirsch's boy."

It took Kirsch a moment to register their faces as belonging to Simon and Esther Gaber, near neighbors from London and occasional dinner guests at his parents' house. The third member of the group must be their son Robin. Kirsch had played with him once or twice when they were small children, and he seemed to remember that they hadn't hit it off.

Kirsch stood up. He attempted a fluid movement but he was unable quite to hide the difficulty that he had in getting to his feet. Mrs. Gaber kissed him on the cheek; lines of sweat coursed like a delta through the powder on her cheeks and neck.

"What an extraordinary surprise!" she said.

The Gabers joined Kirsch at his table. Mrs. Gaber, acting as if the stone-block houses of Rosh Pinah were about as interesting to her as a mural in a "foreign" restaurant of the type she would never enter, launched into an urgent report of the London Jewish social scene as it had evolved in Kirsch's absence. She was about to offer a description of the

Jeremy Goldthorpe–Naomi Samuels wedding when, simultaneously, her husband butted in with a comment on the weather and her son kicked her on the ankle under the table. She remained unperturbed.

"Oh, don't be ridiculous," she said. "I'm sure Bobby is long over Naomi. I don't doubt for a second that he *wants* to hear about the wedding."

Kirsch had no chance to answer, for Mayan and Rosa had appeared on the terrace, menus in hand. Rosa was clearly the less cheerful of the two, and she stared suspiciously at Kirsch from behind a large pair of square black-rimmed glasses.

Kirsch knew that he ought to introduce Mayan, but for some reason he didn't immediately do so, and by the time that he had made up his mind to go ahead, orders had been delivered by the Gabers and the two young women had returned to the kitchen.

"What a pretty little *chalutz,*" Mrs. Gaber said, "the taller one, I mean." She dangled the Hebrew word for "pioneer" like something she might admire as long as it was held at arm's length.

"So?" Mr. Gaber said. "We hear you're a policeman."

"Bobby's a bobby," his wife put in.

Poor Robin Gaber looked as if he might throw himself over the edge of the terrace at any moment. He must have been traveling with his parents for weeks.

"And your parents are well?"

"As far as I know. My cousin Sarah was here. She's seen them more recently than I have."

"Didn't she marry the Cork boy?" Mrs. Gaber put in.

"We moved, you know. To St. John's Wood," her husband continued. "I'm afraid we've been out of touch with most of our old neighbors. We miss your parents. We used to enjoy each other's company. Your father was a wonderful conversationalist."

"Such an intelligent man!" Mrs. Gaber added, and then she sadly shook her head, as if Kirsch's father, bereft and miserable, had passed away once the Gabers had decided to move.

Kirsch sensed that the conversation was about to turn to Marcus's death and his parents' subsequent suffering: these were subjects that he did not wish to hear Mrs. Gaber reflect upon. He turned to Robin, who thus far had not uttered a word.

"How long are you here for?" Kirsch asked.

"We're out for a month. I'm sure the firm could have spared me for longer, but I didn't want to give them the opportunity."

"Don't belittle yourself," Mrs. Gaber said. She had given their tiny conversation a hawklike monitoring. "Robin is a brilliant barrister," she added.

The shadows on the hillside broadened as the sun rose behind the Manor, and its roof threw an arklike pattern onto the garden. Mrs. Gaber went off in search of "the little girls' room" and the three men fell silent. Eventually Robin asked Kirsch a few questions about his work, but without probing overmuch. He wasn't such a bad chap, Kirsch thought, and he even began to enjoy a certain relaxed quality in their conversation, something that he hadn't experienced much since coming out to Palestine. Did Kirsch have more in common with the Jews his own age from his part of London than he had previously believed? Robin Gaber's stories of their mutual acquaintances made him laugh, and he wished for a moment that the hot summer's day were in England, not here, and that he were lying on freshly mown grass under fleecy white clouds without a care in the world.

Mrs. Gaber returned to the table. She stepped over Kirsch's walking stick, which he had placed on the floor beside his chair, but, to Kirsch's relief, she chose not to offer a comment.

"Nice and clean," she said, "everything clean."

Mayan and Rosa appeared carrying plates of chicken and rice. They set them down carefully before the diners. Mayan was no longer smiling.

"Tell me, young ladies," Mrs. Gaber began, "are you here because of persecution?"

Mayan shrugged her shoulders.

"Not at all," Rosa responded, trying halfheartedly to appear both cheerful and accommodating. "My family in Odessa was prosperous."

Mrs. Gaber's face fell; she seemed disappointed.

"Then why on earth did you come here?"

Kirsch was waiting for an opportunity to mention Mayan, but Mrs. Gaber monopolized the conversation while Mayan patiently explained the roots of her youthful idealism. Kirsch noticed that Rosa was staring at him, urging him, or so Kirsch thought, to speak up.

"Look at your hands," Mrs. Gaber suddenly exclaimed, grabbing hold of Rosa's wrist as she went to move a plate of olives into the center of the table. "What kind of work have they made you do here?"

Mrs. Gaber turned Rosa's palms so that everyone at the table could view the calluses on her fingers.

Rosa pulled her hand free.

"It's nothing," she said.

"She worked on the road in Beersheva. It's not a thing to be ashamed of. Women can break stones too."

Kirsch looked at Mayan. He had seen gangs of women dressing stones for paved roads in both Jerusalem and Tel Aviv. They squatted on piles of rocks and chiseled away, chips flying past and sometimes into their faces. They wore long skirts and white headdresses that looked like beehive bandages.

"Well, a good thing she's here now, that's all I can say," Mrs. Gaber told Mayan.

"This . . . this is . . ." Kirsch began to stutter an introduction, but the Gabers had turned full attention to their food. Mayan and Rosa quickly left.

"It is *wonderful* what they're doing here, isn't it? Truly a miracle. Now, Bobby, when are you coming back to England? Your parents must miss you terribly."

Kirsch mumbled a noncommittal reply, sat in silence for a moment or two and then excused himself from the table. He tracked down Rosa in the kitchen.

"Where is she? Where's Mayan?"

Rosa gave him a look of indifference, or perhaps it was disgust. "She's gone."

"Where to? I mean . . . she can't have left."

He moved past Rosa toward the adjoining room. The door was locked.

"Please open this door," he said.

"You can't go in there. It's where the waitresses change."

Kirsch banged on the wooden panels. "Mayan. Mayan. Please. I'm sorry. Please open the door."

There was no reply from inside.

Kirsch turned to Rosa. "I'll just wait here, then," he said.

He sat beside her at the table. For five minutes neither of them spoke. Eventually Rosa got up and unlocked the door. Kirsch pushed past her into the room. It was empty, but a door in the opposite wall had been left flung open to the garden. He crossed the room and looked out. Mayan was nowhere to be seen.

Kirsch made his way back to the terrace and surveyed the view in every direction. He couldn't see her. He was sweating and the drops of perspiration ran down his nose and onto his lips.

Mrs. Gaber sat poised with a sliver of roast chicken on her fork.

"Robert," she said, "you seem to be walking very strangely. Is there something wrong?"

In the evening Robin Gaber came down from the manor and drove Kirsch up to the Arab village of Djuannin. He had borrowed a car from one of the office workers. It was kind of him. At lunch Robin had seen that Kirsch was in a state and he had urged his mother not to pester him. Kirsch had wandered off in search of Mayan, a hopeless endeavor as he lacked the strength to go far and Mayan clearly didn't want to be found. He had asked for her in the local grocery shop, a provisional, cramped box of a place where a young boy slid on a rolling ladder to the high shelves, throwing down tins to the customers like an agile monkey in the forest canopy pelting unwanted visitors. No one had seen her. If Mayan had returned to Jerusalem without him, then Kirsch was a dead man. Toward three in the afternoon, leg-weary and heavyhearted, he made his way back to the hostelry. There, he had collapsed onto his bed until Robin Gaber, holding a hip flask in one hand and a set of car keys in the other, had shown up to suggest a drive. They set off up a narrow track. The car bumped and jolted, then seemed to lower its head and charge at the surrounding hills where the sinking sun curled its red cape over the horizon.

Now Robin and Kirsch sat on a cluster of rocks; they passed the brandy flask between them and watched as the flocks and herds returned to the village from the low pastures. Twenty fat black cows slogged past, a few little calves skipping sideways at their tails. Behind them walked two men incongruously dressed in what looked like Russian peasant outfits: boots, jerkins and black caps.

Robin looked over at Kirsch. "Strangest Arabs I ever saw." He tried to suppress a laugh. "Must be Jewish cattle."

"Apparently there are no problems here," Kirsch replied. "The Jews and the Arabs drive to the same pasture. At least that's what Mayan told me."

There was a clear spring above them that ran into a drinking pool. Kirsch watched the cattle jostle together by the water. He had explained to Gaber how he had messed everything up with Mayan, and now he wished that he hadn't done so.

"What are you going to do now?" Robin asked.

"Oh, I don't know. Find her, apologize. Explain that I'm not the snob that she thinks I am. What else can I do?"

The night came on fast, and the salient points of the landscape by which Kirsch was orienting himself—the manor, the hostelry, Djuannin's minaret—seemed to disappear in the click of a heavenly camera shutter.

"Do you think this place could be home for you?" Gaber asked.

A startled expression crossed Kirsch's face as it occurred to him for the first time that unlike his fantasies of life with Joyce, a future with Mayan (any chance of which he had just blown out of the window) might mean a long-term commitment to living in Palestine. Kirsch remembered the blisters on Rosa's fingers: interim police work had been fine until his troubles started, but he wasn't sure that he was ready to help build a state, or fight for one.

"Home?" Kirsch looked out into the blackness. "Home's England, isn't it?"

"It is for me," Gaber said. "Although I sometimes think," he added ruefully, "that the reason so many Englishmen like to take a turn at running the colonies is that we're in England."

"They're running away from the Jews, you mean?"

"Well, not only us—there are other pariahs, but we're a part of it. Out in India or even here, they can play all the old prewar games, ornament themselves with plumed helmets and pretend that nothing has changed. It's not the foreign peoples whom they despise, especially if they come with a title attached, the prince of Bangalore or the nawab of Patudi, no, it's the 'foreigners' in the England they've left behind, people like you and me who've made it up the ladder. People they didn't want to see on the ladder in the first place, let alone climbing it."

"But here half the colonial staff is Jewish: Samuels, Bentwich . . ."

"Kirsch . . ."

Kirsch laughed.

"Yes," Gaber added, "it's a tricky one. Satraps and riffraff—all Jews. That's a recipe for trouble, don't you think?"

Kirsch didn't know what he thought—and that, he now saw, was a problem. He had set off for his adventure in Palestine as if he were going out to Ceylon or Australia, or any outpost of the empire. He hadn't thought about the Jews much at all; he'd been thinking about himself, and his brother and his parents, and not really loving Naomi, and the prospect of decent weather—that too. Kirsch remembered how he had been ill one wartime winter and a huge icicle had formed outside his bedroom window, hanging from the roof edge like a harpoon. It wasn't long after his recovery that the family received word that Marcus had been killed. Kirsch had gone upstairs, opened the window and hacked away at the icicle until it crashed into the garden, shattering into a thousand crystals.

He looked across at Gaber, then up at the sky, where the moon floated small and distant like a lone jellyfish in the dark waves of the sky.

"I'll drive you back," Gaber said.

Around two in the morning, unable to sleep, Kirsch heard a noise on the path outside his room. He got out of bed and walked to the door.

When he opened it he saw Mayan standing about twenty yards away. He couldn't guess how long she had been there, pacing up and down, poised, it seemed, between flight and return. He called to her from the doorway.

"I'm sorry," he said. "Please come in. I was horrible. I'm sorry."

They made up their discord very gently on the bed. Later, when Mayan was lying in his arms, her sleeping face washed in moonlight, the thought crossed Kirsch's mind that she had forgiven him too quickly. For a moment the sensation of being trapped overcame him, as it had during dinner at the Bassans' when he had suspected them of match-making. But the feeling soon passed. After all, what kind of a catch was he?

He touched his fingers to the scars on Mayan's back. Her body stirred and she turned away from him. She opened her eyes and stared at the wall.

"You want to know how I got the scars?"

"Not if you don't want to tell me."

"What would you like to hear? A Cossack's whip?"

"I think you're confusing me with Mrs. Gaber."

Mayan reached for the twisted sheet, made an attempt to disentangle it and pull it over her, then gave up and threw the linen to the side. She lay back naked on the bed, the length of her small, compact body fully exposed.

"It was a Cossack's saber. I was six years old."

Kirsch lay in silence. Somewhere nearby an electric wire buzzed and fizzed.

"It wasn't a Cossack's saber. It was in a car crash. My father was driving his van on a street that ran near the sea. We had set out to collect a delivery of books at the port: two hundred copies of an English language primer, Jews heading for America were desperate for them. It was raining hard and he skidded on the wet road and drove into a wall. The van's windshield shattered and its glass flew out. I was flung forward and then back into the jagged pieces. I was fifteen. Perhaps some local anti-Semite had thrown a rock at our windshield, who knows? Would it please Mrs. Gaber if that were the case?"

"Don't," Kirsch said. He shifted onto his side and kissed Mayan's face.

"I'm going back to Jerusalem tomorrow," she said. "I have to be at the hospital. What are you going to do?"

It was the same question that Robin Gaber had posed only hours earlier. Then Kirsch had been devastated because he thought he had lost Mayan; now he had her but felt equally unhinged.

"When will you come back to Rosh Pinah?"

"Perhaps I can come again next weekend."

"Then I think I'll stay here," Kirsch said.

He couldn't tell if she was pleased by his decision or not.

It seemed that they had hardly fallen back to sleep when they were awoken by a voice calling from the path outside their room.

"Mila, Mila. Your bus is here."

Mayan rose quickly from the bed. Kirsch sat up drowsily.

"Who's Mila?" he asked.

Mayan had started to pull on her clothes.

"I am," she said. "Ludmila, although only Rosa knows that."

Kirsch nodded. It was common for the new Jewish immigrants to drop their old names and take a Hebrew one instead. It was a way they used to anchor themselves to the place.

"Then I shall call you 'Mila' too."

Was that Kirsch's way of saying no to a life in Palestine? He thought that it might be.

Mayan stopped smoothing down her skirt to look at him. "I wish you wouldn't," she said.

Rosa called out again from closer to the window.

"I'm coming!" Mayan replied.

She took three brisk steps toward the bed, bent over and kissed Kirsch on the lips.

"My Mila," Kirsch said teasingly, but she didn't smile.

Through the open door of his room he could see the headlamps of the dawn bus still shining. The driver shouted something in Hebrew and revved the engine. The last passengers took this, as intended, as a warning of imminent departure and hustled to take their seats.

After the bus had left he saw Rosa walking toward the path that would bring her up to the manor. She had obviously chosen to ignore him. He couldn't blame her.

The rising sun released a burnt-wood scent from under the torn stripped bark of the eucalyptus trees. Kirsch moved to the chipped pitcher and bowl set on a table in the corner of his room and began to splash water over his head. He didn't hear his visitor approach until the young man in uniform had taken two steps into his room.

"Captain Kirsch?"

Kirsch looked up, his face dripping with water.

"Yes, but who are you?"

"Corporal Edward Hiestand, sir. I have orders to accompany you to Jerusalem."

Kirsch remembered the note from Ross that he had thrown away.

"Am I under arrest?"

"Hardly, sir. I believe your help is needed with an interrogation. Shall we say half an hour to get ready, sir?"

"And who am I interrogating?" Kirsch asked even though the question was superfluous. He knew as soon as the corporal announced himself why he was being brought back to Jerusalem.

Hiestand was looking at his briefing letter. "A Mrs. Joyce Bloomberg, sir."

"And what if I don't want to return with you?"

The corporal stood with a slightly bemused expression on his face. His pale skin was covered in freckles. Kirsch guessed that Palestine was his first posting, and that he hadn't been out here very long.

"They said that might be the case, sir."

"And?"

"And I'm not alone, sir. There are three of us."

"That's quite an escort for someone who isn't under arrest."

Hiestand shrugged. "You must be good at your job, sir. Very much in demand."

"Has this request been authorized by Sir Gerald Ross?"

"Couldn't tell you, sir. I got my orders from Sergeant Phipps."

Kirsch, conscious that the corporal was trying to avoid staring at his withered leg, moved away from the washstand, sat on the bed and began to pull on his trousers.

"Give me twenty minutes," he said.

Halfway back to Jerusalem they caught up with the bus in which Mayan was riding. The army vehicle got stuck behind it for almost twenty minutes until, near Jenin, the road widened enough for its driver to overtake. Kirsch, stretched awkwardly in the front passenger seat, strained to catch a glimpse of Mayan, but he was too low down, and in any case, the windows of the bus were covered in a thin layer of dust.

36.

Bloomberg traveled through the night to reach Haifa. Too exhausted to face the drive, he had found a ride in the open back of a lorry that was delivering bricks and asbestos sheets to a building site in Safed. The air was warm and there was little wind, but the calm did nothing to hold down the dust that choked his nose and mouth. Separated from his load by wooden slats, even the driver, a large broad-faced individual with water-buffalo shoulders, had tied a handkerchief over the lower half of his face, like a cowboy. Bloomberg coughed and spat into the road; his chest felt tight but he knew that the deep source of the constriction was poison in his own soul trying to find a way out. Nothing much mattered now except that he locate Kirsch, and Ross too. If he could secure Joyce's release he might at least make partial amends for his years of self-ishness. The thought of her cooped up in the governorate while some threatening boorish officers grilled her for information was unbearable.

The driver, unwilling to make a detour from the main road, dropped him almost a mile from the ticket office. Bloomberg planned to take the first boat over to Cyprus that he could find. He had borrowed a little money from Athill, enough to get him across the water. He hoped he could persuade Ross to finance his return trip: an advance on the painting that was ready to be delivered. He hurried toward the quay as fast as he could and for a moment, on arrival, he was alone there, but as he shuffled forward with his ungainly gait, shouldering his old kit bag with the strap cutting into him, and perspiring from his walk, he heard the gunshot crack of a gangplank on concrete, and before he could reach the window he was swamped by a crowd of new arrivals. He tried to fight his way through the throng of immigrants, some hugging and joyous, but most looking bewildered. The men stood in their white shirts, narrow ties and heavy three-piece suits, tugged at their caps, wiped their brows and stared blankly around as if, in a dream, they had stepped from their homes in Europe intending to go to the office, shop or warehouse, only to find themselves on this blistering, sunstruck Mediterranean quay. Almost all of them clutched landing documents, or smaller scraps of paper that must have listed the names and addresses of their contacts in Palestine. The women, whose long skirts and cotton headdresses seemed immediately more appropriate to the place, shepherded their children, some of whom strained for release while others, dismayed and tearful, buried their faces in their mothers' skirts. Bloomberg's heart raced. Once he had been one of those children, and only the point of arrival was different: the Pool of London. Two years old, he had barely learned to walk, and there he was emerging from the hold gripping his mother's hand and pressing his nails so deeply into her flesh that she cried out in pain. He had no memory of this, only of her later reports, her cherished narrative of arrival, as England moved toward her, the land appearing to sway, the rough voices of waiting longshoremen calling like strange birds, her husband, their family packages strung around his neck, lost somewhere on the crowded deck, and her darling little boy wet-eyed and terrified as she scooped him up and carried him to the gloomy safety of the shore.

The safety of the boat, the *Evresis,* away from the crowd. Bloomberg, his heart still pounding, sucked in air and inhaled deep breaths while the salt spray cooled his face. Beneath his feet the deck throbbed with the sound of the ship's engine. He was ashamed of his immigrant panic, but there was nothing that he could do about it. Perhaps the root of all his anger could be located there: he had tried to fulfill his mother's ambitions for him and claim England as his own. For a while he thought he had succeeded, but the army and his critics had shown him otherwise. He had packed himself off to Palestine because that seemed to be the direction in which they all, including the dead, were pointing him: back on the boat you go, only this time aim your travels to where it all began three thousand years ago. But the truth was that he held allegiance to no place other than the tiny area, indoors or outdoors, where he set up his easel.

He stood by the starboard side rail and watched as the figures, buildings, and ships at anchor dwindled to gray dots, red roofs, and tall masts, then dissolved into the line of hills behind them. In his pocket he held his ticket to Famagusta. He would reach port in ten hours and from there he would find a bus or taxi to take him to Nicosia. In that city he could certainly expect to find Ross; Kirsch's presence was less certain.

There were drinks and snacks available on the freeboard, but Bloomberg rarely went belowdecks if he could help it. On the voyage out from Southampton to Palestine he had spent a good deal of his cabin time vomiting into a bucket. While the sea churned and the ship tipped and tossed, Joyce, who didn't share Bloomberg's susceptibility to imbalance, had sat on her bunk and read, comfortable as in a garden swing. But as long as he could breathe fresh air he was generally fine, and this day was considerately balmy, the cloudless sky an immensity of unstained light.

He hardly noticed the other passengers and he was lost in thought staring into the green and mercifully gentle waves when someone tapped him on the shoulder.

"On the move again so soon?"

Bloomberg turned swiftly. It was George Saphir, the reporter from the *Bulletin*.

"What's the object of your interest this time? Don't tell me, Othello's Tower?"

Bloomberg didn't respond.

"All right then, the ruins at St. Hilarion? Got to be one of the two."

Bloomberg shook his head. "I don't know what you're talking about," he said.

"Well, surely you're not simply taking a holiday? Are you? Or perhaps you're running away. Good Lord, man, a few days ago you were off to see your wife after two months in the desert. What happened? Didn't find someone else while you were away, did she?"

"Something like that, yes."

Saphir had begun to laugh, but he stopped abruptly at Bloomberg's reply. He looked Bloomberg in the face, trying to ascertain if he was joking or not.

Bloomberg smiled and Saphir breathed an exaggerated sigh of relief.

"You had me worried for a moment there, old friend. I know you painter types are wild men—and women—but . . ." Saphir decided not to continue with his thoughts on bohemian life. Bloomberg noted that he was still sporting the faux pioneer outfit that he had seen him in at the Allenby bar.

"How about a sandwich?"

Saphir retrieved a small package from his bag and unwrapped two thick slices of bread, cheese, and tomato.

"No salt, I'm afraid."

Bloomberg refused the offer of food. Despite the placidity of the Mediterranean, his stomach had already begun to churn.

"Then you're not going to tell me why you're on this boat. Don't worry, I shan't press you."

"I'm going to Nicosia. I need to see Sir Gerald. And you?"

Saphir appeared to ponder his options for a moment, then his eagerness to reveal at least part of his news overcame him.

"There's something brewing," he said. "My Greek priest friend Pantelides let me in on it. And Ross is already setting up shop. No longer in Damascus. Well, you know that, of course."

"What's brewing?"

"I'm afraid I can't give you the details. But there are implications for Palestine, and I think I've got a scoop on my hands. I *can* tell you that we share a destination."

"In that case," Bloomberg said, "perhaps you'd like to pay for my taxi fare from Famagusta."

Saphir smiled. "I'm sure the *Bulletin* won't mind," he said. "I hereby appoint you my official illustrator."

The coast of Palestine passed from sight and then there were only the dull bottle green waves to stare at and the steam clouds emanating from the ship's funnels.

Bloomberg stood back from the rail and looked around for somewhere to sit. He didn't want Saphir to know how even the deep easy roll of this ship possessed the ability to make him seasick. He found a spot halfway down the deck and sat, legs outstretched, with his back to a heavy coil of chains. Saphir followed and settled himself a few feet away.

"By the way," he said, taking a bite into his bread and cheese, "you remember you asked me the other day about the De Groot case."

Bloomberg nodded.

"Well, the strangest thing. Right after you'd left the Allenby, in comes a fellow I know from Government House, Fordyce, works for Bentwich, and usually he's pretty careful with me, you know—I am an unabashed fully fledged Zionist and so on—but this time he seems almost eager to give me some news. 'What is it?' I ask. And he starts to tell me about De Groot, says the chap was queer as a coot, used to stalk the little Arab boys and most likely it was one of these poor youngsters' brothers or fathers who decided to exact some heavy revenge. All a personal matter, no politics involved. I ask him, 'Any arrest imminent?' thinking I might be in place for that newsworthy event. 'No,' he says, 'they believe the culprit's long gone. Fled to Egypt or somewhere.' *Finita la commedia.*"

Bloomberg tried to keep his expression neutral. "And who did you think had killed him? That is, before you received the new information."

"Well, everybody was aware that they were looking for an Arab; the whole of Jerusalem knew the police were after a suspect named Saud. And I'm sure I thought along with most people that this was a case of an Arab seizing an opportunity to kill a prominent Jew."

"Yes, but De Groot was not a Zionist."

"Far from it. Do you know what I heard someone say? That the black hats had done it themselves, a ploy to win the sympathy of worldwide Jewry. Taking things a bit too far, I thought."

"And would it have been 'taking things a bit too far' to suggest that the Zionists themselves were responsible?"

Saphir's eyes widened. It seemed the first time that such an outlandish idea had crossed his mind.

"That would be impossible," he murmured. "As crazy as believing that members of his own sect did it."

"But suppose he knew something, something that could threaten the advance of the Zionist movement?"

Saphir looked at Bloomberg. "Do *you* know something?" he asked.

"I don't know anything," Bloomberg replied, "I'm only speculating. It just seems a little convenient, doesn't it—an Arab killer who has disappeared to another country?"

"They hate us, you know, the Orthodox. We protect them from the Arabs and in return they tell us we're blasphemers and infidels."

"I thought the British were protecting them, along with everyone else."

"The British won't be around forever. And it doesn't look as if they've done a very good job. De Groot's dead, isn't he? And there will be Jews dead every day if we don't get control."

Bloomberg could have told him, could have produced the crumpled letter from his pocket, shown Saphir the tunic button that Saud had given him, described what Saud had described—the stabbing of De Groot, the boy's escape and desperate rush down the hillside.

But Bloomberg didn't offer a word. Saphir couldn't be trusted, Jews assassinating a Jew was news that he didn't want either to process or to digest, and besides, as Bloomberg suddenly realized, there was a more vital destination and use for the information that he held.

Saphir finished his sandwich, wiped his hands on its brown-paper wrapping, then went off in search of a drink. By the time he returned Bloomberg had closed his eyes, tipped his gaucho hat over his face, and was feigning sleep.

Real sleep followed soon after, and by the time that Bloomberg awoke the journey was more than halfway over. Saphir was nowhere in sight.

Bloomberg found his way down to the toilet; it had overflowed and in order to piss into the fetid bowl he had to roll up his trouser bottoms and stand in a quarter inch of clouded water. Someone had stuffed an English newspaper behind one of the pipes, undoubtedly for use as toilet paper, but a few words in a headline caught Bloomberg's eye and, even though he knew he might discomfort at least one desperate passenger before the ship reached port, he ripped off the sheet and folded it into his pocket. He emerged, slightly dizzy, through a battery of flies, and felt his way upstairs toward the light breezes of the deck, but, while he had slept, the weather had turned heavy and oppressive and when he reached the open air it offered little relief. Bloomberg gazed down; the sea, a shifting palette of greens and blues, had grown eerily calm, so much so that he could hardly feel the forward movement of the ferry. It seemed for a time as if the captain had changed his mind about the journey and decided to drop anchor.

Bloomberg found a seat and retrieved the sheet of newspaper. The headline that had captured his attention was from London's *Daily Graphic;* it led an exhibition review, almost three months old, that concentrated on the first solo show of one of Bloomberg's former students, Leonard Green. There, beneath the banner head GREEN MAKES CANVAS COME ALIVE, was a photograph of dark-eyed Leonard looking stern and artistic, and a reproduction of one of his recent paintings, a Futurist work that celebrated the factory machinery of an East End garment manufacturer. The reviewer, T. J. Furbanks, was quite certain that Green's art was, as its adopted style implied, the work of the future.

Bloomberg read through the review and, from the writer's descriptions, tried to imagine how the colors of the painting might operate. He found to his pleasure that, however temporarily, he had passed beyond envy: the lavish praise heaped upon Leonard by T. J. Furbanks did not trouble him. Bloomberg's own career, which he reflected upon now without bitterness for perhaps the first time, had not had such an auspicious beginning. Indeed, he had stumbled for years, praised by the few, until his one-man show five years ago at the Whitechapel Gallery had lifted him high and, it seemed at the time, secured his reputation forever. But the euphoria, both his and his critics', had not lasted: a tiny crack in the general appreciation of his work slowly widened to a fissure. The group show of Jewish painters that he had organized restored him somewhat, but by last year the fissure had reached canyon width. Rereading the Green article Bloomberg wondered if anything—a career, a marriage, even a country—that started out badly could ever be put right: the effort to get things back on track was so enormous. It was true that a glowing start such as Leonard's could also quickly fade to black, but at least the chance was there.

The *Evresis* pushed on through a bleak subdued twilight; lone figures, couples, and family groups circled past Bloomberg, who, as the travelers wandered to the rail and back, picked up whispers of conversation, words and phrases in four or five languages that lapped at the corners of his mind. Once, a young boy squatted next to him, peeled an orange, and offered him a slice, but otherwise he remained undisturbed. If he had thought to bring paper and pencil he would have used the opportunity to sketch, but his hands remained idle. His mind, however, was in a fever of expectancy.

Shortly after midnight a slow clanging of bells announced that the boat was steaming cautiously through the narrow pass into Famagusta. Out of nowhere, it seemed, Saphir appeared at Bloomberg's side and the two men watched as the lantern lights of the old harbor city beckoned with false serenity out of the folds of night.

By the time that Bloomberg and Saphir had disembarked the *Evresis* it was too late to find a ride to Nicosia. Both men were in a state of agitation, eager to reach their urgent destinations, and for more than an hour they plied the lobbies of the small tavernas close to the harbor in search of a driver willing to test his skills by moonlight against the narrow inland roads. Eventually, they were obliged to admit defeat, but rather than find a soft bed for the three or four hours that remained of the night they determined to wait outdoors until dawn. They found a bench close to a garage, Fotis Brothers, that offered a motorcar service, and steeled themselves for the journey by consuming a small bottle of ouzo that Saphir had purchased on the ship.

Bloomberg was exhausted, he had a sharp pain in his shoulder from heaving his bag, and his entire body ached. The ouzo burned his throat and, by the third or fourth gulp, had set his mind reeling. He sensed that he was at the end of what had been almost a decade of futile travels, beginning with his sailing from Folkestone to join the fighting in Flanders and culminating here on this hot little island. He had made so many attempts at escape, without precisely knowing what he was looking for, and without conviction.

Bloomberg stood up and immediately Saphir dropped down full length on the bench, half drunk and half asleep. Bloomberg walked with his back to the sea. Not too far away, made visible by the bright moon, he could make out the contours of the town's vast Gothic cathedral. He set off in its general direction, past a train station and through a warren of narrow cobblestoned streets that brought him to his destination. The great wooden doors of the cathedral were closed. Bloomberg sat on the steps in order to catch his breath. And now Joyce occupied all his thoughts; the image of her face glowed like an icon. He pictured her seated in front of the mirror of her dressing table in their West Hampstead flat, brushing her hair back, her lips slightly parted in concentration, an occasional grimace as she pulled through a knot. Her hopeful American face and lively gray-green eyes. The very picture of a Zionist terrorist. Life was mad.

The taxi took Bloomberg and Saphir past Othello's Tower, through Famagusta's medieval fortifications and into a fertile plain that, their driver informed them, stretched between two mountain ranges. There were small tree-covered hills and the occasional river. Two hours later the outskirts of Nicosia were announced by the presence of Greek flags that seemed to hang everywhere from balconies and windows of white-walled houses. Saphir pointed out the profusion:

"It seems we're not wanted here either."

"We?"

Saphir's face reddened. He had slipped back into his British self as easily as putting on a change of clothes, and his embarrassment was profound.

"Where shall I drop you?" he asked.

"I'm going to Government House."

Bloomberg leaned forward. "Do you know where that is?" he asked the driver, who nodded his assent.

The car passed through a series of plantations that after Palestine seemed to Bloomberg almost like an English park, except that the light that the sun threw on them was so intense. In a few moments a long, low barnlike building came in sight.

Saphir and Bloomberg looked at one another.

"There must be some mistake here," Saphir said. "Where are you taking us?"

"No mistake."

"But these are stables."

"No, sir."

The car pulled up fifty yards from a sentry gate that guarded what could now be seen as a small house with white-painted plank walls. There was a flagpole in the garden but, as yet, it seemed, no Union Jack. Bloomberg got out of the taxi.

"Thanks for the ride," he said. "I hope you get your scoop."

"Oh, I will," Saphir replied. "It's not too late."

Bloomberg watched the car turn on the driveway, and then he was alone. His clothes were rumpled and stained with the grime of his long journey: red-brick dust from the lorry, grease and oil from the deck of the boat. He could still smell the urine from the ship's toilet, which despite his precautions, had soaked the bottom of his trousers. He stood for a moment in a shaded grove of silver-stemmed poplars. The heat, if it was possible, seemed greater than in Palestine, although the same antiseptic odor emanated from the eucalyptus trees. He knew exactly what he had to do here: bargain his silence for Joyce's release. De Groot's murderers would go free, but so would Joyce. Bloomberg gathered himself and moved toward the sentry gate where, before anyone could come to his assistance, he collapsed, clutching his chest, and lay motionless on the dirt path.

37.

When Kirsch entered the room Joyce stood up and took three quick steps toward him, but Kirsch was not alone, so instead of embracing him, as she had intended, she returned to her narrow bed with its rough brown blanket and sat on its edge.

For what felt like an age, but was probably only a matter of thirty seconds or so, he stared at her without speaking. Her hair was tangled and knotted, her eyes bleary and circled black from lack of sleep. The staff sergeant had informed Kirsch that Joyce had been treated very well, and offered every chance to "perform her ablutions," but she had passed up opportunities to bathe, just as she had rejected most of the meals prepared for her. In deference, it seemed, to the fact that this was a woman's room, someone had placed a vase of yellow crowned daisies on the windowsill.

"It appears that we have to talk," Kirsch said stiffly.

Joyce looked at Robert, took in his skinniness, his sunken cheeks, his walking stick and the awkward way that he leaned upon it. She felt light-headed but tried to keep her gaze steady. For a moment she had an impulse to play the deranged woman, but if this meeting was to mean anything at all she had to face the consequences of her actions head on. After all, here was Robert, her victim, right in front of her, with his righteous anger and his broken body. Even so, when she opened her mouth to speak, the words of apology that she had planned to utter got stuck in her throat and emerged as a nervous cough.

Athill, who was standing slightly behind Kirsch, stepped forward and stretched his long frame to proffer a half-empty glass of water that stood on the chair beside Joyce's bed.

She drank; the water quelled her cough but couldn't help her speak.

Athill turned to Kirsch. "Perhaps I should leave," he said.

"I'd rather you didn't," Kirsch replied.

Joyce's face showed no reaction. She was wearing, Kirsch noticed, with a feeling of disgust tempered by a residue of desire that he could hardly bear to acknowledge, the same white dress that she had worn on their first motorcycle ride into the Jerusalem hills.

"They say that you asked for me. Here I am. What do you have to tell us?"

She was hurt, but she knew that she had no right to expect civility from Kirsch.

"Come on"—he was working himself up into a fury—"Francis here meets me outside and says, 'She'll only talk to you.' He tells me you specifically requested my presence, that you're willing to spill all your secrets to me, but not to anybody else. So let's hear them, right now. The games, the deceit, the lying, who you've fucked, who you've bought off, who gave you the guns, where they come from, who pays you, who gives you your orders?"

Athill put his hand on Kirsch's shoulder and he stopped his tirade.

"You," Joyce murmured. "I fucked you, that's all."

He was a boy. She saw it as she had never allowed herself to during their intimate relationship. He was an English boy, out of his depth. The short trousers that he had worn when he arrived at her door should have told her, but she had misread the sign and seen a policeman instead.

Joyce sat back on the bed. Whatever she might say was going to be utterly inadequate. Perhaps, she realized, all that she had wanted was to see Robert alive. She hadn't killed him after all.

She heard herself speaking, but it was almost as if the words were coming from someone else in the room. "The ballet," she began.

"The *ballet*? What are you talking about?"

Athill coughed and, once again, Kirsch relented.

"My father," she said, and paused again; her shoulders dipped as if the weight of the air in the room was too much to bear. "Well, he drove me to Miss Nugent's classes."

Kirsch glanced at Athill, who seemed riveted by Joyce. He felt a pang of jealousy and, for a moment, dropped his air of impatience. The two men waited for Joyce's explanation to take on meaning.

"My feet began to get distorted, like a geisha's. But I wouldn't stop. My parents tore their hair out. 'It's over,' my father said. He said he had to be cruel to be kind. The lessons were over." Joyce paused again. She made an effort to look Kirsch in the face. There were tears running down her cheeks. "I can never stop myself. Someone else has to do it."

"Is providing Enfield rifles to anybody who wants to shoot a British serviceman being cruel to be kind?"

Joyce closed her eyes and buried her face in her hands. She caught the smell of her wool coat after the rain as she crammed into Toynbee Hall with the others. A speaker with a German accent. In dreary London it was Palestine Flower Day, someone tagged a miniature flag with a small artificial flower to her lapel, "I am the Rose of Sharon, the Lily of the Valleys."

Kirsch's voice, relentless, unforgiving, returned her to the room.

"And the end justifies the means, I suppose? They justify Cartwright getting his face shot off and Lampard losing his arm, and God knows how many deaths to come, and . . ." Kirsch's voice trailed away.

"And you. You nearly died."

"That doesn't matter," Kirsch snapped.

"Then nothing does," Joyce replied.

Kirsch felt a surge of love for her. It rose in him unbidden and against all his better instincts. He wanted to take her in his arms, just as on the first time that she had opened the door of her cottage to him. He might actually have embraced her, but Athill's presence held him back. And best that it did so.

Athill had moved to the room's single window and was staring out toward the Damascus Gate. The moat that ran alongside it had been entirely filled up with rubbish. In the open square in front of the gate, where four roads met, a larger crowd than usual had congregated for this time of day. It was late afternoon and the hubbub of the throng grew and grew to a positive pandemonium. Athill didn't notice that the women who usually hunted for cheap goods at the close of shopping hours were

conspicuously absent. He saw what he imagined to be impassioned bar-
gaining, the wild song of the city, at once its color and commerce. He
looked across to the high chambers above the gate, the arches with their
machicolated balconies and narrow coupled windows surmounted by
stone cupolas; the wild capers that grabbed at the stones with their mole
claws. He closed the window against the tumultuous din and the rank
stench of open sewers and rotting vegetables, and turned back to face
Joyce and Robert Kirsch. He was about to speak when the first stone
shattered the glass behind his back.

Athill instinctively raised his hands to cover his head. Rocks were
thudding against the outside wall and then more glass shattered onto the
floor of the room. A gunshot blasted through the air.

"Get her out of here!" Athill yelled.

Kirsch, who had been frozen momentarily by the gun blast, as if he
had taken the bullet himself, tried to run forward. He stumbled but
managed to grab Joyce around the waist and drag her to the ground. Together, they crawled toward the door. Athill too was down on the floor,
but crawling in the other direction, back toward the broken windows. He
stood against a wall, removed his revolver from its holster, and leaned
quickly forward to peer through the glass. The gunshot, which seemed
to have come from within the governorate, had panicked the crowd. Men
and boys scattered in all directions, only for a large number quickly to
reassemble in a rough circle. Athill heard a great ocean roar and then saw
a body at first cradled, then almost lifted into the air. A child! It was a
child! Athill saw the bloodstain spread on the boy's shirt, but by then he
had looked too long: a rock thrown aimlessly caught the edge of the
stone window and ricocheted into his face. He screamed with pain and
put his hand to his eye, which had turned to a bloody mess.

Kirsch and Joyce descended two flights of stairs as fast as they could.
Kirsch had lost his stick, and it was he who needed Joyce's assistance.
She shouldered his weight and they exited the building through its basement cafeteria. They headed north, took two turns down streets that
were empty and, ten minutes later, emerged into a blind alley that ended

at a wooden door that was slightly ajar. Kirsch pushed through and Joyce followed. They found themselves in a garden, but one that lay at the foot of a tomb-covered green hill. Kirsch sat down on a grassy knoll to catch his breath. Joyce stood with her back to him staring at the cliff of the hill where, to her eye, the cavities in the rock seemed to form the eyes, nose, and mouth in a rounded skull. At this distance the sounds of the riot were diminished but not extinguished.

Kirsch's chest heaved and his lungs felt as if they were about to burst. Joyce knelt beside him. He wanted to put his arms around her, or rather, have her encircle him.

"Am I still your prisoner?" she said.

"I don't know what you are."

The air was hot and honey-thick, and the late afternoon seemed to be choking on itself, gasping for breath.

Kirsch gestured toward the wooden door.

"Go," he said, "I can't stop you."

"I'll stay with you."

"Oh, you will? Well, I've met someone else."

Kirsch had intended these words for another, quite different, conversation, but they had spilled out now, childishly, unnecessarily. He rose clumsily to his feet and took a few steps away from her.

A shot rang out. The faint noise of the distant crowd subsided, then rose again and seemed now to be coming closer.

"We can't stay here," Kirsch said.

He walked over to Joyce. She rose and brushed the grass off her dress.

"I'll take you somewhere safe," he said.

They passed down narrow half-built silent streets that were strewn with debris and construction materials. As much as he could Kirsch sheltered Joyce with his body and kept her tucked in, barely visible, against the walls of the new buildings. After twenty minutes or so they paused in shadow at the rear of the hospice kept by the French friars. They stood side by side with their backs against the wall. Joyce's mouth was dry and her legs were scratched and bruised.

"We'll go to a hotel," Kirsch said. "Hensman's. The proprietor knows me."

Joyce nodded.

Kirsch took a deep breath.

"I can't forgive you," he said.

"No, but there is someone who needs forgiving. The boy, Saud. He didn't kill anyone. Ross sent him into the desert with Mark. He told Mark everything. Mark showed me a letter. De Groot knew that he was in danger. We did it. Your men. Your policemen. The Jewish police. Mark has a button from one of their tunics. De Groot ripped it off in the struggle, then carried it in his fist. He must have dropped it in our garden."

Kirsch stared straight ahead. He watched a stray cat searching for food on the other side of the street.

"There's a second button," he said. "I have it."

They sat in the candlelit lobby of the hotel, each cradling a whisky.

"There must be people out looking for you," Kirsch said. "I can't decide what to do."

Joyce shrugged. "It's up to you. I'll do whatever you want me to."

Kirsch took a gulp of whisky. "Tell me the truth. Was it you? Was it a gun you brought that I was shot with?"

"I don't know," she said. "I can't be sure."

Kirsch stared at her. Her face, after weeks indoors, had grown pale, but her gray-green eyes still blazed.

"Will you tell me who you worked for?"

The lobby was a sea of shadows.

"Let's go to sleep," Joyce said.

She woke far into the night. Kirsch lay sleeping beside her, his body shaped uncomfortably to the deep indentations in the mattress left by former travelers. He hadn't wanted to make love to her, but had laid his head on her chest. She had offered him her breasts but he had fallen asleep, like a baby, with his open mouth and dry lips at her nipple. She rose from the bed, pulled on his shirt, left the room, and pattered barefoot down a narrow corridor toward the communal toilet at its end. Why hadn't she told Robert that she worked for Frumkin? She wasn't quite sure. She *had* told him that, despite everything that had happened, she still believed in the Zionist cause, but she wanted nothing more to do with violence. It was too late, of course, for that declaration, too late for her remorse, too late for everything.

She sat on the toilet and shivered. A medley of coughs and snores penetrated the thin doors of the other rooms on the floor, and then came the raw cries of a couple at love.

Where was Mark? She had sent him off to find Robert Kirsch, but Athill's men had located Kirsch first. If she told them about Frumkin there was a chance she wouldn't be shot, but even though she hated him she couldn't surrender his name. Why not? She had already betrayed Mark by making love to Robert Kirsch, and betrayed Robert Kirsch by running guns for Frumkin. What would be the point of a third betrayal? Would it stop more men from dying? The guns were already here, and Frumkin, she was certain, must have left the country by now. As to the urgent notion that Peter Frumkin's name could be exchanged for her own life, she wasn't at all sure that she wanted to live; she certainly didn't deserve to.

She pulled the rusty toilet chain, water gushed then gurgled in the pipes. Close by, so close that it seemed to come from deep within the building, a church bell tolled for matins. In the interstices between the sonorous strikes of the bell tongue, someone was calling her name. It was Robert's voice, devoid of fury now, but tuned to the urgency of a parent searching for a lost child. Joyce was on a train. It was winter and the snow packed up high on the railroad embankments. Outside, the sky was smoky blue and the Hudson snaked beneath it like smooth white stone; a lone skater twirled and was gone. She wanted to see him again and ran down the corridor. Instead of the skater she had found the caboose, and scrunched herself in between two giant mailbags. After a while she heard her father's voice, distant at first, but growing ever closer. She couldn't decide whether to stay in hiding or to reveal herself, but at the last minute, when it seemed that he might turn away, she had leapt out and into his arms: "I'm here, I'm here."

38.

Ross and Kirsch sat on the enclosed veranda that gave onto the garden.

"The yellow stone is traditional here," Ross said, gesturing toward the Gothic arcading that formed a low, narrow gallery about a hundred feet long.

Ever the instructor, Kirsch thought. He had taken the ferry from Haifa and arrived, as Bloomberg had on his final journey, by taxi from Famagusta. The driver, supervised by Kirsch, had roped Bloomberg's painting to the roof of his car in such a way that it could not be damaged. Currently, the work, still in the gray sacking wrap that Bloomberg had provided in the desert, stood propped in Ross's lofty new drawing room.

"A drink first?" Ross had said, and Kirsch had been surprised by the governor's ability to defer viewing the fruits of his commission. A drink first, though, seemed to be both a mark of respect and an act of homage to Bloomberg.

Ross sipped at his scotch and soda and waved his hand in the general direction of the gardens. "If the soil were richer and the water adequate . . . it's regrettable."

Kirsch looked over the barren expanse with its scattered trees; he could see why the possibility of roses appeared unlikely.

Kirsch lifted his glass of lemon water to his lips. No whisky for him. He needed to keep his wits about him.

"We've had a heck of time locating a Jewish cemetery," Ross said. "There is only one. It's in Ercan. They tried to establish a settlement there about twenty years ago. Money from a French baron, Maurice de Hirsch. Heard of him?"

Kirsch shook his head.

"Well, what made him try Cyprus God only knows." Ross lifted his tumbler of scotch and turned it around in his fingers. "You'll accompany us there, then?"

"I promised her I would."

"She didn't . . . didn't want him brought back?"

"No. She thought he'd have had no preference for Jerusalem. Or home. I think she almost liked the idea of being able to come here at some future time, and entirely alone, to visit the grave. She's asked me to pay someone for the upkeep."

"For all those years? I wonder if you'll be able to find an individual whom you can trust."

"Yes," Kirsch said. "The years. That's something I'd like to talk you about."

"I thought you might."

"Is there anything that can be done?"

"Not if she won't talk."

"But what if I were to talk?"

Ross stared past Kirsch. Now that the prospective governor was in residence, a subaltern was preparing to run the Union Jack up on the flagpole at the foot of the garden.

"About the boy? I sent him away for his own good. Turned out I was right. I don't think you've got much to go on there. As for the rest, the missing Sergeant Harlap and his missing buttons, well, that's for you and my successor to deal with."

"And Frumkin?"

"Well, you'll pursue him, no doubt, even without Mrs. Bloomberg's assistance. But you're not going to have any easy time. There's nothing to go on, except that he lent Joyce a car. I imagine he's back in California. He's a powerful man. Good luck to you."

"And her confession, doesn't that count for something?"

"It will reduce the sentence by about five years. Look, Robert, you've done all that you can. And so have I. Shall we look at that painting?"

Ross eased himself out of his chair. He looked to Kirsch as if he had lost weight, but perhaps it was a loss of authority that made him appear less imposing. Kirsch followed him into the drawing room. The painting still had one corner exposed where Bloomberg had ripped the sacking outside Government House in Jerusalem.

Kirsch cut through the rope with his knife and revealed the painting.

Ross stood a distance away. His face took on a look of hard concentration. He walked forward until he was only two or three feet away from the surface of the canvas; then he removed his glasses. It was a few minutes before he spoke.

"Well," he said, "I'd be lying if I said that I wasn't disappointed."

Kirsch looked at Bloomberg's swirling browns, pinks, and reds. The place of sacrifice that the artist had been sent to paint was not distinguishable.

"Do you know," Ross said, "I don't think I want to keep this. Why don't you take it?"

"If you don't want it . . . then surely Joyce."

"Well, as the owner, I believe that I can pass it on to whomsoever I please. And in any case, I don't think that Mrs. Bloomberg is going to have the wall space. But if you feel that way, perhaps you could look after it for her."

"I will," Kirsch said.

Ross was still looking at the painting, as if he were trying to puzzle it out.

"I suppose we should be on our way," he said finally. "I'm sorry to rush you."

"Can she at least serve her sentence in England?"

"I shan't have a problem speaking for that. But are you sure that's where she wants to be?"

"I haven't asked her, but I know that she has friends in London. At least she'll have visitors."

"Will you be one of them?"

"I don't know. I haven't decided what to do."

They walked through the dining room. Two servants were unpacking boxes, removing plates and glasses, then gingerly setting them on the floor.

Kirsch and Ross made their way to the front of the house. Outside, a car was waiting for them behind the hearse, its engine idling. The sky held the color of bottled glass. Unlikely though it was, it felt to Kirsch as if it might rain.

They drove for hours, the sky darkening ahead of them. By the time they reached the cemetery a heavy rainfall was in progress. With no trees to resist its passage the water coursed across the ground in a dull yellow streak that stretched as far as the eye could see.

Kirsch and Ross stood by the grave as Bloomberg's coffin was lowered in. When it had come to rest Ross turned to Kirsch.

"I thought you might like to say something," he said.

Kirsch didn't reply immediately. The rain beat down on his head. He looked at the grave next to Bloomberg's. A star of David adorned a simple stone that memorialized Artur Niederhoffer 15.12.1886–2.11.1921. Bloomberg was the colony's last member.

"No," he told Ross, "I don't have anything to say."

December

39.

The day dawned bright and evangelical, and it was hard for Kirsch to resist its redeeming light, its broad white shimmer. The city offered its early seductions: morning bells striking down upon the old walls, newly constructed dwellings and building plots, the nasal call of the muezzin, and, as if to adjust the spirit and bring it to back to earth, Jerusalem's domestic display erupting in color: a woman on the opposite balcony shaking out a big blue-checked tablecloth, and beneath her another woman holding a bunch of blood-red late-blooming roses, flowers that Kirsch suspected she had stolen from the garden at the corner of his street and that she would undoubtedly offer for sale later in the day.

As was habitual since his return from Cyprus three months ago, he had been up for most of the night, kept awake by his ferocious regret. He had paid weekly visits to Joyce. The first time he had simply described the place where her husband was buried, but in their subsequent meetings he had tried desperately to convince her to tell everything that she knew, otherwise her fate was inexorable. She refused to say more than she already had. She believed, Kirsch understood, that she had got what she deserved, and she was prepared, or so she imagined, to spend the next twenty years in what was from his point of view an utterly wasteful atonement. All that was required was her cooperation, and a new life was hers for the asking. In recent weeks he found that her stubbornness made it almost unbearable for him to be with her. He had told her once that he couldn't forgive her for what she had done, but it wasn't so. Long ago, it seemed, she had offered one name, "Saud," and now even a half-whispered dreamlike murmur of the second name would free her. Her silence and her equanimity in the face of her sentence were both incomprehensible to him. In a week, through Ross's intervention, she would be taken back to London to serve out the remainder of her term.

At the first sounds of traffic on the newly opened road near his house, Kirsch rose from his seat on the balcony and went back into his flat. He wasn't alone. As he entered, Mayan's dark form, her belly already slightly swollen, moved across the room. She crouched over the chamber pot and peed into it. She stood, pulled down her nightdress, and returned to Kirsch's bed. He sat beside her on the edge of the mattress. She stretched out her arm and laid her hand, palm up, on his thigh.

"Do you think I'll like England?" she said.

"Do you like dullness and rain?"

"Yes."

"Then you'll like England."

"But if I hate it we can come back here."

Kirsch didn't reply. Instead he put his hand under her nightdress and caressed the stretched skin of her stomach.

Mayan held his wrist.

"Are you going to see her today?"

"I'll give it another try, yes."

She shifted uneasily in the bed.

Kirsch stared over the top of Mayan's head toward the green-silver olive tree outside his window. Mayan drifted back to sleep. For a while he kept his hand on her stomach, and then he withdrew it.

After a few minutes she opened her eyes.

"Was she the great love of your life?" she asked.

"No," Kirsch said. "You are."